The Suicide Society

Book Two

Rational Insanity

A Novel by

William Brennan Knight

Published by Altron Services
Copyright © 2019 by William Brennan Knight

Printed in the United States of America
First Printing, 2019
ISBN 978-1-7339698-0-2
Published by Altron Services

www.authorwbk.com

Dedicated To: William J and Maureen D. Throughout life's challenges, setbacks and accomplishments, no one could have had more supportive parents

Books in the Suicide Society Series:

Chapter One

"What do labels matter anyway, Marshall?" The psychiatrist rose from his chair and walked over to a window where he parted two slats in the blinds and gazed out at the mountains. "Whether you're classified as someone with Asperger's Syndrome, level one or 'high-functioning', you'll still be Marshall Beiner. But you're a different person than the one who walked into my office six years ago."

"Five years ago."

"What?"

"Five years, three months and seventeen days ago. That is how long it has been since my first appointment with you, Dr. Abrams. I saw you on a Monday, five years, three months and seventeen days ago."

"Marshall, try and remember to use contractions in your speech patterns, it sounds more natural. But I swore..." Abrams walked to his desk and picked up a file labelled *Beiner* and rifled through the pages. He found the document he was looking for and ran his index finger down the lines of text.

"My, this has to be a first, Marshall. I'm actually right. Your first visit here was on September 12th, six and a half years ago."

"Let me see that." Marshall approached the doctor, while still keeping a significant distance between them.

"Here it is. Look for yourself."

Marshall reached his arm out at full length and took the document. He glanced at the form and focused on the date.

"This is wrong."

Dr. Abrams shook his head. "Don't get caught up in small details, Marshall."

"This is not a small detail. I remember specifically when I... This is very odd. Lately, there have been several things I remember that others do not."

"Such as?"

Marshall grew quiet as he contemplated the value of further discussion. Despite years of practice, it was still difficult to understand the concept of subterfuge. Yet, experience taught him that revealing the truth at an inopportune moment might bring unpleasant consequences. He filtered through several layers of pragmatic analysis and carefully weighed his answer. "It doesn't matter, doctor. You are probably right. I—must be mistaken."

Abrams smiled and quickly covered the remaining distance between them. He thrust out his hand. "Good luck, Marshall. I believe you're ready to fully integrate into society."

Marshall weakly returned the smile and clasped the doctor's hand with his thumb and forefinger. He hated the feel of human flesh but learned to internalize the revulsion without flinching. "Thank you, doctor. You have been most helpful."

As he reached the door, Marshall paused at the threshold. Without turning to face Dr. Abrams, he asked, "One more thing, doctor. Are you married?"

"Marshall, you know my wife passed away three years ago."

"I'm sorry, it must have slipped my mind." As he left, Marshall closed the door behind him gently.

Walking down the hallway to the elevators, he entered the first car that stopped on his floor. Marshall resisted the temptation to use his mobile phone. Instead, he focused on remaining isolated from his fellow passengers. The elevator creaked and stuttered as it moved slowly down the shaft, and he wondered if there was cause for concern.

"Jeez, this thing seems like a disaster waiting to happen. Hope we don't die." The heavyset man with a birthmark on his cheek went on to make sounds that mimicked an explosion. The other passengers shuffled their feet and smiled uncomfortably. Marshall looked at the man curiously and wondered how anyone could find crashing to the bottom of an elevator shaft funny. In years past, he might have asked, but over time, he learned that when exposed to inexplicable behavior, it was best to remain quiet.

For all his effort, humor was still evasive; an elusive layer of consciousness that escaped him. Wanda once explained it using a math analogy. For Marshall, calculus was as elementary and simple as tying one's shoes. Yet, for others, it was impossible to work through the complexities no matter how much effort they exerted. Some could almost reach the threshold but never fully understood the beauty, simplicity and logic of the essential formulas. Humor was like that for Marshall, and Wanda's explanation had provided some peace.

3

He noticed a woman in the corner of the elevator was trembling. She wore several layers of clothing, which wasn't healthy or stylistically appropriate for a hot July day in Phoenix. Others couldn't see her slight shudders, but Marshall was sensitive to movements, thoughts and actions imperceptible to everyone else. He tried to move to the other side of the small enclosure, but several people already occupied that area of the cabin, so he wasn't able find a personal space. The woman's shaking grew more pronounced, and when her hands went up to her head, the passengers standing closest took notice.

As she turned, Marshall saw the long angry scar that ran from her ear to her lip. She whimpered and grabbed handfuls of her stringy blonde hair and pulled hard. The rest of the passengers moved as far away as possible and pushed up against the others. They experienced this sort of thing too many times before. She slid down the perforated steel side wall until she was in a sitting position with her knees drawn up to her chest.

"I can't stand it anymore. Make it stop. For the love of God, make it stop!"

The eyes of the passengers turned everywhere except in her direction. They looked at their watches, the rolling numbers of the passing floors and the overhead lights, but no one looked over at her as she pulled hard on her hair and shivered in tearless sobs.

"I can't do this anymore. It's—so hopeless. I can't find a job; there are no jobs for me. My baby is hungry, and my mom's got dementia or something. The thugs are in the street every night, and I feel like I'm losing my sanity. I see people in my nightmares... and they tell me to hurt myself. Why is this happening?"

A long, awkward silence ensued before Marshall cleared his throat and spoke softly.

"I don't have an explanation. You are being vague, and I doubt that the duration of this elevator ride is enough time to dissect and solve your multitude of problems. I would say this though: the extraordinary increase in psychological disease in the general population is quite unusual and troubling, so I guess you are right in questioning that phenomenon."

She looked at Marshall with a blank stare. Even the disinterested passengers swiveled their collective heads for a moment and gave him a variety of looks ranging from incredulity to bewilderment. Just as quickly, they returned to their disassociated state.

"What the fuck?" the woman said. "I should rip your heart out for saying something like that to me."

Marshall backed away. "I—am sorry. I thought..." His mind raced until it accessed the mental file that stored the appropriate response for a severe faux pas. He referenced social blunders with accompanying anger and returned his attention to the woman. "Yes, I am very sorry. My remarks were insensitive and rude. Please forgive me."

She continued to glare at him, but her face softened. "Ok, but you should learn to show some feelings for people who are hurtin'. And Lord knows, I'm hurtin'." The sobs began again, this time accompanied by tears.

Mercifully, the elevator reached the ground floor and opened, and the passengers pushed hard to exit as quickly as they could. In these times, no one wanted to become involved in another person's vortex of personal chaos if it was avoidable. Marshall waited until everyone left before he got out and moved over to a secluded part of the lobby. He pulled out his phone and pressed number one on his keypad. The phone rang a single time before it connected.

"Marshall, you won't believe it. I — I can't believe it. I just can't believe it. You were right. You were *right*."

"Kenny, Kenny, slow down. Gather yourself. I need empirical data not hysteria. What did you find out?"

"They all remember it the same way. Wait, I wrote it down." Marshall heard the rustling sounds of a folded piece of paper. "Ok, here it is. Hayden said all three of them recollect the Xib-prime particle was discovered at CERN in 2015, just like you do. None of them remember it being discovered at Fermilab in 2014 as the history books say. Of course, we can't speak for Iglar or Korinth."

Marshall paused as he processed the information. "What about the professors?"

"That's where it gets really weird. Very, very weird. I called Professor Higgins at ASU and Professor Markus at U of A, and they both remember the exact opposite of how our people believe it happened. They remember the false version of the Fermilab discovery. Marshall, how can that be?"

"What about the second item?"

"Well, only two of us remember it, but it's the same thing. You recalled Dr. Portis McFee being named the Head of the Department of Physics at MIT, right?"

"Yes. It happened exactly seven years ago."

"Not according to the faculty guide. If you look at that book, he didn't become a department head until three years ago."

Marshall paused and allowed his mind to work. The colors flowed through him and rippled like waves of air rising off the hot pavement. Red, violet, blue and shades in between rolled and mixed together, distilling his thoughts and filtering the information.

"Ok, Kenny. Tell everyone to meet tonight at my house at seven o'clock. Tell them this is not — isn't an ordinary meeting. We need to understand what this all means."

"Sure, Marshall. I'll call them. This is wickedly strange."

"I know, Kenny. Very strange indeed."

Marshall carefully placed the phone back into his shirt pocket and buttoned the flap over it for extra security. He went through the revolving door, exited Phoenix Tower, and walked down 1st Avenue to the parking garage on Adams. Once he reached the corner, he pushed the button on the streetlight and waited for the sign with the stick figure in motion to illuminate, signaling he had the right-of-way to cross. Mid-morning was not a busy time of day, so he was alone as he walked, careful to stay within the painted lines that defined the crosswalk.

From down the street somewhere, a car started up, and the engine revved, but it was far enough away that Marshall didn't give it any thought as he hurried through the intersection. It wasn't until he heard the screech of tires breaking from the pavement that he turned toward the source of the sound. A large silver SUV accelerated rapidly and headed directly at him.

He froze in the middle of the street and couldn't get his legs to move. For an instant, time seemed to slow perceptibly, and in that moment, Marshall could clearly see the face of the driver. The man sat hunched over, and his hands clutched the steering wheel tightly. With his brow furrowed and mouth turned down, his eyes were focused intently on his victim.

Marshall knew he only had one chance to jump out of the way without giving the driver time to adjust. Instinct told him to dive forward and slightly to his left behind a parked car. Unfortunately, it was a fair distance, and the maniacal motorist probably anticipated such a move. Adrenalin coursing through him, Marshall feinted as though he would lunge to his left and instead leapt in the opposite direction.

Considering the speed of the vehicle, the maneuver provided enough of a distraction that it caused the driver to swerve wildly as he overcompensated. The tires screeched and protested at the severity of the maneuver, and the back end swung out as the wheels skipped laterally across the pavement. For a long second it appeared like the vehicle might recover, but he oversteered again. Turning 180 degrees, the SUV slammed into the exact parked car Marshall had considered hiding behind.

Utterly terrified, he got to his feet and peered through the driver's side window. The man was cursing and pounding on the dashboard. He turned and looked at Marshall, and his level of anger escalated as he pulled at the door release to no avail. As a crowd gathered, Marshall quickly moved around the back of the parking garage and out of the madman's line of sight. He walked up the stairs to the second floor, found his white Civic, and drove down the ramp, making sure he exited on Monroe, well away from the scene of the accident.

His heart beat fast as he headed toward the freeway. The level of random violence seemed to escalate every week, and a simple trip for a doctor's appointment was now a life-threating situation. As he remembered the man's face, Marshall became increasingly disturbed. It was a random act of violence, wasn't it?

***

The "Group," as they called themselves, assembled in Marshall's living room later that evening. They always met at his house because he had the only room that was big enough to accommodate everyone without triggering Kenny's anthropophobia or Hayden's enchlophobia. The others lived in apartments or with their parents anyway, so meeting anywhere else was impractical.

While Asperger's and high-functioning autistic people often had IQs higher than the general population, the social challenges kept some from developing the coping skills they needed to be totally independent. Every personality was different, but it could take years before someone with Asperger's developed the discipline to deal with everyday challenges, not to mention the difficulties that social settings presented.

Marshall Beiner was one of those people. Over time, he perfected the ability to process common greetings, salutations, humor and idiosyncrasies that made no sense to him intellectually. Years of training and countless books on social graces finally allowed him to understand the function and purpose of etiquette on an academic level. While he never truly could grasp the concept of small talk and courtesy, a carefully constructed matrix of programmed responses provided an opportunity to interact in a way that rarely exposed his flaws.

Many of those with high-functioning autism followed a similar path to social integration, but some of the younger ones still struggled. In fact, it was part of the reason Marshall formed the Group. It gave him a sense of satisfaction to help others develop abilities that gave them an opportunity to relate to unaffected people without drawing unwanted attention.

At every meeting, Marshall offered soft drinks and crackers for refreshment, and he placed them on the kitchen table. However, most of the members had specific dietary preferences and usually brought their own food and beverages. In the early meetings, he tried to accommodate them, but this only served to encourage requests for increasingly exotic food and drink. When Hayden Barwin asked for anchovies on Don Bruno Crostini crackers topped with an eight-millimeter slice of Fiscalini Bandaged cheddar, he knew that providing a suitable spread for his guests was impossible. Hence, the Ritz crackers and colas.

Marshall stood at the top of a semi-circle of chairs spaced exactly one meter apart and faced the group. Some autistic people thrived on predictable uniformity, and they were protective of their personal space. Therefore, every meeting was the same; chairs placed in a perfect semicircle. For Marshall, even setting up the chairs was exhausting since the arrangement required such precision, and he always had to move some of his existing furniture into the garage.

All seven members were in attendance tonight, and he turned and faced the assembled group. "As you know, we have a challenging problem to deal with. From an empirical point of view, nothing about this makes any sense. To be succinct, we as a group seem to recall past events differently than the way they were recorded in historical archives or remembered by other people.

"So far, we have documented three specific instances, but there are probably many others. The first relates to the discovery of Xib-prime at CERN. The second concerns the timing of the appointment of Dr. Portis McFee as the head of physics at MIT. Finally, during my last therapy session, my psychologist recorded the date I first entered treatment, which is inaccurate as I remember it."

From Marshall's left, a hand went up slowly. "Yes, Hayden?"

"It is actually much worse than that, Marshall. Much, much worse."

Marshall frowned. "What do you mean? How is it worse?"

"There could be hundreds, perhaps thousands of inaccuracies if you extrapolate from this small sample." A crescendo of murmurs spread through the group. "Wallace, please present the handouts I prepared." Then, turning to Marshall, he continued, "The report was compiled by Wallace and me. Of course, I put the final version together. There is also a copy available on the cloud."

"Get to the meat and potatoes. What does it all mean?" Kenny Flanton was blunt and loud as usual.

"There are no 'meat and potatoes' as you put it, Kenneth. We were simply exploring the possibilities based on the number of anomalies we discovered over such a short period."

Another hand was raised. "Wanda, you have the floor."

A slightly overweight girl with a pleasant face stood up but kept her eyes turned downward. Marshall could sense her unease. "As you all know, I work in probabilities and statistics. Once I learned of this phenomenon, I talked to ten of our friends who are like us but aren't in the group. I compiled a great deal of data from them, and I was able to catalogue fourteen instances of historical variants that totally contradicted official records and the recollections of unaffected people.

"As I discussed each incident with our friends, we realized there was only one explanation: the nature of time itself had changed for us. And reality somehow... shifted."

"Shifted? What does that mean?" asked Hayden.

"We don't know. Statistically, it's clear the outcome could not have happened as records and memories suggest. The chances of ten people remembering an event in a way that differs from documented history is remarkably small. It can't be a mass delusion."

"Where did you conduct this research, Wanda?" asked Marshall.

"At the Lincoln House. I wanted to talk to more autistics and aspies, and as you know, that's the best place to find them." Iglar's head drooped so far down his chest it looked like he was sleeping, but suddenly, his body shifted, and he sat straight up. A soft din ensued as hushed discussions bubbled up among the members.

Recognizing his responsibilities, Marshall brought his hands up to bring the focus back to the group. "Please, please. Kenny, Hayden and Iglar —

12

please, can I have your attention?" He waited for the background chatter to settle down.

"Look, it appears we have stumbled upon something unusual, perhaps extraordinary. But there is much work to do before anyone can approach the scientific community, let alone the authorities. Have we compiled all the anomalies in one master database?"

They exchanged quizzical glances before Kenny spoke. "No, Marshall. Nothing is ready yet. You know I've been working with everyone. No time! No time!"

"Kenny, it was just a question, not an indictment. Wanda, can your IT department coordinate with the others to assimilate the data? We're looking for commonalities here. Dates, times and people. We need to find out if these acts are random or if there is symmetry. Wallace, could you speculate on if there is a quantum mechanics explanation?"

Wallace Thornberry sighed and picked at the skin around his thumbnail. He jerked when he spoke and looked as though he was nodding his head even as his words belied the movement. "Assuming any of this is true, it would radically alter our understanding of quantum physics and even relativity. I have no explanation, but we will work on it."

"Good. Let's adjourn and get some rest. We'll meet back here at seven p.m. in a fortnight.

"Marshall." The room grew silent. Iglar rarely spoke, and he and Korinth could go weeks without uttering a single word.

"Yes, Iglar?" said Marshall.

"Let it alone, Marshall. Just leave the men from Mars alone."

Chapter Two

Marshall found it difficult to concentrate throughout the day as his mind tried to cope with the implications of the group's findings. While he enjoyed his job as a freelance graphic artist, he also had a Ph.D. with an emphasis on quantum and particle physics from the University of Arizona. So it was no wonder these new developments shook his foundational view of space and time to its core.

At precisely three p.m., he saved his work and turned off his Surface Studio. After arming the security system, he locked the door to his house and went out to his Civic. Turning onto 43rd Avenue and eventually Camelback, he drove south until he came upon the Innovation Business Center entrance, which was a hi-tech industrial park on the west side of Phoenix.

Marshall pulled up in front of the Culver Aerospace Corporation building, found a covered parking space, and walked into the lobby. A receptionist seated behind a large curved back-lit stainless steel counter looked up and smiled.

"Can I help you, sir?"

"I'm here to see Wallace Thornberry."

"Do you have an appointment?"

Marshall fought against the impulse to express his annoyance. "Yes, I have an appointment." he said in a controlled monotone.

The receptionist smiled, but it was dripping with sarcasm, which Marshall naturally missed. "Certainly, sir. One moment, please. He picked up the phone and pushed a series of buttons. The line connected, and he talked in a whisper while glancing at Marshall, who avoided eye contact.

"Ok, sir. Mr. Thornberry is on the fourth floor."

"I know what floor he is on. I've been here many times before. I'm always surprised you never remember me."

"Hmmm… I can't imagine how I could forget a person with such a pleasant attitude. Anyway, you enjoy your day, sir."

Marshall turned and walked toward the elevator, once again missing the derision.

Wallace stood at the front door to his office, waiting to greet Marshall as he exited the elevator. The smaller man looked around suspiciously, his exaggerated movements drawing attention from several other people standing or walking down the hallway.

"Wallace, you are making a spectacle. Calm down."

"It's extraordinary, Marshall. Simply extraordinary. Hurry; come in."

As they walked through the office area, Wallace shifted his eyes and swung his head around in every direction while awkwardly trying to remain inconspicuous. However, the unusual nature of his body language had the exact opposite effect. Amid the stares of his coworkers, they reached the lab where Wallace opened the door and waved at Marshall to follow. After his friend entered, Wallace poked his head into the hallway to check for imaginary moles. Satisfied, he closed the door and engaged the airlock, remaining motionless until he heard the audible *click* and *whoosh* of the mechanism.

"Come over here," he motioned for Marshall to an expansive fifty-inch, 8k-HD display. Sitting at her terminal, Wanda Parsens was typing and hardly noticed their approach until Marshall gently touched her shoulder, which caused her to flinch.

She looked up at him and wrinkled her nose. "Oh, Marshall, you have a strong odor. Did you bathe today?" Like many people with Asperger's or autism, Wanda's senses were heightened, and she could be painfully blunt when they were offended.

Marshall lifted his arm and smelled his armpit, which he knew would be the most likely source of the bacteria that produced the offensive smell. "Yes, I did bathe. However, it's late in the day, and my deodorant may no longer be effective in this hot July weather."

Wanda pulled away and scooted the chair. "You know how much I dislike the foul smells on other people, Marshall. I don't like it, I just don't—don't—don't." Wanda balled her fist and pounded the counsel.

Wallace looked at Marshall and said, "There is a bathroom over there. Maybe you could cleanse yourself." He walked over to Wanda and grabbed her arm to stop the pounding. She began to cry and buried her face in her hands. "Wallace, at least you don't smell as bad as Marshall," she muttered.

Slightly perturbed, Marshall walked into the restroom and took off his shirt. He used a paper towel soaked with soap and water to wash his armpits and the rest of his upper torso. The facilities were inadequate for bathing, so some soap residue remained on his body. Later that night, he would experience a maddening itch he blamed entirely on Wanda.

He reentered the room and walked back over to his colleagues. Wanda stayed seated and looked at the floor with her legs crossed and hands folded. "I'm sorry, Marshall," she said in a soft voice. "I know I shouldn't have said anything."

Marshall forced a smile, but the slight squint in his eyes belied the sentiment. "It is fine, Wanda. I had a difficult day, and I should have reapplied my deodorant. I hope my odor is less offensive now." He moved over to her computer but stood a couple feet away. "So, can you tell me what you discovered?"

She pointed at the computer screen. "We documented and catalogued every memory that each group member could recall that differed from recorded and anecdotal history. We then confirmed our version of events with the ten people with high-functioning autism we spoke about last night. Our memories were prioritized by the vividness of the recollection and the number of people who shared the same memory. After we compiled the data base, I sent it over to Wallace."

"And?"

"It's not entirely random." Wallace picked up where Wanda had left off.

"What do you mean?" asked Marshall.

"I said it's not entirely random. There's a pattern, and the events are interconnected. Most would have missed it, and I almost did. But they are layered. In several cases, one change seems to have triggered several others."

Marshall paused to contemplate. "Could it be an astrophysics anomaly?"

"Unlikely. I've considered a variety of quantum mechanics scenarios, specifically super string theory, but this experience doesn't fit comfortably in any of them."

"So, what is — I mean, what's the most likely explanation?" Marshall remembered Dr. Abrams' suggestion that he practice speaking using contractions.

Wallace shook his head. "I don't have one yet."

"There is one more thing," said Wanda.

"Okay?"

"We think one of us may know the identity of an individual who triggered certain events."

Marshall looked up and made eye contact with Wanda. "What?"

"Iglar may have been there when someone caused a change."

"How could that be possible?"

Wallace shrugged. "I don't know. We've tried to talk to Iglar, but he is hard to... Sometimes he makes me feel very bad."

"Me too," added Wanda. "He's — difficult. Sometimes he does — dirty things."

"I know, I know," said Marshall. "But what did he say?"

"Well, when Wanda and I were at the Lincoln House, he mumbled about experiences that were much different than everyone else. We couldn't really understand his disjointed speech patterns, but it sounded like he thought he was actually *there* during change events."

"I know it sounds strange," said Wanda, "but Iglar became more agitated with each question, so we stopped the exercise and left."

Marshall rubbed his temples. "I'm going to have to talk to him. You know that will not—won't be easy."

"Most level twos are challenging," said Wallace, referring to the Autism Spectrum Disorder rating scale.

"Wallace, have you given Hayden the data and told him about Iglar?"

"Yes, I sent it to him, but frankly, I'm worried. When I told him what Iglar said, he started that rapid incoherent talking he does. I think he was hyperventilating."

***

Marshall left the meeting more confused than when he entered. Why would those with high-functioning autism remember events differently than everyone else? Despite the objective evidence, Marshall doubted their assertion would carry any weight in the scientific community. Someone with autism always had to reach a higher threshold to be taken seriously. Marshall experienced it many times in college as well as in the workforce. The discrimination was always subtle but unmistakable.

He pulled his car into the driveway of the modest two-bedroom burnt adobe home in Glendale where Iglar lived with his mother. As he walked up the short brick walkway, he saw a curtain over the front window partially pulled back, and he could see Grace Stone looking out at him. Marshall imagined she wouldn't be pleased he had come to see Iglar, so he expected the usual interrogation. The curtain closed, and the door opened a crack.

"Hello, Mrs. Stone."

"Hello, Marshall. Did your mother drive you here?"

She asked the same question every time he visited. No matter that he passed his written test with 100 percent accuracy and his driving test with a single minor error. Grace Stone was like many others who noticed his unusual mannerisms and assumed he was incapable of engaging in activities conventional people took for granted.

"No, Mrs. Stone. I haven't lived with my parents for several years, remember?"

"Oh, yes, that's right. I think you may have told me that. Even so, do you think it's safe for you to be driving yourself, Marshall? I've never considered letting Iglar drive. Perhaps someday, but certainly not now. You know, with his condition and all. Of course, you also suffer from the condition. Am I right?"

"It's called high-functioning autism, Mrs. Stone. We can talk about it out in the open now. We've come a long way since the 1980s."

Grace Stone pursed her lips and smiled tightly. "I'm aware of the year, Marshall. I just don't think it's wise to bring attention to your—affliction." She drew out the second syllable of the last word for emphasis.

Whatever her intent might have been, the subtle reproaches were lost on Marshall, who wondered for a moment if she was suffering from mild dementia. He paused a moment and thought about asking but decided not to. "Can I see Iglar, please?"

"Yes, I suppose so. He's in his bedroom, but you can't stay very long. I still need to give him his bath." Marshall nodded and moved quickly toward the stairs and away from Grace Stone.

Iglar sat at his small desk, which was pushed up against a wall in the exact position it occupied for

20

over thirty years. He typed furiously at his computer without acknowledging that someone had entered the room. Marshall imagined some might think the sight of a forty-year-old man sitting at a child's desk was comical or pathetic.

"Hello Iglar, is this a good time to talk?"

Iglar continued to stare at the monitor, immersed in an online interactive fantasy game. His long hair stuck to the sides of his face, separated into several greasy clumps that looked like rope. His clothes were wrinkled and stained, and they emitted a stench that smelled like a combination of fresh and old sweat. Iglar's arms and face had some sort of substance smeared on them. *Motor oil perhaps?* It was brownish and gave off a terrible odor.

No, is it feces? Grease and feces? Impeccably dressed and germophobic, Marshall fought against the urge to retch. His body lurched in a heaving motion, and he struggled to control his gag reflex.

Through tearing eyes, he said, "Iglar, it would be polite if you could acknowledge me."

Iglar's upper lip snarled a bit as he paused the game. Without looking away from the screen, he said, "I know you're there, Marshall. But why did you come?"

"I think you know why I'm here. You talked with Wanda and Wallace at the Lincoln House. You know about the memory deviation project we are — we're working on, and you understand the number of incidents exceeds any reasonable control. However, the recollections from the group pertain to distant memories, but I understand your experience is different. Wallace tells me you may have observed certain events in real time. That could only mean you have the capacity to see these changes before they happen... Is this true, Iglar?"

21

Iglar started a raking motion with bent fingers. A few seconds later, deep red marks appeared on his neck. He gnashed his teeth and rocked in the chair.

"This is very important, Iglar. Are you seeing memory deviations as they happen or even in the future?"

Iglar let out a high-pitched yowl. "I can't—can't talk about it. They'll come for me. They'll come for every one of us."

"Who Iglar. Who will come for us?"

Meet Kathy who's been most everywhere from Zanzibar to Barkley Square, but Patti's only seen the sights a girl can see from Brooklyn Heights... Iglar began to sing the theme song from the Patty Duke show, an old black and white television program from the 1960s. He rubbed at his crotch as he sang, a reflexive habit that horrified his mother and created enormous embarrassment in social circles. When he was with the group, no one seemed to notice or care. After all, every one of them had their own idiosyncrasies.

Marshall sat stoically throughout the performance, acting indifferent, which he discovered was the best way to curtail Iglar's aberrant behavior. When the song finished, Iglar grew silent.

"Iglar, tell me who is making these changes?"

Without turning from the computer screen, Iglar said, "They know what's happening, Marshall, and they just change it. I don't know why, but they keep changing it again and again. It's so—painful..."

"Who is doing it, Iglar? Who is changing the memories?"

"I—I don't know who they are. I don't know what they want. But it's getting harder and harder

22

to see through it. Harder and harder to be—me. I'm not sure who I am anymore, Marshall. Help me!" Iglar turned and pushed his rolling chair within inches of where Marshall was sitting. He reached out and grabbed his friend's head with both hands and squeezed. For Marshall, it was uncomfortable and revolting. He avoided thinking about where Iglar had put his hands.

"Help me. The confusion is horrible. Every day, sometimes every minute, it changes. Changes and then more changes caused by the first ones. They're killing me."

"Can you tell me anymore about it, Iglar? I need something to help me find out who is behind it."

Iglar dropped his hands and rolled back to the computer. "It was a birthday party. He snuck an art painting set into the pile of presents. I saw him do it. I don't know why, but Kia now loves painting, and some of her work is getting noticed, and she's only fourteen. It happened six years ago. I don't know why he did it, but she wasn't supposed to get that set."

"Who gave it to her, Iglar?"

"I don't know, but he's one of them. You have to be careful, Marshall. They can see you."

"Wanda tells me you see these changes in future memories before they actually occur. Is that what happened at the birthday party?"

"I see things, but I don't like to talk about it. I don't tell anyone because they'll know. They know, but they won't talk about it because they don't want you to know."

Marshall shook his head slowly. "Please, Iglar, try to be more specific."

Iglar twisted in his chair and grabbed at several papers bound with a clip. He flung them at Marshall, who raised his hands defensively. "Look if you don't believe me. I've been keeping track of them, but I don't dare tell anyone. I told Jonathan Thomas once. But he was too far gone. He understood but then went away for good. Too many changes did it. The smart ones know. You, Wanda, Hayden and Wallace know something about it but not enough. You think you know, but it's just the opposite. The smart ones know. Korinth knows. But they just can't speak of it any more. They know even more than me."

Marshall bent down and picked up the papers as Iglar was talking and shuffled them back into order.

"Okay, so if I understand this right, we have the ability to see the divergent events in hindsight after they have occurred. But you, Iglar, you can see the changes in the future. Is that it?"

Iglar nodded slowly. "Sometimes I see some of them before they happen. The ones happening now; I see those. Others are smarter than me. They are much, much smarter and see all of them in advance. All of them, do you understand!" Iglar moved his chair even closer so his lips were only a couple centimeters from Marshall's. The breath of the disheveled man smelled like he chewed on a rotten piece of fish. Once again, Marshall fought the urge to vomit. The room started spinning; he had to get out soon.

"Tell me more, Iglar? There are others who are smarter than you?"

Iglar pointed to the documents in Marshall's hand. "Read. Then you'll know some of it but not all of it. You can't have everything, Marshall. That would be dangerous. It's very dangerous, but it was predicted, that we know."

Marshall rose from his chair and headed toward the door. "Thank you, Iglar. I'll let myself out. I will read these papers and we will — we'll talk again. Will that be alright?"

"Maybe, but I don't know because it may not happen and neither of us will even know it. Beware, Marshall — he's coming for you too." Iglar began to laugh slowly, but the laughter soon morphed into sobs. He grabbed at his head and pulled hard on his long, stringy hair. Marshall couldn't stand to watch and hurried out, bounding down the flight of stairs and heading quickly toward the front door with Iglar's papers in hand.

Chapter Three

After consuming four 12-ounce bags of M&Ms in one sitting, the sugar rush had long abated, and Marshall felt exhausted and irritable. Plus, he had a terrible itch near his naval from the earlier incident with the soap at Wanda's workplace.

He scooted his chair closer to the table while staring into each face, hoping for inspiration and insight. Instead, he saw nothing of comfort in the blank, frightened stares that looked back at him. Copies of Iglar's documents lay scattered across the tabletop, along with empty soda bottles and snack bags. Wanda, Wallace, Hayden and Kenny had gathered to piece the mystery together.

"So, we have — we've determined that the anomalies are real, and they're only apparent to us. I think it's obvious this is because we have one thing in common — one very important thing."

"Yes, we're autistic," said Kenny.

"High-functioning autistic." Wanda corrected him. "It matters relative to the experience. We're level one on the DSM-5 — except Iglar and Korinth of course."

"Well, we know what Iglar experienced," said Marshall while pointing at the papers. "Has anyone been able to connect with Korinth?"

"She's even more difficult to understand," said Wanda. "I was able to get some useful information, but she's withdrawn and isolated."

"Kind of like you, Wanda," said Kenny while smiling and pushing his glasses over the bridge of his nose. Wanda crouched down in the chair and wrapped her arms around her legs. It took Marshall several seconds to understand Kenny's failed attempt at humor.

"That wasn't funny, Kenny. You hurt Wanda's feelings."

His friend paused a moment before his smile changed into a deep frown. Turning toward Wanda, he said in a low voice. "I'm sorry. You know I like to make jokes, and sometimes they're bad."

Wanda's forehead furrowed as her eyes filled with tears. "It's ok, Kenny. I know I'm ugly... ugly and stupid!" She choked through the last word.

Marshall looked around the table as everyone focused on Wanda. Unfortunately, empathy was a difficult concept for some of her friends to understand, let alone practice. Marshall read many books on the subject, and he memorized the most common responses to awkward situations like this.

"Wanda, I know Kenny is sorry. We, ah, all see your inner beauty. That's why I asked you to be in the group. I — value you."

Wanda looked over at him and smiled weakly. "Thank you, Marshall. I value you too." There was something in the way she said the words that made him pause for just a moment. The feeling was strange and unnerving.

"Okay, I'm glad that is settled. Now, can we talk about Korinth? So, did you get a chance to speak with her?"

Wanda shook her head. "I did, but as I said, it was hard. Korinth got very upset when I started to explain what we experienced. I showed her the incidents we categorized, and she gave me these." Wanda reached into a leather artist's folder with handles and pulled out a small stack of drawing papers. She spread out five illustrations done in charcoal with remarkable detail. Each paper had a date scribbled haphazardly across the top.

"I've studied them thoroughly. They correlate to five specific incidents documented on our list."

She pointed to the first picture. "This is a drawing of a man with a bomb strapped to his body who was apprehended outside O'Hare Airport in Chicago in July 2016 before he could detonate it. There were no casualties. But *we* remember this in an entirely different way. To all of us, the device *did* go off inside the building. The explosion caused nine deaths, including the terrorist."

"If the future held true to *our* timeline," said Hayden, "the security at major airports around the world would have been enhanced, which might have prevented this from happening..." He produced an internet printout that screamed, *Suicide Bombers Detonate Explosives in LaGuardia Airport Killing 139 People*. The date on the story was August 2016.

"But look at the dates on Korinth's drawing." Wanda pointed to the top of the page where *July 2016* was written in bold lettering. At the bottom, in smaller script were Korinth's signature and a handwritten date of April 2014. "Not only did she predict the exact date of the change event, but she drew an accurate depiction of it more than two years before it happened."

Wallace shuffled through the papers Marshall had taken from Iglar's house. He pulled out one of the sheets and placed it on top of Wanda's picture. "This is how Iglar describes the same event. 'In July 2016, the man alerts the police to the one with the bomb in the Chicago airport. The man will disappear again once he knows he has made the change.' Iglar dated this page April 2014."

Hayden scratched his head. "I believe 139 people died a month later in a different bombing that probably never should have happened."

There was silence as they examined Korinth's drawing and Iglar's narrative. Wanda pushed the first rendering to the side and pulled out the second. A woman stood inside the concourse of a small airport next to the same man from the other sketch.

"It took me some time to understand this one. This person is talking to a female aircraft mechanic. She worked at a private airport. You can see the name on the drawing, which catered to corporate jets and chartered flights. That day, a Learjet 70 was scheduled to travel from Newark to Cleveland. It's item thirteen on our list. Three of us recall reading about a crash involving this airplane. However, in the new reality, the plane arrived at its destination with no reported incidents. Korinth drew this in November 2015, six months before the event took place."

Marshall rifled through Iglar's papers. "Here it is. 'In May 2016, the man approaches the woman mechanic in the concourse. He tells her the plane will crash because of a turbine disc failure in one of the engines. She asks him to wait, but he leaves and no one can find him. When she checks the engine, she discovers the broken part.' Iglar's note is dated November 2015."

"It took great effort, but Hayden and I tracked down the five passengers on that plane we believe were supposed to die," said Wanda. "Naturally, the possibilities are infinite when there are multiple people involved. The two who would have had the most immediate impact included a popular Congressman who was in line for an important committee chairmanship and a Saudi sheikh with substantial wealth and a connection to a terrorist cell in America."

Hayden stroked his chin and gazed off in the distance. He rose, but his poor coordination caused his feet to cross. He stumbled and nearly fell to the floor, but Marshall and Kenny rushed over to help him back up.

"I am fine, really." Hayden awkwardly brushed his clothes as he made his way back to his chair. "I have been rehabilitating my apartment, and I think I inhaled mold spores." Hayden took a deep, wheezing breath to validate his claim. "But look, let us not worry about my clumsiness. I am always clumsy, we know this. But it does not change the fact that we have a theoretical physics mystery. In some instances, we recall different perceptions of history from what actually happened. To add a twist, Korinth and Iglar experience these historic diversions before they take place. Based on the laws of the universe as we understand them, this simply cannot be."

"I don't have an answer," said Marshall. "And why is it that only Iglar and Korinth possess this advanced ability? What is it they share?"

"I can only think of one thing," said Wanda. She had their undivided attention and loved a bit of drama.

"So, what is the commonality?"

"As I said before, they're level two on the DSM-5 scale. The rest of us are level one. It's really the only difference."

Marshall's head tilted slightly. "That is an odd coincidence, but I don't understand how that has any bearing on any of this. Theories?"

The room was silent as they looked at each other while searching for answers.

"It gets even stranger," said Wanda.

"How can it possibly become any stranger?" asked Kenny.

Wanda pulled the final etching and set it on the table. The drawing depicted a man in the middle of the street turning just in time to see an early model pickup truck that was about to strike him head on. The driver and passenger had a look of stunned horror with eyes wide and mouths gaping open. On the easement between the sidewalk and street, someone else stood in the shadows of a dimly lit street lamp, shrouded in a full-length trench coat and heavy brimmed hat. At the top of the sketch, written in bold lettering, was the date of July 16th of this year.

Marshall lifted one of Iglar's papers and began to read from it. "'The man will approach someone on a deserted road on the evening of the due date. The victim plans to pass on important information, but the man does not want that transfer to take place. He will push the other in front of the truck.'" Marshall set the paper back down. "The date on Iglar's last note—is July 16th, the same as Korinth."

Kenny jumped up from his chair and began pacing. "Oh my God, this can't be happening. It's sooooo bad. July 16th. That's a couple days from now. Holy Einstein, we shouldn't think any more about this. Just forget it for cryin' out loud. Does anyone want to come over to my parent's house and play Age of Wulin? I enjoy Age of Wulin. I also have the Howl of Freedom. Doesn't anyone else have the Howl of Freedom? Because I do..."

Kenny's sudden emotional reaction affected Wanda, and she hit herself with an open palm. "I can't take it, I just can't take it," she repeated. "It gives me the creeps." Each word corresponded with another self-inflicted blow.

The unsettling actions of Kenny and Wanda caused Hayden to withdraw to a corner of the room, where he slid down to the floor and mumbled to no one in general. "I can recite the entire known nebula by heart. Ghost of Jupiter, Blinking Planetary, Dumbell Nebula, Ring Nebula...."

The situation became chaotic, and Marshall felt that familiar stirring in the pit of his stomach. The panic and fear crawled through his torso and out into his limbs like an aggressive vine in an accelerated growth mode, squeezing him until he couldn't process events in an orderly manner. Breathing deeply and slowly, he reminded himself that the feeling was temporary and would eventually pass. No matter what it took, panic would not get the better of him.

"Kenneth!" Marshall used an angry tone sparingly so it would have the optimum effect when he most needed it. In fact, Kenny froze in his tracks. He stopped talking, turned, and walked back to his seat, folding his hands in his lap. Kenny's sudden silence had an immediate impact on Wanda. She slowed the motion of her open palm, and the impact of the blows to her head lessened. To further calm her, Marshall reached out and took her free hand. Their eyes remained locked together for an uncomfortably long period. Despite the red welts on her forehead, Wanda looked different lately… *better*, in a way that Marshall couldn't explain. He felt a rather unusual sensation that he ruminated about for some time.

"I'm not sure we would have much success talking to either Iglar or Korinth at this point," said Marshall. "So, it seems we have two days until the next incident takes place. In his obscure manner of communicating, Iglar hinted he watched this 'man,' as he calls him, perform these deeds. I'm guessing Iglar will try to follow him on July 16th. We must also be there. I'm unaware of any other way to gain clarity on this."

Wanda broke the ensuing silence. "I'm scared, Marshall. What is going on here? We only catalogued big events we all remembered. What if there were smaller changes too insignificant to recall? There could be hundreds, thousands or even millions… Are we going — crazy? Is this part of our condition? Maybe we don't belong out here by ourselves like everyone says."

"We have to be strong, Wanda." Marshall didn't let go of her hand as he took hold of the other. "We've all had these collective experiences, so it's unlikely we're deranged."

Hayden rose and walked toward the door. "There is a substantial amount of work to do over the next two days. We must catalogue these occurrences and try to find patterns that will help us understand why this is happening."

"Patterns are almost irrelevant, Hayden." Wallace rolled his eyes and curled the corners of his mouth. "It could be random. It could be group psychosis. Who knows?"

33

"Group psychosis? Can that even be possible?" Wanda pulled away from Marshall and grabbed the sides of her head.

"Don't worry, Wanda, it's not group psychosis." Marshall glared at Wallace. "There's an explanation for this, and we will find it. I promise."

***

The intervening days went by quickly as the group carried out their assigned tasks. Wanda and Wallace continued to study the phenomenon and ultimately decided there were three distinct categories. The group recounted origin events with extreme clarity. Secondary events were by-products of the original change, and peripheral events were branches of secondary events that had a dead end.

As Wanda pointed out, there were thirteen origin events they recalled in sharp detail. There may have been more, but participant age tainted the results to some degree. Iglar was the oldest at forty, which made him fourteen years older than Kenny, who was the youngest. In his lifetime, Hayden may have experienced at least three more origin events, but there was no corroboration. Hayden and Wallace worked on quantum mechanics to apply science to the phenomenon, but they weren't having much success.

On July 15th, one day before Iglar and Korinth's prediction of the next origin event, Marshall convened a final meeting to review their collective findings and develop a strategy.

"I think it's clear we've discovered an anomaly that will shatter the precepts of modern science. Either we are hallucinating, which will disrupt the basic understanding of autism, or we recall true events that were changed by some force and falsely recorded in history. If so, the question is, who or what is responsible."

"I am leaning toward the latter explanation," said Hayden. "Wallace and I dug deep into the theoretical physics, and it is possible. In fact, it has always been possible, I suppose. You are all familiar with the many worlds interpretation of quantum mechanics, correct?"

Everyone nodded except Kenny, who mumbled a nearly inaudible, "I'm not."

"Fine," said Hayden as he sighed and gave Kenny a side glance. "For those of you who are *not* acquainted with MWI, it hypothesizes that when two particles interact in a certain way, there can be multiple outcomes. This explains why, for example, an electron may appear to take two paths simultaneously. In the double slit experiment, the electron in one universe interacts with the electron in an identical universe."

Hayden paused. "Are you following me, Kenny?"

"Was that necessary, Hayden?" asked Marshall. "Please don't mock Kenny, if that's what you're doing."

"I was not mocking anyone, Marshall. But it is rather — frustrating — to speak to someone so lacking."

"Just continue without your commentary."

Hayden cleared his throat and peered over his reading glasses. "Over time, the resulting two universes diverge, so the subsequent realities become less similar. Why we seem to recall both sets of events, I cannot say. However, if it proves to be true, we will have redefined quantum physics, essentially discrediting the Copenhagen interpretation."

"All of this assumes an unnatural cause. What could it be?" asked Wanda.

35

"Time travel. If MWI is real, there is no other reasonable explanation. Contemporary physics predicted the potential for traversable wormholes for many years. If a future society discovered how to hold a wormhole open, by a Casmir Vacuum for example, then it is very possible, perhaps even probable given our present circumstances."

"Why are *we* the only ones who are experiencing this?"

"We are different, Marshall. The gene expression in unaffected people is dissimilar in their frontal and temporal lobes while there is typically very little difference in either of our lobes," said Wallace. "Perhaps our brains are more sensitive to these changes, or maybe we simply lag behind in adjusting to these new realities. I cannot say, but it's foolish to dismiss the possibility that our condition is responsible for our sensitivity."

"Shouldn't everyone with autism have these memories?" asked Kenny.

"How do we know they don't?" replied Wallace.

"Well, ah, I guess we would have to ask them. I cannot imagine..."

"We need to deal with the issue at hand," said Marshall. "According to Iglar's writings and Korinth's pictures, the next 'event' takes place tomorrow evening. We must follow Iglar throughout the day. I know others have disagreed with that, and so we haven't arrived at a consensus. I've decided that I will track Iglar whether or not anyone else participates."

"I'm going with," said Kenny. "Yeah, I'm going; I don't believe I just said that."

"No way, no way! It's dangerous, Marshall. Too dangerous!" Wanda pulled and twirled her hair while Hayden mumbled to himself and rocked in his chair. Wallace sat stoically without uttering a word.

Marshall looked at each one of them for a long moment. "I'm going, and it's just that simple. I have to find out where this mystery leads…"

Chapter Four

Sixtus walked to the end of the building and peered around the corner while shielding his body from view. The man he was watching stopped a couple hundred feet north of the intersection between Buckeye and 12th street. He looked in both directions before pulling out a pack of cigarettes and taking out a smoke with his lips. The night sky was lit up in the eerie glow of a full moon reflecting off dark clouds that hung ominously low. The air was thick with the musty smell of summer rain mixed with soot and dust. A single overhead streetlight was dull and lifeless like the sky itself.

Sixtus moved out from the shadows and strode with purpose toward the target. He blinked and called up the visual. The countdown in the corner of his eye indicated there were thirty-one seconds until the Event threshold. The Object faced the opposite direction and didn't notice Sixtus approaching. Smoke wafted up from his cigarette as the glow of the burning ember periodically illuminated part of his deeply lined and haggard face.

The countdown continued: twelve...eleven...ten seconds until the display flashed red and the time elapsed completely. The holographic icon dissipated on his internal HUD just as a blue Ford F-series made an abrupt right turn that caused the tires to squeal. The vehicle hit a small puddle of water that sent a spray of droplets in every direction. The target's attention was drawn to the rapidly approaching truck, so he didn't notice Sixtus until the last instant. The cigarette dropped from his mouth as he realized there was someone stalking him. The Object turned and looked deep into the stone-cold eyes of the antagonist.

"Who are you? No, I..." It was all he had time to mutter before Sixtus grasped him firmly, and with a sudden violent push, shoved him in front of the oncoming pickup.

The victim impacted with the grille of the moving vehicle with a sickening *thud*, and the body hurtled backwards several feet as the driver slammed on the brakes. In that instant, the air appeared to evacuate the space immediately surrounding the truck. A small shudder rippled through the voided area, and for a moment, material reality seemed pliable and elastic.

Positioned directly under the streetlamp, Sixtus evaluated the condition of the body and concluded the target was dead. The collision with the grille opened a massive fracture resulting in a gaping hole in the back of the Object's skull. Blood oozed from the wound, and a large shard of bone sliced into the occipital lobe, which caused a chunk of brain to drop onto the pavement. The dead man's legs were twisted grotesquely, and an exposed femur with a raw jagged edge poked out from his khaki trousers.

Just that quickly, the assignment was over.

All the readouts turned green, and the internals vanished as Sixtus began walking back toward Henson Park. Slamming doors pierced the night air, and he heard two voices clearly in the distance.

"Holy shit, Arturo, what did you do? This guy is dead. *Santa Madre de Dios lo matamos.*"

"Shut up, Rudy. Just shut up. He jumped out into the road, I swear it."

"*Calma mi amigo.* I saw someone else. Did you? Standing right behind him. I think he was pushed."

Arturo dropped his head into his hands. "My God, I killed someone. Call 9-1-1, Rudy. I can't..."

Rudy wasn't really listening. He grabbed his stomach and stumbled over to the shoulder of the road just as he started to heave.

Sixtus reached the church parking lot on Tonto Street, where he left his black BMW 650i. He listened to parts of the conversation from a block away.

The voice was loud and distressed. "Oh, my God. Some guy pushed him right in front of us."

Once he got to his car, Sixtus touched his thumb to the infrared sensor on the handle, but as he prepared to open the door, he heard a high-pitched cackling from behind. He turned to evaluate the potential threat as the holographic display opened and focused on the approaching figure.

The man appeared to be in his fifties or perhaps younger and ravaged by drugs. He hunched over completely naked, a wide grin spread unevenly across his pock-marked face. Extending one hand out, the other dropped to his genitals, and he began to massage and stroke himself. He approached cautiously, mumbling under his breath.

"I saw it. Yes, yes, I did. You pushed him. Boom. Right into its path. Splat, I say splat." He pursed his lips and made a farting noise. "Uh huh, you pushed, didn't you? You think I don't know, but I do. I remember. I remember it all." He tapped the side of his head with a forefinger.

The holographic display buzzed with activity as the vagrant's vitals appeared on the visual. His heartbeat was very fast and irregular, while his systolic and diastolic blood pressure readings were dangerously high. His rate of respiration was indicative of someone with severe asthma or COPD. A blip sounded simultaneously as a two-sentence conclusion flashed. *Subject suffering from severe hypertension, early onset emphysema, chronic and advanced fibromuscular dysplasia. Actuarial data indicates subject will likely die within five years.*

Sixtus closed the car door and walked up to the derelict, stopping about ten feet away. The wretch continued to jerk violently at his genitalia, growing more nervous as the tanned and well-muscled man approached. Reaching into his billfold, Sixtus extracted five one-hundred-dollar bills and held them up in the weak glow of a dim lightbulb mounted on the church eaves.

"I'll give you $500 to forget what you saw tonight. Can you do that?"

The man squirmed and used his free hand to grab at the skin on his face. "I know you. Why are you here? Men from Mars. Ha ha ha... That's what I said, Bunkie, men from Mars."

Sixtus sighed. "Look. I'm laying this money on the ground here. If you pick it up, I'll assume we have a deal. But if you say anything, I'll beam you up to the mother ship for experiments. Very painful experiments."

The gutter snipe backed off, and the smile faded for a moment. The rapid movements of his hand on his phallus did not abate. "I hate you and your kind. Crazy,

crazy, crazy. You're all trying to make us bat-shit crazy." He raised both hands and grabbed at a few strands of his long, unkempt hair and pulled hard. "Get the fuck away from me... Get away."

Sixtus evaluated the threat. To invoke Rule Seven was severe in any instance, but in this case, hardly necessary. Here was another dead man walking; an imbecile with no future. No one would believe him, regardless of what he said. Sixtus left the cash on the wet pavement and returned to his car. As he exited the parking lot, he glanced over his shoulder and watched the naked man pick up the bills just as he ejaculated.

As Sixtus maneuvered the BMW away from the scene of the incident, he caught a glimpse of the truck that struck the Object. A group of floaters surrounded the unwitting accomplices in the assassination. The driver and the passenger attempted to retreat to the interior of the cab, but the mob blocked their path.

They dragged the men out to the middle of the street and threw them down on the pavement, savagely beating them with baseball bats, sticks and metal toed boots. Some fifty feet away from the scene, a squad car sat parked just off the road with its red light twirling and a cautious officer locked safely inside.

Sixtus didn't feel comfortable until he was back on the 202 heading east, which eventually merged with the 101 north. Traffic was minimal, and he only had a half hour drive to his home in Scottsdale's fashionable McCormick Ranch. He pulled into the gated community and waved at the security guard as he drove up to the guard shack. As the gate opened, Sixtus rolled down the window.

"Hi, Doug. How are things this evening?"

"Hey, Mr. Clayton. It's been a night, I'll tell ya. The craziness just keeps coming farther and farther north. We caught someone trying to climb over the fence tonight. He got zapped when he touched the electrodes at the top. When they hauled him away, they found a gun and a pressure cooker filled with nails and explosives. I believe he was going to bomb someone's house."

"Wow...Yeah, it keeps getting stranger. Wish I had an answer."

The gate finished opening, and the whir of the electric motor ceased. "Well, you try to get some rest, Mr. Clayton. You look worn out."

Sixtus smiled weakly. "I know. I've had a long day."

"Oh, and Mr. Clayton, there was someone here looking for you earlier. He wouldn't give me a name, but he looked—uncomfortable. He was professional though. Not a floater. But he was nervous... real nervous."

"Okay, thanks for the heads up. Have a nice night, Doug."

Sixtus entered the extended driveway and parked in the open bay inside the four-car garage. On one side of the BMW sat a new Cadillac Escalade and on the other was a vintage red 1998 Dodge Viper. Everything that surrounded Sixtus was comfortable but not pretentious. He was wealthy but careful about not drawing attention.

After walking up the winding brick pathway, he came into the house, took off his shoes, and reset the security alarm. Taking care to tiptoe quietly, he made his way over to the study and carefully opened the double doors. After settling into the overstuffed leather chair behind the cherry wood desk, he grabbed the decanter on the credenza and poured himself a stiff Oban single malt scotch. Leaning back, he sighed and took a long swallow of the smooth beverage.

Clearly there was something wrong in the future, but he had no way of knowing what it was. His commitment to the program ended a little over five years ago, but he recently received two additional assignments, which could only mean a crisis had developed.

When the dormant overhead display lit up in his mind two weeks ago, Sixtus almost fainted from shock and disbelief. Yet, he followed protocol and carried out the mission. In his original twenty-year commitment, he never was asked to kill anyone directly. The fact that he ended the lives of two Objects in the last fourteen days only confirmed the seriousness of the situation in his own time.

Sixtus raised his glass to drink again but stopped short as someone rapped on the door. The distinctive knock was a welcome diversion. "It's open. Come in."

She walked in and smiled, moving past the edge of the desk. The chair swiveled so it faced her, and she sat on his lap and locked her hands behind his neck. Her scent was unmistakable, and her blond hair flowed in soft curls around her shoulders. Kara Norscone was the only thing that made life bearable in this stench hole of a century. Her smile could still melt Sixtus' heart in an instant, and he thanked the unseen powers that allowed such couplings to occur. He never knew what she saw in him. Yet, despite their age difference and unimaginably diverse backgrounds, he knew she loved him, and that was all that ever mattered.

"Jeffery, how come you're so late?" she asked while pulling back a bit. Her green eyes were penetrating and perceptive. Sixtus only survived her scrutiny because she chose to ignore the obvious contradictions in his life.

"I took a drive to try and relax. I had a rough night at the shelter. Several fights and one guy pulled a knife. More nut jobs roll in every night."

Her expression changed, and Sixtus could sense her concern. He knew Kara learned early on that it was best to avoid prying too deep into his daily activities. She had accepted, albeit reluctantly, his brief and stiff explanation that he was an only child whose parents had died, and an inherited trust fund provided the luxury of not having to work.

Even after they were married, Kara chose to continue her job at the clinic because she was proud of her stature as the Administrative Director at Phoenix General. Sixtus was an occasional volunteer at the Primavera homeless shelter. His so called "profession" may have appeared odd and out of character, but she never pried or checked up on him. Perhaps Kara wanted to avoid discovering something that might upset the wonderful life they built over the last five years.

"It bothers me, Jeffery. There's so much insanity in the world. I live it every day at the hospital. Sometimes I worry that you're not safe."

He grinned and rubbed her back. "I'm fine. Turk, the security guard, is as big as an ox, and nobody messes with him. Trust me."

She shook her head and ran her fingers through his thick crop of black hair. "I'm going to bed now, Jeffery. Any interest in following me?" Her eyes became playful, and she smiled coyly.

"Is that a trick question?" She rose, but as he started to follow, the phone in his pants pocket began to

45

vibrate. "Just a minute," he said. "I'll be right there." She turned and walked gracefully from the room as he pulled out the thin glass slab. The screen changed into 3-D holographic relief. He scrolled over the hologram and opened the newest text message. As he read the note, he felt a rush of panic:

You killed that man, and I watched you do it

Sixtus' eyes widened, and he shoved the phone back into his pocket. He held the glass of Scotch with trembling hands and drank heartily. *Who saw me tonight? That homeless drifter I encountered earlier wouldn't try and blackmail me, would he?*

Getting up slowly, Sixtus went and closed the doors. He sat back down and accessed the internal display. No messages were pending, which was a good sign. Apparently, nothing had changed in the future because of the breach. Moving his eyes rapidly, he used the search feature to determine if there were any anomalies when he compared the theoretical to the real. After several seconds, a red light flashed in the corner of the visual. *One anomaly found.* Sixtus shuddered; this could not be any worse.

He meditated for ten minutes before getting up and walking to the bedroom. Kara was still awake, propped up in bed and reading a romance novel. She looked up briefly as he went into the closet to change into his nightwear.

"Jeffery, something is bothering you. Do you want to talk about it?"

He came out in his pajamas and joined her under the sheets. "There's nothing wrong. It's just one of those days. I'll be alright tomorrow."

She patted his arm reassuringly. "Ok, I know better, but I won't bug you about it... Besides, I have other things in mind." She moved closer and began slowly caressing his thigh. Sixtus felt that familiar warm feeling flow as he cupped his hand over her breast.

While he always responded to any sort of encouragement from Kara, Sixtus remained distracted, and he knew he couldn't hide it from her. Someone was after him, and life was about to get much more complicated.

Chapter Five

Marshall, Wallace and Kenny watched Iglar throughout the day. He left his home in the early afternoon and travelled to the Lincoln House, which was a state-run hospital that provided lodging for over 400 patients with a variety of mental and emotional challenges. Unlike the horrific sanitariums of the past, these facilities were regulated and offered first-class treatment and living arrangements. Still, the Lincoln House was the exception and not the rule. Even with increased scrutiny, estimates put the level of abuse for those with cognitive challenges living apart from immediate family members at nearly seventy percent.

Iglar visited the facility for several hours as Marshall and his companions kept a respectable distance. They occupied a booth in a coffee shop across the street so they could see everyone who entered and exited the facility.

Marshall was lactose intolerant; Wallace couldn't have sugar, and the smell of coffee nauseated Kenny, so it was a challenge to keep their collective focus after sitting at the table drinking water for several hours. When the clock moved past two p.m., Kenny had a panic attack. This drove

Wallace into a dissociative state where he appeared semi-catatonic.

"We missed him. I know we missed him. He left and we're still sitting here. Sitting here—*forever*. It's getting dark now. What if we sit here forever, Marshall? What if we never move from here? Just waiting and waiting and waiting..."

"We won't stay here forever, Kenny. Iglar has not yet emerged, but he can't stay there forever. We have—we've watched the entrance with unwavering consistency. He just hasn't left yet."

"So, why don't we go in and find him? I wish I was at home drinking skim milk. Did you know pasteurization kills 99.2 percent of the bacteria and other microorganisms in the liquid? Do you want me to name the bacteria pasteurization kills? I can; I really can. Campylobacter jejuni, Coliforms, Coxiella burnetii, Escherichia coli O157:H7, Listeria monocytogenes..."

"Kenny—Kenny! I appreciate your knowledge of pasteurization, truly I do, but it's not germane to what we're here for."

"I don't want to be here anymore, Marshall. And why is Wallace shaking?"

After several more uncomfortable exchanges that pushed the trio to the breaking point, Iglar finally left the main building and got into a waiting Uber. The car remained in the well-lit courtesy zone for some time, which probably meant Iglar was having trouble communicating with the driver. Marshall interrupted Wallace as he meticulously removed crumbs and debris from the table with a sanitary wipe and pulled him towards the door as Kenny followed closely behind.

They got into the Civic and turned onto Peoria just as the Uber came out of the horseshoe driveway and started east toward I-10. Nightfall descended, and only

49

the good fortune of a bright Arizona full moon kept the landscape from being plunged into pitch darkness. Still, the visual challenge made the task of keeping the Uber in sight more difficult. To make matters worse, Marshall was naturally cautious, but the Uber driver was the opposite, and the erratic swerves and lane changes created a white-knuckled adventure.

For Marshall, the need to weave through traffic was unnerving, but Wallace and Kenney were in near hysterics.

"Too fast—going too fast. Watch out. Watch out!" said Kenny.

"Arrrgh! No, no, no. Slow down, Marshall." Wallace pushed up against his seat and grabbed at the slingshot handle above the passenger door. "Die, die—we're gonna die!"

"We're not going to die, Wallace. We won't die," said Marshall while swerving into the left lane in a reckless manner that suggested they might die after all.

The Uber cut across two lanes and turned onto the frontage road that funneled into I-10. Marshall hated the freeways and driving over fifty mph could trigger anxiety and apprehension. He swallowed hard and hit the accelerator, merging into traffic without looking over his shoulder. He hoped the other drivers were paying attention and would make room for him, or there might be a horrific crash. Wallace covered his eyes and Kenny disengaged his seat belt and curled up on the floor.

Traffic thinned considerably as rush hour receded, and Marshall was able to keep a safe distance until the Uber exited onto Buckeye. The car stopped near a run-down church in a tough Phoenix neighborhood. Marshall slowed as he saw Iglar exit the car and pay the driver.

They purposely drove past Iglar while trying to stay inconspicuous. Wallace slunk low while Kenny remained on the floorboards in the backseat. Marshall turned onto the nearest side street and parked, exhorting his companions to hurry as they exited and walked a respectable distance behind Iglar on 12th street back toward Buckeye. Almost fifty yards from the road, Iglar stopped in the middle of the church's parking lot, and his back stiffened. He faced Buckeye and looked ahead.

Marshall found a small decorative wall that jutted out from an apartment building across the street from the church, and they moved behind it to stay hidden. Following Iglar's line of sight, Marshall saw a figure in dark clothing almost hidden in the shadows of a dim street light. Directly under the lamp, another man looked around suspiciously as though he was expecting someone. He took out a package of cigarettes and lit up a smoke.

The mysterious man emerged from the murky darkness and walked purposely towards the one standing under the street lamp. A passenger truck rounded a curve in the road and approached at a high rate of speed. The shadow man moved with more urgency while the one with the cigarette looked up and flinched, saying something Marshall couldn't hear because of the distance. Without warning, the shadow man reached out and shoved the other into the street just as the truck arrived. The body hit the reinforced grille and bounced backwards with a resounding *thump.*

Marshall gasped while Wallace shrunk against the corner of the building. Kenny stifled a shriek and started sniveling. Meanwhile, Iglar stood in the same position without moving, but Marshall could hear him laughing even at this distance.

The mysterious man who caused the collision moved swiftly away from the scene, his hands thrust deep into the pockets of his trench coat. He walked away from Buckeye towards Tonto Street and turned sharply into the church parking lot. A black BMW was parked in a far corner of the lot away from the light, and he made his way towards it. Initially, he didn't see Iglar, who started walking diagonally on an intercept course. They eventually made eye contact, and both stopped some ten feet apart and cautiously regarded each other.

Iglar was the first to speak; his voice sounded tense and agitated. Periodically, he cackled and tittered at the stranger. Perhaps most unnerving for Marshall was watching Iglar expose himself. The mystery man remained calm throughout the entire encounter. At one point, he reached into his coat and extracted several bills from his wallet and held them up for Iglar to see. Slowly and deliberately, he laid them on the pavement and backed away, resuming his walk toward the BMW. Iglar scuttled forward and picked up the money but then turned and continued talking and gesturing in an animated way while pointing and swinging at the air with a balled fist.

Marshall remained hidden behind the wall across the street, but he pulled out his mobile phone and snapped several pictures of the BMW as it passed underneath the security lamp in the church parking lot. As the car turned onto 12th street heading north, Marshall took another picture of the back end of the car.

Turning to Wallace and Kenny, who huddled together behind the parapet wall, Marshall wondered why he bothered to bring them out here in the first place. Kenny had one hand over his eyes while Wallace whimpered and blew snot out of his nose.

"It's ok. The incident is finished. It transpired just as Iglar and Korinth predicted. We've confirmed beyond a doubt that both of them can identify deviations in future events before they happen."

"I don't care about any of that," said Wallace while he wiped his nose on his sleeve. "I just want to go home. That man killed someone. I saw it, and I can't forget it happened. It's the same as episode twenty-three, season five from Miami Vice when Tubbs sees Gerry Vincent push the Banker into an oncoming car. Everything is too unnerving!"

"I'm having a lot of anxiety, Marshall," said Kenny. "I mean *a lot* of anxiety. This is just bad. Bad, bad, bad. Bad people doing bad things. Bad people doing bad things. Bad, bad, bad."

"I know," said Marshall. "I'm as frightened as both of you. But we came here to find out if Iglar truly sees the future, and now we're sure he does. We have to fight the urges. This is not us. It's not our autism. In fact, it's our autism that's giving us this insight. I would go so far as to say we're... gifted."

Kenny stopped trembling and moved his hands away from his eyes. "You think so, Marshall? Gifted? You mean we have something that other people don't have?"

"Yes, it appears so. We remember things the way they were originally. Other people don't. And now we've found out that some of those with autism can even remember the future. I don't know what it means, but we must find out."

Wallace wasn't responding to Marshall's appeal to his intellect and curiosity. "This is too much. Too much for me, and I feel like I'm ungluing. The glue is seeping from my seams. I see it rolling down my sides as the seams unravel."

"Okay, let's all focus," said Marshall. "We have a license plate number. Hayden can hack into the Motor Vehicle Department and find out who owns the car. Let's collect Iglar and head back home."

"It's too late," said Kenny, "Iglar left." Marshall turned around and looked at the empty parking lot. The dim street lamp cast a muted orange-tinged light over the surface, but there was no trace of Iglar.

"Alright, let's go then. We have to get out of here." With Kenny's help, Marshall pulled Wallace to his feet, and they staggered over to the car before pushing their friend into the backseat. Police and ambulance sirens grew closer, and Marshall didn't want to answer questions about the crime and why they were at the scene.

He pulled the Civic onto Buckeye, traveled up to McDowell and over to 7th Avenue before turning back onto I-10. Nightfall always worsened the insanity that gripped the downtown area. The heroin and opium addicts lined McDowell, cursing and scowling as Marshall maneuvered his car around them. Oil drums appeared alongside the road, their flames serving no purpose on a hot July night except to intimidate those driving by. As Marshall looked around, the burning pyres provided an advanced glimpse into the future of a broken society.

Slam.

Marshall cringed and looked over to his left where the loud sound emanated. Kenny recoiled toward the driver's seat while Wallace groaned and slunk further onto the floorboards. A wild-eyed man with layers of filthy clothes and a soiled beanie cap pressed his face against the passenger's window while pounding on the roof of the car. Marshall tried to speed up, but several other bystanders left the gathering around the barrel fires and moved out onto the street to block the Civic's progress.

"Not good," said Kenny. "Not good at all!"

The psychotic man continued to pound on the roof. His face contorted, and his ungroomed beard added to the menacing look. "Get out of the car," he bellowed. "Get out and give us what you have! We need it. We *deserve* it!"

Marshall fought the paralysis that crept through his body. He found it difficult to react in situations that involved malicious or violent intent. If threatened, he knew the only reasonable recourse was retreat.

Unfortunately, an escape path was blocked by the gathering crowd. He scanned the street on both sides. The late hour left 7th Avenue nearly deserted, and the opposite lanes were completely open. Marshall pushed the accelerator, and the vehicle swerved, crossing the middle yellow dividing lines into the oncoming lanes. The floaters hesitated a moment and froze as the Civic sped up and drove past the group. Retreating to the side of the road, they threw rocks and bottles that careened off the roof and door panels as Marshall and his companions fled the scene.

With the safety of the freeway just ahead, he pulled onto the entrance ramp and breathed a sigh of relief. Kenny had his fists clenched tightly and was mumbling to himself in loud whispers. Wallace was nowhere in sight. In fact, he spent the entire trip pinned to the floor of the back seat.

They exited the freeway and drove back to Marshall's house, ignoring the threatening distractions along the way. A faint smell of wood smoke tinged the air as they walked to the front porch. Every night, a nearby building burned, and the sirens were so common they faded into background noise most people ignored.

Wallace had recovered somewhat and shrugged off an offer of help from Kenny as they went into Marshall's house. They both made their way to the couch and sat down, but Wallace immediately slumped over and laid his head on one of the cushions.

Marshall pulled up a chair from the kitchen table and collected his thoughts as Kenny and Wallace looked at him, waiting for assurance and direction.

"So, what should we do now?"

"We've got to find out who the murderer is. I think he's connected to the phenomenon in a very important way." Marshall grabbed his phone and called up his contacts list.

"Hello, Hayden?"

"Yes? Is this Marshall? Tell me what happened tonight and include the details."

"We saw a man push someone else in front of a car just as Iglar and Korinth predicted. I've got a picture of the car he was driving and the license plate."

"I can't get much information from home at this time of night, Marshall," said Hayden.

56

"Just get me a name and address if you can. I just sent you the pictures. The last one has the license plate."

"Ok, I see them. Working on it...."

There was a period of silence punctuated by the sound of Hayden typing on his keyboard.

"Alright, I have it. Can you write this down?"

"I have a photographic memory, Hayden. There's no need for creating a hardcopy," said Marshall.

"Ah, yes, I forgot about your ability. Sometimes I discount those with minimal recollection skills as compared to my own. After all, I have memorized the entire Encyclopedia Britannica."

Marshall sighed. "Yes, Hayden, we're all aware of your prowess. Can you please give me the contact information?"

"His name is Jeffery Clayton. His address is 8204 N 75th Street, Scottsdale. Do you need his zip code?"

"No, that's fine, Hayden. Thank you. Do you have a phone number?"

"Naturally."

"Can I have it please?"

"Yes, 480-555-0999. That's his mobile phone."

"Good, thank you again."

"Yes, but I'd like a more detailed explanation if it isn't too much trouble," said Hayden.

"Actually, Hayden, this is the worst possible time. I'll see you soon and tell you everything, alright?"

"Well… I suppose it will have to do."

Marshall heard the abrupt click of the phone and turned his attention back to Kenny and Wallace. "So, we now have his name and know where he lives. We also have his cell number."

"What are you going to do now, Marshall, call him?"

"No!" Wallace jerked forward on the couch. "This is so wrong. We need to forget all of it. Just forget these theories. It would be so much better if we just signed on to World of Warcraft. Let's just do that, ok?"

"We can't, Wallace," said Kenny. "We just can't. We're aware of something no one else knows, and we can't forget it. We need to do something. I have a feeling... A deep, deep feeling that something important is happening. We can't just let it go. My distress level is so high, but I agree we need to learn more about him."

"Why can't we send him a text?" asked Marshall.

"Bad idea," said Wallace. "A terrible idea. He'll know who we are. Who knows what he'll do to us. He killed someone, Marshall. Did you hear me? He killed someone."

"We've got to let him know we are — we're watching him," said Marshall. "If he's aware that we know what he's doing, we might save a life. We might save our reality, who knows? The implications are enormous."

"We also might affect this timeline in a negative way," said Wallace. "We might cause a catastrophe of epic proportions. Leave it alone, Marshall."

"No, send the text, Marshall," said Kenny. "Tell him we're out there and he can't kill again without us knowing."

Marshall nodded at Kenny and then encrypted his number by establishing an SMS proxy channel. He entered the information Hayden provided and paused a moment before typing quickly on the keypad and hitting send before he changed his mind.

You killed that man, and I watched it.

Marshall realized there was no turning back.

Chapter Six

Sixtus was unable to sleep, and his chamomile tea sat cooling on his desk in the study as he stared off into the distance, deep in thought. Instinctively, he tried to access the overhead display, but the processor implant deactivated two hours after completing his last mission. He cursed silently and once again wondered what calamity was unfolding in the future.

Like every Time Sculptor who finished their twenty-year obligation, Sixtus was free to live out the remainder of his life in the assigned era, understanding there would be no further contact from the future. Since the technology required to accelerate massive quantities of neutrinos faster than the speed of light didn't exist in this primitive time, returning home was impossible anyway.

Through extensive simulations and casual experience, the Corporates determined that twenty years was the limit an agent could conduct Time Sculpt missions before signs of psychopathy emerged. Once an agent completed his term, he was permitted to assimilate into that era's society as long as he remained obscure and did not procreate. To eliminate the problems associated with obsolescence and unintended interference, the Corporates briefly considered terminating retired Time Sculptors, but the idea was ultimately rejected out of concern that agents might go rogue when faced with certain death. Sixtus was unaware of any agent who had been called back into service after retirement... until now.

Focusing on meditation, he struggled to control irrational thoughts and achieve balanced placement. At least he was still in this reality, so no one from the future ordered an emergency intervention yet. That meant the resultant time line remained intact and undisturbed. Sixtus sat back and exhaled with relief.

With a clear mind, he turned his attention to the disturbing text message. Rogue incidents happened on occasion, but the infinite levels of thought analysis conducted through the Agency's advanced neural intelligence network made agent exposure highly improbable. *How could something so egregious occur in the middle of an operation?* Sixtus always stuck to the script with flawless accuracy as he was taught.

He pushed the Object in front of the pickup at the precise time identified in his instructions, thus adhering to the letter of the protocol. And yet, someone, or possibly several people, observed him. He could only speculate the problem originated because of careless work in constructing the mission in the future.

Sixtus picked up the phone and scrolled through the call history. The antagonist's number showed up as straight zeros. He ran his fingers through his hair several times. The implications of being discovered might have dire consequences.

What if the miscreant in the church parking lot had gone to the police?

Time Sculptors who altered the past outside the scope of their assignment were said to be eliminated instantly, but no one knew the means the Corporates used to cleanse the system. Regardless of the potential for punishment, Sixtus knew he must find the originator of the text to properly assess the damage.

As a general rule, eliminating someone from the local population was prohibited since the time line might be disrupted with unpredictable results. Still, the Academy was replete with rumors of retired agents killing people who were historically insignificant without consequence. Those from the future often adapted poorly to backward eras, and this inability to assimilate led to exaggerated fits of jealousy, envy and rage.

While acts born of emotion ran contrary to the teachings of the instructors, Sixtus never forgot the rumors, so in this instance, caution was paramount. His preference was to locate the offender(s) and try to dissuade them from revealing their knowledge of last night's Event. In a worst-case scenario, he might have to kill them.

He rose from his chair and walked down the long hallway toward the bedroom. The small Victorian globes cast a soft glow on the Satillo tile, and the leather soles of his Tan Ferro Alto's echoed softly through the house. He used the guest bathroom so as not to disturb Kara and stared at his reflection in the mirror while splashing water on his face. The past 25 years in this time were extraordinarily difficult. Besides the obvious cultural challenges, the effects of existing in the past with no connection to his original conception had begun to subtly erode his cognitive functions in subtle but unmistakable ways.

Before he left his home for good, Sixtus understood that any trace of his existence in the future would be deleted. Everyone knew the price of participating in the

Time Sculptor program was severe. At some point, a Corporate enforcer visited his mother in her own past and ordered her to abort Sixtus as a fetus. Great wealth and riches would be bestowed upon the family without explanation, but she would never know of her son's existence once he was sent back to the past. Like the other Time Sculptors, he would exist in a bubble, outside conventional space-time.

He pulled the covers up and slid into bed, trying his best not to wake Kara. She mumbled a bit and shifted her body, snuggling up to him. He placed his arm around her and pulled her even closer. Kara was the one shimmering bright light in the dark abyss of the 21st century. He contemplated how she'd react if he suddenly disappeared because of a Corporate termination order and couldn't bear the thought. Disturbing images invaded Sixtus' shallow dreams, and he slept poorly through the night.

***

Sunlight crept through the small separations in the vertical blinds that covered the carved French doors leading out to the flagstone-covered patio. Sixtus looked over at the digital clock that read: 5:35 a.m. Moving quietly, he walked to the shower in the bedroom farthest from the master suite. His silk pajamas dropped to the floor, and he tested the water temperature before stepping into the spacious cubicle.

The water cascaded over his body, which always helped calm his nerves. Last night's text was unsettling, and Sixtus decided the best option was to return to the scene of the Event and retrace his steps. Perhaps he might find evidence that would help unravel the mystery. Unfortunately, he no longer had the sophisticated internal computer to reference, replay and analyze the incident, so he would have to employ more primitive technologies.

Pulling Kara's Escalade out of the garage, he drove past the security shack and waved to Emmitt, the day guard. He turned out into light traffic with his mind still preoccupied with the furtive text. About two miles farther down on Via de Ventura, something impacted against the rear quarter panel of the Escalade with a loud *bang*, startling Sixtus and causing him to swerve slightly.

Just as he recovered, he slammed on the brakes to avoid hitting a car stopped directly ahead of him. Gridlock was getting worse every day, but this delay didn't relate to an accident. Gazing left and right, Sixtus saw at least twenty floaters running erratically through the line of cars. Armed with rocks, hammers and tire irons, they attacked people inside stalled vehicles indiscriminately.

What the?

A trio of men nearest the Escalade moved towards it, and one was close enough that Sixtus made eye contact with him, which was always a mistake. Reaching over to the glove box, he pulled out a vintage Walther 9mm, a weapon that violated strict national gun control laws. Right now, Sixtus didn't care about the legal consequences, especially when he watched a golf club shatter the windshield of the car in front of him. The filthy assailant wore rags and sported a long, untrimmed beard. His oily, matted hair hung down to his shoulders, partially hidden under a yellow stained cap.

"Poor-people-matter!   Poor-people-matter!"   he yelled through the gaping hole in the glass.

The woman in the car shrieked as he reached inside and pulled her through the broken windshield. The unsightly guttersnipe dragged her to the side of the road and threw her onto the shoulder. She tried to fight him off by kicking and scooting backwards, but he bent over and punched her hard in the face, which seemed to disorient her. He began to rip at her business suit and pulled hard at her bra until her breasts were fully exposed.

Sixtus saw enough. He cursed under his breath, swung the door open, and jumped out with the gun pointed at the floater. The man's eyes widened in momentary fear, but the look of vicious anger quickly returned. He climbed off the woman and began to stalk Sixtus.

Every Time Sculptor dreaded such a moment. If he fired the weapon, Sixtus would commit an unauthorized time breach, which might trigger the cleansing protocols he so feared. He cursed and mumbled as his hand tightened on the pistol grip. In the background, he heard the distant sound of a siren drawing closer. Every day, the cops' struggle to maintain order grew more difficult, but Scottsdale still had a reasonably effective police department. With the gun ban and new rules that allowed officers to shoot anyone who represented a public threat, the mass exodus of personnel from law enforcement finally slowed. Still, it was a very dangerous job.

Like an agitated herd of deer, the troublemakers stopped their assault and looked in the direction of the approaching squad car. In a situation like this, the officers usually fired their automatic weapons at anyone they believed was involved in the melee. The attacker looked back and snarled before turning and running in the opposite direction. Exhaling slowly, Sixtus returned to the SUV and placed the gun under the seat. If he was lucky, no one noticed he had a weapon. At the very least, he hoped no one would alert the officers when they arrived.

He walked over to the woman, who was now sitting up and trying to replace her bra and fasten her blouse. She looked up at him and cowered, a large ugly black knot was forming under her left eye.

"It's ok, it's ok. My name is Roger Clayton. I'm just here to help."

She stammered while trying to re-position her disheveled hair. "I—I have to get to work. Oh my, I think I'm going to be late. Where's my makeup?" She absently looked around the immediate area, but her purse was still in the car.

"I think you may be in shock. Why don't you just sit there and relax until an ambulance arrives. By the way, can you tell me your name?"

"I'm Carol—Carol Chanis. An ambulance? Oh, for goodness' sakes, no. I must get to work." She started to get up, but Sixtus reached out and gently restrained her. "Ma'am, you have a knot the size of a golf ball under your eye, and it's almost swelled shut. They smashed your windshield, and you have cuts on your arms and legs. Please, just wait here."

She reached up and touched her face. "Oh—oh my God," she said as the reality seemed to sink in. "Why? Why did he do that?" Her hands covered her face as she began to sob just as the squad car arrived.

After a half-hour wait, an officer approached and recorded her account of the assault.

"Are you alright, ma'am?"

"I'm okay, I just have to put my clothes back on," she said while struggling to open her swollen eye. "I don't know why those people do this sort of thing..."

The officer shook his head. "I don't know why either, ma'am. It's getting more dangerous all the time. My wife wants me to quit the force, and some days I just don't know what to tell her... Maybe you should go to the hospital. I wish there was an ambulance, but they're backed up for hours."

When the cop finished, he snapped the tablet shut, shook his head and moved on to another injured motorist. With one hand over her battered eye, the woman used the other to keep her ripped bra in place.

"Look," said Sixtus after the officer left, "I can give you a ride to the clinic. It's just a few miles away."

She smiled through obvious discomfort. "Thank you. But I can make it by myself. I called my husband, and he's going to meet me here."

"Ok then, Mrs. Chanis," said Sixtus while smiling. "Good luck, and I wish you the best."

"Thank you, Mr. Clayton. These are certainly trying times, aren't they?"

"They truly are. Remarkably trying."

Sixtus reentered the Escalade and waited another half hour before the traffic snarl untangled itself. The trip was depressing as usual, and he struggled to dodge the copious quantities of trash strewn across the highway. Hordes of floaters were out in force, their numbers growing exponentially as the government continued to face growing budget shortfalls. A lack of money and resources accelerated the burgeoning mental health problems in the general population, which only served to intensify the rising level of violence.

As he turned onto the 202, Sixtus passed a line of squad cars, their lights flashing and sirens blaring as they raced toward a mass shooting by a Kazakhstani immigrant at a local big box retail store. It was one of three active terrorist incidents in Phoenix today, which reflected the number of episodes happening all across the country.

He maneuvered the Escalade off of the freeway onto Buckeye and drove toward the scene of last night's Event. Sixtus wasn't particularly concerned about encountering a law enforcement investigation at the scene. With resources stretched to the limit, the police probably classified yesterday's death as an accident or suicide by now. In these times, exhausted police officers were always looking for an excuse to lessen their workload.

The parking lot next to the church was empty, and after parking the car, Sixtus got out and walked across the lot, stopping at the exact spot he first encountered the vagrant last night. Closing his eyes, the memories and details of the Event began to return. He categorized them as the Object, the collision, the two men in the truck and the mob. To the best of his knowledge, no one at the scene paid any attention to the retreating figure in the dark clothing.

Sixtus walked a few steps over to the spot where the vagrant stood and confronted him. While the crazed man uttered disturbing words, his thoughts were clearly disjointed and incoherent. Spaceships and aliens were the kinds of things you might expect from someone who developed a psychosis from years of chronic drug use. Sixtus found it difficult to believe he represented a serious threat.

Making a slow, 360-degree turn, he tried to remember every detail of his surroundings and cursed silently while attempting once again to open the overhead out of habit. Before the active display was disabled last night, he was able to download a recording of the Event on his secure server. Maintaining a pirate copy of an Event was illicit, but Sixtus took the advice of another trainee at the Academy and recorded every Time Sculpting activity for his own protection.

He accessed the server remotely and called up the file on his tablet. After it loaded, he pressed play on the viewer, watching as the display matched his movements from the night before. He studied the picture as it moved to the left and completed a 360-degree circle. Rewinding the video, he played it over again. Something didn't look right, although identifying the anomaly was elusive. The second run was nearly complete when he punched the pause button. He used his fingers to toggle the screen and enlarge a portion of the shot.

The white apartment building across the street looked different in the daylight because it blended into the background when cast in the pale shadows of the moonlight last night. Still, he recalled the guest parking spots in back of the building were empty when he first arrived at the church. As he gazed at the screen on his tablet, he saw a single white compact car parked there. It looked like a Honda Civic or perhaps another Japanese subcompact.

Sixtus concentrated on the scene, processing the information and looking for additional detail.

What is that object on the other side of the parapet wall? Applying controls to enhance the clarity and contrast, he noticed an indistinct face poking up past the top of the barrier. *Why didn't I notice this last night?* Whoever it was, they did an effective job of hiding their intentions. In light of the recent text, Sixtus suspected this person was the one who surveilled him. If the culprit was tech savvy, he could have traced the license plate on the BMW and used that information to access a linked cell phone number.

White compact cars were infinite in the Phoenix metropolitan area, so Sixtus knew he needed the expertise of someone who would help him trace the mobile number back to the source. Slamming down the accelerator, he turned onto the freeway and headed north. As the miles passed on the drive home, the question burned in his mind.

Who was this person, and how could he have known about the Event?

Chapter Seven

Wallace and Kenny sprawled across the couch with their legs awkwardly entangled. Kenny's mouth was wide open, and a string of drool leaked from the corner of his lips and pooled into a growing wet spot on the cushion where his head lay. Wallace's eyelids fluttered as he snored, and the whites of his eyes showed every time he exhaled.

They fell asleep after talking deep into the night, looking for answers that simply were not forthcoming. After sending the text to the mysterious man and calling Wanda and Hayden, the threesome settled in and covered an array of subjects centering on the science of time change. While the speculation was interesting, they still had no adequate explanation for the phenomenon.

Marshall stood up, stretched, and looked at the clock. "Kenny, get up. Kenny!" He jostled his friend until he began to stir and open his eyes.

Kenny wiped his mouth and frowned at the red-tinged saliva that covered his hand. "Ugh, that's really disgusting. What time is it, anyway? I have to work today."

It's seven," said Marshall. "I guess you should hurry if you're going to make it on time."

"Seven! Are you kidding me?" said Kenny. "I'm gonna be late. This is the first time I've ever been late before. Oh my, oh Lord, they're gonna fire me. They're gonna get rid of me for sure."

"They're not going to fire you, Kenny. You've worked at the post office for six years, and I don't think you've missed a single day until now."

"They fire people like me if you miss one day," said Kenny, almost on the verge of tears. "They fire people like me."

Marshall walked up to his friend and awkwardly touched his shoulder. The moment was uncomfortable, but Marshall noted another odd sensation he couldn't quite verbalize.

Am I worried about Kenny? No, it's more than worry, perhaps sympathy?

Kenny looked up, and a smile started to spread across his face. "Do you really think it'll be alright?"

"Yes, I do. Just call and tell them you're going to be a couple minutes late. Say it exactly that way: you're running a little late. Don't go into a long explanation unless they ask for one. If they want a reason, tell them you overslept. Keep it simple, Kenny."

Kenny's smile grew wider. "Thanks, Marshall. You're right; it's the first time in six years. They should understand."

The discussion woke Wallace, who was rubbing his eyes and yawning. He looked casually at his watch before the sleep effect subsided. "Seven o'clock. Whoa, I'm late too. This never happens to me." He got off the couch and sprinted down the hall. "I'm using the bathroom first. The thought of using it after someone else eliminates and washes filth from their body is nauseating." Marshall rolled his eyes, but it was a sentiment he shared.

71

Fortunately, Marshall's house had two bathrooms, so it didn't take long for them to bathe and get ready. They reconvened around Marshall's breakfast table and shared a box of shredded wheat.

"Ok, so we know who the murderer is, but what are we going to do about it?" asked Wallace.

"We need as much background information as we can get, so I'm going to call Wanda. She's the one who can get us the information we need. As a forensic statistician, she has access to every police data base imaginable."

"And then what?" said Kenny.

"And then I'm visiting Iglar again," said Marshall as he swallowed the last bite of his cereal.

***

Once he was sure Kenny and Wallace reached their respective bus stops, Marshall turned the car toward Glendale. In less than ten minutes he stood on the porch and waited for Grace Stone to answer the door. She looked dour as she ushered him in. He smiled politely and walked to the stairs, hoping to avoid her predictable probing questions. His foot touched the first stair when he froze.

"Marshall, how did you get here? Did your mother drive you?"

Marshall's back stiffened. He struggled to understand why some unaffected people needed to project purposeful cruelty, but over time, he had come to accept it.

"No, Mrs. Stone, I don't live with my mother. And before you ask, I drive myself. In fact, I have had a valid driver's license for several years, and my driving record is spotless. So, my situation is different from Iglar's, since you won't let him drive."

She straightened up and brushed at the hem of her dress. "I see. Well—I just thought..."

"I know what you think, Mrs. Stone. I hope that clears the subject up." As Marshall turned and walked up the stairs, the smallest trace of a smile crossed his lips.

Iglar sat at his computer as usual, rocking back and forth as he worked on a document of some sort. In the past, when he was more lucid, Iglar was the most highly regarded Scala-12 programmer in the country. However, he became increasingly disassociated in his 30s, and by the time he reached thirty-five, he was acting out on a regular basis. No one in a workplace environment wanted to collaborate with him, and the consulting jobs dried up. Marshall believed Iglar was still writing groundbreaking applications and destroying them upon completion.

"Iglar... Iglar. It's Marshall."

Iglar turned slowly in his chair, nodded, and returned to his computer.

"I'm trying to understand, Iglar. You know what will change in the future. *Please*, tell me how that's possible?"

Iglar stopped typing and sat silently for a moment before swiveling around to face Marshall. "You don't know," he said. "You don't understand what goes on in here." He stabbed a forefinger into the side of his temple. "I—I see things. They flash like colors. Colors, colors, colors everywhere. Boom! Wham! Boom!" Iglar punched at something imaginary to emphasize the chaos of his thoughts.

"It's difficult for you, Iglar. I understand. But I need your help, so try to focus. How can you possibly know these things are going to happen?"

73

"I know because I see it. Others see it more clearly than I do..." Iglar began violently pulling on his ear as though he was trying to rip it off.

"Iglar!" Marshall grabbed Iglar's hand and pried it off his ear. The outer lobe was fiery red from the self-inflicted assault. Iglar's fingers continued to twitch, and Marshall held his wrist to prevent him from grabbing another body part.

"Please, you have to try to stay focused. Tell me about that man who was pushed in front of the truck last night?"

Iglar's whole body started to shake with small tremors, and the veins in his neck bulged. "You couldn't have known that. You couldn't..."

"We were there, Iglar. Wallace, Kenny and me. We saw it too. You wrote about it, and we saw it."

"My papers. My private papers. You looked... You looked!" Iglar began to thrust his pelvis forward as though he was engaged in coitus.

Marshall grimaced and waited for Iglar to stop. "We didn't look, Iglar. You gave them to me, remember? Granted, your message was buried in a lot of text we couldn't understand. But in light of our collective experience remembering the past differently than others, we extracted your predictions. You know how the future will change. How is this possible?"

Iglar rose from his chair. "Do you have a vehicle? A car? Motorized transportation? A motorcycle? A..."

"A car, Iglar. I have a car. That's how I arrived here. A car."

"If you want to understand, you should drive me somewhere."

"That's fine. You tell me where I need to drive, and we'll go there."

Iglar walked to his closet and pulled out a weathered Chicago Cubs baseball cap with a piece of masking tape labeled *Tuesday* attached to the bill. He opened a drawer in his dresser, took out a jewelry box and picked two non-matching cuff links that he held up to the light for inspection.

Marshall couldn't help noticing his friend wore a long sleeve t-shirt without a place to attach the cufflinks. Yet, Iglar wasn't deterred. He took the stud end of both pieces and pressed them into the cotton fabric until the material gave way and created a hole in each sleeve. Iglar pushed them through and opened the binding so they remained fastened. The look itself was rather comical, but Iglar seemed pleased.

Once he finished with his carefully crafted dressing routine, Iglar turned abruptly and left the room. He never signaled he was ready to leave, but Marshall understood as soon as he heard his friend descending the stairs.

"Iglar, where are you going?"

"I'm going out, mother. Marshall is taking me out, so that's where I'm going."

Grace Stone turned back towards the stairs just as Marshall reached the landing. "Marshall, it's a bad idea for you to drive Iglar. After all, with your condition...."

He imagined she was trying to insult him, but after decades of caring for Iglar, she still didn't understand autism very well. Marshall was largely oblivious to innuendo, and he rarely responded to provocations.

"Don't worry, Mrs. Stone, we'll be fine." He grabbed Iglar's arm and left the house before she had time to answer.

Once inside the car, Iglar insisted on inspecting all the safety equipment to verify it was in working order. He tested his seat belt and checked all the dashboard lights to confirm the airbags were active, and no engine malfunction lights were on. Iglar took the manual out of the glove box and turned to the safety features chapter. As his finger traced the pages in rapid fashion, Marshall marveled at his friend's speed and reading comprehension. What should have taken at least five minutes to peruse took Iglar less than a minute.

"Alright, Marshall. I'm ready to go. Step on the gas pedal. Go, go, go."

"Where am I driving to?"

"The Lincoln House."

Marshall glanced at Iglar. "The Lincoln House? We'll go and visit together some time, but right now, we need to stay focused on the matter at hand. Help us, Iglar. How are you able to see the future?"

"Drive, Marshall. Drive to the Lincoln House."

Marshall sighed and pulled the car out onto the street and headed over to the 202, which eventually took them to I-10. They didn't converse with each other while traveling since Iglar carried on multiple conversations with himself. Marshall's body would stiffen every time Iglar let out a periodic shriek or wail. In between these unnerving events, he mumbled and wept.

As the Civic arrived at the Lincoln House, Iglar's mood seemed to brighten considerably. He unhooked the restraint and pushed the door open so hard it rebounded and slammed into his legs as he was getting out, but he didn't seem to notice. Iglar walked toward the entrance, motioning Marshall to pick up his pace. The sliding glass doors opened automatically, and they walked into the lobby and headed for the reception desk. Marshall recognized the nurse sitting behind the counter, but she was clearly more familiar with Iglar.

"Hello, Iglar, how are you this morning?"

"I shit my pants, and I have red bumps on my balls," he said. "Other than that, I'm fine."

She smiled momentarily and then looked away. Based on her passive reaction, Marshall assumed that listening to the patients' brutally blunt and honest answers every day had desensitized her. "Well, I'm sorry to hear that," she said, "but I'm sure everything will get better." Hoping to change the subject, she glanced over at Marshall. "Who's your friend, Iglar? Have I seen him around here before?"

"That's Marshall, remember?" said Iglar with a sweeping gesture toward his companion. "He wants to know why everything is so fucked up, so I'm going to show him."

"Uh huh. Well, I hope you find the answers you're looking for. And it's nice to see you again, Marshall."

Marshall learned the proper response to a friendly greeting was to smile politely, so that's what he did. Since he had near perfect recall, Marshall remembered the nurse's name without having to look at her tag. "Thank you, Nurse Walker. It's a pleasure to see you as well." Her face brightened at the salutation, and she smiled back at him.

Lincoln House was an open facility that didn't use locks or heavy security to control the population, so the pair moved easily through the lobby. Marshall followed Iglar as he walked into a courtyard through a side exit and past a series of game tables, picnic tables and shaded areas that reminded Marshall of a retirement community. Several residents smiled at them, and a few even waved, but only Marshall returned the greetings. Iglar scowled and walked with purpose to the other side of the courtyard and back into the building. He failed to hold the door open, and Marshall quickly moved backward to avoid getting hit in the face.

This was a part of the facility Marshall had never seen before. At first glance, he thought he was in a large cafeteria, but as he looked around, it seemed to be more like a modified recreation room. The padded chairs and tables served as a reminder that this area was reserved for those who were capable of hurting themselves or others. Fortunately, there didn't appear to be any obvious threats in the room. Instead, the occupants looked disengaged and heavily medicated based on their blank stares and periodic nodding off.

Iglar turned back to Marshall. "They probably won't kill you, but it could happen, so stay close and follow me." Iglar made his way between the aisles toward the back corner of the room, where a single occupant sat alone at one of the tables. The patient wore a loose robe that didn't fully cover his white briefs or bare chest, and he stared straight ahead with a look that suggested he had suffered some sort of brain trauma. His hands fidgeted, and he had a deep red hue from what Marshall assumed was aggressive scrubbing.

Iglar's face softened as he stood to the side of the man, and he talked in a low and soothing tone. "Hello, Jonathon, can we sit down?"

Jonathan was a young man who looked to be in his twenties with a sallow complexion and a thin, frail frame. His eyes were wide and aquamarine blue but sunk deep in their sockets. As Iglar sat down, he motioned for Marshall to do the same. Reaching into his pants pocket, Iglar pulled out a crumpled piece of paper he unfolded and smoothed out on the table. He took a pen out of his other pocket and placed it in Jonathon's hand.

"Jonathan, will you tell us what's changed today?"

Jonathan trembled as he looked up at Iglar. His lips contorted, and he gulped air and sputtered. Marshall wondered if he was going to have a convulsion.

"Don't worry, Jonathan. Marshall knows. He knows about it. Not like you and me, but he knows."

Jonathan looked up at Marshall and seemed to calm down a bit.

"Yes, Jonathan, he knows. Tell him what will change today."

Jonathan clutched the pen tightly and moved his hand to the left side of the page, writing in small, cursive letters. His strokes were deliberate and erratic at first, but his writing speed began to increase until he was filling up the page with a multitude of sentences. Small grunts escaped his lips as he reached the bottom of the paper and turned it over. The pen drew sharp lines and curves as he wrote, and the intensity of his efforts grew with every stroke.

As if he was possessed, Jonathan started writing on his arms once he was out of space on the paper. High-pitched squeals punctuated grunts as he wrote on bare flesh.

The level of commotion grew as Jonathan's nervous energy radiated out to the other patients, and Marshall feared they would attract the attention of the attendants. He reached over and grabbed at the pen, but Jonathan held on tight as frothy spittle shot through his clenched teeth.

"Jonathan, calm down. I can't help you if you don't calm down. I need to understand what's going on. Give me the pen—please, give me the pen... Iglar, help me."

Ripping the pen away from Marshall, Jonathan moved down to his leg, gouging through the skin and drawing small droplets of blood as he kept writing. The scene was gruesome and troubling, and Marshall leaned back in his chair, shocked into paralysis and silence.

The tumult intensified and spread through the room as a rising murmur from the other patients echoed off the high ceiling. Off to the left, three attendants assigned to the room made their way over towards the center of the disturbance. A surly looking man with large biceps, a starched white uniform and a nameplate that read, *LaTrelle* stepped up to the table while the other two moved behind Jonathan. The attendant snarled at Marshall before turning the corners of his mouth up in a painful smile. If a civilian wasn't sitting there, his reaction would have been much different.

"Jonathan, I want that pen." Instead of complying, Jonathan continued writing past his thigh and down to his shin. With a nod from LaTrelle, one of the other attendants grabbed Jonathan's arm from behind while another clutched his hand and uncurled the tightly wrapped fingers that held the ballpoint. In the process, Jonathan leaned over and bit down into the man's forearm. The orderly dropped the pen and used his free hand to deliver a punch to the forehead. The pressure of the bite lessened momentarily, and the orderly was able to free his arm. He howled in pain and ran out the door in the direction of the infirmary.

"He bit me. The sick bastard bit me," he screamed. "He *bit* me…"

LaTrelle reached into his back pocket and took out a nylon zip tie while moving behind Jonathan. As the remaining orderly held his free arm and avoided his gnashing teeth, the zip tie tightened on Jonathan's hands. Now incapacitated, they roughly pushed him to the floor where he curled up defensively in the fetal position. Despite the sudden passivity, LaTrelle rolled him over and sat directly on his chest. Meanwhile, the other attendant accessed a locked box on a nearby wall and brought over a restraining mask that he pulled over Jonathan's head, fastening it with a small lock.

Dragging him up to his feet, the supervisor pushed the agitated patient through the door toward the treatment center for those at risk of self-injury. Just before leaving, he turned back toward Iglar and Marshall, pointing and shaking his finger at both. "The rules are very clear that patients in this wing are not allowed to have dangerous objects. You two report to security immediately!"

LaTrelle appeared to look past the duo and notice the mood in the room was growing more frantic and angry. While some patients remained seated and oblivious, others were gesturing wildly and hurling insults at the guard. He leaned over and said something into the small microphone attached to his sleeve.

Iglar stood up and started moving to the opposite exit. "Marshall, time to go. Lockdown's coming." The paper Jonathan wrote on fell to the floor, and Marshall hunched down and grabbed it from under the table and stuffed it in his pocket. He followed Iglar to the door, and they exited just before the automatic locks closed to prevent anyone else from leaving. The recreation room in D-wing was now officially locked down.

Chapter Eight

Marshall walked away from the building while Iglar lagged as though he forgot the melee from a few seconds earlier. Iglar didn't care to be touched, so Marshall kept his hands in his pockets as he encouraged his friend to move faster.

"Come on, it's imperative we leave here now." Marshall spoke with obvious frustration as Iglar stopped to observe an unusual arachnid on the ground. "Are you serious? If you won't move, I'm going to come over there and grab you by the arm."

Iglar needed no further encouragement and followed Marshall out to the parking lot with a sense of purpose. Fortunately, they were partially obscured by the parked cars, so the two security guards who walked outside didn't see them even as they scanned the parkway in both directions. By the time their surveillance reached Iglar and Marshall, they were already inside the car.

"They're going to know it was us, Marshall. We signed in. Trouble, dude."

Turning onto Peoria, Marshall retraced the route back to the freeway and finally exhaled to release building tension as they merged into the anonymity of the highway traffic.

"What was that about, Iglar? Why did you take me there, and why did you introduce me to Jonathan?"

Iglar pulled his cap over his ears and slunk deep in the seat. "You still don't get it, do you, Marshall? It's right there in front of you, but you don't get it. You're not deep enough; none of you are deep enough. You skim the surface but barely see what's above the horizon. You're only slightly more aware than a slug."

Marshall ignored the unintentional insult. "Aware of what? What do you perceive that we can't see?"

Iglar looked away and stared out the window as they pulled up to a red light. Marshall turned toward his companion just as a sharp sound rattled through the car. His peripheral vision registered a shadow that grew larger as he swung his head back around in time to see a floater dressed in a dirty sweat shirt draped across his windshield. Marshall looked at the man's face, which was pockmarked and ghostly white. His bloodshot eyes bulged, and pieces of decayed meat stuck in his ungroomed facial hair. He pressed his nose into the windshield and left a long, oily smear.

"I can't take it, brother," he said. He shook his head and pounded his fist on the glass. "I said I can't take it. Every day... It won't leave me alone. Fear—I feel such fear."

Marshall sunk back into his seat as the traffic light changed to green. "Please move. You need to move!" Horns started honking as the unexpected action escalated into an incident, albeit one that was becoming increasingly common.

"Money. I need money, bro." the man yelled at the top of his lungs. "Money. I'm a vet; give me some goddamn money."

Desperately wanting to find a way out of the situation, Marshall reached for his wallet and extracted his emergency twenty-dollar bill from the hidden compartment. Considering the potential danger for a moment, he cracked the window just enough so he could extend his arm out to the man still draped across the windshield. A dirty hand emerged from the sweatshirt sleeve and grabbed the bill.

"Bless you, brother, but I'd still like to rip off your face. The voices don't leave. They never leave." He slid off the hood of the car and made his way back to the shoulder of the road, cursing at drivers as they tried to go around the stranded Civic in the middle lane. Marshall accelerated so quickly he nearly rear-ended an SUV that cut back in front of him.

Once they were moving again, Iglar looked over at Marshall and smiled. "Bat shit crazy. Everyone is going bat shit crazy."

"Why is everyone going crazy, Iglar? What is it you're aware of that we're not? Tell me." Marshall asked the question, but he knew he was too late. Iglar tuned out and was exhaling on the window and drawing circles in the condensate.

The silence continued as Marshall turned off the freeway and onto Bethany Home Road, arriving at the Stone residence just a few minutes later. He waited until Iglar reached the porch before putting the Civic in reverse and backing out of the driveway. Just as he started to pull away, Iglar called his name. Marshall stopped short and rolled down the window.

"It's better that you leave it alone, Marshall. You can't do anything about it, anyway. I know way too much; I won't keep it together much longer." As if to substantiate the claim, he reached into his pocket, extracted a pill and swallowed it without water.

"If you could just help me understand, Iglar..."

"Leave now, Marshall." Iglar opened the door and disappeared into his mother's home.

Marshall shook his head and threw up his hands. He considered revealing more about the other night when he, Kenny and Wallace followed Iglar and witnessed the murder but thought better of it. Iglar might react negatively to such a provocation, and Marshall wasn't ready to risk losing a friend and such a valuable source of information.

The drive home was short, and he decided to stop and have tempura at a local Taiwanese restaurant since he hadn't eaten in quite a while. The establishment was familiar, and he enjoyed the company of the proprietor as much as he liked the food. A row of bells over the door jingled as Marshall walked in and made his way over to his regular booth. The fiery invective from the kitchen signaled Yao Cong was berating the help as usual, but his tone changed immediately when he stepped into the restaurant to greet his guests.

"Ah, my friend, Marshall. It is good to see you." Even though Yao's accent was distinct, he spoke technically perfect English. Marshall was relatively fluent in Mandarin, which he assumed was the main reason Yao liked him. However, in his establishment, Yao insisted they speak only English. He was a proud immigrant who desperately wanted to assimilate.

"Hello, Cong, how are you this evening?"

Yao shrugged his shoulders. "All day the homeless ones walk in. They have no money and no job. Many of them have the odor and look of the drug death. I give food to as many as I can, but they spread the word, and I am soon overrun. I cannot do it anymore, so they break a window." He pointed to the rear of the building, and Marshall turned around to see a sheet of plywood covering the space once occupied by the glass.

"Have you called the authorities?"

"The police are not very reliable anymore, especially with the violent ones. Besides, the cops would rather harass guys like you and me and eat donuts, right? Yao let out a hearty laugh and playfully cuffed Marshall on the shoulder.

Looking at Yao and then his shoulder, Marshall processed the proprietor's actions, which were difficult to understand. The mild slap was a self-congratulatory reaction to the "joke", which Yao confirmed with his enthusiastic laugh. Marshall learned through experience that the teller of the story usually found the quip far more amusing than the listener. "Good one, Cong," he said. That only made the Taiwan national laugh harder.

"You want the usual?"

"Yes, please."

Yao walked back to the kitchen still chuckling while Marshall leaned back in the booth and sighed. The day's challenges wore him down, and he simply wanted to eat some food and go home to rest. Perhaps with the benefit of sleep, he would clear his head and gain some perspective on his experience with Iglar and Jonathan.

He wondered if Wanda was able to compile any additional data and reached into his pants pocket for his phone. That's when his hand ran up against the paper Jonathan scribbled on at the Lincoln House.

Wrinkled and smudged, he opened it up and tried to smooth it out on the table.

At first glance, the writing was incomprehensible and looked like meaningless gibberish. Jonathan used so much ink, that at a distance, it would be easy to believe the paper was actually blue instead of white. Marshall rubbed his eyes and looked at it again. The cursive was minuscule, and he couldn't make out any letters, let alone words. Even squinting didn't help.

"You far-sighted, Marshall?" Yao returned with a Dr Pepper.

"No, Cong. The writing is very small. I can't read it."

Yao thought for a moment and then held up an index finger. "Wait a minute. I am very far-sighted. I cannot read the tickets sometimes, so I keep a big magnifying glass here. Let me go and get it."

Once Yao returned with the magnifying glass, Marshall held it over the paper and adjusted the focal length until the words came into focus. The small letters couldn't have been more than a sixty-fourth of an inch in height, and he realized as he scanned the text there were hundreds of lines of writing that ran in random directions across the page. At first, he couldn't discern any identifiable symmetry and wondered if the writing was simply the manifestation of heavy medication and a diseased mind.

An accident on I-60 kills three people instead of one.

Marshall's eyes widened as he pulled back and stared at the paper. The phrase was written diagonally from left to right, and another followed immediately after the original sentence.

The Norris Electric plant in Ohio closes down next year… Then the next: *Torry Howard drowns while fishing.* As he began to better understand the pattern of

Jonathan's writing, Marshall started reading in rapid succession.

The car on Third Street in Boise has a head on collision.

James Edgar avoids the falling rocks.

Three people die in the Quartz Park mine in Montana
School lets out early in Highland Park

Jessica Walton marries Edward Milton instead of Harry Brownman.

Genetic sequencing for BRCA2 is halted.

Nicholas Sam wins Lexington mayor race.

Kerry Ann Michaels opens a bakery two blocks away
Max Fontaine wins a Grammy

Oakland mayor appoints Leandra Jones instead of Thomas Schwartz

The partial list of seemingly innocuous events covered less than a half inch of the paper. As his eyes moved to another area, the content was entirely different but just as perplexing. A state senator won an election in Wisconsin; a passenger train running from Boston to Washington was delayed and rerouted; a yacht capsized in the Pacific Ocean and killed a prominent businessman; someone missed their son's birthday; a surgeon was replaced in a delicate operation...

Marshall turned the paper over and looked at the backside content. From the top left corner to the lower right edge, the rambling, disjointed sentence fragments continued, lacking any sense of cogency or order.

Why would Iglar take me to see a person so disturbed he was incapable of rational thought?

Iglar was always challenging, but Marshall was fairly certain he conveyed his purpose. The prognostications were the focus of their discussions.

How could Iglar have misinterpreted? He picked up his phone just as Yao approached the table with a plate of tempura.

"You eat, Marshall. Don't let the food get cold. You look like you had a bad day. You eat. It will make you feel much better."

Marshall shook his head and laid the phone down on the table. He remembered Iglar didn't own a mobile phone because he worried about the effects of residual radiation, and he also believed the government was monitoring his phone calls. Marshall was still looking at his phone when it chirped, indicating he just received a new text.

***

Sixtus sat at his desk and typed rapidly on the keyboard. Ancient computer code was both exceedingly simple and maddeningly cumbersome. He hired a dark web hacker who established the threatening text was routed through the Quasar-mobile network, but it hadn't originated there. Whoever sent the message knew how to cover their tracks. They used a special piece of code to create a spider that leapt from network to network, steering the data through the U.S., Pakistan, Germany, Belgium and ultimately back to the U.S. Sixtus had no doubt he was dealing with a sophisticated adversary.

Rapidly moving the mouse, he called up his contact file. In rare cases, he hired a local security consultant when he needed access to an Object's personal information during an assignment. As he clicked the file and hovered over the number, his phone buzzed. The call came from the front gate. "Yes, Doug?"

When he spoke, the guard sounded slightly out of breath. "Mr. Clayton, there's a man here... He's not in a car. He's on foot and won't give me his name."

"Well, turn him away, Doug. I have no meetings planned, and we don't need someone coming up to the house without an appointment."

"I know, Mr. Clayton. I'm sorry to bother you. But he insists I deliver a message to you."

"What's the message?"

"He says to tell you that he knows you are a... 'time sculptor'. Sounds like a crackpot, I know. And I'll tell you something else, he looks really sick."

Sixtus straightened up, and his eyes widened. Questions bubbled up so quickly they couldn't fully form in his mind. It wasn't supposed to be possible. The breach was unprecedented and extraordinarily dangerous.

"Hello? Mr. Clayton?"

Sixtus put the phone back up to his ear. "I better see him, Doug. We don't need a stranger causing problems in the neighborhood. Tell him I'll be down there in just a minute."

"Ok, Mr. Clayton."

Sixtus grabbed the keys to the BMW and walked into the den. "Kara, an old friend is at the guard shack. I'm sorry for the short notice, but he's traveled a great distance, and I can't turn him away."

She set her tablet down on the ottoman and sighed. "Roger!" Her nose scrunched up in a way he became familiar with over time. It said, *I'll act slightly annoyed because I don't have time to straighten up the house, but I'm not really mad.* "Go and get him, and I'll try to pick up the best I can. But don't you dare take him into the parlor."

He held up his arms in surrender. "Not in the parlor. Got it."

She cocked her head slightly and looked at him with a puzzled expression. "An old friend, Roger? I don't ever recall you bringing a friend to our home."

He smiled weakly. "I guess there's a first time for everything."

Sixtus' mind was not focused on the parlor as he said the words. His hand was shaking while he pressed the start button and the six series throaty V-8 roared to life. He drove with urgency down the driveway onto the winding road that led to the guard shack. Outside the small building near the overgrown oleanders, Sixtus could see the two figures: Doug in his white uniform and blue hat and a second man in jeans and a black t-shirt. Once both men became aware of the BMW, they simultaneously looked at the driver. Doug appeared uncomfortable, but the other man stared at Sixtus with a blank expression.

Sixtus pulled his car up to the building and unlocked the door. He waved at Doug and smiled, which seemed to satisfy the burly guard, and he gave the stranger one last suspicious glance before returning to his position on the stool inside the shack. Sixtus' attention was drawn to the other side of the vehicle as the passenger's door opened, and the visitor got in. Their eyes met, and they instantly exchanged a deep sense of understanding and shared experience.

"I am Daxtar Liss." The man spoke in a low tone. He appeared older than Sixtus, and he was obviously unhealthy. His face reflected a combination of extreme stress and some sort of physical ailment. Deep lines hugged his lower eyelids and curved downward across

91

his cheeks until they met up with more craggy wrinkles near his lips and chin. His complexion was pallid, and angry, red boils with weeping pus covered his face and arms.

He reached into his pocket and pulled out a package of cigarettes but had difficulty getting one out because his hands were shaking badly. After several unsuccessful attempts, two sticks fell to the floorboards, and he hastily reached down to pick them up. He offered one to his companion, but Sixtus wrinkled his nose to convey his distaste. It didn't deter Liss. He struck a match and steadied one hand with the other to bring the flame up to the tip of the cigarette. He took several small puffs before drawing deeply and exhaling slowly.

"How did you find me?" asked Sixtus. Among all his questions, this was the most pressing.

"I do not want to talk in the car. Do you have a safe room?"

Communication with the future was controlled entirely by the Corporates, and Time Sculptors were expected to remain perpetually accessible. That said, there were ways to avoid the eavesdropping by communicating in an area shielded by a Faraday Cage. Sixtus constructed such a room although he never used it before.

"Yes, I have a second den that is shielded. You — you do not look well. Do you need a doctor?"

Liss took another deep drag on the cigarette and wiped his sweaty forehead with the back of his hand. "I am not well, but my condition is not contagious. The only priority is that I convey this information. Nothing else matters." He shook his head slowly and became silent.

"I have a wife. Do you have a 21ˢᵗ century designation?"

"Yes. I am Frank DeTomaso."

Once the six series pulled back into the driveway, they exited the car and entered the house through the service door. Hoping to avoid questions later, Sixtus moved directly to the den only to find Kara still sitting in a chair near the fireplace. She rose, smiled politely and extended her hand to the stranger.

"Kara, this is Frank DeTomaso. We, ah, worked together at Halliburton many years ago. He was my boss."

Liss grasped her hand and shook it lightly. "Mrs. Clayton, it is a pleasure."

"Likewise, Mr. DeTomaso," she replied.

"Kara, we're going to catch up and talk about old times in the library. You're welcome to join us..."

She dipped her head and smiled, trying to hide her revulsion at Liss's appearance. "No, but thank you. Let the boys do their bonding. I'll have Emma bring you tea and coffee."

Sixtus led the way to the shielded library, ushered Liss in, and closed the door behind them. The room was decorated in 18ᵗʰ century neoclassic architecture with walls painted in deep monotone colors of Pompeiian red and pale brown. Rich mahogany wood accented the desk, moldings and book shelves, carved and sculpted in a frieze-like relief.

"You have a nice home, Maras."

"Thank you... Now, why have you come here, and how did you find me?"

"I have a contact at Central. They gave me your information."

Sixtus looked at Liss with alarm. "That's a capital offense. Whoever it was jeopardized their entire family." Turning pensive, he continued, "Besides, there is no way to communicate with the future. The technology isn't available."

"It is if it is arranged in advance."

"What?"

"I arranged it in advance."

Sixtus shook his head. "Not possible."

"It is possible, and you, Sixtus Maras, are in great danger."

Chapter Nine

"How long have you existed in this timeline?" asked Sixtus.

"I only arrived recently out of necessity. I wonder how you could have lived in the cesspool for decades, Maras. The odor alone…" Liss wrinkled his nose, obviously unaware of his own pungent smell.

"Why are you here, Liss? You must know this situation is unprecedented and a serious violation of Time Sculptor program regulations." Sixtus watched Liss' face for a reaction. *I wonder if he knows about the breach during the last Time Sculpt?*

"Let me get to the point." Liss was interrupted by a deep, phlegmy coughing spell. When he finally recovered, he continued. "There is a catastrophe in the future. A revolt has developed, and a new leader has risen up to challenge the Corporates. It is essential that he and his followers succeed."

"A revolt?" Sixtus sat up straight and leaned forward. "How is that even possible? The Corporates control every facet of society. I don't understand."

Liss ran his fingers through his thin hair. He looked at his hand and grimaced while trying to shake off a mass of strands. He appeared befuddled for a moment. "I am losing my hair," he mumbled.

"I'm sorry, Liss. As I said, I can call a doctor…"

"No, no. Where was I? Ah, yes. The forces were able to stay hidden underground in the deserts of the Sahara, and the surprise attack caught the Corporates completely unprepared. The leaders of the revolutionaries have capabilities no one has ever seen before. Within two days, the insurgents controlled three continents. Unfortunately, someone in a key position inside our organization defected, and the Corporates learned the nature of the plan. The fighting continues, but the outcome is not decided."

"Is this why I received two new assignments recently?"

"Yes. The Corporates are desperate. They hatched a sloppy and ill-conceived plan to change the past to prevent the insurgency, but they were unsuccessful and have caused much damage."

"You still haven't explained why you are here," said Sixtus.

"The Corporate Council is trying to engineer the ultimate time sculpt. It is the only way they can ensure their complete victory. This must not be allowed to happen. But my time is short, so I will not be able to prevent the change. I must have your help."

"Have you contacted the other Time Sculptors occupying this space?"

Liss nodded. "Yes, in addition to you, I have made contact with two of them. The third is elusive. Whoever it is has vanished, and we have been unable to find him, or her…"

Sixtus opened his mouth to speak, but a knock at the door interrupted him. "I'm sorry to disturb you, but I have your tea and coffee, sir."

"Come in, Emma." The house attendant came inside, shrugged her shoulders and smiled awkwardly. She walked over and set the tray on the credenza.

"Would you gentlemen care for tea or coffee? Perhaps something stronger?"

Sixtus glanced over at the bar and considered bourbon on the rocks but dismissed the thought. He needed to stay clear headed. "Coffee is good for me." Turning to Liss, he said, "Frank, a beverage?"

Liss smiled at Emma. "A cup of tea with a cube of sugar would be wonderful."

Emma served the beverages as quickly as she could without spilling the liquid. The somber mood was palpable, and once both men had their refreshment, she nodded and left the room, drawing the doors behind her.

Sixtus took a small sip and cradled his cup, absently running a finger around the rim. "Since I am forty-five, the other Time Sculptors must be twenty-five, sixty-five and eighty-five, respectively. How did they react to your assertions, and which one disappeared?"

Liss nodded, but before he could speak, his right hand shot up to his face in a single rapid motion as though he was fighting against an irresistible urge. The same hand curled, and he raked his fingernails over the largest boil on his left cheek. The thin membrane covering the infection burst from the action, and pus and blood squirted out onto Liss' hand and Sixtus' carpet. An oily substance slid down the side of his jawline and traced a path across his neck. Sixtus pulled several tissues from a box that sat on his desk. Liss took them and wiped at his face. He looked back and shrugged.

"Sorry. I am deteriorating rapidly."

"Why?"

"I have no time for a lengthy explanation. Anyway, it is irrelevant. As I said, my condition is not contagious." Liss reached for his tea and blew on it to cool the contents. He brought the cup to his lips and sipped carefully. "Mmmm. That is soothing," he remarked as he set the cup back in the saucer.

"The second oldest Time Sculptor is the one who disappeared, and we have no knowledge of his or her existence in this reality. Fortunately, the Corporates do not know the identities of *any* of the Time Sculptors in this era except you."

"But why me? How could they know of my existence if the data was destroyed?"

Liss seemed preoccupied with the fresh wound and pawed at it for a moment. "Unfortunately, they already identified you as the one who would carry out the final Event before our operatives were able to purge the Time Sculptor data. That is why they need you so badly. Only we know the identities and location of the other Time Sculptors here, but only they know the nature of the mission.

"What is it you want from me?"

"Without access to the other three Sculptors, you will be the total focus of the Corporate's efforts. I have already convinced the older and younger, and they are with us. They will help you disrupt the Corporate's plan."

"So…"

"You must uncover their plot to alter a significant event in this era. It is all our contact could give us. We know these are the time coordinates, and they have a plan to affect a change with enormous implications."

"Liss, your information is not very useful. How can I possibly foil such a scheme without knowing the details?"

"You will soon learn everything. I promise you that."

Sixtus cocked his head slightly and set his cup on the table. "Who is going to share them with me, Liss?"

Daxtar Liss hunched over and clutched his abdomen. "I am bleeding internally. Time is shorter than I thought. Our hope is the assassin will reveal the information you need."

"Assassin? What are you talking about?"

"The Corporates sent an assassin here to direct the final time sculpt operation. At first, he will try to recruit you. If unsuccessful, he will try to kill you."

Sixtus needed to hear no more. He rose and walked to a portrait on the far wall, which was a Marc Chagall original. He pulled on the hinged wood that framed *Jeremiah in the Well*. The painting moved to the side, revealing a recessed safe. Sixtus turned the tumbler until the lock emitted a familiar *click* and opened automatically. He reached inside and took out a Maglite and a loaded Kel-Tec PF9-9mm.

Liss didn't show any particular concern for the weapon, and his face remained expressionless. "I believe the assassin is likely to contact you. He will try to talk you into doing his bidding as he explains his plan to oversee a single massive event. This will cause a ripple through the time line in unimaginably complex ways as it completely transforms reality in the 24th century to make sure the Corporates regain a stranglehold on absolute power."

Sixtus pondered the implications for a moment and stroked his chin thoughtfully. "I don't know... You appear authentic, but your story seems — implausible."

"You do not believe me, Maras? Try to access your overhead."

"I—I can't. It only works intermittently during these last two unscheduled Time Sculpts. I assumed this was part of a hidden protocol."

"Communications are the epicenter of a destructive battle. Sometimes the revolutionaries control them, but the hacks are fierce, and the system is often compromised. I learn of things periodically. Other times, communications stop entirely. I assume during these periods the Corporates have regained control."

"Well, that is quite a story. If I agree, what would you ask me to do?"

"You only need to wait. The assassin will find you. Learn about the mission and work with the other Time Sculptors in the era to defeat it."

"That's out of the question, Liss. I won't put my wife in danger. I have a life here."

"This is much bigger than one person, Maras. You must understand that. The insurgency needs your help. We desperately need you to preserve this time line."

"The Corporates," said Sixtus, "do not inspire any sense of loyalty. I would enjoy seeing our time experience new leadership but only if they are just. Still, I am not invested enough in the outcome to risk losing my life and endangering Kara."

"You are already involved, Maras. I wish it could be different. But the stakes are much too high."

Sixtus rose from the chair and walked over to the fireplace, leaning against the rock and mortar facade. "Well, at least you provided an explanation for a strange occurrence. After my last Time Sculpt concluded, I received an anonymous phone text message indicating that someone had watched me complete the act. It must have been you or the assassin."

Liss' eyes widened. "It most assuredly was the assassin. But it is odd he made no attempt to contact you in person."

"Well, how do we deal with this threat?

Liss started to talk, but the words never left his lips. The room was plunged into pitch darkness. The background hum of the refrigerator, wash machine and mechanical ventilator stopped simultaneously. The silence was unnerving.

"It seems the assassin has arrived." whispered Liss.

Sixtus instinctively ducked under the desk as he processed the situation. "You led him here, Liss! You did it purposely," he said in an agitated whisper.

A thick cough came from somewhere in the room followed by a rasping low voice. "He arrived sooner than I expected, Maras, but we still must stop him. There is much more that I need to explain."

Sixtus flicked the flashlight on and shone the beam in Liss' direction. The beleaguered time traveler used his hand to shield his eyes, peaking through his fingers. For an instant, Sixtus saw the look of death etched in the deep contours of the other man's face.

"Who is the assassin, Liss?" Sixtus whispered. "And who are the other Time Sculptors? I need their names."

Liss shrugged. "I do not know if they are even still alive. I arrived earlier than the assassin, so I am hopeful. I cannot unmask them until I have your solemn promise you are with us."

"I—I can't commit to something I don't fully understand. How do I know..." Sixtus went silent as he heard a rattling noise and a muffled scream coming from the kitchen.

Sixtus motioned for Liss to join him. He placed his mouth near the other man's ear and whispered. "I must try to protect my wife. That bay window opens outward. You are gravely ill, and it's best if you leave."

Liss nodded and moved toward the window while Sixtus walked to the door. Nearly a minute had passed, and it would be another minute before the emergency power activated. Sixtus cursed himself for setting the delay, but he grew weary of intermittent micro-outages that caused his electric panel to burn out when the transfer switch couldn't keep up with the shifting loads.

He didn't want to reveal himself to the assassin and negate the element of surprise, so he scanned for any artificial light that might expose his adversary. Moving slowly, he made his way down the hallway, keeping a hand pressed against the wall while the gun remained drawn.

Sixtus stepped lightly as he approached the theater room. Standing to one side of the door, he pointed the flashlight inward and turned it on. Sweeping from side to side, the light outlined eerie shadows as the beam illuminated different parts of the empty room.

He continued moving through the hallway with the torch extinguished, feeling his way along the contoured David Hicks wallpaper just as the emergency generator clicked on. The lighting was low intensity, but the sensation was still disorienting. He dropped the flashlight and raised the gun as he heard a small voice from the kitchen.

"Jeffery... Help me... Jeffery, please." Kara's voice was unmistakable, and he sensed her distress and emotion.

His first reaction was to sprint to her, but he imagined that was exactly what the assassin wanted him to do. Instead, he approached the kitchen from the laundry room so he could see inside without being detected. He moved quietly through the hallway until he came to the juncture that split into dual entryways dividing the two rooms. Taking slow and deliberate steps, Sixtus reached the farthest door and opened it carefully.

Thankfully, the hinges didn't squeak. Once he reached the other side of the room, he grabbed the handle and pushed the sliding pocket door open a crack and looked into the kitchen. Still hidden, he was able to catch his first glimpse of the assassin.

A man of medium build, he stood with his legs set apart to create a stout base. He was dressed in black from head to toe, which only served to highlight the fringes of blond hair that protruded from his beanie cap. Even with his back turned, Sixtus saw his forearm wrapped around Kara's neck, and a gloved hand held a knife with a 6-inch blade pressed against her jugular vein. He whispered something in her ear.

"Jeffery, please. He says if you don't come out, he's going to kill me." Her shaking voice trailed off, and her last few words were punctuated by muted sobs.

Sixtus couldn't bear to watch anymore. He pushed the door open and entered the kitchen, gun drawn and pointed at the assassin.

Should I take the shot?

The thought passed as the adversary anticipated the action and pushed Kara so she was positioned directly in front of him. She looked at Sixtus with wide eyes bloodshot from crying and fear. Her terror pierced his soul, and he almost cried out from the depths of his anguish.

The adversaries regarded each other for several seconds without speaking. The intruder's face was covered with crusted lesions like Liss but not quite as rancid. Sixtus suspected his complexion had once been smooth and altered on a cellular level to improve his visual appearance. Whatever affliction Liss had, this man had it too, and the corners of his mouth turned down, which created a macabre mask of pain and loathing. The assassin whispered to Kara again without taking his eyes off Sixtus.

"He's serious, Jeffery. If you don't drop the gun, he'll slit my throat." She was so distraught her words were nearly unintelligible as her body began to lurch and shake with fear.

The assassin's sneer deepened. "Sixtus Maras, put down the weapon, or the woman dies." To demonstrate his resolve, he pressed the knife deeper into the soft tissues of Kara's throat.

Sixtus sensed his wife's rising panic and realized he had no choice. If he was a seasoned marksman, he might try to make the shot, but the chance of hitting Kara made the issue moot. He extended his left arm over his head in surrender while placing the gun on the floor with his other hand.

"Push it towards me—gently." Sixtus kept his left arm raised as he complied. The gun clattered as it bounced across the tile until the assassin's loafer stopped its progress. In a single motion, he pushed Kara to the side and bent over to grab the weapon. By the time he stood up, Kara had run to her husband's arms. The assassin pointed the gun directly at Sixtus' head.

"I insist you come with me, Maras, or you will die."

"Who are you? How did you get in here? I have a security system."

"I am Havas Zir. Obviously, we have a schematic of your home, so disabling security was not difficult."

Kara remained in Sixtus' arms but raised her head slightly. "Jeffery, why does he keep calling you that strange name?" Sixtus brought his index finger up to his lips and made a shushing sound.

Turning back to Zir, he said, "Where are you taking me?"

"That is none of your concern. I only need to know if you will willfully comply."

Sixtus looked at Kara, who was still shaking in his arms. Her face was devoid of color, and dark purple circles outlined her eyes. She appeared to be a decade older than when he last saw her a half hour ago.

"I will go with you if you assure me that my wife and my housekeeper are safe."

Zir's upper lip turned up in a slight sneer. "Your 'wife' might be allowed to live. The maid is in the living room. I imagine she has bled out by now."

Kara gasped and pushed further into Sixtus. Her crying grew louder, and the tears flowed freely. "Emma," she said in a soft, weak voice.

Reluctantly, and against his instinct, Sixtus gently pushed Kara away despite her growing protestations. "Listen to me," he said, "I have to go. There's no other way. Don't worry about me, please."

The intensity of her sobbing grew. "I'll never see you again…"

"You'll see me again. I promise." He smiled weakly but knew she wasn't convinced.

"Enough of this," Zir interrupted. "We must go." Turning to Kara, he continued, "If you alert the authorities, he will die instantly. You have no idea how expendable he is."

The words had just escaped Zir's lips when the door burst open and Daxtar Liss stumbled into the kitchen. His eyes were blood red and crazed. His sparse hair stuck to the top and sides of his head, slick with sweat. He panted like a dying man. One hand covered his stomach; the other held a knife.

"Liss, you do not look well." Zir continued to point the gun in Sixtus' direction while wielding the knife he formerly held to Kara's throat in his free hand. "I could kill you on the spot."

"You will not risk using the gun, Zir. Neighbors might hear it and call the authorities. The guard may investigate, and the police could arrive before you escape."

"I am not afraid to use it as a last resort."

"I—I," Liss leaned over even farther and began to cough. A thin string of blood mixed with saliva escaped his mouth and hung like a wire suspended between his lower lip and the floor.

"You are dying, Liss. I will feed your body to the wild pigs when you expire."

Liss gurgled and growled, and when he stood up, he lunged at Zir using his remaining strength. Unfortunately, he didn't have the energy required for an assault, so when he reached his adversary, the other was waiting. As Liss swung the knife, his knees buckled, and he lurched forward out of control. Zir used the fortuitous development to thrust his own blade into the abdomen of the other man as he fell. Liss let out a whimper followed by a bloody gurgle. As they looked at one another for a brief moment, Zir pulled the knife back out, which

106

elicited a second grunt. A small push caused Liss to crumple to the floor.

"Maras, do not believe…"

Zir's eyes flared, and he reached over and stuck the knife back into Liss with a force that conveyed his contempt and rage. He repeated the action several times as the dying man's blood splattered onto his shirt, pants, arms and face. After several more strikes, he withdrew the knife for the last time and stood panting over the still form of Daxtar Liss. Zir looked up at Sixtus as Kara pulled even closer to her husband.

"A vehicle will arrive within the hour. You will instruct the guard to let them through. They will dispose of this body and the other in the parlor. A biohazard crew will remove any furniture contaminated with blood, and they will clean the walls and floors. Identical replacement furniture will arrive tomorrow. Do you understand?"

"But—Emma..." said Kara.

"Let us go, Maras, before I change my mind." Zir waved the gun menacingly for emphasis.

Sixtus kissed his wife and looked at her reassuringly. Kara nodded her head and watched them walk toward the front door as Zir held the bloody knife against the small of Sixtus' back. As they reached the living room, Sixtus encountered the prone form of Emma, her torso stretched out over the Edra sofa. A wet stain of fresh blood glistened in the dull glow of the emergency lighting, and crimson trails dripped off the edge of the sofa onto the hardwood floor.

"You have contaminated this reality, Zir. This woman should not have died."

"Wrong, Maras. This *is* the time line as designed. Now, keep moving." Zir exerted more pressure on the knife to encourage Sixtus to pick up the pace.

107

They walked through the foyer and moved quickly to the front door. "Listen carefully, Maras. We will leave in your vehicle. If you try to resist, you can rest assured your 'wife' will die. More importantly, your true family in the future will die."

"This cannot be. My family is protected. The Corporates..."

Zir interrupted. "The Corporates are finished, Maras. A new leader and a just government have emerged to free us.

"What? Liss said *you* are the agent of the Corporates."

"Bah, that was his ruse. He carried out the cowardly work of the Corporates, not I." As they approached the vehicle, Liss pulled out the gun. "Get in, Maras. I will not hesitate to shoot you if you try something unexpected."

Nodding in acknowledgement, Sixtus went to the driver's side and unlocked the doors of the BMW with his key fob. They both slid into their respective seats at roughly the same time. Once they settled in, Sixtus started the car as Zir wiped beads of sweat off his brow. His complexion appeared waxen, and new boils pushed out from the irritated skin near his lips.

"Where to?" Sixtus asked.

"Take the 101 to the 303 and head out to Route 93."

Sixtus knew the local routes out of town very well, and he pondered potential destinations. "There's nothing up in that direction. Are we going to Las Vegas?"

"Never mind. Just drive. And don't give the security man any signals."

The car moved through the winding side street that emptied onto the main road, ultimately leading to the guard shack. Sixtus waved at Doug as he stopped and waited for the gate to open. He tried to look natural but saw a glimmer of concern on the guard's face as he smiled and waved again as the car passed out onto Doubletree Ranch Road.

Sixtus looked over at his companion, who appeared to be deep in thought. His eyelids fluttered as he massaged his temples. Without opening his eyes, he said, "Stay focused on the road, Maras. We must not procrastinate."

Chapter Ten

Wallace kept staring at the sheet of paper covered with Jonathan's minute writing. "I don't know what to make of it, but it gives me the hives," he said as he scratched at his face and chest simultaneously.

Marshall called a gathering of the Group at a late hour to try to find meaning in the strange ramblings of a troubled man. Wallace, Kenny, Hayden and Wanda sat around a table at the student union at Arizona State University in Tempe where Hayden taught. They collectively looked at the paper with a reverence befitting a mysterious historical document. It was Hayden's turn to pick it up and offer his theory.

"I think it is utter nonsense from a confused level three. Incoherent and filled with unrelated minutiae. He is locked in his mind. 'Gracie goes to the fish market and meets Jim Barley'. What can that drivel be except the ravings of—an afflicted individual?"

Marshall shook his head. "You're probably right."

"I'm more interested in discussing the final results of our analysis," said Wanda as she reached inside a folder and pulled out two stapled pages.

"Wallace and I worked on this for the past two days. We looked for common denominators that might offer a predictive indicator of an event, and we think we've found one."

Marshall closed his eyes and tilted his head backwards. "I'm sorry, but my mind was elsewhere. You've found a predictive element?"

She nodded but already turned her attention to Kenny, who focused on a coin spinning on the slick table. He followed its movements as his head rotated in rhythm until the coin eventually lost inertia and rattled to a full stop. He picked it up and started to spin it again.

"Kenny," she said, "can you please stop that? It's — disconcerting." Kenny looked up, wrinkled his brow and spun the Washington quarter with even greater force.

"Kenny! I said stop it. You're unbearable." When it was clear he was going to ignore her, Marshall reached out and grabbed the coin. Kenny looked at his friend with annoyance and settled back in his chair, crossing his arms in a defensive position.

"I'm tired of listening to her. Besides, she wears the same clothes every time I see her." Kenny pointed a finger in Wanda's direction without making eye contact. Wanda looked down at her pale blue blouse and navy-blue skirt and grimaced. Her eyes welled up with tears.

"I — like my clothes, and I don't wear the same thing every day. I have fourteen blouses and fourteen skirts, so everything is clean, Kenny."

Marshall sighed. "Let's stay on point, please. Wanda, what did you want to present to us?"

She slowly reached back in her folder and extracted the report, sliding copies to Marshall, Hayden and Wallace. Notably, she did not offer one to Kenny.

"The commonality is medication. In every instance where historical events differ from our recollection, there was a marked increase in prescriptions for selective serotonin reuptake inhibitors and antipsychotic drugs just prior to the incident. Notably, citalopram, fluoxetine, sertraline, risperidone, haloperidol and thioridazine."

"How much of an increase?" asked Hayden.

"It steadily rose for nearly a week prior to the change. If they could remember their state of mind at the time, the people we talked to said they felt increasingly despondent and depressed. As the date of the change grew closer, the sense of hopelessness became greater."

Wanda and Wallace provided a visual with a graph that plotted the medication usage by the Group and other high functioning colleagues leading up to a historical change event. There were two lines on the graph that tracked the increase in prescription drug usage categorized by the autism rating on the DSM-5 scale. While there was a noticeable spike in prescription medication among the level-one group, the spike in the level-two group was substantial. In fact, there was nearly a 200-percent increase in usage for that group over the two weeks prior to the event.

"This is extraordinary," said Marshall. A look of delight spread across Wanda's face as she soaked in the praise. Marshall felt better when Wanda displayed happiness, but he struggled to understand why. The sensation differed from the satisfaction he experienced when he completed a successful work project or a gaming victory, for example. Whatever caused it, the feeling was — pleasant.

"So, if we monitor the prescription meds and the level of anxiety from our group and the larger autism community, we may have an excellent gauge of a coming change event."

"Yes," said Wallace. "but it won't tell us *what* will change. So far, we only have Korinth's drawings and Iglar's musings. And trying to understand those two is exasperating."

"There's one more thing, and it's troubling, Marshall." Wanda paused and waited for a response. Over time, Marshall learned that Wanda enjoyed the dramatic pause.

"Well, go on, Wanda. What is it?"

"As we calculated the various historical event changes relative to the psychotropic meds, it became clear there was a correlation. As the dynamics of the event change grew, so did the consumption of various medications."

"So, events with greater significance led to afflicted people taking more pills?" Marshall leaned in closer to her as he spoke. He could smell Wanda's scent, and it affected him in a curious way. Thoughts related to Wanda were confusing.

"Precisely. We assigned a numerical value to the events themselves. Minor events received a 'one'. We assigned a 'five' to the most significant events. We found psychotropic medication usage increased by twenty percent for every numerical escalation."

Marshall looked at his copy of the paper. The brightly colored pie charts and line graphs confirmed the relationship between the medication use and the next change. "This is excellent work, Wanda, but it's just another disturbing facet of this mystery." He glanced over and felt good as she beamed in delight. Marshall wanted to find reasons to compliment Wanda, and it didn't make him as uncomfortable as it should have.

He brought his focus back to the matter at hand and looked over at Hayden, hoping for more analytical input. "What are your thoughts, Hayden?"

"Wha?" Hayden was still staring at the crumpled paper that contained Jonathan's ramblings. "Why is everyone looking at me? I do not care for people staring at me," he said.

Kenny giggled while Wanda, Wallace and Marshall looked away.

"Why are you laughing, Kenny? Are you laughing at me?" Hayden crossed his arms over his chest and began a rocking motion.

"I'm not laughing at you," said Kenny, who halfheartedly tried to hide a slight smirk with his hand.

"See, Marshall, that is what I am talking about. Kenny is always trying to make us seem foolish, and none of us like it, especially me."

Kenny jumped up and scowled at Hayden. "No, it's always you guys making fun of *me*. You're always hinting that I'm the dumb one."

"You *are* the dumb one," mumbled Wallace under his breath but loud enough that everyone heard him.

"That's it!" said Kenny as he started to back away. "I'm done with this group. You're not my friends anymore. If you need a vintage Orange amplifier fixed, find someone else!" Kenny turned and walked away defiantly, but let out a loud scream that reverberated through the large building.

"Kenny..." Marshall called after him.

"He's always doing that," said Wallace. "Always acting as though we're making him out to be stupid. Well, maybe he is."

"You know, Wallace, he can play the entire Bach catalog from the Cantatas through the late contrapuntal work. I hardly believe that qualifies as 'stupid'."

Wallace shrugged. "He doesn't know very much about physics or quantum mechanics."

"So, is that the only measure of intelligence that matters to us? Maybe we should exclude Iglar as well. He contributes far less than Kenny."

"Well, it's hard for all of us, Marshall. We're treated as outcasts most of the time."

"I know. That's why the group is so important and... magical." Almost imperceptibly, Marshall flinched. It was unusual for him to use such a word. He saw their puzzled looks and reconsidered. "Perhaps 'magical' was a poor choice of words. 'Useful' probably describes my sentiments more accurately."

Wallace and Hayden nodded in agreement, but Wanda looked unhappy.

"Is something wrong, Wanda?"

"No, Marshall. But I liked 'magical' better."

"*Ahem.*" Clearing his throat, Marshall shifted uncomfortably. "I think we should move on."

Wanda reached into her valise and took out another paper while Hayden went back to studying Jonathan's writings.

"I've saved the most important news for last." She stopped talking and waited for the suspense to build.

"Ok, Wanda, what else do you have?"

"Well, when we examined the prescription refill history for everyone we surveyed, we uncovered something profound."

Marshall understood his cue. "And what was that?"

"Medication refills have skyrocketed recently. It's at a much higher level than at any other time during the study. When we asked our friends in medicine about it, they said that higher levels of anxiety and depression started building over the last two weeks. It's a precursor to a major event, Marshall. And it's likely to be bigger and more significant than anything we've experienced so far."

"Fascinating," said Marshall. "Let's consider..." Before he could finish, Hayden slapped his forehead and stood up.

"I have it figured out," he said. "How could I have missed it?"

"Figured what out?" asked Marshall.

"Jonathan. I know what his writings mean. My God, I know what they really mean."

***

The BMW moved north on the 101, and Sixtus did his best to dodge the people who lined the side of the highway. While some were passive, the majority tried to influence traffic. Homemade signs dotted the landscape on the sloped banks that surrounded the below-grade freeway. People congregated under the overpasses, and they seemed more aggressive than usual.

Sixtus dodged a projectile launched by a disheveled man dressed in a stained and ragged trench coat. His face was a collection of dirty wrinkles and stray hair that obscured his forehead, mouth and chin. For a moment, he met the man's gaze and saw a maniacal hatred set deep in his hollowed eyes. In the passenger's seat, Zir was also

116

eyeing the floater, and there was a slight but noticeable shake of his head.

"It's remarkable what's happening. It gets worse every day."

Zir looked over as though he was contemplating whether to answer. "You have no idea."

Another pause followed. "What do you mean?"

"What century are you from, Maras?"

"The early 24th."

The edges of Zir's mouth turned up in an almost imperceptibly. "If you lived in the late 24th century, you would not recognize the world you came from."

"Hyper-change affected society since the 22nd century. That's nothing new."

"I was not referencing hyper-change."

"Then what?"

"Never mind. Just drive."

Sixtus held the accelerator steady for several miles before breaking the silence. "Where are we going? If you're going to execute me, I know a remote location that's close and heavily wooded. No one will find my body for months."

"I have no intention of executing you, Maras. At least not yet."

"How did you find me? I took great care to create an identity that never showed up in historical records."

"We were able to partially penetrate the Corporate's neural network before they purged the system. They knew more about you in this time than you suspect. Since I knew your location, I just waited for Liss to show up. I knew he would try and persuade you."

"You knew Liss was here and did nothing to stop him?"

Zir shrugged. "Liss is not important to us. He was near death anyway, so dealing with him was unnecessary."

"What value could I have to the Corporates — or whoever is now in control of society?" said Sixtus.

"You have a great deal of value, Maras. In fact, you may have the ultimate value."

Sixtus paused and considered his next question. "Liss claimed you were sent back to assassinate the living Time Sculptors in this era. Is that true?"

Zir pointed at an approaching freeway sign. "Get on I-17 and take it to the seventy-four."

Sixtus drifted over to the lanes that routed traffic onto I-17. Once he reached the junction where the two freeways merged, traffic quickly ground to a halt. They both tried to look out their windows, but the bottleneck was not in their line of sight.

As they inched forward, Sixtus heard a cacophony of sirens accompanied by flashing red and blue lights. In the distance, he could make out over a dozen people running in different directions under the bright quartz-halogen streetlamps, shouting unintelligible words while gesturing wildly. Outnumbered by nearly fifty to one, the police officers moved hesitantly through the crowd with their hands on their weapons. The gathering quickly morphed into a mob as those who took up a position just off to the side of the freeway acted with extreme hostility, tossing bottles and rocks indiscriminately into the center of the crowd.

"This is taking too long," said Zir as he opened the passenger window and tried to see past the endless gridlock.

"There's isn't much I can do," said Sixtus. "The traffic snarls are a way of life now. There's always some group protesting something."

"Run up on the shoulder and go by it."

"I can't do that," said Sixtus. "I'll be pulled over and ticketed. Maybe even arrested."

Zir fidgeted nervously. "Nonsense. It is obvious the police are outnumbered. They count on a frightened herd mentality to control the masses. They are preoccupied with that mob. Just go."

"But..."

"I am not asking, Maras." To emphasize the point, Zir raised the barrel of the gun.

Shaking his head slightly, Sixtus pulled off the highway and onto the shoulder as the sound of the rumble strips invaded the cabin and irritated his already frayed nerves.

"Faster!" said Zir, and the car lurched forward. Motorists stalled in one of the three westbound lanes looked on with incredulity as the BMW passed them rapidly. In several minutes, they covered a distance that should have taken an hour to traverse under the circumstances. Headlights appeared in the rear-view mirror, and Sixtus glanced back, quite sure it was the police ready to hit their sirens and lights.

Zir turned and looked at the trailing cars. "*Hah.* I told you they were sheep. Look at that. We have three or four cars right behind us. Call them the bold sheep."

"That's fine, but there's a problem up ahead..." Sixtus couldn't get the words out before a loud thud echoed through the cabin from a rock that landed on the roof. Stunned momentarily, Zir and Sixtus looked at each other just before an even louder bang caused them both to flinch as a bigger boulder crashed into the hood, leaving a large dent and deep scratches in the metal.

119

"It is coming from up there." Zir pointed through the passenger's window to a spot higher on the slanted freeway sidewall. Sixtus couldn't see the instigators, but the car was being peppered with rocks, so he was fairly certain Zir had pinpointed the cause. "I suggest you go faster, they are running down the slope toward us."

"I can't go any faster without risking driving off the road. It's dark out here."

"Well, if you don't drive faster, they will swarm the car." Sixtus pressed further on the accelerator just as a fist-size rock smashed into the windshield, causing an angry lattice of jagged cracks to form in the safety glass.

"Oh crap, there's a squad car blocking the way." Sixtus watched as a black and white up ahead veered toward the shoulder and stopped, cutting off any chance of escape.

"What should I do now?"

"You need to go around it."

Sixtus looked at the traffic and shook his head. "Are you crazy? I can't go around it."

"Rev the engine and ride up on the embankment."

"That's at least a thirty-degree angle. The car will roll."

Zir leaned over and yanked Sixtus by the shoulder. "It should work out fine if you have enough speed. Now, quit talking and do it."

At that moment, a large crowd moved from the road and surrounded the police squad, and several people walked to the back of the car and pushed it into an area where the asphalt met the sloped dirt of the manmade roadside hill. Now, they truly had no escape.

120

Zir screamed and pounded the gun on the dashboard in frustration. "We are going to have to walk," he said. "We will get past the police car and then steal one from somebody caught in this gridlock."

"That's crazy. We'll get arrested for sure."

"Listen, Maras, I am not arguing with you. Either follow my instructions or die. It is your choice."

Sixtus nodded and turned off the engine. As he opened the door to exit, he noticed the mob gathered around the squad car had started to rock it. Several others were beating on the windows with sticks, pipes and other objects. The glass exploded with an unsettling sound that reverberated down the long line of stalled cars.

Multiple arms reached inside the police vehicle, and Sixtus could see the head and torso of the struggling officer emerge through the driver's side window as they grabbed his body, hair and clothing. His right hand held a service revolver, and he got off four shots before they pulled him out and threw him to the ground.

Like a swarm of mindless piranha acting entirely on instinct, the mob assaulted the fallen lawman with unimaginable viciousness. Multiple floaters kicked him repeatedly while others fell to their knees and punched him in the face. One bloodthirsty vagrant ripped away the officer's shirt and sunk his teeth deep into the flesh of the other man's forearm. He shook the arm like a rabid Doberman.

Zir placed his hand on Sixtus' shoulder. "Start the car and be ready. We may get a chance to go around them after all. Listen for my signal."

Sixtus gulped air and clutched the steering wheel. There was no way this could work.

Chapter Eleven

While the crowd focused on the fallen patrolman, a floater slipped away from the mob and got into the squad car. The sound of the slamming door attracted several others who joined him by jumping into the back and passenger's side of the vehicle. With lights flashing and sirens blaring, the patrol car drove along the shoulder as several others started to chase after the cruiser for reasons that were unclear.

Meanwhile, the fallen officer managed to grab hold of his radio and desperately called for help while writhing around on the ground in obvious agony. Two of his fellow DPS bluecoats abandoned the primary melee and jumped into a different car, driving through the mass of humanity, who pounded on the vehicle and yelled vile epithets.

Sixtus realized this was his best opportunity to get around the emerging riot, and he piloted the BMW on the shoulder in an attempt to get past the bloodied cop before the cruiser could cut them off a second time. It appeared he could make it, but one problem remained. The downed officer was still prone on the pavement, and the surrounding crowd fanned out into their pathway. Sixtus had no choice but to slow down.

"Faster, go faster!" yelled Zir.

"I can't. I'd have to plow through them."

"Then do it. We need to get past this."

Sixtus hesitated, but another large rock landed on the roof of the car, and the metal buckled as the liner sagged and touched the top of his head. He pushed on the accelerator but slowed once again as a small group of floaters grabbed the semi-conscious cop and roughly pulled him away from the shoulder and back into the road. The assault took on a new sense of viciousness as a rotund man straddled the officer's chest and repeatedly hit him in the face with a crowbar. Others spat on him as the injured patrolman feebly raised his hands to fend off the assault with his waning strength.

Without hesitation, Sixtus punched the gas pedal, and the car thundered past the mob at full throttle. As they drove by, Sixtus watched the besieged lawman reach out his hand for help. His eyes conveyed a desperate sense of hopelessness and resignation.

For an instant, Sixtus considered stopping, but the sound of the approaching squad car jarred him back into the moment. They passed the mob scene just as the patrol car skidded to a halt. Armed officers emerged from either door, and as the crowd turned and began to stalk them, the cops didn't hesitate. The crack of gunfire pierced the night air, and bodies began to fall. Sixtus pulled off the shoulder and back onto the road, finally free of the gridlock. The fading sound of weapons fire continued well after the chaotic scene was out of sight.

They continued driving in silence for a while, but when they reached the juncture of I-17 and Route-74, Zir said, "We're going to Route-93 north. Just stay on it and I'll tell you where to turn."

Sixtus was now certain they were heading for Las Vegas, but he said nothing. As they merged onto Route-74, he looked back to Zir.

"I remember we were talking about Liss. He believed you wanted to eliminate the retired Sculptors."

Zir laughed. *"Retired?* You're never retired, Maras."

"But they deactivated my neural processor. If they wanted to maintain surveillance, why didn't they just keep it functioning?"

"The chip works both ways. You could access their systems as they tracked you. If you became aware something was amiss, you might try to affect the future... Turn on 93 north when we get there."

"Okay, 93 north. So, you don't intend to assassinate me and the other three Sculptors?"

"You ask too many questions, Maras. My mission here is confidential. But the world as you remember it no longer exists. I am part of a group that is trying to restore a sense of order and justice to our time. Perhaps you will play a role in that process."

"Who is this 'group'?"

Zir hesitated before speaking in a low voice. "You are not familiar with them, so giving you a name has no relevance."

Sixtus' mind raced as he tried to find some angle that would buy time so he could free himself from this dire situation. "The Corporates are no longer directing the societal operations of the planet?"

"There is a conflict. I'm sure Liss told you about it. The Corporates cling to power, but the insurgents have made great gains."

"Who is directing the planet?"

Zir shook his head. "You do not want to know, Maras. It is better that you do not know."

***

Hayden pushed Jonathan's notes back to the middle of the coffee table. He looked up at the group to make sure he had everyone's attention. "It came to me as I was thinking of Iglar and Korinth and their ability to predict these deviations in advance. As we examined each event, we ignored something just as important."

"Which was?" asked Marshall.

"The sheer number. Iglar remembered other deviations the rest of us could not recall. As I thought about it, there was only one explanation."

"Which is?"

"He is more sensitive to the changes than we are."

Wallace slapped his forehead with the palm of his hand. "Of course. It's the degree of his autism affliction. Iglar experiences secondary and subsequent impacts that are far more subtle."

Hayden pointed at the notes. "Marshall, Iglar took you to see Jonathan for a specific reason. I imagine he is a 'marginal' level three on the DSM scale, and I believe what he wrote reflects the multitude of simultaneous changes in the timeline as he was experiencing them in that moment."

Wallace picked up the paper and began reading. *"They closed the Eisenhower, so Michael Parks takes the Kennedy and is late for a job interview.* Everything he wrote is like that. Minor details that have no obvious relevance or purpose. Overlapping ripples in the fabric of space-time resulting from the original change. He's perceptive enough to consciously experience far more of the different resulting realities than we are."

125

"Can you imagine what it must be like to have this running through your head?" said Hayden.

"Torture," replied Marshall. "In fact, it might be enough to..."

"To drive someone into a near catatonic state." Wanda finished his sentence. "If Jonathan experienced this many variations in such a short period, I wonder how he could process all of them without completely shutting down?"

"Maybe that's what happened," said Marshall. "We might have finally stumbled on autism's true cause. What if we're tuned to a higher level of sensitivity in space-time? As the vibrations increase, we lose our ability to cope with the overwhelming volume of the changes."

"This could explain many things," said Hayden. "There has never been a definitive cause established for autism, we know this."

"And no explanation for the continuing growth of the condition. In 1970, it was one out of every 2,000 children. Now, it's one out of every hundred," said Wanda.

Marshall rubbed his temples and sat back in his chair. "These are extraordinary implications. It suggests the frequency and the severity of the timeline distortions are becoming worse, and that may be why the incidence of autism has increased so dramatically in the last fifty years. Apparently, our brains can't cope with these primary and secondary changes very well."

"Perhaps the increased sensitivity relates to the variance in gene expression in the frontal lobes." said Wallace. "The synaptic functions of unaffected brains might have a dampening effect."

"Yes, but no one is completely immune to the effects, right?" asked Wanda.

"I do not think so," said Hayden. "It just means that their immediate reaction may not be as pronounced. The higher the frontal lobe expression, the less they are aware of the changes."

"If enhanced sensitivity leaves level three's essentially catatonic, what is the long-term effect on those who are 'normal'?" asked Marshall.

"Well," said Hayden as he deliberated. "I believe the end result would be the same, but it could take a much longer time to unfold."

"Unless... unless the volume and severity of changes rose," said Wallace. "It would become progressively more difficult for the person to remain lucid as the deviations increased."

"Why?" asked Marshall. "Why would time deviations result in mental collapse?"

"I imagine it's sensory overload," said Wallace. "Our brains are primarily conditioned through experience. It shapes our personalities and the way we react to future events. When the past is altered artificially, the brain might 'glitch' a bit. The mind instinctively wants to react in a way that's based on the original experience, but it's forced instead to consider the alternate reality. This could be especially destructive if the same event changed multiple times."

"I'm not sure I understand. Give me an example."

Wallace stroked his chin and adjusted his glasses. "Alright, consider this. I think everyone agrees that 9/11 was an event that had an extraordinary impact on society and every individual who experienced it.

"For decades, it's affected the way people thought and acted. Security protocols changed radically, and the lives of millions of people were impacted, including the families who lost loved ones. Governments adopted policies that changed how they functioned internally and externally. These were all secondary effects based on the original event."

"So, what's your point?" asked Marshall.

"What if it never happened?"

"I'm sorry?" Wallace had everyone's attention.

"Imagine if someone changed the timeline and 9/11 never happened. What if the imprint of the event was still in the subconscious of every person who experienced it, but no one consciously remembered it because, in a different reality, it never happened?"

"I—don't really know." Marshall's eyes narrowed in a slight frown. "I imagine it might..."

"... Drive you mad?" said Wallace. "Now imagine that impact times one thousand or one million."

"Oh my," said Wanda. "Is that why the violence outside keeps getting worse? How does this end?"

A silence fell over the group. Finally, Hayden spoke in an uncharacteristically small, weak voice. "It ends with a world in utter chaos. Over seven billion psychotic people expressing fear, paranoia and aggression without ever understanding why they felt that way. As they deteriorate, the subconscious mind might provide subtle reminders of the many different realities it experienced, yet none of it would make any sense."

Marshall sat back and sighed. "And how did this all begin?"

Hayden shrugged. "Who knows? In light of the circumstances, let us assume our descendants have figured out how to overcome the physics involved in traveling to the past. If that is the case, we must assume they were unaware of the effects of their actions. It is important to remember that every event we recall differently than how it actually transpired was relatively minor. None of them were earth shattering. I assume the changes were tightly focused."

"To what end? What motivates them to change the timeline?" asked Marshall.

"It is anyone's guess." said Hayden with a shrug. "Maybe they were looking to improve certain things in the future without disrupting their reality or ours."

Wallace pulled on his long nose hairs, a habit he exhibited during periods of extreme stress. "Changes that minute? Hundreds of them as Jonathan documented. Who knows what period his writings cover? It could be years, months, weeks..."

"Or seconds." Marshall interrupted while lacing his hands behind his head. "I'm not sure how often these changes are taking place, but the prospects are frightening. I mean, what if this conversation has transformed multiple times since we started it?"

Hayden grabbed his head and ran his fingers through his buzz cut. "It is too much. I cannot think that way, or *I'll* be driven mad. Anyway, what can we do about it?"

"I don't know, but we better think of something quick," said Wanda. "If my study is correct, and the consumption of anti-depressants correlates to the size of the event, there's going to be a huge disruption in this reality very soon."

"It starts with Iglar and leads to Jeffrey Clayton," said Marshall. "I'm going back to talk to Iglar one more time. Since I now understand his riddles, I might finally learn the truth."

"What should be we doing, Marshall?" asked Wallace.

"You and Hayden work on finding Jeffery Clayton. Wanda, you try to learn more about this earth-shattering change and when it will happen." He glanced at his friends and sensed their concern as they looked back at him with uncertainty.

"I have no answers. I'm not even sure if we are — we're asking the right questions. But I know our autism is now a strength that we must use to uncover the truth. I fear much depends on the outcome."

***

"Exit here." Zir pointed at a sign that signaled a turnoff onto an obscure road marked as Highway-97. He rubbed his eyes and wiped sweat from his forehead.

"Where are we going, Zir, and what awaits us? This is the middle of nowhere."

"I—I have struggled with finding a way to explain this to you." He again wiped at his brow with a handkerchief and appeared to refocus his eyes. "Maras, this will be difficult for you to comprehend. As I told you before, a catastrophic event occurs in the future, less than a decade after you left on your mission. The Kren class revolted, and for a time, it appeared they might overthrow the Undulates and the ruling Corporates.

"However, the Corporates regrouped and used their control over the power and data sources to suppress the rebellion. Millions died, and hundreds of millions were left to starve and perish. No one realized the Corporates retained the terrible weapons of the 21st and 22nd century. They unleashed them on the public indiscriminately, killing both rebels and innocent citizens."

"No, that can't be. The Corporates banned mass destruction weapons in 2164."

"I'm afraid it is true. Directed energy weapons and even a nuclear bomb."

Sixtus leaned back in the seat as his eyes widened. "Impossible. They imposed the ban."

"Meaningless to the Corporates when they felt threatened. The struggle was valiant but in vain. We believed we would prevail and release those in bondage for two centuries. You understand, Maras. Your family lived in a state of repression until you were chosen to become a Time Sculptor. When you left, their lives improved, but they never enjoyed the freedom they deserved."

Zir stopped talking long enough to cough up a quantity of bloody mucus he expelled out the open window. After wiping his mouth with a handkerchief, he continued. "We tried to change it, but to no avail. And then our leaders discovered a way."

"What do you mean 'a way'?"

"A way for us to triumph and banish the Corporates forever. It is why I am here, Maras. The people we are going to see hold the key to our triumph and securing a future we could only dream of. You must ensure they succeed in their quest. But—it will seem abhorrent to you at first."

"I still have no idea what you're talking about."

"You will soon understand. Please hurry, we do not have much time."

The road was poorly lit and covered with tumbleweeds. Thick vegetation encroached from the shoulder, a sign that the county maintenance crew had given up trying to keep the pavement unobstructed a

131

long time ago. Eventually, they reached a junction, and Zir directed Sixtus onto an even more desolate road identified on his GPS as route 96. Switching to high beams, Sixtus stayed alert as he looked for wild animals that might be traveling through the barren countryside.

They moved down the road for several minutes before Zir placed his left arm across Sixtus' body. "Slow the car down."

The vehicle decelerated and covered nearly half a mile at a crawl before coming to an intersection with a two-lane road. A faded street sign leaned badly to the left. One side of the sign was sun bleached and unreadable, but the faded letters on the back side identified *Lindal Road* as the other street.

Sixtus turned off the pavement onto the dirt, moving cautiously as a cloud of dust enveloped the car and made visibility difficult. After a short distance, they crept over an unstable bridge that spanned a dry wash called the *Burro Creek*. On the other side, Sixtus could see a faded sign hanging off its anchor poles. It read: *Desolation*.

Beyond the town boundary, he could see several structures in the silhouette of a half moon. He couldn't make out any details, but a single dimly lit building stood in the distance.

"There, that is where we are going." Zir pointed directly at the light. Sixtus drove toward the single dim streetlamp, passing several rows of dilapidated shacks in varying degrees of disrepair. If he hadn't noticed a gas station with a working pump, he would have thought this was a ghost town.

As they pulled up in front of the building, the headlights illuminated a weathered and tarnished bronze plaque set inside a brick pillar that read, *Office of the Mayor and City Council*. Even though his vision was limited, Sixtus wondered if this was the only habitable place in the town. Zir opened the passenger's door and exited, piercing the dead silence that surrounded them.

The summer air was hot and dry, and Sixtus could smell the aroma of mesquite and Palo Verde as they approached the building. Zir turned the 1950s-style doorknob, which creaked with a palpable agony as the dull light from inside the room bled out just as the BMW's headlamps turned off.

Sixtus stepped inside and looked around at furnishings that were sparse, worn and old. A faded red velvet couch sat in a corner with its springs exposed as many generations of rats had re-purposed the interior stuffing as nesting material. A single desk occupied a space against an exterior wall, a missing leg replaced by several volumes of stacked books. Entryways for several antechambers appeared throughout the exterior of the room, but it looked as though most of them hadn't been opened for years. The desk hosted an old gooseneck lamp, which appeared to be the source of the lighting they saw from the road. The monitor from a computer lit up the area in an eerie green glow.

"Over here," Zir called from across the room. Sixtus walked carefully on the cracked tile floor until he reached his companion, who stood by a small illuminated plastic ring set into the wall adjacent to a nondescript door. Puzzled by the obvious juxtaposition of ancient décor and modern technology, Sixtus wondered what purpose the touch-sensitive button served. Before he could weigh his theories, the door slid open to reveal a modern elevator carrier.

"Where are we, Zir? What is this place?"

"Never mind, Maras. You will find out soon enough."

With some hesitation, Sixtus entered the cabin. He watched as Zir pushed the button labeled *down* on the interior panel, and the elevator began a rapid descent that took almost half a minute before it began to decelerate.

The doors slid open and Zir stepped out, motioning for Sixtus to follow. He looked around in awe at the breathtaking surroundings.

What is this terrifying place, and why am I here?

Chapter Twelve

Sixtus stood for a moment and gazed around the huge room, stunned by the opulence that stood in stark contrast to the rotting buildings that lined the streets of this decrepit town. These walls were hand plastered and painted in rich pastels. Original paintings adorned much of the space, depicting gruesome scenes of torture, debauchery and sexual deviation plucked from the worst of the middle ages. Based on the oversized morion helmets worn by the soldiers in several of the scenes, Sixtus assumed these were portrayals of the Spanish inquisition.

As he walked, the sound of his footsteps echoed off the fine marble tile floor. The lighting was dim, but he could still see the ornate carvings on the baseboard and crown moldings in stunning detail. The edges of the dadoes over the doors were fashioned into grisly otherworldly creatures that Sixtus could not place. Mouths gaping and eyes flaming, each of the beasts seemed to stare directly at him with a fixed gaze that caused extreme discomfort. He continued to trail behind Zir, who was having trouble maintaining his balance. The color drained from the time traveler's face, and he appeared to struggle with simple motor functions. The afflicted man used a handkerchief stained with fresh blood to dab at his forehead periodically.

They made their way toward a double set of doors across the far end of the main vestibule that were wider and at least four feet higher than the others they encountered. The wood was darker, and these carvings were particularly disturbing. Countless depictions of demons, serpents, snakes and horned devils engaged in acts of sexual savagery merged into one huge bas-relief. Looking over the top edge of the doorframe, Sixtus detected a single penetration in the wall itself. As he suspected, a small camera tracked their movements.

Without breaking stride, the doors swung open automatically, and Zir motioned Sixtus to follow him inside. They entered a kind of underground subterranean bunker of mammoth proportions. The height of the ceiling must have been at least thirty-five feet, which amplified even the slightest sound and sent multiple reverberations in every direction. The furnishings were lavish, and Sixtus suspected that many pieces were centuries old and not reproductions.

In the center, a high bench not unlike those seen in legal courts occupied a large space. The top of the bench reached at least 10 feet, so those standing below would appear small and insignificant. Down its length, Sixtus counted seven chairs, but there were only three occupied.

The man seated to the left looked like he was in his late twenties, perhaps early thirties. His long, unwashed auburn hair hid an acne-ravaged complexion. He picked at his visage, squeezing an inflamed postulant with one hand while a half-smoked cigarette dangled in the other. He radiated boredom mixed with mild curiosity.

An older man sat to the right of center, and he appeared to be a professional, perhaps a lawyer or financial advisor. The cut of his suit said Fioravanti, Abboud or Merrion, and his shirt was crisply creased with the tie positioned in a perfect custom Windsor knot. His hair was salt and pepper, groomed so that every strand lay perfectly in place. The toned skin on his face was tanned, but not dyed.

Yet, it was the man in the middle seat that Sixtus found most unnerving. While small in stature, his presence dominated the room even though he appeared to be sitting on a cushion to create an illusion he was taller than everyone else. He looked thin and frail with loose black clothing that hung off his slight shoulders. Thin, red lips contrasted with his pale skin, suggesting they were coated with ruby lipstick, but Sixtus could tell they were natural and not painted. A wide-brimmed fedora hung low and hid his eyes.

The unsettling figure regarded the pair before leaning forward and placing his elbows on the bench, resting his chin on top of his clenched hands. "Well, Mr. Greene, I see you have brought us a visitor. Who do I have the pleasure of addressing?"

Zir stepped forward and bowed. "This is Sixtus Maras. He goes by Jeffery Clayton in this time."

"Ah, Mr. Clayton, it is a pleasure to make your acquaintance." He stretched his thin arms out in a gesture of welcome. "Mr., uh, 'Greene' has told us you may prove to be an asset in our effort to bring stability to a vile and contemptible world."

"I know nothing of this," replied Sixtus. "'Mr. Greene' has spoken out of turn. I am a philanthropist and nothing more."

"I told you he would pull this shit," said the filthy one with the red hair. "Let's kill them both and get on with it."

"Alan, not now." The well-dressed man on the opposite end of the bench spoke up.

The thin one in the center hushed his companion and then turned to Zir. "Indeed, Mr. Greene. Why shouldn't we just kill him if he doesn't intend to cooperate? In fact, I'm also wondering why we don't kill you as well?"

Zir looked uncomfortable but didn't flinch. "I explained to you that without my help—his help, your plan will surely fail. You already have confirmed my authenticity. I could not have knowledge of your plans without the benefit of my resources."

The pale man carefully removed his hat and peered at Zir for several moments before shifting his gaze to Sixtus. His eyes appeared to smolder and glow as they focused, and Sixtus felt the stare morph into something more sinister. Odd sensations beset his mind, and he responded to subtle suggestions and probing questions not of his origin. The sensation was strange and disquieting, but once he was aware of the assault, Sixtus resisted and employed the mental disciplines he learned in Time Sculptor academy training. Thought manipulation was growing more common in his time, much of it aided by cybernetic implants.

Sixtus relaxed and shut the gates to the various passages into his occipital lobe and frontal cortex. Even as he denied access, the strength of the foreign effort surprised him. Once he blocked all available avenues, the slender man smiled slyly before withdrawing from his subject's mind.

"Who are you?" asked Sixtus as the intrusion ended.

The smile widened. "It astounds me you and your companion don't know the answer to that question. My name," he said as his lips curled in a condescending sneer, "is Mr. Cox."

"What were you trying to accomplish with your cerebral incursion?"

"My *cerebral incursion?* If I wanted to violate you mentally, you would be mindlessly drooling all over yourself by now."

Sixtus turned his head toward Zir. "What is this? Why am I here, and who are these people?"

"This — man," said Zir while pointing at Mr. Cox, "has certain unique abilities. He assembled an extensive network of powerful individuals who control critical institutions in government, academia, economics and religion. He has a plan — a rather vile plan — to fracture the foundations of society. When the campaign is complete, he will step from the shadows, and armed with his impressive talents, his organization will assume global authority."

"And how will he carry this out?"

"For decades, he sowed the seeds of hatred among races, classes, sexes and ethnicities. The plan will culminate by detonating several small nuclear warheads. When the third bomb explodes, it will obliterate the last remaining thin strands of order."

Sixtus paused a moment and shifted in the chair. "Obviously, this effort will fail. No nuclear detonations took place after 1942; you know this."

"You are wrong, Miras. Were you told about the 1942 detonations in your own time? Of course not. In less than a week," said Zir while nodding toward Mr. Cox. "Their organization will detonate two nuclear bombs within twelve hours of each other. It is already part of our history, but this information was sanitized and buried by the Corporates. He planned on detonating six bombs, but something stopped him just before the third explosion."

"You—you lie, Zir."

"I do not lie. Ask them."

The distinguished man pulled his chair up and carefully evaluated Sixtus. "Sir," he said, "we are as baffled by this as you appear to be. My name is Xavier Watts, and I handle the operational aspects of our organization on Mr. Cox' behalf. I assume you understand the precarious nature of your situation. In fact, the lives of both you and your friend hang in the balance. However, what he says is fundamentally correct, except we do not anticipate any disruption to our plan. We *do* have the ability to detonate six nuclear devices over a three-day period."

"It will be glorious!" added Mr. Cox.

"Fuckin' cool," chimed in the young man referred to as 'Alan'.

"Why would the Corporates have kept this information hidden?"

"Come, Maras, surely you have learned of many things concealed from us in the future. It is all about control. They want to discourage any thoughts of rebellion. If a violent history was ever revealed, the Kren class might have organized a revolution."

Sixtus turned toward the bench. "No one has answered me yet. How does this affect me? Why am I here?"

"We need you, Maras. Our future society needs you," said Zir. "My time here is short. I fulfilled my mission by contacting these people and finding you. It is imperative you believe me."

"Why is your time here short?"

"Look at me. Like Liss, I am dying. The Corporates destroyed the Casimir Vacuum technology required to traverse the Kerr rings during the conflict. The only way to pierce the space-time barrier was to travel through an Einstein-Rosen bridge."

"But that is defective technology. You would suffer enormous radiation exposure. You couldn't survive…"

"Exactly. I am expiring as we speak. It is why Liss was already near death when he came to your home. He arrived here earlier than I did. As such, you need to help these people succeed in their most despicable efforts. The third bomb must detonate so the future survives and the Corporates are defeated."

"That… that is insanity, Zir. We're here to conduct minor changes in the timeline for the convenience of the Corporates. The vast majority of the changes are so subtle they're functionally irrelevant. The Time Sculptor program was deliberately designed that way. Minor changes only. Suddenly, over the last two weeks, I'm called out of retirement to kill two people, and now you ask me to facilitate three nuclear explosions? Millions of lives lost? I—I couldn't possibly participate in such a thing."

"And yet you must, Maras. If you refuse, all hope is lost. The future will hold nothing. The beautiful countryside is in ruin. They treat our people like animals and force them to live in the streets and drink tainted water and eat spoiled food."

"But such a horrific act… How can you justify something so terrible?"

"Think of your family, Maras. The Corporate's special police killed your mother. They forced your brother into mercenary slavery and made him serve an

Undulate lord. I will not tell you of the unspeakable acts your sister suffered…"

"Enough!" Sixtus' controlled emotional veneer fractured, and raw anger spilled out. "There's no proof. I can't just take you on your word. Several hours ago, you were threatening to kill my wife."

"As you know, there is no way to transport inorganic material through an Einstein-Rosen bridge. Therefore, I cannot provide the proof you require. Watch as events unfold over the next week. I assume that when you experience the first detonation, you will believe."

"How was their plan thwarted?"

Zir shrugged. "No one is sure. Even the Corporates micro-history department could not fully ascertain the methods used to foil the plot. The only history we could access before the data purge identified a detective from Seattle as the person who uncovered the scheme and intervened, but it is improbable that he acted alone. There must be someone or something else involved."

"I don't know what to believe, Zir," said Sixtus. "Before he died, Liss warned that you would lie. You both claim to represent a rebellion against the Corporates. How do I know his version isn't truthful since it directly contradicts yours? He foretold of a catastrophic event that must not happen. This timeline must be preserved no matter what the cost."

"Liss was a Corporate agent; you must know that. I w — I warn you, Maras." Zir's eyes grew wide as a spasm contorted the muscles in his face into an exaggerated expression of pain and confusion. Sixtus rose from the chair, but Zir motioned him to sit.

"My time is close, Maras..." Zir gasped for breath and clutched at his chest. "The other Time Sculptors living in this reality will try to neutralize you. Liss corrupted two of them, and only he knew their identities. I'm sorry, but you may be humanity's last hope."

"How am I humanity's last hope?" asked Sixtus with incredulity. "I must ensure that three nuclear detonations take place in order to 'save' humanity? It's almost impossible to understand…"

"If you succeed, it will be the last time change, and the people will finally live according to the principles of justice and liberty." A sudden coughing fit caused Zir's face to swell as the flesh momentarily discolored for lack of blood flow. The spasm lasted for nearly a minute before he regained his composure.

Zir picked up a plastic bottle of water and fumbled with the cap. He took a drink, but just as he set it down, he expelled a mixture of water, mucus and blood that sprayed across the floor as remnants dribbled from his mouth and onto his shirt.

Everyone looked on in horror, except Mr. Cox who leaned forward and licked his lips. Zir peered at Sixtus and opened his mouth, but there was no sound as his jaw clenched tightly.

He stood up and took a step forward, but his equilibrium was affected, and he stumbled erratically. Reaching out blindly, Zir grabbed a handful of Sixtus' shirt and pulled him close. "I tell the truth, Maras. The knowledge is now yours." Before he could finish, Zir crumpled back into his seat. His breathing was ragged, but somehow, he focused through his pain and nodded slightly.

Instantaneously, Sixtus' internal processor rebooted, and his mind was crushed by a massive data dump. As the screen flashed a bright green, he attempted to petition the system to establish a connection with the Ark complex. However, before he could gain access, the caretaker denied his request and instead directly accessed his AMPA receptor deep in the hippocampus. An incomplete history of Mr. Cox and his minions flashed before his mind's eye. In less than a second, everything Zir knew about Mr. Cox and his organization transferred to Sixtus. As the download completed, the processor disengaged, thwarting his repeated attempts to gain access.

After moving uncomfortably in his chair for several seconds, Zir crumpled to the floor. He raised his arm and motioned Sixtus closer. In a weak voice he whispered, "Beware of the second Time Sculptor. He is…"

Zir never completed his sentence. He uttered a single rasping sound while exhaling a final breath before his body went limp. Sixtus reached over and grabbed Zir's wrist, checking for a pulse as his bowels and bladder evacuated.

He looked up at the three men on the bench. "Mr. Greene is dead."

Chapter Thirteen

"How fucking disgusting!" Alan Ziminski recoiled as the pool of blood grew beneath Zir. As gravity took over, a small stream started to flow across the floor, tracing a path to the bench and pooling near the red-haired mongrel. "Get that stiff outta here! His piss and blood are making a puddle right in front of me. I can smell his shit!"

As Xavier Watts picked up a phone and talked in a hushed tone, Mr. Cox left the bench and turned toward Sixtus. "Mr. Clayton, let us retire to the conference room to continue our discussion."

Sixtus rose and walked to his left as he watched Cox and Ziminski also moving in that direction. A short time later, Watts hung up the phone and followed. Almost simultaneously, a maintenance crew entered from the opposite end of the room and approached the dead man lying in the middle of a significant quantity of accumulated bodily secretions. Sixtus wasn't sure how they would dispose of Zir, but frankly, he didn't care.

One of the single doors off the main room opened as Cox approached, and automatic lights flickered in anticipation of his arrival. Sixtus entered a deceptively large room with a massive conference table positioned near the back wall. Directly to the side, a lectern and microphone were set up for speaking along with a large powered screen and ceiling mounted projector for presentations. The conference room resembled those found on upper management floors in prestigious Fortune 500 companies.

"Please, sit." Mr. Cox motioned to a chair on the far side as he took his own seat at the head of the conference table. Watts and Ziminski soon joined them.

"It appears Mr. Greene was in poorer health than we imagined. In any event, his death only complicates matters. I want to clarify that everything he told you was essentially true. We intend to cleanse the world and purge the rot that has infiltrated every corner of the planet.

"Mr. Greene knew certain highly classified details, which made us consider his authenticity. He told us about his impending demise and explained that he believed you were the only one who could ensure our plans would come to fruition. Do you have the same knowledge, Mr. Clayton?"

"Yes, I have Zir's knowledge, but I'm not still convinced I should help you. Your reign over humanity could be ruthless and cause much harm."

"Perhaps," replied Mr. Cox. "But according to Mr. Greene, a successful revolution in your future might ultimately result in the benign leadership group you both thirst for. Frankly, what happens in the 24th century doesn't interest me. Right now, I am only living in the moment. If I can trust you to carry out Mr. Greene's will, I will welcome you into my little 'family.' If not…"

"If not, then what would happen to me?"

"I will erase your memories and return you to your upper-class existence. We will go on with our business, and you will remember nothing."

"Why don't we just kill him?" asked Alan.

Mr. Cox shook his head and exhaled. "His death would serve no purpose when I can simply wipe his memory. We must remember it is highly unlikely Mr. Greene could have such detailed knowledge of our organization and plan if he wasn't privy to some extraordinary resources. If he was from the future, we are wise to heed his warning that we need Mr. Clayton to succeed."

"Bullshit!" said Alan. "Why do we need him? Let's get rid of him now and move on."

"You hear but do not listen, Alan."

"I need time to consider the possibilities," said Sixtus. "I am not discounting Zir's narrative. I want to do the right thing for this time and my own."

"Of course, Mr. Clayton. Return to your home and carefully think it through. We will be in touch with you in due time."

Sixtus stood up and faced Mr. Cox. He looked at the floor and spoke in a low tone. "I don't want you inside my head."

Cox smiled and folded his hands. "You know what you must do, Mr. Clayton…"

Just before he exited the room, Sixtus could hear the red headed punk in the background mutter, "We should have just killed him."

***

Marshall sat and watched Iglar traverse the Twisting Nether realm, his face no more than six inches away from the computer screen. Interrupting Iglar during a gaming session was usually forbidden, but in this case, there was no choice.

"Please, I need you to let go of the mouse and keyboard and look at me." Iglar ignored the request and continued to stare straight ahead. Marshall hesitated before reaching out and touching the exposed flesh on Iglar's left arm. The result was instantaneous, and the loud shriek echoed throughout the house.

From downstairs, Grace Stone yelled, "Iglar, are you alright? Marshall, what's going on up there?"

"Nothing, Mrs. Stone. Everything is fine." Iglar left the computer and scurried to a corner of the bedroom where he sat with his knees drawn up to his chest. His eyes conveyed a sense of fright and trepidation. At least Marshall had his attention.

"We figured it out, Iglar. We know what Jonathan's writings mean. The greater the degree of autism affliction, the more sensitive that person will be to changes in the timeline. Some become so sensitive, they experience all the overlapping repercussive secondary changes leading to complete sensory overload. Am I right?

Iglar pulled his legs up tighter and wrapped his arms around them. "Yes. You riddled the riddle, Marshall. You see it now. They change the past. The aliens; the men from Mars. So many changes the special ones can't stand it. Always in our brains; it never stops. I feel them every day. Once, twice, sometimes ten times. But Jonathan feels them hundreds of times every minute. Those with the most damage are in such pain they can't speak at all. Many feel it thousands of times a minute or maybe more. One change causes ten changes, which cause 100 changes, which cause 10,000 changes, which cause…"

"Okay, Iglar, I understand."

"… Until—boom! Then it's over, and their brain short circuits. Even in the womb, the sensitive ones are bombarded every day." Iglar shook his head.

"So, the larger question is what's happening to those without our unique condition? The 'normal' ones. What are they experiencing on a subconscious level? I wonder how it affects their behavior?"

Iglar let out a short howl of laughter. "Look around. Crazies everywhere. Crazy as I am. It's killing everybody, Marshall. It takes longer for the conventionals, but it's just as deadly."

"So, the imprint of each new reality remains in the subconscious as a vague memory. It's possible some people could have lived in hundreds of different realities depending on how many time changes they were subjected to."

"Now you get it, Marshall. The mass murderers, terrorists, serial killers. They overload; no pressure valve. Some just turn off the switch and tune out."

"It explains why so many begin as perfect babies and eventually end up as maniacal killers."

They sat in silence for some moments until Iglar got to his feet and cautiously moved back to the chair in front of his computer.

"This is very disconcerting, Iglar, and I desperately need your help. How can we stop this and put an end to the time changes?"

Iglar shrugged. "They are wicked people, Marshall. It's not just the ripples. They are causing a lot of changes. Big changes. Six just this month. Stay away from them, Marshall. Here, look at this."

He handed over a sheet of paper. Iglar's writing was terrible, but Marshall read through a list that resembled an incident report, except the first five episodes had a line drawn through them.

1)   *6/4: Thomas Duran murdered in Connecticut*
2)   *6/12: Jenna Duran suffocated in Rhode Island*
3)   *6/16: Tomas Jelinek hit by a car in Prague*
4)   *7/19: Olusegun Obi poisoned in Abuja Nigeria*
5)   *7/25: Grayson Baltis killed by a truck in Phoenix*
6)   *7/28: Curtis Roberts man from Mars who makes the changes suicide in Seattle*
7)   *7/31: Chicago — The End*

Marshall glanced at Iglar before continuing to examine the list. "So, it's not just echoes of past events, it involves active events. They're doing it as we speak."

Iglar nodded. "Sends out more ripples each time. Ripples crash into ripples, people bounce like a pinball. One reality — two, three, one thousand or one million. Until — bat shit crazy like me!" Iglar cackled and grabbed a handful of his hair.

"Who are they, Iglar? Who should I stay away from?"

"No, I can't tell you," said Iglar. "They will evaporate me."

"Is one of them Jeffery Clayton?"

Iglar gasped and slid his chair backwards. "How could you know that?"

"It's not important. Who else makes these changes, Iglar? Who else?"

"I won't say. They'll kill me if I say. Don't, Marshall. Just don't." Iglar had buried his head in his hands and started humming the melody to Stars and Stripes Forever. Marshall tried to get him to refocus, but every time he talked, Iglar increased his volume.

The sound grew loud enough that Marshall could hear Grace Stone's footsteps coming up the

150

stairs. She opened Iglar's door and looked at her son and then at Marshall. Her hands went to her hips and deep frown lines formed on her face.

"What have you done to upset Iglar?" she asked with a hint of contempt in her voice.

"We're fine, Mrs. Stone. We were just talking. Sometimes Iglar just…"

"I know what you're going to say, Marshall Beiner, and I won't have it. You and your friends think you're better than Iglar because he's more retarded than the rest of you. Well, none of you are normal; do you understand me?"

Marshall stood up and walked past her to the bedroom door. "I understand you, Grace. I've always understood you. The only one who has castigated and disparaged your son is you. Maybe if you treated him like someone with special abilities instead of someone who is defective, Iglar might be more self-confident and happier."

Her face went scarlet, and her eyes flashed with anger. "Well, who are you to tell me how to raise a child with such problems? You don't understand what I've been through."

Marshall walked down the steps, and when he reached the first floor, he turned back and said, "Yes, Grace, always put yourself ahead of Iglar. Oh, and by the way, the term *retarded* is insulting. Why don't you at least learn to use language that doesn't degrade Iglar? He has a developmental disability, and he's just as valuable as you. In fact, he's far more valuable than you are."

As he closed the front door, he could hear her sputtering with rage. She tried to answer, but her words were incoherent.

Marshall typically avoided conflict, but Grace Stone's offensive negativity simply couldn't go unchallenged. While he might rationalize her resentment intellectually, it didn't make it any easier to understand. Still, the far more pressing issue was Jeffery Clayton and whoever else was manipulating time. The only obvious course of action was to confront Clayton and try to convince him to stop his devastating time altering actions.

While he drove, Marshall pulled his phone from his pocket and hit number one on the speed dial. Kenny answered on the first ring.

"Hello, Marshall. Why are you calling? I'm too dumb to be around you special people, remember? Why do you want to talk to a dummy?"

"Kenny, you're being very emotional. It's unnecessary. I understand you have hurt feelings."

"Hurt feelings? You don't know how it feels, Marshall. Everyone likes you, but I'm the dummy they all make fun of."

"You're talking about Hayden and Wallace. Seriously, do you care what they think? Kenny, you're the one who speaks to the outside world on our behalf. You're the one with a personality. A *real* personality. When someone talks to you, you understand what many of the inflections and expressions mean. I have to study textbooks just so I can give people a learned response. Wallace and Hayden are terrible at reading people. They walk into a room, and 'normal' people, as you put it, search for the first excuse to walk far away from them. Do you want that, Kenny?"

"Well, no…"

"Then recognize your own value and gifts. You're more intelligent and creative than most

152

people, and you have the bonus of being able to interact with everyone."

"I—I never thought of it that way."

"Well, you should start. Look, I'm just calling because I wanted to let you know I'm on my way to Jeffery Clayton's house."

"*Jeffrey Clayton?* The man we watched murder someone? Marshall, no! He is a dangerous person."

"I have to go there, Kenny. We know a lot about the events and what's causing them. More importantly, we understand their devastating effects. I have to at least try to stop it. Please call Wallace, Wanda and Hayden and let them know what I'm doing."

"Marshall, part of the reason I left last night was because I'm scared."

"I know, Kenny. I'm frightened too."

"Please be careful. You are my only… friend."

"I understand, Kenny. I'll call you when I'm finished."

Marshall drove the Civic along Camelback toward the freeway, periodically checking his surroundings in case an aggressive floater was nearby. Random violence was commonplace, especially in this neighborhood. Fortunately, traffic was light mid-morning, and most of the agitators still slept under the bridges or in the ramshackle tent cities. The GPS highlighted the route through Phoenix and into Scottsdale, an area that Marshall rarely visited. The houses were upscale, and for the area's elite, the North Valley was the only place to live.

He exited on Indian Bend and turned north on Scottsdale Road, letting the GPS direct him to the guard shack that served Jeffery Clayton's neighborhood. Unlike some communities that only monitored entry and exit during the evening, Clayton's enclave had a human guard 24/7. Marshall pulled up to the shack and waited. The uniformed attendant on duty opened the window and smiled.

"What can I do for you?"

"My name is Marshall Beiner. I'm here to, ah, fix Mr. Clayton's computer network."

The guard nodded, closed the courtesy window and grabbed the wall phone. Marshall watched the man talking to someone while pointing repeatedly in his direction. When he placed his hand over the receiver and slid the window open, he was far less friendly. "Mr. Clayton says he didn't schedule a computer repair appointment."

"Yes he did. Tell him we met two nights ago at Buckeye and 12th Street at around 10:30 at night."

Emmitt, the day guard, looked at Marshall with suspicion as he appeared to weigh the potential of irritating an important resident with another nuisance call. He rolled his eyes and put the phone back up to his ear. It only took seconds before the glass re-opened.

"You can go up to the house. Do you know how to get there?"

"No, but I have a GPS on my phone."

"Okay, but watch when you reach the roundabout. Your GPS is likely to show it as a four-way stop. La Canada is the second turn off on the right."

"Thank you." Marshall smiled weakly because his conditioning generated the automatic response. He drove past the guard house and moved onto Via Linda, which served as the main service road through the neighborhood. As he scanned the landscape, he absorbed the richness and beauty displayed in the immaculately manicured median and surrounding grounds.

Colorful flowers covered the entry monument, which bordered a waterfall that emptied into a manmade lake. Vivid, evenly cut green grass blanketed virtually every square inch of ground not otherwise landscaped. As a middle-class kid growing up in Phoenix, he rarely saw this kind of scenery. The desert was barren, and the only landscaping he was familiar with included dull rocks and unattractive cactus.

Marshall followed the guard's instructions and took the second right on the roundabout onto La Canada, alternating his view between the GPS and the upscale homes that lined the street. Jeffery Clayton's house was the second on the right with a long and steep driveway that could easily be mistaken for another road. He pulled up to the house, trying to figure out where to park in the massive landing area before deciding to leave the car near the detached garage.

He got out and looked around, marveling at the concrete statues of a lion and lioness surrounded by beds of blooming Desert Willows. Approaching the massive iron gates that hid a large courtyard, Marshall reached out and pushed the doorbell. He wasn't nervous in the conventional sense but felt apprehensive.

Several seconds passed, and he brought his hand up to the button to ring the bell again, but the door opened automatically. Eyeing the inside suspiciously, he walked into a courtyard of great splendor. Vibrant flower beds lined a winding walkway of pavers that looked as though they were straight out of the late 19th century. The property left little doubt that Jeffery Clayton was rich.

In the middle of the courtyard, another fountain spouted multiple streams of water that changed colors along with the lighting. Marshall could only imagine the expense involved in keeping delicate vegetation thriving in such heat. He came upon a second set of doors, more ornate than the first. Maybe there was a knocker somewhere? Unsure of what to do, he pushed the button yet again. This time, a single door opened, and Clayton was standing in the threshold holding a firearm pointed directly at Marshall's chest.

"What do you want?" he asked in a dull monotone. Clayton's face was expressionless, and while his hair kept its shape and cut, he obviously hadn't bothered to comb it today.

"Mr. Clayton, we need to talk. I—I know it was you who pushed that man into traffic the other night."

Sixtus' eyes narrowed and his grip on the handgun tightened.

Chapter Fourteen

Sixtus regarded Marshall for a moment. He brought his gun hand up to his chin and scratched at the stubble that formed overnight. Shaving was not a top priority right now.

"I'll give you one minute to explain who you are and what you want. But I warn you, I'm in no mood for subterfuge."

"My name is Marshall Beiner. I was there when you pushed that man in front of the truck two nights ago."

For just a moment, Sixtus' eyes widened. "You're mistaken. I was nowhere near that area on Wednesday night."

"No sir, you were there. I recorded your license plate number. I also have pictures of your car leaving the scene."

Sixtus pursed his lips and continued to rub the gun against his whiskers. "So, it was you in the white compact car. Well, at least you saved me the time of having to track you down. What is it you want, money?"

Marshall glanced at his shoes before looking up. "*Money?* No, that's not it at all. I'm not sure how to explain this to you. If I'm wrong…"

"Is your name really Marshall Beiner?"

"Yes, that's my real name."

"Well, Marshall Beiner, now you have less than thirty seconds. If you want to say something, I suggest you do it quickly."

Marshall sighed and tried to collect his thoughts. "I don't think you killed that man for revenge, money or personal gain. I think you killed him to change something."

The gun dropped to his side, and Sixtus raised his eyes to meet Marshall's. "What do you mean, *change something?*"

"I mean, I suspect you wanted to change history. I don't know why or what eliminating that man might accomplish, but I believe you murdered him to alter the future."

Sixtus evaluated the awkward young man standing in front of him. He seemed normal enough, but there was something different he couldn't quite put his finger on it.

This couldn't be the youngest Time Sculptor Zir and Liss warned me about?

"Please, come inside."

Sixtus led Marshall through the expansive house, making several turns into hallways that made the journey resemble a maze run. At one point, Marshall saw a woman wrapping a glass vase and placing it in a cardboard moving box. She looked up briefly but tried to avoid making eye contact. Sixtus turned a final corner and opened the doors to his den. Once inside, he went over to his desk and motioned for Marshall to take a seat.

"Changing time? How did you arrive at such a bizarre conclusion?"

Marshall rubbed his temples for a moment. "My friends and I — we are not the same as other people. The medical term is 'autism'. Autism Spectrum

Disorder or ASD to be precise. We have altered brain chemistry that makes us more sensitive to changes in our environment, circumstances and perception."

"I'm not following you… Can you be more specific?"

"It's not uncommon for those of us with this condition to detect even the smallest modifications in our regular routine. For example, my mother might move a chair to vacuum the living room, and then she'll put it back in almost the same location. When I enter the room later, I'll know immediately that she moved it and how far, down to an eighth of an inch."

"I see… Well, that's interesting, but how does it relate to what we're discussing?"

"Changes, Mr. Clayton," said Marshall. "You are changing the natural course of events in this time. Unnatural alterations that are affecting the future. Every time one of these changes takes place, we recognize it. We remember events as they originally occurred, and the changes you are making are abnormal, disturbing and damaging to our mental health."

Sixtus raised his eyebrows and rubbed his neck. "So, are you saying everyone with autism believes time is being altered?"

Marshall shook his head. "No. Some are not affected enough to remember the original events, while others are far too sensitive. They perceive every change and the multitude of secondary effects that ripple through the new reality. Their brains become overloaded, and they shut down."

Sixtus set the gun on the desk and puffed his cheeks as he exhaled. "How did you discover this, Marshall?"

"I suppose it was luck as much as anything. It started with a discussion I had with one of my friends regarding an event I remembered differently than

159

everyone else. Those unaffected by autism remembered it one way, but I remembered it another. However, my friend also recollected it the way I did. We compared our memories with others in our group and made note of the differences. Ultimately, we came to a disturbing and indisputable conclusion. Someone or something was altering time."

"Would you care for something to drink, Marshall?"

"Yes, sir. Water is fine. My throat is quite dry."

Sixtus got up and walked over to a built-in refrigerator. He took out two bottled waters and handed one to Marshall. "That may explain how you came to your conclusion, but it doesn't explain why you were at Buckeye and 12 Street on Wednesday night."

"One of us—this is extremely difficult to explain… One of us remembers the future."

"What?"

"He seems to know about events that are going to change before they actually happen. He remembered you would kill that man long before you actually did it. You encountered my friend as you were leaving that night."

Sixtus scratched his head and looked up. "Not that floater in the church parking lot?"

Marshall nodded. "Yes, his name is Iglar."

"Iglar—that's fitting." Sixtus leaned up on his elbows. "Tell me, was it you who sent me the text?"

"Yes."

There was a slight pause before Sixtus climbed up on the desk and leapt at Marshall, throttling his neck with both hands. "You're one of the Time Sculptors, aren't you? What do you want? Are you here to assassinate me? What is your designation? *Talk…*"

Marshall choked and sputtered as he futilely grabbed at Sixtus' wrists. His windpipe was almost closed off, but he was so horrified, he couldn't speak anyway. After several seconds, Sixtus released his grip on Marshall's throat as he sensed the rising terror in the slight man under him.

A massive panic attack gripped Marshall as he gasped for air and raised his fingers to his neck to count his heart rate. He sucked desperately to get oxygen into his lungs and huffed like a man without a mask in a soot fire. Unsettled by the convulsions, Sixtus got off Marshall's chest and brought over his water. Lifting it to his lips, he poured a small amount of the liquid into the panicked man's mouth, watching as he coughed and spit it out. A second try cleared some phlegm, and a third swallow was successful.

Finally sitting up, Marshall looked over at Sixtus with abject fear. While trying to calm himself, the reality of the assault set in, and he started to cry. Among his feelings of violation, shame and humiliation, Marshall experienced a crushing sadness.

"Why — why did you do that?" he wailed.

Sixtus tried to place his hand on Marshall's shoulder, but the young man recoiled and skittered back several feet.

"I'm sorry. Truly, I am very sorry. I thought… You aren't a Time Sculptor, are you?"

"No, I'm not. What's a 'Time Sculptor', anyway? I told you why we followed you. It's the changes." Marshall used the back of his hand to wipe his watering eyes.

Sixtus pulled a tissue from a 19th century holder and handed it to his guest. "You've complicated things for

161

me. Could I convince you that you and your friends are wrong?"

Marshall got up from the floor before returning to his seat. "We're not wrong. We did the research and cross-referenced the events multiple times. Over the last half century, your name is one of three that appeared repeatedly when the change events were important enough for historical documentation. That's what you're doing, isn't it, Mr. Clayton. You're from the future, and you're changing time."

Sixtus regarded the scholarly young man for several moments. He knew little about autism, but there is something slightly off with this one. "Let's assume I confirmed your suspicions. What would it accomplish?"

"We could begin a dialog that might save everyone."

The statement startled Sixtus. *Does he somehow know of the revolt against the Corporates? How could a primitive possess such insight?*

"If I explain who I am, will you divulge everything you have learned about me and these — changes?"

Marshall looked away for a moment. "I'm not sure if it's right, but I'm also out of options, so yes, I'll tell you."

"Well, you won't be unsure when I'm finished."

For the next twenty minutes, Sixtus divulged the basics of the Time Sculptor program, providing no more detail than was absolutely necessary. He covered qualifications for entering the academy, the safeguards to prevent time disruptions and the fundamental intent of the program, which was to improve the lives of the Corporates. The explanation was short and to the point, and Sixtus weighed his leverage in divulging information relative to the value of what he would receive in return.

For his part, Marshall sat silently, riveted to every word Sixtus spoke. He focused entirely on the narrative while avoiding the temptation to fantasize or speculate. When Sixtus sat back in his chair and took a swallow of water, Marshall finally relaxed.

"I have so many questions. You know the future. Do people still die? Have we conquered disease? Are starships exploring the galaxy? Is there other life in the universe?"

Sixtus held up his hand. "I can't answer any of those questions. Even telling you what I already have violates the essential tenets of the program and could further contaminate the time line. You wanted honesty, so I've given it to you. Now, I need the names of the other people involved in the change events your group discovered."

"But it's not enough. I am talking to someone from the future. There's so much I want to know and so many mysteries you can solve."

"You aren't supposed to know any of this, Marshall." Sixtus tone conveyed his growing annoyance. "I'm already on unstable and dangerous ground here. I can't tell you any more specifics about the program."

Marshall paused and looked out the window. "Then something must be wrong."

"Wrong? I don't understand?"

"Discussing the program with anyone from this time could result in extraordinary consequences for you, personally. In fact, secrecy must be a fundamental rule unless the program is compromised."

Sixtus stared at Marshall as their eyes locked. "Yes, something has gone wrong. That's all I can tell you."

Marshall shrugged and his shoulders slumped a bit. "Ok, so I'm trying to understand. These timeline changes affected every millennium from the dawn of civilization, but they're limited and isolated, so they should have no impact on the natural progression of history, right?"

"Yes. The changes are made to enhance the prestige and position of the privileged class in our time and their future generations."

"So, why are these changes causing society to collapse?"

Sixtus shook his head. "They're unrelated. None of the changes we've made affected societal evolution. As I explained, they are minor, focused alterations designed to enhance status. They are also very rare."

"Something isn't right, Mr. Clayton. There have been four significant changes made just this month alone. Two more will happen within the next two days. The cumulative effect is that your future society is tearing this one apart."

"No, that can't be. The Corporates ran sophisticated simulations. And six substantial changes in the last month? That's not possible."

"It's more than possible, it's happening," said Marshall

"The Corporates made sure of the efficacy of the program…"

"Then they missed something, or someone is tampering with the formula. With all the advanced technology from your time, you clearly haven't considered the effect your actions are having on the psyche of the people from this time."

Marshall pointed at the side of his head for emphasis. "These changes are creating micro fissures in the time line. Obviously, you're unable to detect the smallest ripples as they fan out from the original splash. They leave imprints on the subconscious part of the brain that affects memories and decision-making. As the changes multiply, we believe it triggers a neurosis and often violent psychosis."

Sixtus thought carefully before answering. "Do you have any evidence that supports your theory?"

"Evidence? Look around yourself. Everything is falling apart. There is no consensus anymore, only anger and hate. Violence in the streets every day with growing numbers. I was assaulted this morning on my way over here. Certainly, you have experienced it too. If I'm not right, how do you explain it?"

"I admit your speculation is interesting, but it hardly serves as proof."

Marshall reached into his back pocket and pulled out a crumpled piece of paper. He walked over and handed it to Sixtus.

"What is this?" He held the paper at arm's length to focus. "It looks like gibberish. I see some words in sentences that make no sense."

"Yes, it might look that way. This was written by a man named 'Jonathan'. It represents some of the memories he has of changes in the timeline. Look at the number of micro changes he experiences every minute of every day due to the alterations your 'Time Sculptors' have made. They drove him to madness. The orderlies at the facility had to restrain him because he was writing on his own body when he ran out of space on the paper."

"And this man suffers from autism?"

"Yes, but he's only level two on the Autism Spectrum Disorder of the DSM-5 scale."

"My God, what do those with higher levels experience?"

"They mentally freeze up, Mr. Clayton. Many of them stop functioning early in life and never recover. The constant bombardment is too much. But whether the effects are immediate as the sensitive ones experience, or long term like the general population, humanity is deteriorating into utter chaos. You must travel to the future to stop this."

Sixtus leaned over and mumbled, "I can't"

"You don't understand. You must. Everything depends on it."

"It doesn't work that way, Marshall. I'd need access to advanced technology and massive energy to travel through space-time. This age is far too primitive. Once we're here, we can't leave. We're allowed to make a life for ourselves in our assigned era as long as we remain low profile and don't alter the timeline. Only spacecraft that could travel at near the speed of light could reach the future. Again, the technology does not exist here."

Marshall drew his fingers across the length of his face, stretching the skin. "This is terrible, Mr. Clayton. We have discovered a barometer for significant events, and we predict that a very large and substantial change is coming. Based on what we know, it could prove catastrophic. Do you have plans to create a major change soon?"

Sixtus forced himself to remain motionless. *Has he also stumbled on the large-scale Event foretold by Liss and Zir?*

166

"No, my term has ended. I'm no longer in contact with the future."

"Then—then who causes the change, and how can we stop them?"

"You mentioned there were six events of substance this month? How would you know this?

"Like I said, it's Iglar. He has an insight far deeper than anyone else, and he's still lucid."

"You must let me see this list of events. You asked me to trust you, and I did by revealing far more than I should have. But these are extraordinary circumstances, and I need that information."

"Is there a conflict in the future, Mr. Clayton? Is that what you're dealing with?"

"… Yes, there is a devastating conflict, Marshall. A terrible crisis. And the actions I take may have an enormous impact on everyone and everything."

Chapter Fifteen

Marshall pulled out the second sheet of paper and handed it to Sixtus, who unfolded it and started reading.

1) 6/4: *Thomas Duran murdered in Connecticut*
2) 6/12: *Jenna Banner suffocated in Rhode Island*
3) 6/16: *Tomas Jelinek hit by a car in Prague*
4) 7/19: *Olusegun Obi poisoned in Abuja Nigeria*
5) 7/25: *Grayson Baltis killed by a truck in Phoenix*
6) 7/28: *Curtis Roberts man from Mars who makes the changes suicide in Seattle*
7) 7/31: *Chicago – The End*

He repeated the last two lines of Iglar's list out loud.

"That's what Iglar said about you, Mr. Clayton. He called you, 'the man from Mars who makes the changes. Is Curtis Roberts one of your Time Sculptors?"

"This can't be true, Marshall. The Time Sculptor who replaced me five years ago couldn't possibly travel to all these places in such a short period. Anyway, the Corporates rarely give us more than one assignment per year."

Marshall pondered the quandary. "What if a Time Sculptor recruited others to carry out the acts?"

Sixtus shook his head vigorously. "That would completely violate the program's primary rule. That individual and their entire family in the future would die immediately."

Marshall scooted up to the edge of the chair. "What if the protocols in your time are damaged?"

"I can't even begin to imagine…"

There was a knock on the door, and Kara walked in, which broke the tension that hung thick in the air. "Jeffery, I have everything packed. If you don't hurry, we'll miss our flight."

Sixtus held up a hand. "Just give me a few more minutes."

Kara looked at the stranger and hesitated. She nodded slowly and closed the door behind her.

"Marshall, you've done a great service to humanity by confiding in me. The information you provided is invaluable. I will use it to—correct things, but now it's time for you to return to your normal life. Any further involvement could jeopardize your safety." Sixtus stood up and motioned towards the door.

Marshall lowered his head and nodded slightly. Sixtus' response was not unexpected, so he rose to his feet and awkwardly extended his hand, which the other man accepted and shook with a firm grip. Marshall walked slowly toward the door and rested his hand on the knob, standing for some moments with his back to Sixtus.

"Is there anything else?"

"I can't leave, Mr. Clayton," said Marshall without turning around. "I know too much to just go home and eat alone at the local Japanese restaurant every night. Let me help you."

"That's just not possible, Marshall. I have to preserve as much of the existing timeline as possible. Anyway, I'm not even sure if I can improve the situation."

Marshall turned and faced Sixtus directly. "I have something else. Something quite compelling."

"Go on…"

"Not unless you take me to Seattle.

"I never said I was going to Seattle, Marshall."

"But you will go there, won't you? You're going to see Curtis Roberts from Iglar's list because the event that involves him hasn't happened yet."

Sixtus sighed and looked away. "It's too dangerous, and the time line contamination is already severe. You could only make it worse."

"Then I'll go myself, and I will take several of my friends who know about this with me. I can't guarantee that one of us may not go to the authorities."

"You don't understand what you're involved in. You might die; your friends might die."

"I underst…"

Sixtus stood up, flattened his palms and banged them on the desk. "No, you don't understand at all, Marshall. This isn't some damn video game. We're talking about violating the basic constructs of the universe. It's not just humanity; everything could be destroyed. You and your friends worry about a few micro fractures in the time line. What if it's a tidal wave?"

"It *will* be a tidal wave, Mr. Clayton. We've discovered a leading indicator of the intensity of change events. It's based on surveying the psychotropic prescription drug use of those of us with high-functioning autism. The spikes

170

correlating to past events were two to five percent. But recently, the spike is up thirty-five percent and rising. There is a lot of anticipatory fear out there. A major event is coming soon."

Sixtus exhaled and stood up behind the desk. The "major event" that Marshall spoke of was most likely the bomb he would either detonate or help deactivate depending on whether he believed Liss or Zir. The imbecile he met in the parking lot had correctly identified Chicago as the location and provided a critical date.

Sixtus looked at Marshall and marveled at how much this primitive person with autism understood about him, his mission and the future. He still might have to kill him, but not now. Not when his friends knew of the time distortions. For the time being, Marshall had more value alive.

"I suppose you have me at a distinct disadvantage. You must understand that your chances of surviving this 'adventure' are minimal. You'll most likely die at my hand or another's." He turned and glared. "Do you still want to go?"

Marshall swallowed hard and looked up with a kind of resigned sadness. "I—I don't have a choice, Mr. Clayton. I'm not entirely sure who I am. Have the time changes altered my own life? How soon before the effects leave me catatonic? I have to help stop this."

Sixtus sat back down and faced his 32-inch computer monitor. He moved the mouse and made several clicks while scrolling through different screens. When he had accessed the site he wanted, he entered the required information and hit the return button with emphasis.

"Ok, you've convinced me. Meet me at the airport at 6:30 tomorrow morning in terminal three. I've booked us two seats on a flight to Seattle."

"Flying? I have a terrible phobia about flying."

"I'm sure you have a prescription. Take a couple pills. We need to go to Seattle to find this person your friend Iglar says will soon have his life altered."

Marshall regarded the proposition. Next to fear of a doctor or dentist, he hated flying the most. "Alright, I'll be there."

"Fine, Marshall. I also think it would be a good idea to somehow debunk this whole thing with your friends. The more involved they are, the more likely it is that they might get hurt. Give them a plausible explanation so they don't become suspicious."

"You're right. I'll figure out something to tell them. They're very intelligent and inquisitive, but I'll do my best."

"It sounds like you have hacking expertise in your group; is that right?" said Sixtus.

"Yes, of course. In fact, we have one of the best cyber hackers in the country."

"Good. We'll need someone to investigate the other incidents on your friend's list. If we're lucky, most of the victims are alive or never existed in the first place. Despite what you say to the contrary, if this 'Iglar' is the same person I ran into in the church parking lot the other night, I'm not convinced he isn't deranged."

Sixtus rose and left the den, peering over his shoulder as he made his way towards the foyer. It took Marshall several seconds to realize he was being ushered out. After traversing the long hallways, they stood silently in the doorway, searching for the right words.

"Get some sleep and don't talk to anyone about this, okay?" said Sixtus.

"Yes, I understand." Marshall again held out his hand awkwardly. Sixtus shook it and walked back into the house. As the door closed, Marshall stood alone on the porch, confused, frightened and overwhelmed.

***

Marshall eased his car back down the long driveway to the side street that led to Scottsdale Road, fighting the blinding light from the setting sun. He was extremely self-conscious as he passed the guard shack, aware that the attendant was staring at him suspiciously while Marshall tried to avoid eye contact. He wasn't able to shake a crushing feeling of dread until he reached the freeway and began the trip back home. Clayton was right; he would need at least two benzos to calm down. His hands clenched the steering wheel tighter, and as he drove, he realized it wouldn't be prudent to take anything in the morning that would alter his mind. He shuddered at the thought of flying cold turkey.

The Civic reached the on-ramp to the 101 when his cell phone rang, startling him out of deep thought. He glanced at the dashboard screen to see the number. The call was coming from Iglar's house, which meant it had to be Grace Stone. Iglar became very agitated when anyone mentioned the phone. No matter who called, Iglar believed the voice on the other end of the line was an alien imposter.

"Hello?"

"Marshall, it — it's Grace Stone."

"Good evening, Grace..." Marshall let the last word trail, anticipating she would get right to the point.

"We had words earlier today, and I'm sorry for that. But I need your help, Marshall. Something is wrong with Iglar."

Marshall ignored the apology. "What do you mean, Grace?"

"He's—not responding; just sitting there staring at that damn computer screen. He hasn't eaten and won't even take water. He's tuned me out before but never like this. I'm very worried, Marshall."

He could hear the concern in her voice. In these instances, sympathy was in order. He summoned the appropriate set of actions from memory. "I'm sorry, Grace, this must be very difficult for you. Have you considered taking Iglar to the hospital or calling an ambulance?"

He heard soft breathing, but it sounded strained and thick, a sure sign she was crying. "I can't do that, Marshall. You know what they'll do to him in the—sanitarium. You're the only one he communicates with anymore. Please, I'm afraid."

A person with a different psyche might feel sympathy, but Marshall didn't. However, Iglar proved himself to be a reliable acquaintance. In fact, one might say 'friend'. Also, he possessed an extraordinary gift that Marshall believed was essential to unravel this mystery.

"Certainly, Grace. I'm on my way." Then, as an afterthought, he added, "And don't worry, we'll figure this out together." His contrived sympathies had the desired effect.

"Oh God, thank you, Marshall. This means a great deal to me." She began to sob openly. If Iglar

174

recovered, hopefully he wouldn't have to deal with Grace Stone's less-than-subtle insults anymore.

While some would have sped up to reach Iglar sooner, Marshall was fastidious in obeying traffic laws. He maintained the speed limit throughout the trip, which took about twenty-five minutes in light evening traffic.

As he pulled up into the Stone's driveway, he saw Grace waiting near the porch, a half-smoked cigarette in her hand. Two floaters lay inside a cardboard box on the front lawn of the abandoned house next door. A third was in a row of hedges in the middle of a bowel movement. Marshall exited the car but stayed behind the door. "Grace, please extinguish the tobacco product. I have severe allergies."

"Yes, I'm sorry, Marshall." She stubbed out the cigarette with her foot as her jaw clenched a single time. "Please, come in."

She led him through the living room and up the stairs to Iglar's bedroom. Upon entering, Marshall noticed a change in the way it smelled. Iglar spent so much time in his room it always had the aroma of his unique body order, despite how much air freshener Grace used to cover it up. But this was different. There was something else buried beneath the smell of stale air freshener and sweat. Almost like the rot of decaying meat but not exactly. It struck Marshall as a faint wisp of death.

As Iglar stared at the blank monitor in front of him, Marshall walked over and grabbed one of the arms of his chair and swiveled it around so he could see his friend's face. The sight was unexpectedly unsettling, and he pulled back and grimaced. The corners of Iglar's mouth turned down sharply, and his chest heaved in rapid and uneven gasps. His eyes were blood red, and the pupils dilated so they covered the entire iris.

"Iglar, it's me, Marshall. Can you hear me?" Iglar's breathing grew more ragged and shallow. He moved spasmodically in the chair while shifting from side to side. The movements were unnatural, and his struggles looked like an attempt to escape from phantom chains and shackles. Marshall looked over at Grace, who had her hands up to her mouth while she stifled small gasps.

"Iglar, I have much to tell you, but you must communicate with me. I know what's happening to us. There is a solution, but I need you to help me. We can make it all stop. Please, Iglar, help me."

As Marshall talked, Iglar's level of agitation escalated. His face grew red, and veins stood out prominently in his neck as his struggle intensified. With an open mouth and lips curled in a grotesque mask, it appeared he was about to have a seizure.

"You're making it worse, Marshall. Oh my God, he's going into convulsions!"

"I'm not sure, Grace, but you might be right. You better call 9-1-1."

Marshall flinched as his friend momentarily doubled over in obvious pain. He looked past the discomfort and met Iglar's tortured, bloodshot eyes.

"Marshall."

"Yes, Iglar."

"Mar… shall." Iglar reached over and grabbed Marshall's shoulder with surprising strength.

"What is it, Iglar? Tell me."

"The — the Dark One. He came, Marshall."

"The Dark One? Who is that, Iglar?"

Iglar's grip tightened, and his face took on a deep reddish hue as blood coursed through engorged arteries. Spittle flew from his mouth as he sputtered and stammered unintelligibly. Marshall looked down as a wet stain spread through the groin of Iglar's gray sweat pants. His body shook with spasms, and it appeared as though he was having a heart attack. Marshall turned to Grace Stone for help, but she appeared frozen in abject terror.

"Grace, you need to call an ambu…" Marshall didn't finish the sentence as he felt the iron grip on his arm relax, and the noise from the thrashing stopped. By the time he turned around, Iglar was back in his original position with his arms resting on the manchettes of the chair and his hands curled down over the supports. His breathing slowed, and he resumed the blank stare at the computer monitor. Marshall and Grace made several attempts to engage him in conversation, but they proved futile.

"He was in so much pain when he spoke," said Grace as she held a crumpled tissue to her eyes. "I suppose it's a good sign that he talked."

"I don't know. He only said a few words, but as you say, he seemed like he was in terrible pain. Iglar needs a doctor's care."

Grace teared up again, and a short groan escaped her lips. "He'll be committed, Marshall. I won't take him to that place."

Marshall raised his eyebrows and looked down at his shoes. "Don't jump to conclusions, Grace. He might come around. Even if it takes a while, the Lincoln House is a wonderful facility."

"The Lincoln House? I have no money for that. Iglar will go to a state facility."

Marshall couldn't look her in the eye. He heard stories about the abuse autism victims classified as level two or three suffered in some state facilities. Cruelty and neglect were not uncommon, and many of the institutions were under-funded and inadequately staffed. He really had no answer, so he thought it was best to change the subject.

"Grace, do you know what Iglar meant by 'the Dark One?' He said it twice."

She shook her head. "I have no idea, but it gave me chills."

Marshall stood up from the bed. "There's nothing else I can do for him, Grace. And he has, uh, soiled himself, so…"

She lifted her head and straightened her back. "I'm sorry, Marshall. It's embarrassing. Let me walk you out."

They left the room and went down to the first floor in silence. Reaching the front door, Marshall took a step outside before stopping. He felt like walking straight to his car without saying anything, but something told him it wouldn't be right. He turned back to Grace, and without thinking, he extended his arms out to her, inviting a hug. She responded and put her head on his chest and cried. Deep sobs of sadness and fear wracked her body.

"Grace, it's going to be all right." The words were neither forced nor memorized. They came from somewhere buried inside a place Marshall didn't know existed until this moment. He was exploring the feeling and analyzing its meaning when a tortured wail came from upstairs.

"No, no, leave me alone! Man from Mars! You're the man from Mars."

Grace pulled away from Marshall and ran back inside the house. "Iglar," she said in a whisper. Marshall followed and found himself taking two stairs at a time to keep up with her. When he

178

reached the top of the landing, she was already in Iglar's room. A terrified scream filled with a desperate angst echoed through the house, and time slowed perceptibly. Marshall's legs were heavy, and it took an eternity to climb the last few steps, but when he entered the room, he knew Iglar was already dead.

In his peripheral vision, he could see Grace Stone crumpled to the floor. She looked like she was screaming, but Marshall couldn't hear any sound. Her entire body pulsated in motion as she grabbed handfuls of her medium-length blond hair and pulled hard. Standing next to Iglar's chair, Marshall reached up and grasped the high back, slowly spinning it around.

What has Iglar spilled down the front of his shirt?

As he stared in stupefied silence, Marshall paused for several excruciating seconds before realizing fresh blood was spreading through the material. It blotted out the colors and printed words on the transfer. Against his will, he traced a path from the bloody stain up to Iglar's face. When he saw the silver letter opener protruding from Iglar's temple out through his left eye socket, Marshall joined Grace and started to scream.

Iglar's eye was punctured and lay on his cheek, surrounded by a bloody gelatinous-like substance that was coagulating. Despite the gore on the left side of his face, the right side was far more unnerving. The other eye was still intact, and it blinked periodically. After some time, the eyelid fluttered, and the eye itself glazed over with a dull film. Marshall pulled out his mobile phone and called 9-1-1, talking in a calm voice as he gave the dispatcher the clinical facts. Apparently, after he finished the call, he dropped the phone and fainted.

As Marshall lay on the floor in a state of semi-consciousness, he started to hallucinate. The shadow of a man, or something that looked like a man, sat across from him in a corner of the room. He wore a long black coat and a wide-brimmed hat, and he looked at Marshall with eyes that burned like red-hot coals. When they connected visually, a slow grin spread across the man's thin lips, revealing unnaturally white and perfectly aligned teeth. Marshall would later recall the deep sense of dread he felt before losing consciousness.

Chapter Sixteen

"It's out of the question, Jeffery, or whoever you are." Kara's voice trembled as she spoke. "You were the one who told me we're in danger and need to leave town. Renting a cottage in Taos makes perfect sense. It's eight hours away, sparsely populated and isolated. Now you tell me you're going to Seattle without me? There's no way that's happening."

Sixtus understood her fear but knew there were no good options. "I have something I need to do. You must believe that I don't have a choice with any of this."

"You better tell me what's going on, Jeffery. I'm about to have a breakdown. A man had a knife to my throat, and another died in my house. Instead of an ambulance, he's put in the back of a cleaning van along with Emma, and they've both disappeared?" She took a step backward as though she just experienced a sudden revelation. "My God, who are you?"

Sixtus moved forward, but she recoiled, so he stopped short. "Look, Kara, I can't tell you what I'm involved in. None of this was supposed to happen, but it has, so I have to deal with it."

"He—he called you Maras. Sixtus Maras. Is that your real name, Jeffery?"

"I'm Jeffery Clayton, that's the only name you need to know."

Her eyes welled up and a large tear rolled down her cheek. "No, you are Sixtus Maras. What kind of name is that, Jeffery? What nationality? Or Daxtar Liss or Havas Zir? And what about the man who just left our house? Tell me, or you can leave right now."

Her pain was palpable, and Sixtus struggled to maintain his calm veneer. He reached into his pocket and pulled out a plastic sleeve that contained several credit cards and a number of documents. "I want you to take this, Kara. It holds important things you'll need until I return."

"Jeffery, you're scaring me. What are you involved in? How serious is this?"

"It's as serious as it gets, Kara. There's a good reason why I can't say any more about it."

She turned away from him and started fiddling with her luggage. "If you can't be honest with me, we have nothing. It's as though you've been leading a secret life all this time. If you won't tell me who you are and what you're involved in, that's it, Jeffery, I'm going back home."

Sixtus knew "back home" meant Lincoln, Nebraska, where she was raised. Kara never liked to talk about her upbringing. For many, growing up in Nebraska meant you left for good or stayed and worked in agriculture. In Kara's case, her father was an accountant, and she attended the University of Nebraska, earning an undergraduate degree in literature.

However, her decision to move away from Lincoln to San Diego and later Phoenix upset her close-knit family. Her siblings remained within driving distance of her parents' house, and Sunday dinner was mandatory. According to Kara, the separation strained their relationship so much they banished her from the family. In fact, it was a subject rarely discussed in their house. There were no Christmas cards, birthday greetings or casual letters. Sixtus never met or talked to a single member of her family. If Kara was moving out and going back to Nebraska, she was effectively ending their relationship.

"Kara, are you sure this is what you want?"

She turned around; her eyes were flashing. "No, Jeffery, it's not what I want. But someone almost killed me, and our maid and another man are dead. You owe me an explanation, or I'm going back home."

Sixtus sat on the couch, leaned back, and folded his hands together. "The more I tell you, the more danger you'll be in. I'll be leaving in the morning. Perhaps it's best you go to Nebraska. Make sure you tell no one of your plans." He offered her the sachet again. "Take this, please." With reluctance, she accepted the packet and spread the contents out on the table.

"My God, Jeffery. A fake driver's license with my picture? Fake credit cards? A fake passport? Who the hell is *Katherine Nelson*?"

"Katherine Nelson is who you will be until I say otherwise."

"I won't…"

"You will, damn it! You will if you want to live." Sixtus stared at her with anger he rarely displayed. His eyes were hard, and a weariness spread through his face that created creases and deepened lines.

She appeared anxious but gathered up the contents and put them back into the packet. "Okay, Jeffery."

"I mean it, Kara. It's the only way. You must avoid conducting any transactions in your true name."

"That's — impossible. My name defines me."

"Not anymore. *Katherine Nelson* has a bank account with $250,000 in it. That should be enough money to sustain you for a while. But you can't use your given name from tomorrow forward. And when you get to Nebraska, find your own housing."

Kara regarded him for several seconds before the tears returned. "Well, if it's that serious, I won't put my family in danger. Maybe it's best I get in the car and just drive to a new location."

"Yes. Now you're finally being sensible. Keep driving until you reach a place where no one will find you. A corporate housing unit or an extended stay hotel might be best. Most importantly, don't tell me where you're going."

She hastily gathered up her bags. "Oh, don't worry, Jeffery. You'll have no idea where I'm staying."

Sixtus got up and walked to the den. Once inside, he shut the door and sat at his desk. He maneuvered through his bookmarks and logged into the proxy server he used to maintain a semblance of anonymity. After confirming the two airline tickets to Seattle, Sixtus cried for the first time since he was four years old. How he hated living in this primitive, God forsaken time.

He only had one purpose now, and that was to figure out whether he should detonate or deactivate the third nuclear device. He accessed the overhead display and started analyzing the information Zir had given him.

***

When he arrived home, Marshall sat in the corner of his bedroom with the lights off and a blanket pulled up to his chin. He rocked back and forth as he tried to calm himself without using a

184

prescription drug. That was a slippery slope, and Marshall walked the path many times. The short-term relief from his crushing anxiety was often not worth the long-term depression that followed.

Consumed by the dilemma, he wondered what he could do to combat an enemy so powerful. If those in the future were manipulating the past, it was conceivable they knew his every move before he even made it. They only had to consult historical records to know if he played a significant role in any of the events they influenced. That he was still alive served as somewhat of a comfort, but he felt vulnerable, almost as though he was naked and being watched.

A sudden knocking pierced the silence, and Marshall stiffened as an irrational moment of terror spread through his body. He waited a few seconds before managing to shuffle to the door. Without opening it, he said, "Hello?"

"Marshall, it's Wanda. Are you alright?"

"Hello, Wanda. I'm—physically fine."

"How are you, ah, mentally and emotionally?"

"… I'm struggling."

"Can I… Can I come in?"

Marshall leaned his head against the door. "I'm not sure if that's a good idea. You should leave for your own good, Wanda."

The silence lasted long enough for Marshall to believe she left with hurt feelings. He turned and walked back to the dark corner.

"Marshall?"

He stopped and slid into a sitting position once again. "Yes?"

"Would you *please* invite me in?"

In that moment, several of Marshall's social phobias emerged with crushing intensity. Years of conditioning on how to deal with nonexistent threats that emanated from an overactive amygdala didn't help. He summoned his coping mechanisms: separating himself from the feelings and observing them from a distance, reminding himself the odds of a negative outcome were minimal and focusing on positive experiences.

Using each strategy in succession, he somehow mustered the inner strength to go back and open the door. Wanda stood outside looking at her shoes. Several seconds passed before Marshall said softly, "Come in."

She walked into the living room, and he turned on a table lamp, which gave off enough light to avoid tripping but still cast long shadows. Wanda settled in the Lazy Boy recliner, so Marshall sat on the couch across from it.

"You have a nice place, Marshall. I like how you've decorated it."

Marshall looked around the room and shrugged. His furnishings were utilitarian and sparse. His mother, who lived in Virginia, was always prodding him to buy wall hangings and other such superficial items, but Marshall only appreciated original art by the masters.

"Thank you. But you've been over here many times, so I'm wondering why you've chosen this moment to comment on the furnishings."

His rebuff shook her, and she twisted her hair, which was a sign Marshall recognized as nervousness. "I—I guess a person doesn't notice the furnishings much when it's a bigger group that's only talking particle physics." He forced a smile, and she responded in kind. Her hand dropped away from her hair.

"We're worried about you, Marshall. Kenny called and told us what you were doing. How could you meet with Jeffery Clayton by yourself? What if he hurt you?" Her inflections sounded different. He couldn't tell what it was, but her tone was softer and more soothing than usual.

"Well, there was no point in endangering anyone else. I wish we never stumbled upon any of it." He lowered his head and sighed. The next sensation he experienced was the light touch of her hand on his shoulder. Wanda moved from the chair to the couch and sat so close he could smell her distinctive scent. Ordinarily, a human body in this proximity was repulsive to him. However, in this instance, his small flinch went unnoticed. When he opened his eyes, Wanda's face was less than a foot away.

"What happened, Marshall? Tell me what happened."

He looked into her eyes and explored their depth, something he never noticed before. Was the soft lighting affecting his visual perception? "Iglar — Iglar is dead." The emotion welled up from a place he didn't know existed. Tears fell freely, and his eyes grew red and swollen. His body lurched with every wracking sob, and he buried his head deeper into his hands.

Supple arms enveloped him, and instead of experiencing disgust, Marshall found the sensation oddly comforting. She tugged gently, and he didn't resist. Then his head was lying against her breasts, and she rocked him tenderly.

"Shhh. It's okay, Marshall. Everything will be okay." She continued the motion, and Marshall relaxed until he felt her lips on his forehead. She kissed him. A real kiss, not like the cringe worthy kisses he received from his mother and shriveled grandmother. When either of them tried to "get some sugar," he pulled away, sometimes violently. Yet, this was different. The kiss was — pleasurable.

When Marshall tilted his head up, her face was so close he could feel her breath on his cheek. Before he could process these strange feelings, she leaned over and kissed him full on the lips. Marshall didn't flinch this time, and a slight brush of her tongue followed.

Odd feelings surged spontaneously, and their intensity overwhelmed his familiar reticence and loathing. He returned her kiss, and soon afterward, his passion matched her own.

Their actions were awkward as they fumbled with buttons, zippers and belts. The unrelenting hunger overcame embarrassment, and Marshall placed his rational mind on hold as he relented to his primal instinct. When they reached the point where he had unsnapped her bra, and she had pulled off his briefs, Marshall shut out his reservations and phobias and allowed himself to meld with Wanda.

Perhaps they weren't the most attractive couple; he being noticeably slender with effeminate, narrow shoulders; she being overweight with a nose that was a bit too large for her elongated face. However, when she finally pushed him down and straddled him, they gazed at each other through the mists of wanton desire. At that moment, they were the two most beautiful people in the world.

Ultimately, Marshall succumbed and let her do most of the work. She reached over and grasped him, and he responded so completely he thought the moment might end before it began. She successfully guided him deep inside her, and after a few clumsy and graceless moments, they found their natural rhythm. Marshall watched her face contort in transcendent ecstasy, and guttural sounds escaped his own lips as he lost himself in the moment. Their thrashing grew more frenzied as the pressure mounted until it culminated in a massive release of desire, emotion and years of repressed frustration.

As their movements subsided, Marshall could feel the fluids draining out of her onto his body, and he instantly retreated from the surreal state to his familiar reality. The revulsion rushed back like an angry foe launching a counter attack from the brink. Wanda must have seen the rising panic in his eyes because she quickly got off of him, grabbed her blouse and covered her breasts. She dropped her head, and strands of long black hair fell over her face. Despite an overwhelming urge to run into the shower, Marshall fought the rising anxiety.

"That was… wonderful, Wanda," he said quietly.

She tried to remain composed but couldn't hide her obvious joy. "Really, Marshall? Did you like it? I never did that before."

Marshall recognized the physiology involved with a woman's "first time," and he knew he must avoid looking at his torso at all costs. Most likely, there was blood on his genitals, and seeing it might compel him to vomit.

"This was my first time too, and yes, it was— prodigious. Could you get me a towel? They're in the hall closet."

She smiled, stood up and went out to fetch the towels. As she was walking, Marshall reached over to his pants and pulled his cell phone from the front pocket. He punched up his Uber app and selected an XL ride without concern for the cost. Looking down the hallway, he watched as Wanda wiped the residue from her body before pulling out a second towel she brought back to Marshall.

He grimaced while wiping his torso, removing as much of the liquid as possible. After searching through the couch, he found his briefs and pulled them on. Next came his pants, and when he finished fastening the belt, he put his shirt on and buttoned it up tightly. Only when he was done dressing, and that included his shoes and socks, did he look over at Wanda. She still sat naked, and the perpetual look of sadness had returned to her face.

"Everyone knew Iglar was struggling," she said. "All of us struggle sometimes, especially Hayden. But I wonder why Iglar would do that? It's so horrible."

He sighed in relief, thankful she pivoted away from their recent coupling to a different subject even if it was a tragedy. "I don't know why he did it. I can only speculate that the input from the changing timeline was a relentless torture he could no longer endure."

Wanda was putting her clothes back on slowly, but Marshall wanted to speed up the process. "How can we find good news in this nightmare? But at least after meeting Jeffery Clayton, I'm convinced there's nothing more we can do."

"Are you sure? What did you learn from him?"

"Actually, nothing. He thought I had some sort of derangement syndrome and denied pushing anyone in front of a truck on Wednesday night."

"But you were there," she said.

"I know. But did we write down the wrong license plate number? I didn't even see a BMW when I was at his house. He seemed very sincere."

"So that's it? We're dropping the whole thing? We're going to let those in the future change and manipulate our lives?"

Marshall shrugged. "I don't know what else can be done."

"We're just going to accept we have no self-determination? What if — what if our lovemaking never happened? The moment we just shared... gone. I don't want that, Marshall..."

"I don't like it any more than you do. Maybe we should strategize when I get back."

"Get back?" She raised an eyebrow sharply. "Get back from where?"

"I have to go to Houston for a graphic arts conference tomorrow morning. I didn't tell you?"

"No," she said with a note of suspicion in her voice. "Did you tell anyone? This is the first I've heard of it."

Marshall opened his arms and flattened his palms apologetically. "Well, I'm sorry. I made plans several months ago. It's a huge show and a chance to pick up new business. I must become more comfortable in social settings. It will be good for me."

"How long will you be gone?"

"A few days or maybe a week. I'll return before next weekend for sure."

"Will you call me?" She asked the question without looking at him.

"Yes, of course," he said.

Wanda sat motionless for some time as Marshall tried to rationalize her reaction. In all likelihood, her silence related to their earlier sexual encounter. He imagined she wanted him to show compassion and commitment. Unfortunately, he was neither mentally nor emotionally capable of either right now. Levels of self-loathing were rising, and he obsessed over the sticky feeling on his abdomen as the residual semen dried. He felt like the substance was eating through his skin, which triggered a fight to maintain self-control.

Mercifully, the Uber driver lit up his phone with a text message. "I, uh, called you an Uber, and he's right around the corner." Either she didn't understand what he said, or she chose to ignore it because she remained seated.

"My alarm is set for five a.m. so I can make my flight on time tomorrow. I'm sort of tired right now."

Wanda finished putting on her shoes, and when she glanced up, Marshall was already holding the door open. Without looking at him, she stopped just inside the doorway and whispered, "I guess I should go now. Goodnight, Marshall." She turned her head up, and he expected she might try to kiss him again, so he extended his right arm out, which created a space between them. Hesitantly, she reached out and shook his hand.

When she didn't leave after the handshake ended, Marshall turned and gave her a gentle shove onto the front porch. Her head hung low, and her hair covered her face, so he couldn't tell if she was crying. Once she was outside, he quickly closed the door, and the loud, high-pitched shriek he heard as she walked to the Uber car removed any doubt.

Chapter Seventeen

Marshall sat down and turned the television to the PBS station as he processed the events of the day. The myriad of feelings that welled up after his first sexual encounter confused him, especially since he knew he handled the post coital interaction with Wanda poorly.

He picked up his tablet, accessed a search engine, and typed, "post coital tristesse in men." Several pages of responses showed up, and Marshall selected an article that explored the physiological differences between male and female orgasm. As he scanned the piece, he realized his indifference likely resulted from residual testosterone levels and dopamine receptors that wouldn't fully recover for hours or days after the intimate event. To compensate, he should have made an effort to "cuddle." This was not a particularly pleasant thought considering how much Marshall disliked physical contact, but if he was to continue his relationship with Wanda, he would have to overcome the revulsion.

Still, despite his apprehension, their coupling was somewhat pleasant, and he knew he would continue pursuing her if she forgave him for his insensitivity. He felt something quite powerful when he thought about Wanda. In fact, his feelings continued to intensify to the point where he could hardly focus on anything else. Even the horrific death of Iglar faded into the background.

Marshall finished the cup of warm skim milk he prepared, turned off the TV and moved to the bedroom. After tending to his meticulous grooming, he put on his pajamas and crawled into bed. Sleep was elusive as he tossed and turned for several hours, watching the digital clock numbers slowly turn. At some point, he must have dozed off because the shrill sound of his phone ringing startled him, and he jerked forward into a sitting position.

"Hello?" He stabbed his finger on the screen through bleary eyes until he got a connection.

"Marshall? It is—Hayden." The voice sounded dull and lifeless; the words had the thickness of heavy sedation.

"Hayden? It doesn't sound like you."

"It is me, Marshall. I have taken a few secobarbitals. Perhaps more than a few…"

Marshall stood up and rubbed his eyes. "How many have you taken, Hayden?"

"Does it matter? What is the point, Marshall? We know what is going on now. They control our lives, not us. One change and poof, it is all different. You are different; I am different. We might not even know each other in a new reality."

"I believe they only make small changes. It doesn't appear like they tamper with the fundamental timeline."

"Bullshit! He threw a guy in front of a car. That is not a small thing. Most of the events we remember differently had nothing to do with the original change, anyway. They were the consequences. If the changes are minor, that only benefits them. Their changes may be small, but for us, it is Russian roulette."

"I'm coming over, Hayden. You have to keep it together."

"It is too late. Wanda told me about Iglar. They are picking us off one by one..." The last few words trailed off, and Marshall sensed Hayden's deep depression.

"Stay calm, Hayden. I'll be there shortly."

"Ok—I… Wait a minute. Someone is here. They are in the kitchen, and I hear the microwave. What is that sound? … Is someone making popcorn?"

"Who's there? What do you hear? Hayden? Hayden!"

There was a rustling noise, and Hayden must have put his hand over the phone because everything sounded muffled. Several seconds passed, and Marshall heard more commotion before Hayden's hand came off the mouthpiece.

"Who are you? No, no please, do not… My God, no!"

"Hayden? What's happening there? Hayden?"

The line remained open, but only periodic static punctuated the silence, until a sinister sounding voice whispered, "Hayden is—indisposed."

"Who—who is this? Put Hayden back on the phone right now." Slow, rhythmic breathing followed until a *click* signaled the call had ended.

After redialing, Hayden's phone went to voice mail, and Marshall uttered a rare expletive. He grabbed a t-shirt and tried to pull on his pants while hopping toward his wallet and keys on the kitchen table. In this case, multitasking didn't work, and he toppled over, slamming his shoulder into the tile.

195

Marshall grimaced in pain and began to breathe deeply while trying to collects his thoughts. If he reacted without thinking, it would only complicate matters. *Should I call the authorities and alert them to a potential emergency? Could Hayden actually kill himself on the same day Iglar took his own life?* Marshall recognized the chaos caused by overreacting to a nonevent. He decided to check on Hayden before taking any further action.

His friend lived only 10 minutes away, so Marshall took surface streets from his home out to Peoria. Although it was dark, he encountered little resistance as he drove west on Thunderbird. At the stoplight on 51st Ave, he gasped when a loud *bang* rattled the Civic as a rock hit the car on the passenger's side.

At 59th Avenue, two middle-aged men with long beards and matted hair rushed the car as it sat alone at a red light. One held a tire iron above his head, and the other had a splintered wooden baseball bat cocked and ready to swing. The man with the tire iron had a gash across his forehead that leaked blood down his nose and around the sides of his mouth. As they approached, Marshall prepared to run the light, but it changed well before they came within striking distance.

Minutes later, he pulled up to the *Rosewood Terrace*. The building was old and poorly maintained, and the vegetation overran the entry sidewalk, poking up through cracks in the neglected parking lot. A dirty sign faced the road with a single floodlight that lost its intensity over time. It advertised *Free Cable* to whoever drove by. Marshall doubted it was enough of a deal to attract anyone who wouldn't have rented there anyway. The apartments were cheap and one of the few choices in the neighborhood for people living on meager wages.

Marshall parked his car and made his way through the complex. The experience was unsettling since the walkway was dimly lit with most of the courtesy lights that spanned the pathway either burned out or broken. He heard several voices in the distance, so he made sure his sneakers emitted no sound as he walked. After turning the corner, he took the stairway, climbing two steps at a time. Upon reaching the landing, he knocked loudly enough that the voices below stopped talking. They knew someone was nearby.

Marshall knocked again with more urgency. Now the voices spoke with aggressive inflections, and he listened to the clatter of approaching footsteps. Another knock, but still no answer. He could make out their words as they came closer.

"Who the fuck comes here after dark?"

"I don't know, but somebody better answer the door or this guy's gonna get fucked up."

Marshall's breathing intensified as the familiar fear rose from his clenched stomach. Instinctively, he reached down and grabbed the doorknob and twisted. The bolt retracted, and the door opened as Marshall slipped inside the apartment.

"Hayden, your neighbors are terrible. Why do you live here? You make more than enough to move into a nicer neighborhood. Come out; I'm nervous."

Marshall closed the door, waited, and looked outside through the peephole, recoiling as a malevolent face, exaggerated by the optics of the lens, looked back at him. "You better stay in there you little freak. You come out here and we'll fuck you up good." The young anarchist in a gray hoodie thrust his middle finger up in front of the peephole and punched the door with his fist

197

before sprinting away to join his friends, who were already looking for a new victim.

Marshall sighed and took a couple steps back. He focused on his breathing, inhaling through his nose and exhaling through his mouth as he gathered himself. "Hayden, where are you?"

A muffled groan reminded Marshall why he was here. He straightened up and ran into the bedroom. The sight that greeted him sucked the air from his lungs as he dropped to his knees.

***

The rapid knocking startled Sixtus, and he lifted his head from the desk and blinked several times to clear his vision. His arms spread out in a stretching motion, and he knocked the empty bottle of Dalmore Scotch to the floor. Another rap at the door revived his senses, and he rubbed his face and took a deep breath. As he exhaled, the smell of stale alcohol invaded his nostrils and caused him to cringe.

Sixtus looked over at the wall clock through red, bleary eyes and saw it was nearly two-thirty in the morning. His first instinct told him it was Kara coming home despite their argument the night before. Even though he let her live a lie for all that time, he held on tightly to an irrational hope she might look past it all and come back to him. On the other hand, it might be the double shots of Scotch doing the talking.

His steps were uneven as he approached the door, trying to clear the cobwebs from his mind. The knocking returned, louder and more urgent than before. This seemed to sober Sixtus somewhat. Kara wouldn't have knocked since she had an app on her phone that controlled the lock. In the event she thought Sixtus had changed the code, she would use the physical key hidden in a cement flower pot next to the doorway.

Another series of knocks. The urgency was now desperate.

Sixtus approached the small video monitor that provided surveillance for the front porch and pushed the button to get the feed, but the screen was jet black, signaling someone disabled the camera. Pressing the intercom button, Sixtus said, "Who's there?"

No answer.

He walked to the desk and picked up the Kel-Tec he recovered when Zir died. With slow and deliberate footsteps, he walked back to the door when the familiar ring of his cell phone pierced the silence. Sixtus cursed silently as he reached into his pocket and pulled the device out. The number was unfamiliar.

"Hello?"

"Listen, Clayton or Sixtus or whatever your name is, I could give a shit about you, but I was told... I mean asked by Xavier Watts to keep an eye on you. There's a guy breaking in through the back door. Who knows what he's after, but it doesn't look good to me. I'd go through the service entrance and get out. Just sayin..."

"Who the hell is this?" Sixtus looked again at the caller ID before glancing at the ceiling for cameras.

"Never mind, but I wouldn't spend a lot of time talking. He's walking down your hallway now."

Sixtus punched the *end call* button and turned toward the service entrance used by the landscapers and pool maintenance people to access equipment stored on site. He crouched at the sound of approaching footsteps just outside the guest quarters, but it was too late.

"Maras, I come to warn you."

Sixtus got up and sized up the intruder. He was about 6'2 and in his mid-to-late 30s. His blue eyes were devoid of any emotion except extreme intensity. A ball cap with the word *Orioles* sat perched on his head, gangsta low. Shoulder-length blond hair sprouted from the hat and hung in clean, but uncombed, wispy strands. His jeans looked stained from oil, and his shirt was ripped on the elbows.

"Who are you?"

"One of your co-workers sent me. They have a message that I'm supposed to deliver to you."

Silence ensued, and Sixtus realized the man wasn't going to offer information freely. "Who was it that sent you? Only a few people know of my true identity. What is the message?"

"I cannot reveal a name Sixtus Maras. But the message is simple. You must confirm you will not follow the foul words and directions of Havas Zir."

Sixtus regarded the stranger, who appeared extremely tense and agitated. "I'm in the process of evaluating the information I received from Zir. I haven't made a decision yet."

"Wrong answer, Maras. I am here for a resolution. My employer demands a resolution."

Sixtus was already drawing his own revolver as the man's Glock 9-mm came into sight. Without thinking, Sixtus assumed a shooters stance and squeezed off two shots. One hit the intruder in the shoulder; the other struck him somewhere in the abdomen. His eyes grew wide, and his mouth opened in surprise. The gun dropped to the floor and clattered on the rough tile in the hallway. The wounded man clutched his stomach with his free hand as the other arm fell limply to his side. He stumbled forward, locking eyes with Sixtus, who stood in a state of shock.

After falling to his knees, the stalker reached up; his hand glistened in fresh blood that dripped off the ends of his fingers. "Maras, you must not embrace the Corporates. The insurrection is the only hope…" He toppled over and fell face first onto the stone floor with a sickening, dull thud. Almost simultaneously, Sixtus' phone rang yet again. He grabbed it from his pocket.

"What?" he said in a whisper.

"Hey, there's a couple more coming from both sides. I see you have an exit to the courtyard in the second bedroom down the east hallway. You better get going, or they're gonna fry your ass. Oh, and by the way, that guard in the shack just called 9-1-1. If you're really quick, you might go around the side and get out to your car."

"Who are you, and why are you helping me?"

"Who knows? I guess you're important to us. If it comes up, tell 'em Ziminski helped you out"

Sixtus glanced at the phone and shook his head before putting it back into his front pants pocket. A silver letter opener sat on a wall table a few steps away, and he picked it up and slid it into the same pocket that held his phone. He turned off all the lights he could find in this wing, which included those in the hallways leading to many different rooms in the house.

He wore Timberlands, so there was no sound from his footfalls as he moved across the tiled floor. In contrast, his pursuer's hard rubber-soled shoes broadcast his location with every step. Based on the sound, Sixtus knew he entered through the garage.

If the other one came from the opposite end of the property, he might encounter one or both before he could leave through the French doors in the bedroom.

A moonlight reflection flashed off an object at the end of the hallway. Sixtus couldn't see a person, but it served as a warning, so he ducked into a guest bedroom and moved swiftly to the window. He quietly twisted the latches but couldn't avoid the sound of the rails against the frame as he raised it up. Rapid footsteps reverberated off the tile floor; someone was running. Sixtus reached back and cocked his leg, and with a swift motion, kicked out the screen panel. The opening was large enough for him to fit through, and he slid outside just as the antagonist entered the room.

"Hey!" the intruder called out while raising his gun. Without hesitation, Sixtus ran from the house with the other man in close pursuit.

He turned a corner and ran toward the fence, which wasn't hard to climb but did slow him down. Unfortunately, there was enough moonlight to allow the pursuer to see him from a distance. Once on the other side, Sixtus veered away from the fence and took a path adjacent to his neighbor's house, staying parallel to the boundary. The attacker detoured as well, but the sudden change in direction confused him for a moment. The additional distance, plus a row of hedges with untrimmed branches, allowed Sixtus to remain obscured just long enough to dart through a break in the bushes he knew the kids in the neighborhood used as a stealthy passageway.

The kids called it "the secret skyway," and it led from his fence to an easement between his house

202

and his neighbor's property. He used to laugh about it with Larry Stengle over a beer at one of their many backyard barbeques. After some discussion, they decided to leave it open because the kids seemed to enjoy it so much. Sixtus never suspected the secret skyway might someday save his life.

As he ran down the easement, hidden by the line of bushes and the fence, he heard the assailant muttering nearby. The opening was hard to find in the daylight, but at night, it was almost impossible.

When he reached the corner of the property, Sixtus followed the fence line back toward the front of the house. This was the side the garage was on, and his BMW was sitting inside it. He pushed past the bushes and HVAC equipment until he came to the side entrance. After punching in the code to the automated lock, it disengaged with an audible click. He was about to slip into his car when he felt a hand grip his shoulder hard.

Without flinching, Sixtus whirled around, knocked the hand away, and shoved the attacker backwards. With only a moment to size up his opponent, he realized this man was bigger and burlier than the first. The push caused the aggressor to stumble back awkwardly, so Sixtus rushed and caught his opponent off guard. They tumbled to the ground, half on a small cement walkway and half in decorative rock that covered most of the front yard.

The bigger man used his weight to pin Sixtus down as he pulled out a knife and pushed a button that snapped the blade into place. He raised his arm high, and his intent was clear. This was no kidnapping; the Time Sculptor was in a fight for his life. Fortunately, his arms were free, and Sixtus used his left hand to grab the man at the wrist just as he began the downward motion with the knife. While the struggle continued, he was able to unleash a vicious punch to the assailant's left eye with his other hand.

Pressure from the arm that held the knife eased for a moment as the man brought his other hand up to his face. Getting to his feet, he stumbled backward as his eye instantly swelled. Sixtus found the letter opener in his pocket and pulled it out, tightening his grip on the shaft. While the wounded assailant struggled to see, Sixtus leaned up and swung the converted weapon hard at his adversary's lower abdomen.

His training and muscle memory positioned the stab wound in such a way that it ruptured two vital mesenteric arteries. The shaft sunk deep into the right side of the gasping man's stomach. As Sixtus extracted the letter opener, the intruder's hands switched positions as he felt the side of his damaged abdomen while the good eye rolled to the back of his head. The pain centers were reflecting the extent of the injury.

Sixtus fought to quiet the growing panic inside him. He got up and pulled the mask off the intruder before checking his pockets. The man was about forty and probably of African-American descent, but he didn't carry any ID.

Quickly moving to the BMW, Sixtus waited impatiently as the garage door slowly opened. The tires squealed as he backed out, creating enough noise that it attracted the attention of the third assailant. A shot rang out, shattering the passenger's side mirror and causing the car to jump a curb. A second followed but missed the car entirely.

Moving at high speed toward the guard shack, Doug looked terrified and confused as

Sixtus smashed through the wooden gate. Just before he pointed the car onto Scottsdale Road, he heard the blaring sirens of squad cars approaching. McCormick Ranch residents would have fodder to talk about for years to come.

Chapter Eighteen

Marshall cautiously stepped into Hayden's bedroom. The only light came from a 1970s style lamp set on a nightstand next to an old twin bed with a sunken mattress. The tattered, weathered blinds filtered the street lights and cast the room in long gray shadows. A comforter lay crumpled on the floor along with piles of discarded clothes, and several empty bottles of liquor were scattered around the room. This raised Marshall's awareness because Hayden normally didn't drink.

With a sense of dread, he looked over at the bed. Hayden sat propped up against the headboard while bent at the waist with his legs splayed open, revealing a large wet fecal stain in the crotch of his underwear. A combination of fresh and drying blood, along with a brown viscous material Marshall assumed was vomit, discolored his shirt. The oppressive, nauseating smell in the room confirmed his suspicions.

Hayden's left arm hung limp against his side, and his other arm was bent at the elbow and raised up. He held a fork covered in fresh blood in his right hand. That side of his face was gouged and mangled, and Marshall noticed multiple puncture marks from fork prongs dug repeatedly into the flesh on his cheek and neck. Based on the pattern of imprints, Marshall imagined Hayden had stabbed himself at least a dozen times.

"Hayden, Hayden, it's me, Marshall. Put the fork down. I'm calling an ambulance."

Hayden looked up at Marshall as he slammed the fork once again into his butchered face. Blood bubbled up from the new wounds and further coated his hand as it ran over his temporal bone, down his cheek and onto his shirt. "I did not agree to it, Marshall. I fought it with everything I had. Almost, almost…"

Marshall approached with his hands up in a non-threatening manner, but after the third step, Hayden raised the fork back up to his face. "Stay back! It is over… It is over. You do not get it; we cannot fight them. They are in our heads—my head."

"Who's in your head, Hayden? Think about this carefully. You've suffered from depression for years. Are you taking your medication?"

Hayden emitted a series of chuckles that morphed into a shrill laugh. "My *medication*? They are changing our reality on a whim, and you think my problem is *medication*? This me might not exist tomorrow. This me might never have existed if they were not manipulating our reality." Hayden turned his head to the ceiling and shouted, "Leave us alone, you tormentors! Leave us alone…" His words trailed off as he slumped over on the bed, his body shaking and heaving.

In that moment, Marshall knew the choice was clear: he could either try to talk Hayden out of doing further harm to himself or attempt to physically restrain him. Without coming to a conscious decision, Marshal ignored his revulsion and sprinted to the bed. He jumped onto his startled friend, grabbing the hand that held the fork while using the other to push his torso down on the mattress.

The shock of the assault didn't immediately register, which gave Marshall time to swing his leg across Hayden's body. The startled man tried to rise, but Marshall pushed his head back down. He noticed a slick rubbery material between his fingers, but he couldn't see what it was. It gave, and his hand slid off Hayden's face. When he looked down, Marshall realized he had a chunk of Hayden's bloody cheek wedged between his index and middle fingers.

Hayden screamed as the perforated flesh tore easily away from his face, exposing the lower jawbone and two rows of interlocking teeth. Marshall tried to counter a sudden surge of strength as Hayden moved the hand that held the fork back towards his face. Even though Marshall was marginally more muscular, he couldn't stop the movement entirely.

Their hands shook with the forces of opposition, but it was clear Hayden's single-minded purpose was prevailing. With a fork prong moving dangerously close to his jugular vein, Marshall had no choice but to abandon his hold on Haden's torso and use his free hand to help keep the fork from further damaging his friend.

Free from Marshall's leverage, Hayden used the opportunity to twist his body so they lay parallel to each other as the struggle continued. Hayden pushed Marshall away with surprising force and dug his fingernails into exposed flesh. Marshall yelped in pain and tried to fend off the assault to his

208

midsection. His grip on the fork loosened, and it once again moved back up to the bloody man's face.

After one final moment of equilibrium, Marshall's grasp weakened further, and Hayden's hand broke free. He turned and looked directly at his friend.

"You cannot beat them, Marshall." The words sounded slurred, and he struggled with consonants as the air whistled through the hole in his face when he talked. Only a small shard of flesh hung down over his exposed cheek, jiggling with every movement of his head. Hayden flexed his facial muscles as the unaffected side of his mouth curled in a sardonic grin. "You do not even know what you are dealing with. It is much bleaker than you could imagine."

Hayden's eyes grew wide and dark as vantablack as he plunged the fork into the soft tissues of his neck and buried it deep into his main carotid artery. Blood poured freely from the newly inflicted wound as Hayden's hand shook, and his body convulsed spasmodically. The fork wiggled as if it was stuck in a slab of pulsating jello.

The dying man raised his hand to seek out the embedded utensil in what was probably an involuntary action, but he didn't have the strength to pull it out. Gurgling through blood collecting in his mouth, he tried to form several words with his torn lips, but there was too much disruption in his synaptic pathways.

Marshall climbed off him and stood silently as his friend writhed in agony. Each spasm was slightly less violent and shorter than the one before. Finally, after what seemed like an eternity, the ravaged body went limp, and its lungs exhaled a long, tortured breath. Like something out of a nightmare, Hayden's clothing and the bedsheets appeared drenched in a dark burgundy paint.

For several long minutes, Marshall's brain locked up as he couldn't turn away from the gruesome sight of the fork protruding from Hayden's neck. He staggered backwards until he reached the wall and slid down into a sitting position. Blackness closed in from both sides, accompanied by an overwhelming nausea. He remembered wondering if someone was laughing in the distance as he lost consciousness.

Unaware of how much time passed, Marshall blinked rapidly as the fog cleared from his mind. Apparently, he vomited while cataleptic, and he spit out chunks of partially digested fish and rice that remained in his mouth. Functioning on adrenaline and pre-programmed responses, he pulled out his cell phone to dial 9-1-1. He punched in the number "9" when he heard the voice from behind him.

"I wouldn't do that if I were you."

Marshall stiffened and stopped dialing. Every muscle in his body seemed paralyzed, and he fought to fill his lungs with oxygen. Somehow, he managed to shuffle his feet and turn to encounter whoever issued the warning. Marshall gazed in disbelief at the sight of a man, no, thing that stood before him.

Indeed, it appeared to be humanoid. That is, it had two arms, two legs, a torso and a head. But there was something exceedingly unusual about its appearance. The being seemed to excrete malice from its pores and created an aura that was black and palpable. Marshall finally concluded the gender was masculine.

The man was short, slender and slightly over five feet tall with skin that was a ghastly shade of white and long fingers that showed off exquisitely manicured nails. His eyes might have been hazel, but they were tinged with deep red that almost blotted out the iris. When he smiled, his perfectly aligned bleached-white teeth chilled Marshall to the bone.

"You seem overwhelmed, Mr. Beiner, or should I call you, Marshall? I wonder why? Surely you knew Hayden was sick. I can't imagine this is surprising to you."

"Who..." Marshall couldn't overcome his vocal paralysis.

"It doesn't matter who I am, Mr. Beiner. What matters is the situation you find yourself in. You're covered with blood; your fingerprints are all over the room, and poor Hayden has a fork sticking out of his neck. It's a touching scene, and your struggle was entertaining, but it may not reflect well on you."

"I was only trying to help Hayden."

"Well, you know that, and so do I, but the police won't know it. Do you want to become embroiled in a major criminal investigation? In fact, don't you have an appointment in Seattle tomorrow?"

"How did you find out about that? I never revealed it to anyone."

"What you say to others doesn't matter; it's what you're thinking that counts. I know about you and your group and what you have discovered. This information evaded me, and it is an unsettling feeling. I must learn more about this phenomenon."

"If you were here, why didn't you stop Hayden? You could have saved him."

"*Save* him? I was here to help him complete the task he started, just like your friend Iglar. They both were weary of the struggle. Much as you are, Marshall."

"What?"

"Oh, you hide it well, but you understand what crushing depression feels like. The sense of

211

hopelessness. It's what draws your little group together. You try to talk yourselves into thinking you're slightly superior because of your unusual talents, but it's the sense of isolation that binds you. I'm right, am I not, Marshall?"

"No, we enjoy each other's company. We are — friends."

The small man's smile grew wider. "*Friends*? You have difficulty even saying the word. You're all outcasts, Marshall, and you know it. You're not capable of the deep feelings that normal people have, so it's impossible to understand how others bond so easily. You're isolated, alone and frightened, just like Iglar and Hayden."

Marshall lowered his head. The self-loathing he worked so hard to address in therapy emerged through gaps in the mental dungeon, where he kept it locked away. The familiar doubt crept into his psyche like a reunion with an old unwelcome companion. "I — I know we have problems. But we *are* friends."

"No, you are far from friends, Marshall. Let's not forget, two of your 'friends' are dead. More importantly, you lack the capacity to understand the emotions associated with friendship, or even love, for that matter. Let it rise up from within, Marshall. Don't you want to join your colleagues, especially since you are already involved in two separate suicides today? Imagine the suspicion; the scrutiny. You will be all over interconnected media."

"I don't like attention. Crowds are intimidating to me. I couldn't stand the publicity of people thinking I killed Hayden. It would be horrible."

"That is exactly what will happen, Marshall. Wouldn't it be easier for you to just bring an end to it all? Finish what you started with me? It would be so much easier…"

"Finish what I started? Yes, I know. It's much easier to swallow a handful of pills. I've gone over my exit plan so many times I've memorized every detail."

"Well, perhaps this is the right time. Go look on Hayden's nightstand. There's nearly a full bottle of sleeping pills just sitting there. Or, you could just walk outside and jump off the balcony. I'm fairly certain a fall from thirty feet would do the trick. Then again, maybe you want to follow Hayden's lead and use the fork." His pale hand made an exaggerated stabbing motion into his neck.

Marshall walked robotically over to the nightstand and pushed aside the discarded candy wrappers and soda bottles until he found the pills. He looked at the label and saw it was a prescription for a common antidepressant. Marshall pushed on the safety cap and twisted it off. The pills inside the bottle were mesmerizing, and he experienced a compulsion he couldn't understand.

Marshall poured the contents into his cupped hand and flexed his palm while watching the pills move and shimmy. A flat carbonated soda, half empty, sat on the nightstand. Ordinarily, placing something to his lips contaminated by the saliva of another would have led him to purge, but in this instance, he overlooked the probable germ content.

As if he was an automaton, his mouth opened in anticipation. He ran his tongue over the smooth surface of the pills as they started to dissolve in the liquid that would wash them down. He started to swallow, but the creature's voice interrupted the hypnotic state that enveloped his psyche.

"Of course, there might be a better way…"

213

Marshall reflexively spit the pills and soda on the floor, gagging and coughing as a result. He turned to face the pallid man. "What do you mean 'a better way'?"

"Wouldn't you like to be normal? To understand subtlety and immediately recognize the meaning of expressions and gestures? Wouldn't you like to love deeply?"

Marshall shook his head slowly. "Naturally, I would. But that's impossible for me. Some people with autism are capable of a full range of feelings, but I am not."

"I know who you are, and I'm aware of your deficits, but none of that matters. I can help you experience these things."

Marshall was about to answer when he felt an unusual tingling in the farthest reaches of his extremities. A mild burning sensation started in his fingers and toes and spread up through his torso and limbs. Somewhere between his heart and stomach, the separate filaments creating this odd sensation converged.

The mass held its position for a moment, but he could feel spikes of energy emerging from its center. He looked down at his midsection, almost expecting to see glowing iridescence through his shirt. Gently touching the area where the mass converged, it ruptured on contact as coils of energy unfurled into the furthest recesses of his body.

The most potent tendril snaked up through his spinal cord to the medulla oblongata, mid-brain and ultimately the corpus callosum, amygdala and cerebellum. His frontal and temporal lobes were saturated by the stream, and Marshall experienced a sudden rush of emotion and awareness that spread like food coloring dropped into a clear glass of water. The sensation was impossible to put into words, but his burgeoning enlightenment was exhilarating.

In an instant, he instinctively knew every nuance those without autism took for granted. His mind was bursting with rapid fire memories of encounters with different people through the years who tried to communicate by using expressions, gestures, verbal inflections, sarcasm and the myriad of other refinements that defined everyday human interaction. In an instant, Marshall understood the unspoken meaning that eluded him. His responses were often correct, though they were devoid of any real meaning. He wished he could revisit those situations since he now understood the consequences of his cold interactions.

Perhaps the most startling revelation was the depth of emotions he experienced. Sorrow became a cloak that shrouded him as he relived the loss of his father from cancer. His mother faced exhausting challenges and loneliness while raising him since she had no chance to establish another relationship. Few men wanted a woman with an autistic child in tow. Anger, humor, happiness, despondence; Marshall cycled through the full range of human emotions in a few seconds. As the journey concluded, he found himself in a place where all searches for meaning and purpose end. The most fundamental of all emotions... love.

In those moments, Marshall felt a sensory overload as the myriad of diverse manifestations of love washed over him like a rogue ocean wave. The love he had for his mother; how much he loved the boxer/pit bull mutt who slept in his bed when he was a child. Even the love he had for his friends coursed through his psyche. Once he peeled back all the different layers, he looked into a huge, glowing pool of contentment and optimism. He

215

felt lightheaded and overcome with excitement, delight and a sense of completeness.

Underneath the overwhelming pull of these enormous forces, there was a single version of love far more powerful than the others, but it carried a sense of insecurity with it. At that moment, Marshall knew he was hopelessly in love with Wanda. He could see her in his mind's eye, and she was utterly beautiful. In his vision, Marshall watched her raven black hair flowing and shining in the soft light. Her skin was glowing, and he gazed into those deep and soulful brown eyes.

He reached out to touch her, but she was elusive. He moved forward with his arms outstretched, but she started to recede and fade. Simultaneously, the depth of the other emotions he acquired also started to dissipate. Just as they had rushed through his body, they retreated as quickly. The energy mass lingered in his midsection for a moment before scattering out through his extremities, leaving a tingling feeling in his toes and fingers long after the effects had passed.

The sudden emptiness was overwhelming, and Marshall doubled over with both arms crossed over his midsection. He fell to his knees and lowered his head. For several seconds, he remained motionless, the vast familiar emptiness was far more painful than it had ever been before. He now had context, and the hollow abyss seemed deeper and wider than he could ever remember.

Marshall slowly raised his head and looked at the strange being who stood before him. The smile was so wide Marshall wondered if the man's lips might split, and his eyes blazed so brightly that the red fringe of his iris nearly consumed the now jet-black center.

"Well, I imagine that was quite an experience. Did you enjoy it?"

"It was... exhilarating."

"And now?"

"Now, I feel empty and worse than ever before. My reality is so bleak..."

"Well, the pills are on the floor. You can still take them. Or, you can have those feelings permanently. I can help you."

"How is that possible? How can you have such power?"

"It doesn't matter how I can do it; just accept that I can. If you cooperate, I can do many things for you."

"What do you mean *cooperate*?

"I run a large organization. It's very challenging, and my time is valuable. I am addressing some — issues that require my attention, and I need someone to monitor certain individuals. You have already encountered most of them. I may contact you periodically for updates and give you instructions. In return, I will endow you with a full array of emotions, and I will bestow the ability to interpret nonverbal communication when I am convinced of your loyalty and cooperation."

Marshall scratched his head and said, "If I refuse?"

The pale man's smile faded, and he shrugged. "That is up to you. You can continue to live your shallow life, or..." He glanced sideways at the bloody, ravaged dead body of Hayden lying on the bed.

Marshall slowly rose to a standing position. "Who are you?"

"You can call me... Mr. Cox." He tipped his hat, smiled widely, and walked out the door.

Chapter Nineteen

Sixtus imagined he had about two hours before the police issued an APB for his arrest. Unless the surviving assailant somehow found time to remove the body and scrub the crime scene, Sixtus and his wife would soon be fugitives. Hopefully, Kara was somewhere safe and dealing with the locals under an assumed name.

He drove over to 23rd Avenue near I-17 and pulled into the darkened Knoll-Highland industrial center. The car rolled slowly through the parking lot until it arrived at a building near the interior of the complex. Sixtus reached inside the BMW's glove box and pulled out a remote control for the roll-up delivery door. He swept the area for security cameras before pulling the car inside a nondescript warehouse and closing the door behind him.

After removing the license plate, he took out all the identification and registration documents from the glove compartment and fed them into a commercial metal shredder located against a far wall. The motor strained a moment as it ground up the contents. When the whine of the engine subsided, he opened the collection bin and looked at a clump of blackened material composed of shards of paper, plastic and metal.

In an adjacent bay, another vehicle had a tarp over it, and Sixtus removed the covering to reveal a late model white Ford Escape. He opened the driver's door, slid inside and rifled through the various contents of the glove box, pulling out a driver's license, social security card, passport, several credit cards, a new phone and a birth certificate. Each of the cards and documents bore the name, *Mark Simpson*. A new identity could provide cover until he made sense of this mess. Hopefully, he might resume his life as Jeffery Clayton someday. He tried to stay optimistic, but a nagging feeling told him he shouldn't count on it.

The Mark Simpson persona was strategically placed into various government, insurance and banking databases in case an unexpected emergency arose. Time Sculptors created multiple identities in strategic positions of power and authority as soon as they arrived in their assigned era. The implant made hacking into primitive cloud-based servers easy, and Mark Simpson was one of several unique personas Sixtus set up. Simpson was a pedestrian man who dutifully paid taxes, conducted personal transactions and stayed out of trouble.

Over the years, Sixtus periodically slipped into each of the different characters to maintain their relevance and preserve their existence in the system. The only suspicion he encountered was from the auto salespeople when he traded in a car every three years with less than 200 miles on it.

After destroying the rest of his Jeffery Clayton identification, Sixtus returned to the Escape, raised the hood and removed the cables from a trickle charger.

After re-connecting the device to the BMW, he got into the other vehicle and powered up the new phone. He accessed an app on the old device, and after making a few menu selections, all his contacts, pictures and documents transferred over. Before leaving, he threw the old phone in the metal shredder.

A few minutes later, he drove out of the industrial park and back to the freeway. The new cell phone lay on the passenger's seat, and he picked it up and scrolled through the contact list until he reached Marshall's name. He tapped the screen, and the phone autodialed. Even though he wouldn't recognize the number, he hoped the kid would answer.

On the third ring, "Hello?"

"Marshall, it's Jeffery Clayton." A long pause ensued.

"... I'm here."

"What are you doing? Are you at home?"

"Actually, no. I'm at a friend's house. He — never mind. I was just getting ready to leave though."

"Look, there's been a slight change in plans. We have to leave for Seattle tonight instead of tomorrow morning. I booked a 2:15 a.m. flight. Can you meet me at the airport?

"Well, yes, I can do that. I'll need to shower and pack, but I should be able to get there by one o'clock," said Marshall.

"Good. I'm sending you your ticket now. I'll see you at the boarding gate, and please, don't be late."

"I understand. I — I need to leave here, anyway. Don't worry, I'll be there on time."

Sixtus ended the call and lay the phone back on the seat. As he drove, an overwhelming urge to call

Kara welled up inside him, but he knew they would end up fighting, and he didn't want to endanger her even more. Despite a desperate sense of hope, he suspected the relationship was over, and short of telling the complete truth, nothing could salvage it at this point.

He yanked the wheel sharply to avoid hitting a floater who erratically stumbled onto the road. The woman was wildly scratching herself, no doubt the result of the genital rash epidemic that spread unchecked through South America and later the entire world. Health care in a declining civilization deteriorated in stages. While everyone had free health care, only the extremely rich could afford to see a doctor.

In the future, chaos and fear served as the foundation of an environment that led to the Corporates assuming total control. Humans were in such despair they had little choice but to sacrifice their freedom for simple necessities. Ultimately, the corporations became more powerful than governments, and eventually, they seized total control. The long-standing globalist goal of one world order was finally realized. As the Corporates power solidified, their escalating wealth and social reach changed the meaning of equality to shared misery.

Sixtus swerved again as a second floater ran out from the shadows. The man waved one hand and tried to hide a huge boulder he was holding with the other. For a moment, Sixtus considered changing lanes but decided instead to drive directly at him. This caused the transient to drop the rock in the highway and sprint back toward the shoulder. By the time Sixtus passed, the floater was shaking a fist and cursing loudly at the Escape.

The balance of the trip on the 101 to the 51 was relatively uneventful, at least in the context of these times. A man sawed through the head of a dog with a dull knife while two people cut themselves with razor blades under the freeway at the 202 interchange. The gangs and street bums were out in force, and despite the relentless Phoenix heat, they huddled around burning oil drums and talked endlessly about their gnawing emptiness and growing hate.

The crowds of disheveled malcontents grew bigger every day, and they no longer limited their activities to the night. The anger was palpable and festered under the surface. Something was terribly wrong with the world. Everyone knew it, but no one could quite put their finger on the cause.

After merging onto Route-43, Sixtus drove to the East Economy Parking lot. He found a space easily, and he took the registration and other documents out of the car before spraying the inside with a DNA disinfectant. Neither Jeffery Clayton nor Mark Simpson had a profile on record, but preventing the authorities from establishing one might slow the effort to apprehend him. After removing his carry-on bag and placing the strap over his shoulder, he made his way toward Terminal Four.

Once inside the building, Sixtus viewed his surroundings suspiciously as his training dictated. He looked around to confirm no hostile threats were in the vicinity before walking over to the security checkpoint where he took his place in line. The digital wall clock read 1:10, which gave him plenty of time to make the flight. The TSA attendant scanned and accepted the barcode for the boarding pass on his phone, and he breathed a sigh of relief since a degree of paranoia surrounded the Simpson identity.

After passing through the metal detector, he moved down the walkway to the gate where they serviced AirWest 216 in preparation for the flight to Seattle. Over in a far corner, Marshall Beiner sat motionless in the last seat on a row of hard plastic chairs. The kid's back was rigid, and his head remained still as he stared straight ahead. Once again, Sixtus flashed his phone under the barcode and entered the gated area. Marshall's eyes shifted after he came into full frontal view.

"Two of my friends committed suicide tonight." Marshall broke eye contact with Sixtus and resumed his straight forward gaze out the window to the tarmac.

"Marshall, I'm truly sorry. How…"

"It's not a coincidence, you know."

"What do you mean? You think it has something to do with our situation?" said Sixtus.

"I know it does. There's no doubt in my mind about it. Someone is involved; he has to be from the future. Maybe many people from the future are here, and some have extraordinary powers. Do you have such powers, Jeffery?"

Sixtus noted that Marshall no longer called him, "Mr. Clayton." He rubbed his chin and looked off into the distance. "Telepathy, telekinesis and other thought manipulation sciences were a burgeoning area of study. But we only perfected the ability to close off our minds defensively. We could not manipulate the thoughts of others."

"Either you are wrong, or they have come from a future more distant than your own."

"What do you mean?"

"I met him. He is very powerful, and he invades your mind."

Sixtus frowned and shook his head. "I'm not sure I understand. It's theoretically possible there could be other Time Sculptors here, but it's unlikely. Recently, those who have attempted the jump to the past have absorbed lethal doses of radiation."

"What about the more distant future? Why couldn't they send someone here?"

"Again, it's unlikely. We assumed the program terminated in the 25th century. A barrier prevented us from traveling past 2436. Our engineers tried everything imaginable to penetrate the obstruction without success."

"But wouldn't your changes affect them as well?"

Sixtus shrugged. "Perhaps, but it's impossible to know for sure. They may have found a way to compensate for our changes. Alter space-time so what we did in the past wouldn't affect them." He shrugged his shoulders again. "They are secretive and obviously very advanced. We never were able to communicate with them."

"Well, someone is here, and he has enormous power."

Sixtus looked up as the doors to the jet bridge opened, and the passengers began to board the plane. He stood up and motioned for Marshall to follow. They flashed their passes and made their way into the cabin. Sixtus showed his e-ticket to the flight attendant, who smiled and beckoned them to follow her to the business class section.

Marshall marveled at the luxurious nature of the seats on a domestic flight. He found his place next to Sixtus, stretched his feet out, and connected his earphones. Phoenix to Seattle wasn't a long trip, but it was late, and he experienced an extraordinary range of emotions today. Despite his crushing anxiety, Marshall was sound asleep before the plane reached the runway.

By contrast, Sixtus remained deep in thought. He wondered if another Time Sculptor from a distant future was here to meddle in the affairs of the 21st century. Maybe Marshall Beiner was simply displaying characteristics of mental illness. In any event, he needed to stay alert to future developments. He slid down in his spacious chair and positioned a pillow behind his head. Sleep would probably remain elusive, but he knew he should at least try.

***

The screech of the wheels hitting the runway jolted Sixtus out of a light slumber. He was momentarily disoriented because it felt like he never really lost consciousness. After rubbing his eyes, the soft snoring coming from the chair next to him attracted his attention. He gently shook Marshall until his companion woke up.

It took a moment to realize where he was, but Marshall jerked forward in his seat, craned his neck and looked around the cabin with a sense of uncertainty.

"Where — are we?"

"We've just landed at Sea-Tac, and they're getting ready to disembark."

Marshall yawned deeply, pulled the buds out of his ears and put them in his pocket. As passengers moved by, Sixtus stood up, grabbed their bags from the overhead, and pushed against the gathering bodies until he was standing in the aisle. This created space for Marshall to walk ahead, and they moved through the jet bridge and ultimately past the gate.

When they entered the airport, Sixtus walked to the directory and located the rental car pickup zone. Moving down an escalator to the baggage claim level on the south end of the airport, they joined several other passengers waiting for the shuttle. It only took a couple minutes before the brightly colored vehicle pulled up to the curb, and the doors opened with an audible sound from the hydraulics. Marshall followed Sixtus inside, and they took their seats on a long plastic bench that ran along the sides of the vehicle.

Sixtus looked over at his companion, who still seemed agitated. He reminded himself that he was dealing with a person with a difficult condition who probably didn't travel often. He patted Marshall's leg reassuringly, but that only seemed to further irritate his shaken cohort.

"You know, you're doing something very courageous, Marshall."

"Courageous? I have no choice. My friends are dead because of this—thing. I have to do something."

The surrounding air crackled for an instant and left a faint smell of ozone.

"You know, you're doing something very courageous, Marshall." Sixtus experienced an odd sensation as though his brain had seized momentarily.

"Courageous? I have no choice. My friends are dead because of this—thing. I have to do something." Marshall looked over at Sixtus, who held his gaze. "Wait a minute; didn't we just repeat the exact same sentences?"

"Yes, how strange."

226

"It felt like déjà vu only real, and we both experienced it simultaneously," said Marshall.

Sixtus opened his mouth to speak but instead his attention was distracted by another man who crossed the shuttle's narrow aisle. He positioned himself next to Sixtus even though the van had plenty of open space. Looking over, the man grinned and inched even closer until his leg touched Sixtus. The body odor and stench of his breath were overwhelming. Face pockmarked with bulbous acne, unwashed burnt red hair falling across his face, the passenger was an unnerving sight, especially when the smile plastered across his lips exposed stained, yellow teeth.

"Hello, friend," he said in a low voice. "Remember me?"

Chapter Twenty

Sixtus leaned back and regarded the stranger, scrutinizing him from every angle. He wasn't quite sure, but there was something familiar… "No, actually I don't remember you."

"Ziminski. Alan Ziminski. We met a few days ago. You came with a friend of yours who, uh, kind of died. Remember now?"

Sixtus straightened up, glanced at Marshall, and looked directly at Alan. "What? Ziminski? What in the hell are you doing here?"

Alan shrugged and tilted his head slightly. "Well, I don't get out much, so I volunteered to meet you in Seattle to help out. After your fracas back in Scottsdale, I figured you could use my help. After all, I pretty much saved your life."

"Yes, I appreciated the help, but we have everything under control here. Wait, how could you know I was coming to Seattle? Are you monitoring my movements?"

Ziminski reached into his pocket and pulled out a pack of cigarettes before remembering there was no smoking on the van. "Damn it, no smoking everywhere… Uh, what were you asking? Oh yeah, we're just looking out for you, Mr. Clayton. Or should I just call you 'Sixtus'?"

"You don't need to call me anything. In fact, once we get off this shuttle, I don't want to see you again, do you understand?"

"Aw, Mr. Clayton, such a lack of gratitude. Why don't you tell me where you're going, and I'll be on my way."

"Get out of my way, you…"

Ziminski suddenly thrust himself forward with aggression, placing his face half an inch from Sixtus. "Listen to me, you worthless piece of shit. You may have the rest of these people convinced you're some 'man of the future', but I ain't buyin' it." He pushed a stiff index finger into his Sixtus' chest.

Without conscious thought, Sixtus' hand shot out and grabbed Ziminski's finger and twisted hard. The action forced a howl of pain as Alan turned his entire body awkwardly to relieve the discomfort, which caused him to lose his balance and fall to the floor of the van. Background conversation stopped as the unfolding scene drew the attention of the passengers. The driver looked at the panoramic rear-view mirror and scowled.

Sixtus released the finger, and Ziminski clutched his hand and whimpered. "Why the fuck did you do that? I wasn't here to mess with you, but now you've pissed me off!"

In a low tone, Sixtus replied, "I could have broken your finger. Stay away from me."

Ziminski rose to his feet and grimaced. "You'll be sorry for this, asshole."

"Is there trouble back there? Do I need to call security?" The driver began to brake as the van pulled up to the drop-off zone near the rental car building.

229

Sixtus rose and motioned for Marshall to follow. "No, no, we're fine," he said while smiling weakly. He turned back and glared at Alan, who was sitting on the bench nursing his hand. After grabbing Marshall by the arm, they disembarked and quickly walked into the building.

Once they were out of view, Ziminski began to laugh while still holding his throbbing finger. He picked up his phone and pushed a button. "Yes, Mr. Watts, it's Ziminski. They're here, and everything is right on schedule. But that guy's a real asshole."

The rental car counters hugged the exterior walls of the circular building, and Sixtus took a moment to identify the company where he reserved a car. After exchanging pleasantries with the check-in attendant, he produced the required documents and his driver's license. She punched the information into the computer and waited for a confirmation number to appear on her screen, smiling at him awkwardly as almost a minute passed.

"Yes, Mr. Simpson, you're all set," she said finally, "and your car is reserved until Wednesday. You've declined the insurance, roadside assistance and the gasoline top off service. Please initial on these lines and sign at the bottom." With an inauthentic customer service smile, she added, "And how do you care to pay for that?"

"American Express." Sixtus reached into his wallet and pulled out his credit card embossed with the name, *Mark Simpson*.

After signing the papers and getting the key, they were transported back to the parking lot where they maneuvered through the massive collection of cars before reaching an indistinct Nissan Altima sitting in its assigned space. Sixtus slumped in the seat and stared straight ahead as Marshall got in. They pulled out of the airport and headed to Route-518, which eventually emptied into I-405 north.

Darkness still surrounded them, but signs of a bustling city coming to life were already evident as the delivery trucks and long-haul semis tried to beat the impending rush hour traffic to their destinations. Sixtus glanced over at Marshall repeatedly, aware that his companion was slipping further away. Considering the potential danger that loomed ahead, keeping him engaged was essential. In that moment, Sixtus regretted bringing him along. Yet, it was extortion that brought him here, wasn't it? Marshall had Iglar's list of change events, and Sixtus needed it.

"Marshall, I know you're upset by the death of your friends. These are troubling times. Over half a million people die every day, and the numbers keep growing. If the Time Sculptors caused this, it will only get worse."

Marshall hung his head. "I think my friends were compelled to commit suicide. They wanted to give me important information that could have helped us. They tried to tell me about the big change coming in the near future."

"Do you have any idea what they were talking about?"

"No. The 'Dark One' stopped them. He's very powerful and seductive. He knows what I'm trying to do, and he will stop me too. Unless…"

"Unless what, Marshall? Who is 'the Dark One'?"

Marshall sighed and rubbed his face with his hands. "I can't talk about it. Leave me alone."

Sixtus gripped the steering wheel harder as they rode in silence for several miles. Finally, he said, "I wouldn't have suspected, you know."

231

"Suspected what?"

"That you have an affliction. Autism is a neurodevelopmental disorder, isn't it? I had no idea that someone could have it but appear unaffected."

"You mean 'normal,' don't you, Jeffery? I may appear normal, but if you were around me enough, my behavior would lead you to pause."

"Perhaps. But under the circumstances, you seem pretty well-adjusted. I imagine you faced many challenges."

"*Challenges?* Most of my days as a child felt like I was living in a torture chamber erected especially for me. The bullying was relentless, and I didn't understand why the other children hated me so."

A morning chill permeated the cabin, and Sixtus paused to adjust the heater. "So, you were educated with everyone else? I thought they had special classes for people with developmental difficulties."

"You've just recited the politically correct version of my existence, Jeffery. It's too bad you weren't around when I was growing up. They called me a retard, freak and worse. Those were not fond memories."

"I didn't mean… Surely, your parents were aware of your—challenges."

"My father died when I was very young, and I was exhausting to my mother. She grasped at any straw that might convince her I was normal. This included putting me in special needs twice, but she always insisted I go back to regular classes since my grades were superior. I don't think she ever wanted to acknowledge I was different from the other children."

"Tough childhood. How did you survive it?"

"I'm not sure, really. My mother says I became obsessed with learning the proper response in every situation. I cataloged the different social circumstances I encountered and learned what I should say in common situations. After a while, I started to fit in a little more."

"Very clever."

"I suppose. But I still don't understand things instinctively. You can raise your eyebrow a certain way or use a tone of voice, and everyone knows exactly what you mean. But I don't, at least not on that deep intuitive level everyone else experiences. I mean, I didn't until…" Again, Marshall's voice trailed off.

"Until when, Marshall?"

"Nothing. I didn't mean anything by it."

"Has something changed with you? Are you able to read people now?"

"No," said Marshall in a tone that conveyed annoyance. "I said nothing has changed. Please just keep driving."

The car moved through the interchange at I-5, and Marshall looked out the passenger's window while remaining silent. Finally, he said in a low voice, "What's it like to grow up in the future?"

Sixtus pondered the question. It was important to answer in a way that avoided revealing details that could further compromise the timeline. "It's very different. Societal rules are strict and serious. Childhood involves a great deal of training, especially if you're selected for the Time Sculptor program."

"What happens then?"

"You're tested in every conceivable way. Your entire life is focused on mental, intellectual and physical preparation. The candidate must know protocol and understand how to respond to every potential unexpected event. Hundreds enroll every year, but only one out of 100 million is selected for time travel."

"Are all the spots taken?"

"What do you mean?" said Sixtus.

"Were people sent back to every time period?"

"No. Some eras in human history were not exploited. There are certain ages—the Dionysian era, for example—where it was impossible to affect a change that would impact the future with any sort of precision. In most instances, it was easier to make the changes in the late 20th and early 21st centuries on the North American and European continents."

Marshall closed his eyes as he tried to measure the potential for paradox. In the end, he doubted he could ever fully understand the mechanics of the program. "Did you have a happy childhood?"

"Our existence is not measured by happiness," said Sixtus without hesitation. "That's an emotion people rarely experience in the early 24th century. Actually, it's hard to put into terms you would understand. The structure in the future is rigid and extremely detailed. Technology has advanced to the point where no one dares deviate from group thought. It leads to sterile and superficial relationships, even among family members. I can't remember anything resembling the closeness I've experienced here."

The car exited the 405 onto Park Avenue and moved through traffic until reaching the intersection with Union Drive. Sixtus made a left turn and drove a few blocks until he found 10th Street. As he looked down the road, he saw a weathered sign that identified the Sun Valley mobile home park. The Altima entered the driveway at low speed, avoiding the potholes in the cracked pavement. The trailers on the grounds were old, rusted and in a general state of disrepair.

"This is a very poor neighborhood. I imagine we've traveled all this way for nothing. How could a person living in this kind of squalor have any impact on the timeline?" said Sixtus as the vehicle rolled to a stop in a common parking area.

The sun was beginning to rise, which cast a soft light on the unpleasant landscape. "If Iglar identified Curtis Roberts as being important, you can rest assured he is. Besides, most people live like this now," said Marshall as he undid his seat belt and opened the car door. "It's all they can afford."

Sixtus exited the driver's side and unwittingly stepped on a rusted car engine part of some sort, nearly twisting his ankle. Old appliances, plumbing fixtures, battered furniture and other unidentifiable objects filled the parking lot and nearby grounds. The weeds covered much of the refuse, but the socio-economics were obvious. In the middle of the complex, a weathered and broken stone angel stood in the center of an old, dry cement fountain.

Most of the lots were empty, and the majority of the trailers were moved or abandoned long ago. The occupied ones were relatively easy to spot since their windows weren't cracked or broken. Sixtus looked around until he identified trailer number 12, which was a half a block down the street. He signaled to Marshall, and they followed a path up to the single-wide Fleetwood. The exterior was a faded, oxidized white color, and numerous rust spots appeared where the paint had worn away. Sixtus knocked several times without anyone answering. As he debated whether to open the door without permission, he heard a weak voice from inside.

"Who is it? What do you want?"

"Curtis Roberts. My friend and I have traveled a great distance to talk to you. May we come in?"

"… Are you the angel?"

Sixtus looked at Marshall, who raised his eyebrows and shrugged. Turning back to the door, he said, "Curtis, can we come in and talk about it?"

"You can come in, but I have nothing left. I told him that."

Sixtus twisted the knob and pushed on the warped door. The hinges squeaked as it opened. The smell burst through the opening and filled the outdoor air with the odor of mold, urine and rotting food. Stepping through the threshold, his eyes confirmed what his olfactory senses detected. The interior of the trailer was covered in layers of hoarding-style filth. Empty food containers were strewn everywhere, and garbage covered much of the floor so only an occasional glimpse of faded red carpet peaked through.

Marshall hesitantly followed, stepping over unidentifiable foodstuffs that had begun to liquefy from decay. The buzzing of flies created a low drone that only added to the disconcerting atmosphere that permeated the flimsy structure.

As he stepped through the debris, Marshall fought a rising nausea that wrapped him in a shroud of panic and anxiety. He reached out and grasped Sixtus' arm until he turned around.

"I—can't stay here. I recognize several cultures of infectious bacteria, and I suspect there are thousands of others. We need to find hazmat suits and alert the local health authorities."

236

Sixtus looked at his companion for several seconds before realizing he was serious. At that moment, Sixtus understood how people with high functioning autism could be humorous even if it was inadvertent. Despite the dire circumstances, he fought the urge to laugh.

"I don't think we'll catch something from such a short exposure. Follow me and avoid touching anything." Sixtus turned around and continued moving forward through the kitchen area, stepping carefully to avoid the multitude of putrid substances.

Marshall looked around for a moment and considered leaving, but he remembered why he was there and knew he must follow the mystery wherever it led. He took a step and felt something wet squish under his shoe. He turned to his right, saw the flattened fresh feces, and retched. A swarm of flies left whatever decaying substance they were consuming and gathered over his fresh vomit.

Sixtus stopped again and turned around. "Ok, Marshall, you expelled it from your system. Let's move."

They reached the bedroom, but the door was closed. The bathroom was across a short hallway, and the odor was so noxious that Sixtus forced himself to compartmentalize his sense of smell so he wasn't overwhelmed by the distraction. He turned the doorknob and entered the bedroom, hoping Marshall was still conscious.

A man sat upright on the bed, his bare white legs extended and spread open. He appeared to be in the early stages of old age, perhaps mid-sixties, and he was clad only in a stained t-shirt and a pair of white briefs. His sparse hair was dirty and disheveled, glued to the flesh on his face with a thick layer of sweat and oil. One arm lay limp to the side, but in his right hand, he held a gleaming silver handgun. He pressed it hard into his chest, and Sixtus sensed this was no idle threat.

The man's body stiffened, and he looked over at the intruder. His facial expression softened after a few moments, but he didn't move the gun.

"Are you the angel?" Without taking his eyes off Sixtus, he reached over and grabbed a bottle from the nightstand with his free hand. He took a hearty pull and placed it back on the table. Sixtus couldn't see the label, but the thick smell of alcohol that cut through the stench said cheap gin.

"I'm here to talk with you about something important, Curtis. Can you please put the gun down?" Marshall slipped in behind Sixtus to see what was happening. He wasn't sure he could endure a third suicide in less than twenty-four hours. The smells and filth suddenly seemed much less important.

"Who are you?" asked Roberts without moving the gun. "If you're not the angel, then tell me who you are?"

"Curtis, my name is—Sixtus Maras. Does that mean anything to you?"

Curtis Roberts stiffened and pushed himself up against the headboard. "Sixtus Maras. That's a very strange name. Where do you come from, Sixtus?"

"I come from a distant place, Curtis. You might say I'm from a distant time as well."

"A distant time?"

"Yes, a time so distant that you may be familiar with it."

"Who do you answer to, Sixtus Maras?"

Roberts asked the operative question, which was part of the extensive training Sixtus received when he was in the program. In the unlikely event that two

Time Sculptors came in contact with one another, they were instructed to ask the operative question. *Who do you answer to?* If they both acknowledged being part of the program, they must immediately move a minimum of one continent away from one another and avoid any future contact. However, these were different circumstances, and normal protocol no longer applied.

Chapter Twenty-One

"I answer to the Corporates."

Curtis Roberts' eyes grew wide, and he used his feet to push up against the headboard, almost as though he was trying to burrow into it. "This — this can't be. Another Time Sculptor? How did you find me? And, who is he?" Roberts pointed at Marshall and emphasized the word *he*.

Sixtus held up his arms with palms extended. "He is with me, and he has extraordinary insight into our dilemma. Please, it's important that we talk. Can you put the gun down?"

The admonition only seemed to agitate Roberts, and he responded by pushing the gun further into his chest for emphasis. "You should not be here, Sixtus Maras. They warned me you might resist. You stand by the Corporates, so someone must stop you. They've caused this horror."

"Who told you about me? Whatever you believe, it is false. I only came to learn. You have been in this time forty years longer than I have. Tell me, what is your era of origin?"

"I came to this time from 2364. A populist movement within the Corporates emerged just before I left. They wanted to end the program. Who knows if it continued or not?" Roberts shook his head. "I have seen so much. Almost everything has changed since I arrived in the late-20th century, and yet, still so primitive…"

"Late-20th century? How old are you?" asked Marshall.

Roberts looked up and glared. "He's eighty-five," said Sixtus.

"Eighty-five? That's impossible. He only looks like he's in his fifties."

"The aging process is slower in people from our time. At least those in the Undulate class, and naturally, the Corporates. Since we were in the Time Sculptor program, we also received life protraction treatments, which primarily consist of genetic freezing and telomere extension. Once we reach forty, we age at half the rate of the people from this time."

Marshall pulled back slightly as his eyes widened for an instant. "Amazing."

Sixtus turned his attention back to Roberts. "Curtis, can I at least have your designation? I know how much it affects me when I hear my birth name. I had almost forgotten. Until recently, my true name wasn't spoken for decades."

Roberts hesitated, and the pressure on the gun lessened noticeably. "My name is… Glendnar Raczor." He smirked, and his body heaved slightly from the effect of a stifled laugh. "I have difficulty saying my own name."

"I'm glad you shared that, Raczor. Obviously, the first question is why? Why do you have a gun pointed at your chest?"

Raczor rolled his eyes and emitted a half sob. "They're in my head, Maras. I've spent the majority of my life alone in this horrible place. They told us to create a new beginning after our mission ended, but I never fit in. These people are primitive, ignorant, superficial, and most of them are psychotic. Nothing in this time interests me, and I hated this era from the moment I arrived. Europe, America; it made no difference."

"Yes, I can imagine you suffered."

"You have no idea. There were no useable computers here until the late 1980s, and even those were toys. They drank copious quantities of alcohol and inhaled smoke from burning tobacco. Social gatherings focused on gossip. These primitives never discuss anything substantive. They disgust me."

"I see. Did you develop any hobbies? I found I enjoyed boating and photography."

"*Boating and photography?*" Raczor scoffed and let out an audible grunt. "Why would I want to take photos when my overhead could provide three dimensional renderings of anything I looked at? And boating? I lived in an underwater city in the 24th century."

"Your life has certainly been lonely and secluded. It's no wonder you feel despondent."

"I wasn't prepared for the loneliness, although we were warned and trained to accept the condition if we did not adjust well. As you're aware, suicide was encouraged in such situations. Until now, I could never bring myself to do it.

"Raczor, we can still accomplish much in this era. You are a valuable resource."

"A valuable resource? To whom? I lost the overhead so many years ago I can hardly remember how it operated, and without it, I lost my edge. My money vanished through lavish spending and bad investments. I tried to recall history. Who won the Super Bowl in 2016? Was it Carolina? No, it turned out to be the other team. I couldn't remember which stocks to buy and which ones to sell, so I ended up penniless and alone. Then there's this." Raczor waved his arm in an expansive motion.

"What, Raczor?"

"This whole — society. It's going to hell, and it looks like it will only get worse."

"I understand. In fact, we may have caused it," said Sixtus. Both he and Raczor had unconsciously slipped out of formal enunciation of their era to the common vernacular of the day that included contractions.

"What?"

"That's why my friend Marshall is here. He and his associates discovered a link between the time sculpts and the deterioration of the collective psyche. We're leaving imprints of past realities on these people every time something changes. It's a cumulative effect. We're driving the indigenous people insane."

"But — the program. The simulations showed no net effect."

Sixtus' jaw clenched slightly. "They were wrong. It's subconscious, but there nonetheless."

"If it's subconscious, how does he know?" said Raczor while nodding at Marshall.

"Because he is more sensitive than most. He suffers from autism, which apparently increases perceptive abilities. Some of them are so sensitive they experience and recall every minute fluctuation in the altered time

243

line. We've created so many overlapping currents that many succumb to complete withdrawal."

"And let me guess. You're here to change it all and save humanity. Isn't that right, Maras?"

"Certainly, we hope to do the right thing, Raczor."

"And what is the 'right thing' exactly?"

Sixtus shuffled uncomfortably while Marshall moved over and sat in a wooden chair propped up against the wall near the door.

"I assume you talked to Daxtar Liss?"

Raczor pushed the gun deeper into his chest at the mention of Liss. "Many people have visited me. I don't recognize the name."

Sixtus furrowed his brow. "Come now, Raczor. I suspect you do recognize the name. Liss told me he already visited two of the four Time Sculptors in this period. That means you had to talk with him."

"What's your point, Maras?"

"Liss told you of a catastrophic event that's supposed to occur very soon. He told you this event must be stopped at all costs. Isn't that right?"

"I know nothing…"

"Stop with your denials. Liss was clear, and my friend Marshall confirmed it. A cataclysmic event is forthcoming, and I believe you may have vital information that could help us avoid the calamity and possibly decontaminate the timeline."

Raczor again reached for the gin bottle. Taking another healthy pull, he swirled it around in his mouth before swallowing. "Liss found me as he found you. He explained the circumstances, and as you say, they are very dire. But I have no knowledge of the details of the crisis. Liss did not give me that information. Did he give it to you?

"No, he didn't."

"But we know what it will be." Marshall inserted himself into an awkward pause in the conversation.

"Marshall!" Sixtus turned and looked at his companion. His eyebrows arched, and his lips pursed tightly.

"What?" Marshall pleaded. "Why can't we tell him? We need his help to reverse this. He must have initiated several of the significant time changes. Maybe he can help us undo the worst of them."

"How did you find this information, Maras?" Raczor leaned forward, and the gun dropped to his side.

"I can't tell you. But I need you to join me on this journey to uncover the truth. You must tell me the identity of the second and fourth Time Sculptors."

"I pray you're on the side of right, Maras. The Corporates must lose this battle; Liss convinced me of that. Tell me more about this 'event' you speak of."

Sixtus ignored the question. "Liss did not convince me. I encountered another traveler who arrived later and also took a high dose of radiation. Havas Zir said he was from a time farther in the future than Liss, and he also claimed to be working with the rebellion against the Corporates."

Raczor did a poor job of hiding his obvious surprise. "I am unaware of another time traveler, Maras. Are you making this up? I suspected you might not cooperate." He grabbed the gin bottle, and after draining the last of the liquid, he tossed it on the floor. "I am weary, Maras. It has been a hard life, and I've questioned my sanity. Am I affected by the time changes as well? Supposedly not, but another visited me, and it was frightening. I hoped you were the angel, but I see now you are not." He hung his head, and a sad look crossed his face.

"Who else has visited you, Raczor."

Without looking up, Raczor replied, "I was visited by 'the Dark One'."

Marshall's eyes widened, and he leaned forward so far that he nearly fell off the chair. He steadied himself, stood up, and stepped backward until he was up against the far wall of the bedroom. "Who did you say visited you?"

"I said, The Dark One."

"His name. Tell me his name."

"He said his name was—Mr. Cox."

Marshall's knees buckled, and he grabbed the sides of his head with his hands.

"Does that name mean something to you, Marshall?" said Sixtus.

"No. I—I have no idea..."

Raczor pointed a finger at Marshall. "He's visited you too? Did you consider his offer? I..."

"No!" Marshall inched closer to the door. "I said I don't know. It's your hallucination, not mine."

"He's malevolent, Maras. You do not want to encounter him."

"I have already met him, but not in the same manner you did, Raczor. Did he speak of the coming catastrophe?"

"No, he came to offer me something. I assumed he was a delusion as your friend suggests. Who knows? I am old and weary, and my mind is failing." In a rapid motion, he raised the gun and pointed it at Sixtus. "Liss warned me you may have been corrupted, Maras. You must not intervene on behalf of the Corporates. That much is clear. I have to stop you."

"Wait, Raczor, think this through. How can we trust Liss anymore than we can trust Havas Zir? We

246

must investigate; find the second and fourth Time Sculptors and talk to them."

Raczor's body tensed. "There is no time for that. The second Time Sculptor is rumored to be in Africa. You don't have the stomach to defeat the Corporates, so they will probably destroy humanity's future."

Marshall froze in fear. He wanted to run, but his legs felt heavy and weak. Sixtus backed up toward the door of the bedroom. His hands were raised as he muttered about the need for calm. The veins of Raczor's neck swelled, and his hands began to shake. A large ball of snot shot out of his left nostril as he winced.

"I didn't want it to end this way. Why did I agree to come to this barbaric time? They never explained the loneliness." Raczor's eyes welled with tears, and he dropped his head into his hands, which twisted the gun so it pointed at the ceiling.

The momentary lapse was all the advantage Sixtus needed. He jumped onto the bed and grabbed the hand that held the gun. At the same time, the fingers on his other hand wrapped around Raczor's neck, and he squeezed hard. Once past the initial surprise of the assault, the older man fought back viciously and with surprising strength, using all the training he learned at the academy to counter his younger, stronger opponent.

His teeth chattered as he snapped his jaws and tried to tilt his head down to bite Sixtus' arm while twisting and turning to buck him off. Even though his head remained stationary, Raczor flexed his wrist and turned his hand so the gun barrel pointed at Sixtus.

Raczor struggled to push his index finger through the trigger guard, and with extreme effort, he reached the cold steel of the curved piece of metal. He tried to squeeze the trigger, but Sixtus desperately pulled his hand in the opposite direction. Raczor focused every

247

ounce of his waning strength on his gun hand while trying to fire the weapon into Sixtus' lower abdomen, but he couldn't have anticipated his opponent's sudden release of the gun hand.

Once relieved of the pressure, Raczor's arm curled inward until the barrel of the gun thumped against his chest. The momentum of his hand was sufficient enough to cause his finger to flex, which applied enough pressure on the weapon so it discharged at point blank range. Outer layers of skin on his chest tore away like a rancid scab on a festering wound. Splayed raw meat exposed his ribcage and showed briefly before a surge of blood covered it.

Raczor sputtered and coughed; his eyes were wide with panic and fear as he looked up at Sixtus. He dropped the gun and clutched the gaping wound with both hands, but the blood oozed through his fingers and ran down the sides of his body in multiple streams filled with bits of bone, tendon and muscle.

"I—I never wanted to be here. I always hated this place. An angel said he was coming to help me." Raczor's eyes grew wide, and he leaned forward and grabbed Sixtus by the arm with surprising strength. "You must fix this, Maras. Something has gone horribly wrong. Beware of the Dark One. I think he…"

A sudden rapping on the front door ended the conversation as they collectively looked toward the source. Raczor gripped Sixtus' tighter. "They have found you, Maras."

The subsequent knocking was louder and more urgent. "Who are the other Sculptors, Raczor? You must tell me. It may be our only chance."

Tears welled up in Raczor's eyes, and the grip on Sixtus' arm relaxed somewhat. "I can't tell you. Liss was adamant that your interference in the event would ensure catastrophe, yet I know you remain unconvinced. No one knows what happened to the second Sculptor, but I hope the fourth kills you if you betray the cause."

The sound of the knob turning jarred Sixtus from his exchange with Raczor. He got up from the bed and motioned for Marshall to follow. They moved swiftly into the hallway and ducked into the second bedroom just as the front door opened. Sixtus closed the bedroom door silently as the sound of two sets of footsteps walked tentatively through the trailer.

Marshall leaned against the bedroom wall in abject terror. He needed to take an anti-anxiety dose, but he dare not make a sound. He heard the heavy breathing of the people outside as they grew closer. Every squeak, creak and whisper grew in intensity, and Marshall thought he could feel the sweat bubbling out of his pores. He wanted to flee but could not move his limbs as his throat tightened and became increasingly constricted. *Am I going to have an asthma attack?* He could barely draw a breath when he heard their first words.

"Jarad, call 9-1-1!" Marshall didn't know what he expected, but the man's voice sounded ordinary. "Curtis? Curtis Roberts, can you hear me?"

The answer came from a delirious and mortally wounded Raczor. "I — want to go to heaven."

"Of course, Curtis. You'll go to heaven. But help is on the way. Hang on." The first voice spoke again.

"I rejected him... I didn't give in. You promised I would go to heaven."

"Didn't give in to what, Curtis? Who?"

249

While Marshall listened intently to every spoken word, Sixtus was having difficulty following the conversation. An audible gasp followed a struggle for breath before Raczor replied, "The Dark One."

"Who—who is that, Curtis? Curtis..." The first voice sounded alarmed.

"Shot myself in the chest... Tell them to study my brain; find out what's wrong with me."

"Nothing is wrong with you, Curtis. Tell me about the Dark One. Who is he?" A sense of urgency came from the unidentified speaker.

There was no answer, and instead, Marshall heard long, rasping belabored breathing. He was certain Raczor was dying. Sounds from the other room conveyed commotion and turmoil, and he envisioned someone trying to resuscitate the fading Time Sculptor. The frenzy reached a crescendo before dying out completely.

"Jesus, Zach, is he dead?" This was a different voice that sounded deeper and anxious. Marshall took note of the names: Jarad and Zach. Another long pause followed before the first man spoke, confirming what Marshall suspected.

"Yes, he's gone. Something frightened him. I wish we could have found out more."

Chapter Twenty-Two

Marshall heard more commotion coming from the front of the house. The door opened a second time, and someone walked in and crept cautiously through the living room. Sixtus moved to the closet, opening the sliding door slowly and motioning for Marshall to follow. Despite the near paralysis that caused his muscles to seize, he slipped into the small space and immediately noticed a new repugnant smell.

"I think someone else came in," Sixtus said in a soft whisper. "I hear more footsteps. We don't have any choice but to stay here and hope we're not detected."

Sixtus strained to hear what was happening in the other room, but the voices sounded muffled and unintelligible. By contrast, Marshall could hear every spoken word with perfect clarity.

"Gentlemen, raise your hands and please move away from the body." The new voice was confident and authoritative. "I am Detective Jose Munoz from Seattle PD. I'm telling you to move away from the body."

Marshall leaned over and cupped his hand to Sixtus' ear. "I think the first two are being arrested."

The one Marshall identified as "Zach," said, "If you're going to shoot me, just do it. I've seem more misery over the last year than anyone should see in a lifetime. This man just died, and it sickens me."

"Who are you?" said the one named Munoz.

"My name is Zach Randall. This is my friend Jarad Anston."

Marshall committed the surnames to memory.

More shuffling followed, interrupted by the sounds of voices talking over each other. Finally, the one named Munoz signaled for quiet.

"All right, exactly what are you doing here? How do you know the victim?"

"We don't know him—not personally," replied Randall. "But we were aware he was trying to commit suicide. We didn't get here in time."

"How would you know something like that, Mr. Randall?"

"I can't explain it in a way that you would understand, Detective. I just knew."

"Mr. Randall, I'm going to ask you again to move away from the body and join your friend. The forensics people will be here shortly, and we prefer that you didn't contaminate evidence. I must be honest; you both are in a lot of trouble."

Marshall wondered how Zach Randall could have known that Curtis Roberts, or "Gladnar Raczor" as Sixtus called him, had planned to kill himself. Renewed conversation interrupted his thoughts.

"Were you here before the victim died?" said Munoz.

"Yes, he was still alive when we came into the bedroom." said Randall.

"Did he say anything to you prior to his death?"

"Yes, he did. He mentioned something about resisting someone or something. He was trying to tell me more, but…"

"Did he give you any names?"

"No. He only said something about someone called the Dark One." Marshall stiffened at the mention of the mysterious name.

"I still need to know why you two are here, Mr. Randall. I'm going to have to see some ID as well."

A momentary pause followed where Marshall envisioned Randall and Anston handing over their driver's licenses.

"It's hard to explain in a way you would believe," said Randall. "Sometimes I just know that someone is in real trouble. I knew Curtis Roberts was in trouble, so I came to help him."

"All the way from New Mexico? That's quite a story, Mr. Randall. You just knew that Curtis Roberts was going to kill himself, and so you came from New Mexico to stop him? Quite a story indeed. Is this going to be your official version? Because if it is, I have to tell you, I think you and Mr. Anston need a lawyer."

"He's telling the truth, Detective," said Anston. "Except that we came from Las Vegas. I know it sounds bizarre, but I swear it's true. Look at the grip of the gun; check for fingerprints. Would I have called 9-1-1 and waited for the police to arrive if we had killed him? I never saw this man before today."

"Very few suicides shoot themselves in the chest."

"He said he wanted his brain intact so it could be studied," said Randall. "Based on what he experienced, he must have thought he lost his mind." Marshall wondered what Randall might say if he understood the *real* reason Roberts killed himself.

Marshall's breathing almost returned to normal when the sound of the front door slamming into an interior wall caused him to stiffen. Another person was entering the house... No, it was two people based on the intensity and number of footfalls pounding along the flimsy floor. The small trailer was suddenly very popular. Marshall looked over at Sixtus who merely shrugged and shook his head slightly.

"This is the FBI! Everyone down on the floor!" Marshall tried to make sense of these seemingly unrelated events. Munoz appeared to be a municipal cop, so it was unlikely he contacted the FBI. The time frame didn't fit either. Other units couldn't respond to the 9-1-1 call this quickly. Had these FBI agents staked the place out? If so, they must know he and Sixtus were inside the trailer. Marshall's heart was beating so hard he was sure a left ventricle rupture was imminent.

"I'm Detective Jose Munoz of the Seattle PD. I'm going to reach into my jacket and give you my credentials."

"Don't bother. I need you to lie on the floor and spread your arms and legs just like your friends are doing." The tone of the FBI agent was brusque and deliberate.

"Can you identify yourself?" Munoz asked.

"I'm going to tell you one more time to lay down on the floor with your arms and legs spread. This is an order not a request."

"This is a crime scene, Agent. It's been called into dispatch. There are black and whites on their way here now. Do you really want them to find a dead detective on the scene? Now, I'm going to carefully pull out my credentials. As I open my jacket, you'll see my service revolver. I won't make any attempt to draw it out, so you won't misunderstand me."

An interminable period of silence followed, and Marshall heard nothing except the distinctive squeak of hard-soled shoes against the unstable floor. Finally, the FBI agent spoke. "Sorry Detective, but we didn't realize that SPD knew about this. Who called it in?"

"Well, the victim called in a suicide attempt earlier, but it was canceled before a unit responded. I came to check on that. Apparently, these two found the body before I arrived, and one of them called it in, although I don't know which one."

The FBI agent's tone changed dramatically. "I'm sorry for the misunderstanding, Detective. I'm Agent Goldblume; this is Agent Sanchez. Obviously, we're not here for the suicide. It's those two; we've come to apprehend them."

Munoz paused, and when he spoke, Marshall's conditioning helped him recognize a sense of suspicion in the detective's tone. "I see. Just what are they wanted for, Agent Goldblume?"

"They're wanted for questioning involving the murder of a prominent businessman and an FBI agent in Las Vegas."

Anston and Randall murdered an FBI agent? Marshall wondered what horrific crimes Gladnar Raczor perpetrated. Could the killings have been time sculpting assignments?

"Tell you what, Agent Goldblume. I'll take these two into custody and bring them to the station. You can interrogate them there. I assume you weren't expecting to run into me here, and unless you have the paperwork, the jurisdiction is mine."

The conversation halted for an uncomfortably long moment, and when the agent spoke, he dropped the polite veneer. "I'm afraid that won't be acceptable, Detective. We need to take these two into custody immediately."

Even crouching in the closet, the mounting tension from the bedroom was palpable. "That doesn't work for me, Agent Goldblume. If you can't produce the paperwork, we're going to the station."

Waves of raw emotion drifted out of the bedroom and permeated through the trailer until the conflict exploded with a crash and loud *oomph* as one person apparently slammed into another. The signs of struggle were obvious as the sounds of furniture toppling and glass shattering pierced the silence. Numerous grunts, snorts and loud obscenities gave Marshall the impression there were multiple skirmishes occurring simultaneously.

Since these law enforcement people were armed, it was no surprise when a loud gunshot rang out, followed almost immediately by two more. At that point, all sound from the bedroom ceased. The eerie quiet was unsettling, and Marshall stood up as the fear became suffocating, but the strong grip of Sixtus pulled him back to the floor. He couldn't tolerate the confined space of the closet much longer, but a glowering look from Sixtus sapped Marshall's will.

The violent struggle subsided for a moment but then returned with a vengeance as another gunshot echoed through the mobile home, shaking the walls and ceiling tiles. After the last reverberation died out, Marshall listened for movement until he heard the patter of uneven footsteps walking out of the bedroom towards the front of the house.

"Let's go." The voice was quiet and subdued but sounded like Munoz. "They'll be coming soon.

There's no time to waste. We need to get away from here quickly."

"Ok, Detective. We'll follow you," replied Randall.

It appeared that Munoz and the other two men had survived, and they left with urgency. The front door slammed shut, and Marshall and Sixtus were left alone in the house. Motioning for quiet, Sixtus set a timer on his watch, and the digital numbers began to count backwards from thirty. When the watch hit zero, he reached down and dragged Marshall to his feet.

"Okay, I believe they're gone; we should leave right now." Sixtus opened the closet without hesitation. As the distant sound of multiple sirens grew louder, he was already in the hallway before realizing Marshall wasn't following. Walking back into the bedroom, he pulled his reluctant companion out of the closet.

"Marshall, we've got to get out of here. Those sirens are getting louder. There's something wrong with all of this."

Nodding his acknowledgment, Marshall forced his stiff legs to move, taking one challenging step after another. As they passed the master bedroom, Sixtus stopped and looked inside. Two men in black suits were lying on the floor in unnatural positions. Pools of blood had gathered around each of them, although the heavy set one seemed to be bleeding out much faster.

On the bed, Raczor remained propped up against the headboard as though he was sleeping, except that his shirt, pants and nearly the entire bed were soaked with copious quantities of fresh and drying blood. It seemed surreal to the point that Marshall might have believed he was on the set of a Hollywood "B" horror movie. Every time he took a breath, the distinctive smell of death reminded him this was his reality.

"Should we—should we make sure they're dead? Marshall continued to stare at the bodies.

Sixtus shook his head. "No time. The police are getting closer. Let's go!" He grabbed Marshall by the arm and pulled him away from the gruesome crime scene. If it wasn't for Sixtus' sense of purpose and direction, Marshall imagined he might suffer a complete nervous breakdown in that moment. Perhaps he was having one, anyway.

Feeling the firm pressure of Sixtus' hand clutching his arm, Marshall had no choice but to move forward in tandem until they were outside the trailer. Walking at a borderline trot, they made it to the rental car, and Sixtus opened the passenger's door and pushed Marshall into the seat. He sprinted around to the driver's side and slipped in. As the first squad car turned the corner onto Union Drive, Sixtus pulled onto 10th and traced a different path back to the 405.

They drove in silence as Marshall looked absently out the passenger's window while Sixtus muttered to himself and chewed lightly on his lower lip. Finally, when they reached I-5 on their way back to the airport, Marshall turned and blurted out, "I want to go home."

Sixtus looked over, squinting and working his jaw muscles. He was ready to lash out, but he saw the abject fear in Marshall's face. With only a laymen's knowledge of autism, Sixtus was learning on the fly. The kid could appear unaffected at times, but on other occasions it was apparent there was something very unusual in the way he perceived the world.

"Marshall, you can't…"

"I want to go *home!*" The words tumbled out of his mouth, and his bottom lip began to quiver. Tears welled up in his eyes, and Marshall was as terrified of the emotions that flooded his body as the chaotic circumstances that overwhelmed him. He wondered if he was developing a psychosis.

One minute he looked at three dead bodies with only superficial feelings of sympathy, and now he was gripped by a sense of dread and doom that was utterly devastating. For a second time, tears fell and left tracks over his cheeks. He tried to calm himself and evaluate the experience from a distance, but he simply could not control his mind, and so he wept openly.

"Marshall, calm yourself. I understand this is extremely disturbing, but you're going to have to deal with it. I can't afford to become sidetracked."

"This is too much for me, Jeffery. Death, death and more death… For the past three days that's all I've seen. I just need to get home and forget any of this happened."

Sixtus rolled his eyes and rubbed his forehead. "That's not possible, and I think you understand why. You're deeply involved with a Time Sculptor, and you're keenly aware the timeline is being manipulated. You could wreak havoc on the future and potentially unleash a catastrophe event worse than what we're dealing with."

Sixtus paused and softened his tone. "Look, I tried to persuade you to stay home, but you insisted. You're here now, and I need your help."

Marshall slumped over and wrapped his arms around his stomach. For a moment, he felt like he might purge again. After several deep breaths and centering his mind, a semblance of calm began to return, and his inflamed psyche relaxed a bit.

"What kind of help do you need from me?" he asked, hoping Sixtus would suggest a meaningless task that would provide a dignified way to exit this nightmare.

"We're going to split up."

"So, you're sending me home?" said Marshall.

"Not at all. We've got two separate leads, and we must follow up on both. You have friends who can hack dedicated networks for information, right?"

"Yes. It's child's play to them."

"Then you'll follow the two who came in immediately after Raczor shot himself during the struggle. Did you happen to catch their names?"

"Yes. Zach Randall and Jarad Anston. I heard them clearly."

Sixtus nodded. "You must have extraordinary hearing. The conversation was muted to me."

"A hearing test indicated I'm endowed with a twenty-decibel advantage over the average person."

"Uh huh, that's excellent." Sixtus tried to hide his impatience. "Can your associates find out where these two came from? We need to know who they are, and how they knew Raczor?"

Marshall paused. "I'm not sure if I can do it. Being alone… it's so dangerous. I thought you were going to send me home."

Sixtus sighed deeply. "There's no other way. There's nothing else to go on. I have no idea where the second or fourth Time Sculptors are, and the details for the upcoming major event are sketchy at best. You must help me, so going home is not an option."

"You already know about the event? Then the conclusions we drew based on the anxiety index were correct. The event — I need to understand it better."

"Not now, Marshall. Perhaps I'll tell you at a later date. But not now."

Once they exited the freeway, Sixtus pulled into a hotel parking lot adjacent to the SeaTac airport. He'd been awake for over twenty-four hours and wanted to find a place to regroup and get some sleep since his ability to reason was suffering. Marshall also desperately needed the respite.

"What are we doing here?" asked Marshall while looking up at the national chain hotel sign.

"We need food and rest, and I'm not thinking clearly. I'll get checked in, and we'll get something to eat at that restaurant next door. Then we'll start planning on what we should do tomorrow."

Marshall nodded and got out of the car. After they grabbed their bags, Sixtus checked into the hotel using Mark Simpson's credit card. He insisted on adjoining rooms and opened the connecting doors once they dropped off their bags. After getting settled in, they took the elevator to the lobby and walked across the parking lot to the *Pirates Cove* seafood restaurant.

As they slid into a booth, Sixtus checked his watch. It was already 5:30 p.m., and he hoped he could keep his eyes open through dinner. As he looked over at Marshall, he wondered how the fate of space, time and reality could rest on the shoulders of a kid with autism.

Chapter Twenty-Three

Marshall sat on the edge of the bed in his hotel room with the lights off. Dinner with Sixtus was awkward, and he struggled more than he normally did with idle talk. His companion wanted to avoid discussing the future, but the timeline was so thoroughly compromised Marshall couldn't understand his reasoning.

The baked Tilapia was delicious, and he would have eaten more under different circumstances, but focusing on food was difficult. Mercifully, the service was efficient, and they were able to finish dinner quickly and return to their rooms. Sixtus left his connecting door open, but Marshall chose to keep his shut, relishing the privacy.

Pulling his phone out, he scrolled through his caller ID list and saw Wanda's number appear numerous times. In fact, the volume of calls bordered on compulsive, which was a destructive trait Wanda often battled. While her phone number dominated the list, Kenny also called several times over the same span.

Staring absently at the phone, Marshall's mind drifted, and he lay back against the pillow propped up on his bed. He pictured himself sitting on a park bench in a wide-open space. The sun was shining, but a gentle breeze kept the temperature cool and comfortable. Large trees swayed as the wind rustled through their leaves, and they created a symphony of sound punctuated by the melody lines of chirping birds. As Marshall looked at the scenery, he didn't care if the trees were deciduous or coniferous. The species of the chirping birds was also unimportant to him. How odd… He closed his eyes and enjoyed the sensation until he felt a gentle touch on his arm.

When he looked around, he realized that Wanda was sitting beside him. She smiled, and her skin looked radiant. They stared into each other's eyes for some time, and Marshall relished her pleasant scent. Somehow, his sense of reason no longer functioned, but oddly, it seemed unimportant. Words were unnecessary in this place, and thoughts and feelings flowed freely between them. Marshall experienced an almost indescribable sense of bliss, and Wanda reached out and gently wiped a tear from his cheek.

Slowly, she leaned in closer as her eyes began to flutter and close. Marshall also leaned in and pursed his lips. They joined together tenderly, and the soft kiss soon gave way to a more penetrating and primitive longing. Wanda's tongue pushed his lips apart and entered his mouth, and he felt stimulated as an urgent passion rose within him. The intensity of the feelings was stunning, and Marshall became lost in desire and lust.

Her tongue continued to dance with his, probing and exploring, growing more deliberate and insistent. For a moment, Marshall grimaced from the force she

263

used to push her tongue deep into his mouth cavity, but she quickly withdrew it and returned to her previous sensuous play. Then it happened again, but this time she didn't stop. Her tongue seemed to morph into a hard, solid shaft that slowly changed from the sweet flavor of amaretto to the repugnant taste of copper. She drove the long rigid rod down his throat as she grabbed the back of his head and pulled it close with surprising strength. Marshall gagged, and his arms thrust out to push her away, but she was too powerful and maintained her strong grip.

His eyes opened wide, and what he saw at such close proximity was horrifying. This wasn't Wanda at all, but a creature whose pale skin was rancid and pockmarked. Numerous tiny lesions opened and closed simultaneously, and Marshal thought he could see slimy maggots crawling out of the wounds. In utter disgust, he screamed and pulled back hard until finally free of the creature's grip. He spat on the floor several times and wiped his mouth as the thing across from him began to laugh. When Marshall regained focus, he realized he was looking into the blazing eyes of Mr. Cox.

"You! How did you get in here?"

"Ah, Marshall, I can go anywhere I want. But admit it; you liked it didn't you? Admit it. When you thought I was Wanda, you became quite aroused, didn't you?"

"I — I don't want to talk about it. I was asleep. It was a nightmare."

"Oh yes, hot and bothered. I felt you smoldering. It can be like that for the rest of your life, Marshall. You can experience feelings. Deep, deep feelings. I'm counting on you. Or maybe it's time for you to follow Iglar and Hayden and finally finish things."

Marshall tried to jump from the bed, but the jarring action made him gasp for breath. He was breathing heavily as he glanced around the empty hotel room. Looking down, the cell phone was still in his hand. Apparently, he dozed off while resting on the bed. Yet, it all seemed so real. Mr. Cox was in his head, and Marshall wasn't sure how to remove him.

As he tried to process the disturbing dream, the cell phone lit up and vibrated in his hand. He saw the number was Wanda's and knew he couldn't avoid her indefinitely. Still rattled by the dream, he answered.

"Hello?"

"Marshall, it's Wanda."

"Yes, I have your name and number in my contacts list."

"Are you—alright?"

"I'm alive and not injured if that's what you mean." He said.

"I'm glad, but I meant more than that. How is your mental and emotional state?"

Marshall's head dropped, and he ran his free hand through his close-cropped hair. "I'm falling apart mentally and emotionally. And now I think I'm hallucinating."

"Marshall, come home. Come home right now."

"I—can't. You have no idea how complex and destructive this phenomenon is, Wanda. It's so much bigger than we suspected, and I'm deeply involved. This reality—all reality is at risk. That's all I can say. I don't want to endanger you any more than I have."

"Marshall… Hayden is dead. He killed himself."

"I know," he said.

"How could you know that?"

"I was there when he did it. He called me, but I got there too late."

"Hayden's mother found the body. She said the scene was unimaginably gruesome. She's gone into seclusion." Marshall didn't answer, and there was a long silence before Wanda continued. "Something is wrong with Wallace."

"What do you mean?"

Her tone was somber. "He's despondent. Even more than normal. I don't understand what's happening here, but I wish you would come home."

Marshall sighed. If she only knew how much he wanted to come home. "I want to, but I can't."

"Do you… do you miss me?" Another long silence followed.

"Yes." Marshall spoke in a voice that was barely above a whisper.

"Marshall, will I ever see you again?" Her voice quivered as she spoke.

"I'm not sure. Really, I'm just not sure. You know how serious this is. Another change could alter the time line so that we never met, let alone…"

"… Made love?"

"Uh, yes." Marshall blushed, and his throat suddenly felt dry. "Look, I have to go. It's a long day tomorrow, and I need to get some sleep."

The sadness in her voice was palpable. "Alright… Marshall?"

"Yes?"

"I think I love you."

"… Thank you, Wanda. Goodnight."

Marshall hung up the phone and lay back on the bed. Why did he have such a difficult time expressing his feelings to Wanda? Was it because he couldn't trust them? Were they being manipulated by Mr. Cox? Did Mr. Cox even exist? Disturbing thoughts ran through his weary mind as he fell into

266

a deep sleep without taking off his clothes or even moving from his original spot. He wouldn't sleep well, but at least the night would be dreamless.

***

Sixtus pulled up the overhead display as he lay back in bed. He still could only access the small memory dump Havas Zir placed into his internal system just before he died. The frustration was maddening since the overhead remained inactive except for this limited packet of information.

He called up the official documents yet again and scanned through them to find the most relevant accounts of the time-altering incident. The Corporates kept tight control over historical archives, and they usually eradicated subversive events from history. So, the entire episode included just two pages of analysis accompanied by three news reports preserved from the days of the ancient internet.

The first report recounted the initial explosion, which would detonate in less than twenty-four hours in Istanbul, Turkey. A second blast would follow in Mumbai, India, twelve hours later. Naturally, there was much confusion relating to the cause and consequence of the detonations. World leaders desperately tried to calm the public by rationalizing the first explosion, but the terrifying second bomb caused the delicate fabric of global cooperation to tear deeply, and only a few remaining strands stood between social order and utter destruction.

As Sixtus scrolled through Zir's last document, he noticed it was much shorter than the previous two. Since the plot to detonate the third bomb was foiled, details about the incident were sparse and incomplete.

The official version identified an unnamed law officer from Seattle who defused the Chicago device. Days earlier, when Sixtus first looked at Iglar's list and saw Curtis Roberts was living in Seattle, he wondered if there was a connection. Unfortunately, Zir's report created more questions than answers.

How could a Seattle detective stumble upon a conspiracy to destroy world order when none of the major intelligence agencies from around the globe were aware of the plot? Was it possible the person who identified himself as "Detective Jose Munoz" in Raczor's trailer was the same law enforcement official in Zir's data file? While the vagueness in the latter's report on the third bomb was frustrating, it was also predictable. The Corporates desire for strict censorship and suppression of information was so thorough, Sixtus wondered how Zir's agents had secured *any* information about these incidents.

He closed the overhead and lay his head on the pillow. *The third nuclear bomb is in Chicago; of that I am certain. The city is mentioned in Zir's report, and it's the last entry on Iglar's list.*

While he was sure of the city, Sixtus had no idea where the bomb was physically planted. Chicago encompassed a vast expanse, and unless he was able to find the Seattle detective mentioned in Zir's report, there was little or no hope he would locate the nuclear device in time.

Even in the event he found the bomb, Sixtus still had no idea what he would do about it. Zir and Liss provided conflicting accounts of the battle for control of time and the future, and neither man convinced him they were telling the truth. He wondered about the other two unidentified Time

Sculptors out there. Where were they, and who were they working for?

As Sixtus nodded off, he began to finalize his plans and settle on a course of action that gave him the best chance of stabilizing the future and improving the plight of billions of people who struggled every day just to survive. With Marshall following Zach Randall and Jarad Anston, Sixtus would track Jose Munoz in an effort to find the bomb. It wasn't much of a plan, but he had essentially nothing else to go on.

***

The morning sun peaked through the small gaps in the vertical blinds, but Sixtus was still asleep. His dreams were vivid and troubling, with haunting images of Kara standing in front of a building Sixtus knew had the nuclear bomb hidden somewhere inside. He ran towards her, shouting for her to leave, but she just stood there, smiling and waving at him.

Running in quicksand through a thickening mental fog, he tried to get there in time to pull her away, but just as he came within arm's reach, the flash of the explosion vaporized her as the frames interpolated, and time slowed until it stopped. He saw the look of confusion and terror on her face, followed by the sight of her skin burning amidst the ugly red flames and oily black smoke. In slow motion, her eyes were the last part of her body to catch fire, and she looked at him with utter contempt before the fireball consumed her.

Sixtus woke up with a start and repositioned himself on the side of the bed so his feet touched the floor. He rubbed his head and tried to shake the unsettling images from his mind while rising and walking over to the shower. Once the water was steaming, he stepped inside

269

and let it cascade over his body. The heat from the water cleared his mind of cobwebs and refreshed his frayed nerves.

Stepping out of the shower, he grabbed a towel and proceeded to commence with his regular grooming routine, dressing in a casual pair of kakis and a polo shirt. All the while, he wondered how much of the story he should tell to an already fragile Marshall. He walked up to the double connecting doors and knocked. The door on the other side opened so quickly Sixtus let out a small grunt and stepped backwards. Marshall was fully dressed and ready. He looked like he hadn't slept at all, which was awfully close to the truth.

They made their way down to the lobby and over to a large room that served as a meeting spot for executives throughout the day and the breakfast cafeteria during the morning hours. They went their separate ways to gather their food and met back at a table in a corner of the room to get some privacy. At this early hour, there were only two other people in the cafeteria. They looked like married travelers eager to eat and get on the road.

Walking over and sitting down, Sixtus was glad to see his companion eating some corn flakes and drinking juice. He looked at his own plate and began buttering his toast.

Marshall carefully laid his spoon down and looked at Sixtus. "Why didn't you tell me you knew Mr. Cox?"

Sixtus grabbed a small container of grape jelly and shrugged. "How could I anticipate you already knew him? When did you first meet?"

"I — I'm not sure. I think Cox was there in Hayden's room when he committed suicide. He's been inside my head. I wasn't even sure he's real."

"Oh, he's real alright." Sixtus paused between bites. "I'm about to tell you far more than I should, Marshall. I'm not sure if it's the right thing to do, but with this reality so compromised, I don't see much of a choice."

Marshall nodded.

"There are two nuclear explosions that will take place within the next thirty-six hours, and Mr. Cox is behind both of them."

"Nuclear explosions?" Marshall moved closer to the table and leaned in. "Where?"

"No, I'm only telling you the absolute minimum you need to know. You're not in danger, and that's all that matters to me."

"But…"

"No, and that's final. I can't take the chance that you might have a relative or close friend in the blast zone and alert them to the coming catastrophe."

Marshall opened his mouth to protest, but logic overrode his guttural reaction. "Of course," he replied softly.

"The third bomb is the key. Depending on whether it detonates, new leadership might emerge in the future. This is the outcome we need to happen."

"So, my friends were right. There is an imminent catastrophic time change event coming. The use of prescription anti-depressants within the autism community is a valid predictor of these changes."

Sixtus swallowed a bite of a rubbery tasting scrambled egg and laid the plastic fork on the paper plate. "Yes, it appears your group has been right all along."

271

"And Mr. Cox is behind it? Obviously, we have to find and dismantle all of those bombs." said Marshall.

"It's not that simple. I have no clarity on the bomb. There are conflicting accounts from the visitors from the future about the consequences of interference."

"Well, is there any question here? Nuclear explosions? Millions will die unless we intervene."

"That's exactly why I'm so reluctant to discuss this with you. You're thinking about these events from a selfish standpoint, as someone from this time would. I'm thinking of it on a much broader scale. Interfering in these explosions could damn the future to unending totalitarian rule."

Marshall leaned back in his chair and considered the argument before he took a deep breath and exhaled. "Logically, I understand it would be selfish to think only of the present. But how can we sit idly by and let millions die?"

"You must think of this on a macro level. If we diffuse the bombs, there might not be a future," said Sixtus.

Marshall lowered his head and nodded almost imperceptibly.

"Good. You're the only one who can help me in this time period. As I said last night, we have to split up. You must follow the two men who entered the trailer first. I believe you said their names were..." Sixtus flipped open his cellphone and called up the notepad. "... Jarad Anston and Zach Randall. Is that right?"

"Yes, that's right."

"Follow them and try to learn more about their intentions. How did they know Raczor? I sense they play a role in this; perhaps an important one."

"I'm not a sleuth, Jeffery. I'm a graphic artist and scientist. How would I know how to go about such a thing?"

"Oh, c'mon, Marshall. You've done nothing but detective work since this began. You discovered the timeline anomaly through detective work. The way you tracked me down would impress any self-respecting gumshoe. You have the intelligence and intuition to pull it off."

Marshall moved his chair back. He was unaccustomed to compliments outside the world of science or commercial drawing. "Well, I suppose I could try and look into it."

"Excellent, I knew I could count on you."

"And what will you be doing while I'm following Randall and Anston?

"I'll be following the detective. The one named Munoz. I have a feeling he is a key part of the time sculpt."

Sixtus reached into his pocket and pulled out a second cellphone. "Here, take this. I'm on the speed dial as number one. This is a secure phone that no one can trace. Don't use it to call anyone but me; is that clear?"

Marshall nodded.

"Give me one of your credit cards."

Marshall reached into his wallet and handed Sixtus a Visa card. Sixtus picked up his phone, punched in several numbers as he navigated to different screens before handing back the card.

"I've just transferred ten thousand dollars to your account, which should be more than enough to cover your expenses. No matter what, you are to cease all your efforts at noon two days from now. At 12:01 p.m. on that day, you go home, and you purge this entire affair from your memory. Do you understand me?"

"Yes, but that can't be the end of it."

"No, that is definitely the end of it, Marshall. Once this is finished, you go about your life as if nothing happened."

Chapter Twenty-Four

Sixtus got up from the table and motioned for Marshall to follow. After returning to their rooms and packing, they checked out of the hotel and began the short drive back to the airport.

"I'll drop you off at the car rental building so you can get your own vehicle," said Sixtus.

Marshall used his left thumb nail to push at the cuticle on his right hand. "Ok, but I'm uncomfortable dealing with people in those kinds of situations."

Sixtus looked out the driver's side window as he spoke. "I'm sorry, but you'll have to deal with the phobia. We don't have time for any of that now. You'll need a car to track down Randall and Anston. It's as simple as that."

Marshall nodded while pushing harder on his cuticle. "I suppose I'll manage, but I won't go there right away. The airport has secure routers I can hack into, so I'll try and track down Randall and Anston first. They may have left Seattle for all we know."

Sixtus agreed. "Ok, that makes sense. I have faith you can get it done. While you're at it, see if you can find out any information on Detective Jose Munoz that might be helpful."

"Of course."

Sixtus pulled the car up to the drop off area in front of the main terminal. As Marshall opened the door, Sixtus patted his arm reassuringly. "Good luck, Marshall. Remember, you must not interfere with their movements in any way. Your role is limited to surveillance. Do you understand?"

Marshall nodded while looking at Sixtus' hand. With a small shake, he freed his arm from the uncomfortable touch.

After grabbing his bag from the back seat, he made his way across the busy terminal departure roadway onto the sidewalk. Marshall turned back toward Sixtus and waved awkwardly before walking through the revolving doors. Inside, he checked the airport directory and located the computer lounge, which turned out to be a large room with numerous cushioned chairs positioned around the perimeter. Two long rows of workstations divided the room in half.

Marshall looked around, and as he hoped, there were less than a dozen people occupying the large space. This gave him a chance to find the most remote station where he could work without drawing attention. After fumbling with the latch, he pulled out his laptop and booted it up. Within seconds, he located the secure airport network and hacked into it, ignoring the public Wi-Fi.

Once inside the system, he activated the packet sniffer, Kismet, which immediately began the process of identifying the WLAN and calling up a list of associated clients to the access point. After initiating an ARP replay attack, he waited until

Kismet created a dump file. Then Airsnort took over, mining the data dump to recover the encryption key. The process would take over an hour, but it was not especially difficult. Marshall was always surprised by the outdated security protocols large bureaucracies left in place long after they were obsolete.

After the handshake was complete, Marshall activated the private intranet accessible only to the Group. He opened Bleep, which was e2e encrypted for video chat and sent out a summons to Wanda and Wallace. He knew they were tethered to connected devices, so it didn't take long for both of them to appear on his screen.

Deep frown lines creased Wanda's forehead, but Marshall was more focused on Wallace. He looked tired and haggard. His hair was bunched together in an unruly knot, and dark circles rimmed his lower eyelids. Wallace was clearly under a lot of stress, but there were more pressing matters at hand.

"I need your help, but I want you to know up front I can't answer any questions," said Marshall. Wanda stared blankly while Wallace shifted around in his seat as he reached for a cigarette and awkwardly lit up.

Wallace is smoking? Isn't he allergic to tobacco?

"Sure, Marshall," said Wallace before launching into a coughing spasm that lasted for several seconds. "You leave and lie to us about going to a graphic arts convention, and now you want a favor."

"I'm sorry, but I don't have time for all that..." Wallace cut him off mid-sentence.

"Wanda tells me you know Iglar and Hayden are dead. Do you even care? Iglar's funeral is tomorrow, and they're holding services for Hayden the next day. Will you even be here?"

Marshall lowered his head and whispered, "No."

"Then why should we help you? You don't even care. Have you checked on Kenny lately?"

"Wallace, that's enough," said Wanda in a small but firm voice. "Marshall must have his reasons. And if he needs our help, it must be important."

"Thank you, Wanda."

"Yeah, ok, well what is it then?" asked Wallace.

"I need information and the whereabouts of three people: Zach Randall, Jarad Anston and a Detective Jose Munoz from the Seattle police department. I'm sending you their names, but the spelling might not be right."

"Where do they reside?"

"I'm not sure. It may be Seattle. I really don't know…"

"That's not much to go on," said Wallace.

"I understand. But it's all I have." Marshall's mouth was dry, and he swallowed hard. "With so little information, what I'm going to ask will seem absurd. I want to know where they live, what they do for a living and where they are right now. Can you do that for me?"

"We'll try," said Wanda while twisting strands of hair. "It helps you have *three* names since we can find points of intersection that will eliminate a lot of background noise. But why is this so important?"

"Please, don't ask me any questions. I need to know what their connections are to each other and a man named 'Curtis Roberts,' who lives in Seattle."

"Curtis Roberts? Wasn't he on Iglar's list?" asked Wanda.

Marshall hoped she had forgotten the names on the list, but he should have known better. "Yes, it's the same one."

"This could take some time. I mean, there's a lot of work here. How long do we have?" asked Wallace.

"I'm in the airport, and I'm at a dead end unless you two can find Randall and Anston."

"Okay, Marshall," said Wallace with a hint of indifference. "I'll do it because the work is important, but that's the only reason."

"Wallace, please. That was unnecessary," said Wanda

"Yeah, ok, I'm sorry. Wanda, do you want to come over here, or should we meet at your lab?"

"Let's meet at the lab; the processors are more powerful there. Plus, we'll be able to maintain anonymity."

"Ok, that's fine. Give me eleven minutes and I'll be on my way. My body is signaling a bowel movement is imminent." Wallace clicked out of the connection without bothering to say goodbye, which was typical.

Marshall looked at Wanda on the small laptop screen. His ability to read the emotions of another was always inadequate, but the events of the past few days had brought a new insight. The encounter with Mr. Cox was revealing, and the residual effects of the emotions the Benefactor gave him seemed to linger on. As he looked at Wanda, he could sense, no, he could *feel* her pain. In the past, he might have abruptly ended the conversation, but this time he impulsively blurted something out.

"I—miss you."

The simple three-word sentence caused her to tilt her head, and a smile spread slowly across her lips as tears filled her eyes.

"What did you say?"

"I'm certain you heard me."

"Say it again."

He hesitated and looked away from the screen. "I said I missed you."

Her smile widened even further. "I wanted to hear those words, Marshall. You do care. I knew deep down inside you cared for me."

"Wanda, I've been thinking of you a great deal. But the whole idea of having a—relationship frightens me."

"What we have is a *good* thing, Marshall." She paused as though she was carefully considering what she would say next. "I have a business trip tomorrow, and I'll be back in three days. Will you be finished by then?"

"Yes, I hope so," he replied.

"Good. Because I don't care about the future. I just want to enjoy what we have now."

"If, no, *when* I return, I want to see you," said Marshall.

"I'd like that very much."

Wanda continued to smile shyly as Marshall considered the best way to end the conversation without the usual cold abruptness. "Well," he said, "I better let you start your research. Wallace should arrive soon, so I'll check back at three o'clock, which will give you nearly four hours to come up with something."

"Okay," she replied, but he could sense there was something more. "Marshall, I—I love you." The picture went dead as she signed off from the video chat.

Marshall sat for some time as her words echoed through his head. She told him she loved him once again. From adolescence through adulthood, he never envisioned anyone saying those words to him, let alone meaning it. Unexpected warmth flowed through his body, and it felt extraordinarily soothing.

What's happening to me? Am I being manipulated by Mr. Cox? What will become of me if I turn down his offer?

For a moment, Marshall wondered if he loved Wanda back. He couldn't deny his feelings were powerful and unsettling. He shut the laptop and slid lower in the seat, thinking of Wanda and whether he would ever see her again.

***

Sixtus left the airport without a clear idea of how, or even if, Detective Munoz might provide insight into the mystery he was facing. Havas Zir's report lacked important details, but it identified an unnamed Seattle law enforcement official as the person responsible for diffusing the Chicago bomb. Could Detective Munoz, the Seattle cop who showed up at Raczor's trailer, be that man?

He merged onto the 518 from the Airport Expressway and made his way over to I-5 North. His plan was still developing, but the first order of business was to find Detective Munoz and determine his level of involvement.

The GPS locked in on Seattle's police headquarters, located just up the road at 5th Avenue. The condition of the main north-south freeway in Seattle was really no different than the highways in Phoenix or any of the other major cities. Homeless vagrants clustered together along the shoulder, often stepping onto the roadway itself. Human waste, debris, the mentally ill, drug addicts and those who had nowhere else to go clogged the overpasses.

Fortunately, the floaters seemed relatively passive at the moment, and only two rocks were thrown at his vehicle. He passed several angry drifters shaking their fists, hurling fresh feces or shooting snot at the passing cars, but this was nothing out of the ordinary.

Cruising up the freeway, his mind wandered absently. When he wasn't thinking about the Time Sculptors dilemma, the image of Kara crept into his thoughts. Sixtus couldn't help but wonder how she was getting along and if she traveled to her father's home in Nebraska. He pulled out his cell phone and called up the speed dial list. Kara's number was in the first position.

His finger moved to the screen and rested on number one. Although he warned her against calling his alias, he privately hoped she would. The pressure on the speed dial button increased as he passed the sign for Jefferson Park and the Jefferson Park Golf Course.

As the names of the facilities registered, Sixtus' dropped the phone to the floorboards. The car swerved as he moved over one lane and took the Columbian Way exit. He directed the vehicle onto Spokane Street and drove to Beacon Avenue, which divided the park from the golf course. He looked at the large signs on either side of the street that identified each attraction. Sixtus ran his hand through his hair and tried to control his breathing.

How could the signs be wrong? The names were changed years ago.

In the early 2000s, Seattle societal elites had planned to honor an older local philanthropist by naming the park and golf course after him. However, right before the renaming resolution came to the floor of the city council, a woman from the man's past stepped forward and accused him of rape. Although the incident happened a little over seven years prior, the victim had strong evidence she preserved, including a medical report and DNA. At the time of the assault, she decided to keep the episode silent, but a monument named after the monster who attacked her was too much to bear.

Ultimately, the cascading effect of the revelation affected the philanthropist's immediate family. His son's trucking business lost customers and subsequently filed for bankruptcy. A brother lost financing for a construction project that went into foreclosure. As often happens, a single act can affect an entire family's lineage for generations. In this case, the name of Claude LaRue was permanently tainted.

Although long forgotten, the cumulative consequences of the LaRue scandal affected the standing of an Udulate family in the distant future. By changing the outcome of this one event, the family would enjoy more privilege and status.

For Sixtus, the mission was minor and relatively simple compared to many of the others. After stalking LaRue for a couple weeks prior to the assault, he tracked the assailant as he moved silently through the back alleys of the Pike Place Plaza on the night of the rape. LaRue followed the victim as she left a renowned downtown theater and made her way to a parking garage to fetch her car.

Sixtus knew LaRue would accost her on the deserted second level, so he hid behind a support pillar. The elevator door opened, and the woman began walking towards her car. Sixtus paused until she was far enough down the aisle before he moved away from the pillar and toward the stairs. Right on cue, LaRue reached the second level.

Before he could react, Sixtus jumped on the man and hit him in the solar plexus with a punch from the Kenpo discipline. LaRue doubled over, struggling for breath. He clutched his chest, but his hands were spastic as the punch struck the largest and most complex nerve in the center of his abdomen. Sixtus grabbed him by the hair and pulled his head up so they were staring at each other eye to eye. LaRue's face was a mask of terror.

"You pathetic scumbag," Sixtus recalled saying. "If I ever see you within five miles of that woman or any other woman except your wife, you won't get away with just a single punch. Do I make myself clear?"

LaRue nodded and held up a weakened arm to protect against another blow, but Sixtus pushed it away and slapped him hard across the face. "Do you understand?"

Whimpering in a high-pitched voice, LaRue said, "Yes," just as his intended victim drove past. She slowed, but Sixtus looked up and smiled, which seemed to offer enough assurance. She drove away, apparently not inclined to interfere in the affairs of two men in a dark downtown parking garage late at night.

Since the assault never took place, LaRue went on to gain notoriety as a philanthropist and model citizen. The incident had frightened him so thoroughly he kept his perverse sexual fantasies to himself and instead privately immersed himself in rape porn. As a result, nearly seven years later in the mid-2000s, the park and golf course were renamed the "Claude S. LaRue Park" and the "Claude S. LaRue Golf Course" respectively.

Yet, the time change had somehow unraveled. Jefferson Park and the Jefferson Park Golf Course kept their original names. Someone had deconstructed his mission, or was it another manifestation of the fabric of time collapsing?

The tires on the Altima squealed as Sixtus accelerated. In his mind, the scales were tipping slightly in favor of Zir's explanation. If the contaminated timeline wasn't altered in dramatic fashion, it seemed an unchanged reality would ultimately lead to the Corporates.

***

"Whaa?" Marshall opened his eyes and tried to reconcile the repeated ringing of a chime on his computer. He didn't think he'd fallen asleep, but a quick glance at the clock on the far wall confirmed he was out for several hours.

He blinked and rubbed his eyes as he woke the device from standby mode. Wanda and Wallace were already connected, and he could see the look of concern on their faces.

"Marshall, are you ok? You look terrible," said Wanda.

"I'm fine." He cleared his throat of phlegm. "What did you find?"

"Well," said Wanda. "It took a while, but we got it."

"You two do exceptional work. Who are they?

"They're both accountants from New Mexico. One works for the IRS; the other is in business for himself. No priors, no arrests."

"Ok, where are they?"

"They're both in Portland in a safe house under the jurisdiction of the Seattle police department. But we're not sure if the Chief or ranking officers know about it."

"Tell me how you were able to find them?"

Wanda smiled. "Based on what you said, we questioned whether they lived in the local area. We did a search through the airline database, and sure enough, we found two tickets in their names originating from Albuquerque via Las Vegas. In seems they rented a car in Randall's name. As you're aware, these rental companies equip their vehicles with hidden GPS devices to keep track of where and how their customers drive. We hacked the system, found the rental agreement and traced the energy GPD identifier to a house in Portland."

"It's not where they are, but it's who they are that's most disturbing," said Wallace as he dragged on a cigarette.

"What do you mean?"

"We're not sure," Wallace choked out words and smoke simultaneously. "But we think these two guys are obsessed with people who commit suicide."

Chapter Twenty-Five

Sixtus arrived at Seattle Police Headquarters with a sense of frustration. He parked in an adjacent public garage and pondered exactly how to find Munoz. Walking in and asking to see the Detective might arouse suspicion since he didn't have a legitimate reason to talk to him. Naturally, he couldn't reveal the true nature of his interest.

Am I wasting my time with this? Should I focus on finding the other two Time Sculptors? But where would I start since I don't have leads on them either? Unsure and hesitant, he decided to stay and wait for Munoz. Hopefully, he might even get a call from Marshall.

As if on cue, his phone rang, except it wasn't his companion. Sixtus froze when he saw the number on the screen. Kara was calling from the secure phone he gave her.

"Kara, I—I'm so sorry." There was no point in wasting precious time with senseless greetings.

She mumbled softly, "I'm sorry too, Jeffery, and I feel the same way. I called because… because I miss you, and I need you."

Sixtus' heart nearly seized when he heard her words. Could this be a dream? Was he the victim to a cruel prank?

"I love you, Jeffery bear."

He melted. "I love you too, Kara bear. I miss you terribly, and I'm so sorry. I should have been more honest. I wish…"

"There's no need for any of that. I'm sure you just wanted to keep me safe, and I probably wouldn't have believed you, anyway. Let's put all that behind us."

"Kara, it's *not* safe. That's the whole problem. There's nothing I want more than to have you near me, but I can't put you in danger."

"I don't *care* about any of that. I just want to be near you."

"I — can't. I…"

"Dammit, Jeffery. If we're not in this together, we have nothing. I won't spend the rest of my life without my soul mate. If you can't trust me with all of your secrets…" She paused before speaking in a very soft voice. "Jeffery, I said for better or for worse."

How could he argue with her? The last of his emotional defenses dissolved into rubble. *What if this time line suddenly changed, and she disappeared from my life completely? The time we have left together is all that matters.*

"It goes against my better judgment, but I want to see you so badly, and you're right about everything. I'm — I'm in Seattle."

"Seattle? What are you doing there?"

"Kara, you already know enough to endanger your life, and I won't make it worse. If you want to come here, I'll pick you up at the airport. But it's a very treacherous situation."

"I'll come, Jeffery. But when I do, you're going to tell me everything."

He sighed. "Yes... everything."

Her tone brightened considerably. "Good. I'll make the reservation right away. There are several flights to Seattle out of Portland International."

"You're in Oregon? I don't understand. I thought you were going to your family's house in Nebraska?"

"You suggested I stay away from there. And you're aware of the problems I have with my family. I called a college friend who still lives in Portland, and she invited me to stay. I guess it's just fate we're so close."

"Yes, fate. That must be it. I—I'm not great with expressing my feelings. But I do love you, Kara. I hope you understand that. My life is utterly meaningless without you."

"I love you too. But you've got to tell me everything."

"I understand... I'll see you soon."

Sixtus sighed and laid the phone on the seat. Kara was coming back to him, and she would soon be in his arms. Everything suddenly seemed brighter and full of renewed hope. Maybe it would all work out after all. Lost in pleasant thoughts, Sixtus was startled when the phone lit up again. This time it was Marshall.

"Well, well, it's the ace detective. I've been waiting for your call. What have you got for me?"

Marshall frowned and looked at the phone, choosing to ignore the "chummy" greeting. "The two guys at Curtis Roberts' place are accountants from Albuquerque," he said. "One works for the government, and there's nothing to indicate they had anything to do with Curtis Roberts before yesterday."

"So, they flew in from Albuquerque. Is that where they live?"

"Yes. They've lived there for many years. They actually flew to Seattle from Las Vegas, but I have no idea what they were doing there."

"Hmmm… Why would two accountants from New Mexico fly in to visit a suicidal vagrant living in a trailer park in Seattle with a stopover in Vegas, no less?" Sixtus was asking himself as much as he was asking Marshall.

"I'm not very good at figuring out what motivates people to carry out perplexing actions. Could they have known he was a Time Sculptor?"

"I don't see how that's possible. Do you know where they went?"

"Yes. They rented a car and drove to an address in Portland. As I'm sure you know, every rental car has a hidden GPS, so they were easy to track."

"*Portland?* Why go there?" Sixtus rubbed his neck. It had to be a coincidence that Kara was in the same city as the two fugitive accountants.

"Again, I don't have a clue. But there's something unusual about their destination. The house is owned by a Carlos Munoz. It's not hard to speculate that he is a relative of Detective Jose Munoz'."

Sixtus let the information filter through his mind. He was thinking out loud again as he spoke. "Two FBI agents confront Detective Munoz and the New Mexico accountants. They kill the agents, and Munoz stashes his new friends, or accomplices as the case may be, in a relative's house. Strange indeed. Do they have any warrants?"

"No warrants or arrest records for either of them," said Marshall. "They're just very average people that led average lives until a few days ago.

"Then how did the FBI know about them?" asked Sixtus.

"My friends found nothing on that, but they're still checking."

Sixtus pinched the bridge of his nose. "Did your friends uncover anything on Detective Munoz? I really need more intel on him."

"No, not yet. They prioritized Randall and Anston, but they're working on Munoz too."

"Okay. I'll continue to monitor police headquarters to see if our detective shows up. If there's something urgent, call me right away… And stay safe."

"I'm trying. But my anxiety is oppressive. I—I can't even move from the chair. I feel like I'm burning alive." Marshall's skin was clammy, and beads of sweat formed on his brow.

"Look, Marshall, you must get out to that house and find Randall and Anston. I'm sorry, I understand this is hard, but you have to do it."

"… Marshall? Marshall, are you there?"

"… Yes, I was able to stand up."

Sixtus took a long, deep breath and puffed out his cheeks as he exhaled. "Good… er, that's excellent, Marshall. So, you're not going to fly, right?"

"I can't fly again. I won't make it."

"Alright, then you need to put one foot in front of the other and get yourself to the rental car desk. Can you do that?"

"Yes, I think so. I'm going to take some gabapentin. It helps with my anxiety although the side effects are debilitating. It's crushing me right now."

"You can do this, Marshall. Call me when you reach the house in Portland. Remember, park down the street and stay out of sight."

Marshall let out a long sigh that signaled his annoyance. "I'm not imbecilic, Mr. Clayton. I recognize the importance of remaining covert in such an operation."

"Ah, okay. Sorry."

The flash of anger Marshall experienced seemed to drive the anxiety away for a moment. He used the respite to quicken his pace, and he robotically followed the pathway that took him to the shuttle and ultimately the rental car facility. Working entirely on autopilot, he blocked out the distractions by consciously isolating his rational mind from the feelings of panic.

After enduring the painful wait and the excessively positive attitude of the woman behind the counter, Marshall finally received his paperwork packet and the keys to the rental. The counter woman beamed as she handed him the documents folded sharply and placed inside a durable envelope. Her cheerful smile was beyond annoying, and when she said, "Thank you so much for choosing Fast and Quick Rent-A-Car. Here is your paperwork and the keys to your Corolla," Marshall had to restrain himself from delivering a blow to her perfectly painted lips.

He turned from the counter and started walking to the car lot when a cold chill passed through his body and spread out to his extremities. The flesh on the back of his neck rose up in small bumps signaling primordial fear.

Mr. Cox? Marshall felt nauseous, and his eyelids fluttered. The disorientation lingered briefly before the sensation passed. When he opened his eyes, he was standing back at the rental counter.

"Thank you so much for choosing Fast N Quick Rent-A-Car. Here is your paperwork and keys to your Corolla." The counter woman smiled exactly as before while handing him the documents and keys.

Stunned, Marshall looked down, but both his hands were empty. He succumbed to another chill, but this one came from a sudden spike in his anxiety. *Is this déjà vu again? Am I losing my mind?*

Tentatively, he reached out and took the envelope and keys. The counter person's smile never wavered. He turned to walk away but didn't reach the door before the same disorienting sensation returned. When the mental fog parted, he was back at the counter for a third time.

"Thank you so much for choosing Fast N Quick Rent-A-Car. Here is your paperwork and keys to your Chevy Cruze." Her mannerisms were identical, down to the slight raise of the left eyebrow when she finished the sentence. However, this time there was something different. She gave him a Chevy Cruze instead of a Toyota Corolla. He contemplated asking her if she remembered the last two encounters but instinctively knew she wouldn't.

They stood staring at each other for some moments until the silence and lack of action became awkward. Her smile faded only slightly. "Sir, is there a problem?"

"No, I…" Again, he took the keys and the envelope and ambled slowly away. Sometime later, he realized the price for the mandatory insurance had doubled between the first rental event and the third. However, in hindsight, it was easy to figure out why.

This time he was able to reach the door without a glitch and walked out to the parking lot. A shuttle picked him up and drove him over to a silver Chevy Cruze sitting in its assigned slot. The driver of the shuttle let him out, tipped his cap and mumbled, "Be safe out there."

Once Marshall placed his bag in the car, he immediately pulled out his phone and dialed Sixtus, who picked up on the first ring.

"I felt it, Marshall. Time rewound twice. The whole timeline is falling apart."

"Why is it only you and I are experiencing this?"

"I imagine we're not the only ones. You are hyper-sensitive to the changes because your mind is tuned differently. Perhaps your friends are experiencing the glitches as well. Some dismiss it as strong déjà vu. I am aware of all time-related anomalies because I exist outside of conventional space time."

"What are we going to do? This is serious and frightening."

"I know. But there's nothing we *can* do except follow our leads and hope we're not too late."

Marshall entered the address Wanda had given him into his phone and let the GPS plot a course. Moving the car out of the airport, he turned out onto 188th Street toward I-5. He couldn't have been fifty feet outside the protective fenced perimeter before a floater came running at his car with a large, fresh lump of feces in his hand. Marshall pushed on the accelerator just as the floater threw the disgusting projectile. The *splat* sound on the roof confirmed the launch was successful, and the floater jumped for joy and cursed wildly. Marshall sped away, fighting his gag reflex.

While driving through the city, he recoiled at the sudden surge in the number of homeless people out on the streets. The radio was on, but he could clearly hear the crying and screaming of distressed children, women and men lying on the sidewalk and shoulder of the road. The surrounding buildings looked to be in greater disrepair than when he arrived. Where only a few people wandered the streets before, now large crowds of floaters lined both sides of the road and moved aimlessly in and around the many shuttered businesses. They seemed more agitated and angry than he remembered, and they pelted passing cars with a steady stream of stones, bottles and excrement.

The underpass at I-5 transformed into an endless city of makeshift cardboard and blanket shelters. The bridge offered some relief from the elements, but the glut of humanity occupying the small space grew twenty times larger since he arrived.

Could this be because of the time glitches? Are they degrading the timeline and creating even more misery?

He pulled onto the freeway just as his phone buzzed. Wanda was calling.

"Marshall, did you just experience really strong déjà vu? It seemed so strange, and it happened twice, I'm not sure how to explain it. Wallace felt it too."

He hesitated before answering. The last thing he wanted was for Wanda to become more frightened. "Ah, no, I didn't notice anything."

"Really? I wondered if the time changes caused it, but this was different. Wallace said people in the Lincoln House are tearing the place apart. It's all over the news."

"How strange. I hope everyone is all right over there." Marshall tried his best to sound calm and natural.

"How are things outside where you are? Since the déjà vu, I think it's become much worse here."

"Every day things are becoming progressively worse. I'm seeing a lot more homeless people, and the level of violence is greater. No one seems to notice it though. Except those like us, I guess."

"I'm sure you're right," she said. "I suppose it's nothing."

"Wanda, I have to go, but for God's sake please stay safe."

"I will… Marshall, I have something else I need to tell you. It's the real reason I called."

"What is it?"

"It's Kenny. He's losing his mind or something. Since Hayden and Iglar died, he's been despondent. He wants to come and see you."

"Uh, uh, not now, Wanda. That's just not possible."

"If he doesn't come out there, I'm afraid he might do something to himself. He already tried…"

"What? To kill himself?"

"Yes. Luckily, his father called him right after he overdosed on anti-depressants. The paramedics arrived just in time. Now, he's saying he'll do it again if you won't see him."

"Wanda, I can't. You have no idea."

"I have every idea, Marshall. You're in great peril, and I know this entire timeline could change at any moment. We might not know each other, and I might not exist. It's driving me mad, but I'm still very worried about Kenny. I just…" Her words trailed off, and Marshall pictured her frantically twirling her hair into a knot.

"I understand, Wanda. But this is the worst possible time."

She didn't say anything for several seconds. "You'll have to see him. He's landing at the Seattle airport in an hour."

"*What?* That can't happen. I'm on my way to... Wait a minute. How did you find me?" Before the words were out of his mouth, he recognized the folly in asking. Of course they found him. Wanda and Wallace were two of the best source trackers in the world. Even with its enhanced security, tracing a direct connection on Bleep was child's play for these two.

"We traced your feed back to the airport."

"That was—deceitful... Look, I'm not a medical practitioner. I can't help Kenny."

"I hope you're wrong, Marshall. He mumbles about something he says only you would understand. He keeps saying, 'the dark one,' over and over again. It really scares me. I've upped my dosage, and I'm crumbling into nothing here. Do you know what he means?"

Her question caught Marshall off guard, and he brought his hand up to his forehead. First it was Igler, then Hayden and now Kenny. Mr. Cox was targeting his friends. "Uh, no. It sounds like Kenny is hallucinating or something. What time did you say he's supposed to arrive?"

"His flight will land in a little over an hour."

"Ok, Wanda, I'll meet with him because you've left me with no choice. But you don't know what you've done."

"Don't stress me out any more, Marshall. I can't take it." Her last words tailed off in obvious anguish, and she disconnected the phone.

By the time Marshal turned around and headed back to SeaTac, he realized driving to Portland today was impractical, so he made reservations at the same airport hotel they stayed at the previous night. His plan was to stabilize Kenny and get him on a plane back to Phoenix in the morning. Then he would set out to find Randall and Anston.

As he drove back into the city, the sun was setting, which brought out the mentally unstable people from the shadows in numbers. The fires in the empty oil barrels were lighting up, and the ominous glances from those huddled around the flames signaled their contempt and unspoken threats. Marshall noted there were few vehicles on the road. In this altered reality, driving at night was too dangerous. He wondered if picking up Kenny and checking into a hotel for the night might have saved him from a potential confrontation with the growing population of the angry, disenfranchised and the unbalanced.

Marshall arrived at the airport just as Kenny's plane was making its final descent. Once inside the terminal, he went to the security checkpoint and glanced up at the screen. The passengers arriving from Phoenix were just beginning to disembark. Several minutes later, he noticed the unmistakable shuffle of his small friend, lagging behind the main group as he moved down the slight incline towards the main terminal.

As he approached, Marshall noticed the anguish on Kenny's face. While the Group was never a gathering for the jovial, Kenny brought a badly needed sense of humor and optimism. But now, his face looked pale, drawn and troubled.

When their eyes met, a smile replaced Kenny's somber expression for just a moment. Marshall smiled back, but he couldn't hide his obvious concern.

"Kenny, I'm glad you're here, but your timing is curious."

"I'm sorry, Marshall. I had to come. I needed to see you and talk to you in person. I'm having some—difficulties since you left."

"Yes, so I've heard, but we can discuss all of that later. I booked us two rooms at a hotel across the street. You can relax and tell me what's bothering you."

"Ok. There's a lot to tell. And I have an important message for you…"

Chapter Twenty-Six

He didn't know it at the time, but Sixtus missed Marshall by only a few minutes as he arrived back at the airport to pick up Kara. After parking his car and making his way to the terminal, he verified her plane was on time and moved over to the passenger arrival area. When he saw her walking down the exit ramp from the plane, he wondered if he might faint. The loose folds of her full-length skirt followed the slow sashay of her hips, accentuating her natural curves. Radiant was the only way he could describe her.

Kara never needed a lot of time to primp. Her beauty was intrinsic, and sometimes Sixtus wondered if makeup only concealed her natural elegance. She moved slowly and scanned the crowd waiting at the arrival gate. He waved and tried to catch her attention, and on the third pass, their eyes locked. Kara smiled, waved back, and quickened her pace.

As she reached the end of the ramp, Sixtus moved through the crowd and grabbed her with both hands, pulling her tight against his chest. She returned his embrace with a hint of hesitation that only Sixtus could have noticed, but he hardly cared.

"My God, I missed you," he said.

She looked up and smiled warmly. "I missed you too, Jeffery." As the hug lingered, she placed her hand on his chest and gently pushed away. "We have so much to discuss."

Kara didn't have any luggage except for a carry-on bag, so they left the airport and took a shuttle to the same hotel where he stayed the night before. Sixtus wished he booked a room at the Marriott on the waterfront, but time was not permitting. Kara's presence was a distraction he could ill afford, and inviting her here was utterly selfish. To assuage his guilt, he remained close to the airport and Detective Munoz. She would leave in the morning, and he would continue his quest.

They walked over to the lobby of the 4-star hotel, and Sixtus left her seated in a recently reupholstered oversized chair. The environment was geared for business travelers rather than romance, but with freshly polished marble floors, abundant vegetation and general cleanliness, the setting wouldn't be a distraction either.

He went to the front desk, got his room key and walked back over to Kara. She didn't see him approach and appeared to be looking away deep in thought. He noticed her eyes were dull, and her expression hardened in a way he never recalled seeing before. When she sensed his presence, her face instantly lit up again, and the warm smile returned. He took her hand and led the way to the elevator, and after a brief ride, they exited on the 11th floor. Unlike last evening when Sixtus opted for two basic rooms with queen beds, tonight he reserved a deluxe suite with a spa and separate bedroom.

He let her in and followed as the door closed softly. Sixtus already had Kara locked in a passionate embrace before the latch bolt engaged with a muted *click*. The next few moments were blurred as they struggled to shed clothing while continuing to kiss and clutch at newly exposed flesh. When Sixtus felt her hands grasping at his belt buckle, he fought against the rising fire that begged for sweet release. Every touch of her skin was a sensuous explosion of passion that sent shivers through his body.

He pushed her down on the bed with purpose and lowered himself onto her. Sixtus marveled at how their bodies fit together perfectly. In fact, everything between them seamlessly meshed as though they were two halves of a complete whole. Their intellectual interests, creative passions and philosophical journeys were always complimentary and congruous. Sixtus often felt that if the universe had constructed the perfect mate for him, as the Corporates often did for themselves, it would have been Kara.

After some moments of close intimacy, she guided him inside her, and they assumed a slow rocking rhythm. This was how she liked it, so Sixtus continued the tease, bringing her close to a climax and then easing off. He watched her eyes flutter and mouth open slightly as he increased the urgency of his thrusts. Closing in on the point of no return, he considered slowing again, but by the time the thought crossed his mind it was too late. Even if he wanted to, he was aware of Kara clawing at his back and wrapping her legs tightly around his torso.

"Don't you dare stop," she said. "Fuck me hard. Don't you goddamn stop."

"You like it, don't you, you little slut? Tell me how you... I'm—argh…"

"Yes, yes," she whimpered as her long nails raked his back to the point of drawing blood. She grabbed him and pulled him close as they both released, but he stayed in her arms, needing her as much as he needed air, food or water. Sixtus really didn't exist in any meaningful way without Kara. He knew it, and so did she. Still, he was never sure if her commitment was as strong or as desperate as his. At those moments when he was honest with himself, Sixtus realized he already knew the answer, but it brought a sense of pain he couldn't face.

With those disturbing thoughts running through his head, he withdrew and rolled over on his side. Kara lay panting, her arm draped across her forehead. After a few moments, she reached over and reassuringly patted his chest while snuggling closer. They remained motionless for some time, enjoying the endorphins that flowed through their bodies. Finally, he rose and walked to the mini bar.

"I think this calls for a bit of a splurge. I'm opening the wine."

"That sounds great," she replied. "A good vintage?"

"Ah, it's a house cabernet." He shrugged.

"That's fine. As long as it has alcohol in it, I'm good."

They laughed as Sixtus removed the cork and filled two glasses from the cabinet and brought them back to bed without spilling. After giving her one, he held out his arm in a classic pose for a toast.

"I'm so happy to see you, Kara. To us: may we spend the rest of our days together." She smiled, and they touched glasses. The wine was thick, bitter and grossly overpriced, but Sixtus couldn't care less. He was with Kara, and everything else was background noise.

She looked thoughtfully at her glass and swirled the wine around, glancing up at him several times before lowering her gaze as her long blonde hair fell and obscured her face.

"So, Jeffery," she said, "I think it's time you tell me what's going on here. I can't live a lie any longer. It seems like I know everything about you, but then I realize I don't know you at all."

He sipped the wine and swallowed slowly. "You know everything that matters. How I feel about you. That part is true."

"That's the only reason I'm here, Jeffery. But there's so much I don't understand." She paused a moment and then inched closer to him. "Is your name really Sixtus?"

His thumb rubbed absently against the rim of the wine glass. The pressure he applied was so heavy, he was afraid it might break. "Yes," he whispered. "My name is Sixtus Maras."

She remained close to him, but her expression didn't change. "That's such an unusual name. *Sixtus Maras*. I suppose I can understand why you changed it to Jeffery Clayton."

"Yes, it always drew unnecessary attention." A single nervous laugh followed.

"Is that an ethnic name? I can't place it."

"Yes, it's — Italian. Roman actually."

"I see. Is the name 'Daxtar Liss' also Italian? Or 'Havas Zir'?" Are they Italian too?"

Sixtus hung his head and didn't reply.

"In Italy, are they ruled by 'The Corporates' or are they controlled by the 'Kren', Jeffery?"

He raised his head slowly. "How do you know about those things?"

"I have ears. I turned on the intercom and listened to your conversation with Daxtar Liss in the den. I was worried, and something struck me as odd about him from the beginning. You don't have old friends, Jeffery. No scrap books, photos or phone calls from people in your past. In five years, he was the first. That worried me."

"So, how much do you know?"

"I couldn't hear very well. You talked about a catastrophe that affects the future or something like that. I wasn't entirely sure. Then, when I was grabbed by that horrible Zir, I understood you were in serious trouble. What is that trouble, Jeffery? Who are you, really, and where are you from?"

"If I told you, I imagine you would think I was insane."

"Try me. Not knowing is making me wonder if what's going on with you isn't far worse than insanity."

He sighed deeply. In his training, nothing carried more importance than maintaining the secrecy and integrity of his identity and missions here in the past. In a best-case scenario, she might believe he was deranged and would leave him for good without ever talking about his delusions with anyone. With the fabric of time itself resting in the balance, he should resist telling her anything related to the 24th century. Giving Marshall a glimpse into the future was unforgivable, but this was much worse.

She looked at him with those large, doleful blue eyes, and his good sense and resistance crumbled. "You know my name, but what you don't know is that I am from the future…."

***

Marshall sat across from Kenny and sipped his iced tea while staring at the cold food that sat on his plate. The restaurant was nearly empty, occupied by a young couple reluctant to end their date and an older gay couple sharing a double-scoop chocolate sundae. Kenny was looking down at his pot roast and scalloped potatoes, his elbows resting on the table. He held his head up by using the thumb and forefinger of each hand placed symmetrically on his forehead.

"I can't take it anymore, Marshall. It's driving me insane. Everything changes all the time. I don't know if I'm still me from one minute to the next. Iglar killed himself and now Hayden. We're dropping like flies. There won't be any of us left soon."

Marshall recognized his friend's fragility without actually sensing it. "Kenny, we're all struggling with this. I'm just trying to make sense out of what's happening and hoping to find a way to stop the changes."

"Tell me, what are you working on, Marshall? Will it save us? Please, I need to know."

"I'm sorry... I can't. I can't tell you what I'm involved in. I won't endanger anyone else."

"I'm your best friend, Marshall. And I'm hurting. I'm so depressed and anxious, and the hole is so deep I can't climb out of it. I keep dividing by six. 37,345 divided by 6 is 6,224. 37,346 divided by 6 is 6224.3. 37,347 divided by..."

"Okay, Kenny, okay. You don't have to do the division thing."

Kenny stopped and shook his head. When he spoke again, his voice dropped an octave and was barely above a whisper. "I wanted to do it, Marshall."

"Do what?"

"I wanted to kill myself."

Marshall leaned back and rubbed his face. "You can't talk that way. If you're in crisis, let's get you some help."

"You're the only one who can help, Marshall. I— What's happening to me?"

Marshall reached over and picked up the receipt and his credit card from the check tray. "C'mon, Kenny, let's go to the hotel." He rose from the table while Kenny remained seated with his head still bowed and held up by his hands.

"Kenny, let's go." With what appeared to be an enormous effort, his friend got to his feet and followed Marshall out to the parking lot. The night air was cool, damp and crisp, and Marshall felt traces of a shower as small droplets periodically tickled the skin on his forearms and neck.

They walked through the dimly lit parking lot next to the hotel and across the street from the airport. It wasn't safe to be out at night anywhere anymore, but the fires from the oil barrels were off in the distance, and it didn't seem likely they would encounter any trouble on the short trek back to the hotel.

"So, tell me what led you to want to commit suicide," said Marshall.

Kenny shrugged and thrust his hands deep into his pants pockets. "Losing Iglar and Hayden was terrible. And then… I had no one to turn to. You left me alone."

Kenny stopped walking and tilted his head. It took Marshall a few steps to realize his friend was no longer beside him. He looked back at Kenny, who had a peculiar look on his face.

"What's wrong? Why did you stop?" Kenny continued to stare, but his expression hardened as his eyes widened. He raised his hand and extended his index finger, pointing directly at Marshall.

"You should have told the truth, Marshall. I gave you every chance to tell me the truth."

"What are you talking about? Kenny, let's go. I don't like it out here in the dark. Those homeless people aren't that far away. Let's go to the hotel."

"You denied him. You had the chance to pledge your loyalty, but you denied him. That isn't right. You shouldn't have done that."

"Denied who? Denied what? You're not making much sense."

"Stop acting like you don't get it." Kenny backed away slowly, but his arm remained extended, and the finger straightened further with an even greater sense of accusation. "You were going to commit suicide too; you're no better than me."

"I never said I was better than you, Kenny. I'm not better than you now. But how—how did you know?"

"About how you wanted to kill yourself? From the Benefactor, of course. He knows everything, Marshall. He's the Dark One, and he's there to help anyone who's dug in so deep they're suffocated by the despair."

"You mean, Mr. Cox? There's something very sinister about him, Kenny."

"He offered all of us gifts, including you, Marshall. I'm not the dumb one anymore. My head is filled with so much smart stuff it hurts. But I don't mind. He gave you emotions. You felt normal for the first time in your life. Are you going to give it all up?"

"I don't know…" Marshall pushed his hand through his hair a couple times. Kenny's revelations were troubling and unsettling. Mr. Cox appeared to be omnipotent.

Who in God's name is he?

"Kenny, let's talk at the hotel. Just walk with me. This dark parking lot is stimulating my limbic system, and it's causing me great distress. Let's go back, please."

Kenny didn't move, but his expression softened. His arm dropped to his side, and he retracted the finger.

"That's it. Walk with me. We're best friends, remember?"

The last words brought a smile that spread slowly across Kenny's lips. He shrugged sheepishly, which was his usual way of acquiescing, and he started walking again. "Ok, Marshall. We'll ta — ."

Kenny never finished his sentence. Marshall felt the cold chill creep through his body as the black fog rolled in and obscured his vision and cluttered his mind. He fell, no, stumbled backwards a couple steps before the confusion cleared, and his eyes regained focus. When he looked around, he saw Kenny was once again standing behind him with the same scowl and pointed finger from moments ago.

Words flowed out of Marshall's mouth he couldn't control. "You mean, Mr. Cox? There's something very sinister about him, Kenny."

"He offered all of us gifts, including you, Marshall." Kenny grimaced and repeated the identical words from before. "I'm not the dumb one anymore. My head filled with so much smart stuff it hurts. But I don't mind. He gave you emotions. You felt normal for the first time in your life. Are you going to give it all up?"

They stood silently looking at each other. Kenny brought his arm slowly back down to his side as a look of panic replaced the hostility.

"Oh please, not now," said Kenny. "You felt it, Marshall. Don't deny you felt it. Time just reset again. It happened back in Phoenix yesterday. Something's wrong here, and it's getting worse."

"Kenny, calm down. We're both alright. We're not even sure if these echoes affect anything."

Kenny shook his head and mumbled. "No, no, no. I can't do this anymore. It's driving me crazy. Now time is repeating itself. Am I the same person I was before? There's no point to this, Marshall."

"Kenny, we can talk it out. Come with me."

"No, Marshall, I can't. Are you with Mr. Cox? Are you *with* him? You know he's the only answer."

"I—I don't know that, Kenny. I'm not thinking about it right now. I just want to get back to my room."

Kenny kept backing away, and Marshall started to follow, but his agitated friend pushed his palm forward as a caution. "Don't. Don't come any closer. It's too late. I can't stand this anymore." Suddenly, Kenny broke into a sprint across the parking lot in the direction of the freeway and the floaters standing around the burning barrels a hundred yards away.

Stunned, Marshall stared blankly as Kenny ran at full speed. His fight/flight response activated instantly, and his instinct screamed to avoid the danger presented by the violent homeless people up ahead. Yet, Marshall's sense of loyalty overruled his doubt, and he set out after his friend with no chance of catching him.

Kenny ran toward the throng of floaters in wide-eyed terror while screaming unflattering epithets at the top of his lungs. A group of vagrants moved slowly forward to intercept him with a sense of indifference. In these times, Kenny's behavior was all too commonplace among the millions addicted to PCP, fentanyl, sterno and other lethal drugs.

Marshall continued to pursue his friend, not realizing he too was yelling. Desperately shrieking Kenny's name and pleading with him to stop, the effort proved futile. The gap between them was widening, and by the time Kenny plunged into the floater crowd, Marshall was still at least thirty yards away.

Arms, legs and balled fists greeted the small man with obscene violence both primal and brutal. The first punch landed to Kenny's midsection, and he doubled over and clutched his stomach. A blow to the back of the head sent him to the pavement, and the bloodthirsty heathens swarmed. They unleashed a torrent of kicks and punches, and Kenny cried out in horrific shrieks of pain and terror that echoed back to Marshall. The beating continued for several minutes until his screams mercifully subsided and then faded away completely.

Marshall watched in stunned silence as several floaters grabbed Kenny by the limbs and carried him to the roadway, tossing his corpse in front of an approaching eighteen-wheel semi-truck. The horn blared, but the driver had no chance of stopping. Even thirty yards away, Marshall heard the sickening crunch of multiple bones as several sets of wheels ran over the body. Once the semi passed, Marshall could see severed chunks of raw meat scattered along the highway with portions of Kenny's torso flattened against the pavement.

With their bloodlust engorged and rage enflamed, the mob turned its attention to Marshall. Realizing his own life was in grave danger, he turned towards the hotel and sprinted as fast as he could. He didn't stop to look back until the foyer's double glass doors swished closed behind him.

Chapter Twenty-Seven

"I don't know, Jeffery. It's an incredible story, but it sounds preposterous." Kara took a sip of wine and regarded Sixtus from behind the glass.

"Maybe it might be easier if I said I worked for the CIA or NSA? Those men in our house were real, Kara, and they wanted something from me. So, I guess you'll either have to believe me or not."

She spoke without looking at him. "I have to admit it would explain a lot. You said you were a volunteer at a shelter, but you hardly ever talked about it. We always had money, and I never questioned where it came from. I'm sorry to say this, but I *do* almost wish you told me you were a drug dealer or something nefarious."

"Did you see any evidence of that? Strange phone calls, large quantities of cash? I doubt I could hide such a high-profile activity from you for five years." Sixtus shrugged.

"That's true." She drew out the last word as she pondered his revelation. "Let's assume, and I mean I'm being entirely hypothetical, that you are from the future. Why were Zir and Liss so eager to find you?"

He picked at a stray thread on the blanket while carefully choosing his words. "Because something terrible might happen soon, and they both were trying to persuade me to do their bidding."

"*Terrible?* What does that mean? What's going to happen?"

He shook his head. "I can't tell you that. It could be catastrophic; that's all I can say. Liss wanted me to let the original timeline play out and protect it against tampering. Zir wanted me to change the timeline. They both claimed the survival of the future depended on it."

"You realize that if you were anyone else, I might think you were insane, right?"

"I know. That's why I kept it to myself. How could I possibly explain any of it to you?"

She stood up and walked over to the window, which looked out over a beautiful courtyard lit up in a dazzling array of colored lights. "This is very frightening, Jeffery. To think reality could change at any moment—it's unsettling and terrifying."

"None of the events initiated by the Time Sculptors should have radically changed the timeline. They were always subtle, precise and tightly controlled to avoid contamination."

"And yet, it's so out of control you're concerned there may be no future."

"Or present for that matter. The outcome could have catastrophic consequences for everyone living in this time," he said

"What do you mean, Jeffery? What are the choices Zir and Liss presented, exactly?"

"I shouldn't talk about that. Really, I mean it. I've already told you too much."

She looked at him and scowled. "You promised to be truthful. I want all of it."

He exhaled with emphasis. "Do you believe me?"

She took another sip of wine and closed her eyes for several seconds. "Since I can't come up with any explanation that makes more sense, I suppose I'll have to believe you. Is it so preposterous that someone from the future could discover a way to travel back to the past? Three hundred years ago, no one thought air travel was possible, so I'll keep an open mind."

"Are you sure?" he asked. "You really want to know everything?"

"You agreed no more secrets. Talk to me, Jeffery." She leaned forward and stroked his hair tenderly.

"There's no easy way to say it. A series of nuclear bombs will detonate soon. Once the first explosion takes place, the next two will follow in twelve-hour intervals. The last one is scheduled to go off somewhere in Chicago. In the established timeline, someone deactivates the bomb before it explodes."

"Oh my God. That's horrifying. Thank God at least one will be deactivated," she said.

"Not according to Havas Zir. Remember I told you about our rulers, the Corporates? Zir claims detonating the Chicago bomb will cause the collapse of the government and the emergence of a new world order that ushers in an era of peace and benevolence."

"And what did Liss say?"

"Exactly the opposite. He says we must preserve the timeline so the insurgency will succeed, and the Corporates will be defeated."

"So, they both claim these oppressive 'Corporates' will lose power if you follow their direction. No wonder you're confused. What do you think, Jeffery?"

"I'm not sure, really. I've been trying to figure everything out without much success."

She paused before speaking but continued stroking his hair. "Isn't the solution obvious? Surely you can't allow a nuclear bomb to explode in Chicago. Millions will die, and it might destroy the future at the same time. In fact, we should try to stop the first two."

Kara moved her hands and began massaging his temples, and he mumbled, "That's the same thing Marshall said."

"Marshall? Who is that?"

Sixtus purposely left his autistic companion out of the discussion. "He's just a kid from the shelter. No one, really."

Eager to avoid further prying, he continued talking about the information he knew would interest her the most. "I know the cities where they placed the bombs but not the exact locations. I only have time to focus on the third bomb in Chicago. It's possible I have the identity of the person who deactivates the device. When he goes to disarm it, I need to be there."

"Who is he?"

"Some police officer from Seattle." He said.

"So, *that's* why you're here." She paused. "What's his name?

Sixtus sat up and looked at her quizzically. "Why is his name important?"

"Just curiosity, I suppose." She shrugged and propped up the pillows. "But just to be clear, you won't kill the policeman or do anything else that would allow that bomb to explode, right?"

"Kara, I can't make any guarantees. The Corporates are completely corrupt. I must make the right choice so the people in my time can live their lives in peace and with some sense of happiness."

"No, Jeffery, that's not good enough. You have to promise me you'll keep that bomb in Chicago from exploding. *Please*."

"I'm sorry… I just can't commit to that right now." Sixtus put his glass on the nightstand and leaned against the headboard. "Trust my judgement on this, Kara."

She shook her head. "I'm shocked, Jeffery. No matter what the consequences, I can't believe you'll allow millions to die in Chicago."

"I said I'm sorry. I wish I hadn't told you."

Kara stood up and walked into the bathroom with her purse in hand. She returned in one of the hotel's white terrycloth robes. Even though the thick folds covered her body, Sixtus still thought she looked striking. She moved back over to the bed and sat next to him, staring into his eyes as though they might reveal an answer to a perplexing question.

"Is that your final decision, Jeffery?" she asked

"I—haven't made up my mind yet if that's what you mean. I'm unsure…"

She slowly placed her right hand inside the left sleeve of the robe. "Please, Jeffery, you have to find the bomb and make sure it's disarmed."

He pursed his lip and sighed. "I'm sorry. I didn't mean to upset you…"

When Kara pulled her hand out of the robe, it wasn't empty. Her fingers were wrapped tightly around a pearl handled stiletto with a gleaming, fully extended blade. "You, bastard!" she screamed. "You're going to let all those people die?"

"What the fuck?" he yelled while rolling off the bed. She violently swung the weapon and barely missed her target as the blade plunged harmlessly into the soft cushion of the mattress.

Kara pulled the knife out and coiled to strike again. Her eyes were wide and full of contempt. When she spoke, spittle flew from her lips. "Sixtus Maras, you are a fool. We gave you every opportunity to do the right thing, but you continue to disappoint."

"Kara... I... What is this?"

"Stop calling me Kara, you dolt. I am Ninyas Yarmskis, and I am the fourth Time Sculptor..."

"*Whaaat?*" Darkness clouded his vision, and the room suddenly became oppressively hot. Sixtus wondered if he might faint as the heat continued to intensify. He used his legs to push himself back against a side wall. His breathing was heavy and labored.

"Don't act so dumbfounded, Maras. I was sent back by the Corporates five years ago to watch you. Both sides knew the pivotal role you play in determining our reality. You are a wild card. We suspect you won't interfere when the bomb is diffused, but there are more variables in this cycle, and you are conflicted. As this time line continues to deteriorate, I needed to confirm you would make the right decision."

Sixtus used the wall to steady himself as he rose to his feet. Standing there stark naked, he felt completely exposed. His instinct for survival clashed with the emotional devastation that descended on him amidst rising shock and panic.

"Kara, you are the fourth Time Sculptor? It can't be..."

"Oh, it's true, Maras. I've been with you for the last five years carrying out missions, creating back fires to stop the raging inferno you and the other Sculptors started by changing the time line. Within every loop, I tried to undo some of the accumulated damage. There's so much devastation it's almost beyond repair."

"You — you deceived me."

"Secrecy was critical to the success of the mission. Something you should understand. You see, I carried out time sculpt interventions, but I also monitored you. In the end, I needed to ensure you didn't interfere in the bomb's deactivation."

"So, are you a Corporate, Kara? Was Havas Zir right? Were you playing along with Zir when he held a knife to your throat?"

"Goddamn it, Jeffery. I said I was sent by the Corporates, not that I was aligned with them. Zir only knew of *your* identity in this reality. The imbecile had the fourth Time Sculptor at knifepoint and didn't even know it."

"This is muddled and confusing, Kara. You must have an idea who defuses the bomb? Is it the Seattle detective?"

"He's a *detective*? Thank you for another piece of vital information. No one in the future is sure who deactivated it. The Corporates manipulated history to obfuscate his or her identify. No matter how many cycles of this timeline transpire, the details of the explosion remain largely hidden. Do *you* have his name?"

Sixtus ignored the question. "Kara, don't you see what's happening? You already know the timeline is disintegrating. The more it's tampered with, the worse it gets. Every change creates multiple distortions resulting in further contamination. We must do something dramatic to stop it. I can't help but wonder if allowing the bomb to detonate might give everyone a chance at a new beginning."

"The time change contagion has corrupted you, Maras," she said. "Detonating the bomb would be a global catastrophe for the people in this time and those in the future. It also guarantees the continuation of the Corporates reign of terror. You truly are a rogue as Liss warned. I'm—sorry." The words hardly left her lips before she bounded onto the bed and used the recoil action of the mattress to launch herself at Sixtus with the knife raised high and slashing through the air.

He reached out and grabbed her wrist, but she balled her free hand into a fist and punched the side of his head as they toppled to the floor. Kara slid her leg around his and sunk a hook while rolling her body into an upright position. When she grabbed his foot and pulled back in a perfectly executed calf slicer, Sixtus grimaced and slapped the carpet repeatedly because of the intense pain.

Her move was classic academy training, and she would expect him to pull at her exposed arm to free himself. Instead, Sixtus used his weight advantage and MMA techniques from this era to rock backwards and reduce the pressure on his leg. Once he had the calf slicer neutralized, he wrapped his hand around her exposed neck and tightened it into a guillotine.

As Kara struggled to free herself, Sixtus felt like he was fighting a badger. She shrieked and gouged his skin with her nails and swung the knife wildly. Somehow, she managed to pull her head out of the guillotine and bit into the well-defined muscle in his forearm. This time, he howled in pain and instinctively slammed his fist directly into her eye, which immediately blackened and swelled.

They lay panting and regarding each other in a kind of stalemate before she pulled out of the calf slicer and kicked at his groin. Scoring a direct hit, the pain was almost unbearable, and Sixtus could only drive an elbow into her solar plexus in reply. With his eyes still shut from the pain, he heard her cough and gasp for air, and she dropped the knife while grabbing at her constricted throat. Sixtus loosened his grip on her wrist and rolled off while still clutching his damaged privates.

Her good eye blazed with anger; the other was discolored and swollen shut. It looked like half a boiled egg sat underneath her cartoonish purple and off-yellow eyelid.

"Kara, what is it you want?" he asked while panting heavily.

"It's too late, Maras. You can't be trusted."

She picked up the knife and lunged at him again, screaming and cursing like a crazed maniac. Sixtus blocked the attack and slammed his forearm in between her neck and shoulder. Before she could react, he landed another punch to the wounded eye, which caused her to grunt and reflexively pull back. The blow altered the trajectory of the knife so it missed his chest, only creasing the top of his shoulder. Still, the blade opened a nasty gash that bled profusely.

Largely unaware of the wound, Sixtus saw the blood smeared across the knife as she drew it back. The second punch to the face stunned her, and her functional eye started blinking and watering as her head lolled to the side. Sixtus rose from his knees and jumped at her, pulling the knife out of her hand as they fell to the floor. He straddled her torso and raised the weapon high over his head and looked down at her. Kara feebly put up her

321

hand defensively and shuddered. A gasp escaped her lips as tears leaked from her good eye. For a moment, Sixtus wavered.

"Jeffery, please don't," she said. "I—love you. Please understand, I had no choice. Liss said he would kill my family in the future if I didn't cooperate. Help me, Jeffery. I don't know what to do."

He looked at her for a moment and then dropped the knife, collapsing in exhaustion on top of her. Sixtus burst into tears and shook his head as he buried his face into her bosom. He only needed to hear that she loved him, and everything else became instantly irrelevant. Kara cradled his head with one arm and uttered soothing whispers of love and encouragement in his ear. He was so absorbed in her affection that he didn't notice she reached out and grabbed the knife, holding it a few inches below his left shoulder.

When she thrust it into his body, Sixtus winced as the six-inch blade punctured his lung and severed his left pulmonary artery. The deoxygenated blood hemorrhaged from the right ventricle and gushed out of the wound. He gasped for breath, but the blood loss and sudden depressurization led only to a sputtering that escaped his lips in a gurgle of spit and blood. Kara pushed him off and got on her hands and knees as crimson droplets fell off the knife she still held in her hand.

"Why?" he gasped.

"You had to die, Maras. When I realized you wouldn't work with us, there was no other choice. The good news is that it will be quick. Based on the blood loss, I suspect you'll be dead in less than two minutes."

Sixtus continued to look straight at her as the blackness closed in from the edges. His thoughts became disjointed and incoherent, and he knew his mission to save humanity had failed. As consciousness faded, the feeling of betrayal lingered.

He opened his mouth to speak, but his vision suddenly fractured and he felt a jolt of pain followed by a deep cold chill inside the recesses of his brain.

This has happened before. Desperately, Sixtus fought to reorient himself.

"Jeffery, please don't. I—love you. Please understand, I had no choice. Liss said he would kill my family in the future if I didn't cooperate. Help me, Jeffery. I don't know what to do." Kara involuntarily spoke the same words once again as a look of confusion spread across her face.

Sixtus arched and flexed his back. The pain was gone, and as he looked at the floor, he didn't see any blood. He straddled her body with his arm raised high over his head, and he held the knife firmly in his hand as Kara squirmed underneath him.

Time reset again; I'm not dying. We're back to where we were a few seconds ago. She hasn't stabbed me yet.

"Oh no," cried Kara, "it's happening again, Jeffery. Please, I love you." Ninyas Yarmskis looked up at him with alarm but didn't utter another word as the knife thrust deep under her ribcage and directly into her heart. Sixtus twisted the blade and watched as Kara's good eye bulged open before she exhaled a last breath that lingered for seconds.

The fabric of time seemed opaque and malleable. In a surreal moment, Sixtus stumbled backwards as he gazed at the lifeless body of his deceased wife on the floor.

Were her last words sincere?

She killed him with malice, and if time had not unexpectedly reset, Sixtus would be the one lying there dead.

The emotional devastation was indescribable. The shock of the last few minutes mercifully suppressed some of the anguish, but the impact of the event affected him deeply. Kara was dead, and he had killed her. Except she wasn't Kara at all; she was Ninyas Yarmskis, a tool the Corporates or perhaps the Revolution sent back to monitor his movements and undo the damage caused by the Time Sculptor program.

Without Kara, he knew there was no purpose to his life except this final mission. If she was somehow persuaded to kill him, the forces that wanted the Chicago bomb diffused were extremely desperate. Finding Detective Munoz was now imperative; the matter had become personal.

Still in a state of shock, Sixtus walked into the bathroom and pulled the shower curtain down as the snapping metal rings sounded like machine gun fire. He brought the plastic sheet out to the main room and spread it out on the carpet. Already, a great deal of blood seeped from Kara's wound.

He dragged the body onto the curtain and wrapped her up inside. After filling the tub, he laid her in the water and used one of the nightstands to keep her submerged. Hopefully, this would delay the decomposition process long enough to allow him to complete his assignment before the smell attracted attention.

Sixtus walked over to the living room and stared at the phone. Immersed in the assignment as a way to subjugate his grief, he called the front desk and extended his stay for an extra two days, making sure

324

to request complete privacy and no maid service. After turning the air conditioner down to further slow the decay of the body, he started to pack. As he placed his shirts and socks into his bag, his cell phone shattered the silence and caused his heart rate to elevate.

He looked down at the caller ID and breathed a sigh of relief. "Hello?"

"Mr. Clayton, uh, Sixtus, it's Marshall."

"Where are you?"

"I'm in the hotel we stayed at last night. My friend, who was very disconsolate, tracked me down here."

Sixtus spoke through clenched teeth. "Goddamn it, Marshall, you're supposed to be tracking Randall and Anston not hanging out with a friend."

"I—I had no choice, and honestly, I don't appreciate your tone, Mr. Clayton. My friend is dead. He deliberately ran into a mob of street people, and they tore him apart. That's the third friend I've lost in three days."

Immersed in his own grief, Sixtus had trouble feigning sympathy. "I don't know what I can say, Marshall. I—I have experienced a horrific loss myself today. I'm sorry I snapped at you. Honestly, I think I'm still in shock."

Marshall ignored the apology. "We were leaving a restaurant, and while walking back to the hotel, time jumped again. Did you feel it?"

"Yes. They're happening more frequently now. This timeline is unraveling at a rapid rate, and it's more imperative than ever that I complete my mission. What room are you in? I'm also in the same hotel, but I need to leave immediately."

"You're here too? I'm in room 1403."

"Stay there," said Sixtus. "I'll come up in a few moments. Pack your things. We'll be leaving soon."

"Are you in trouble, Mr. Clayton?"

"We're all in trouble, Marshall. All of humanity is in trouble, past, present and future.

Chapter Twenty-Eight

Marshall hung up the phone, sat down at a table positioned near the wall and opened his computer. He hacked into the hotel's network, called up Bleep and paged Wanda. After about twenty seconds, her image appeared on the screen, but she looked disheveled, and dark circles hugged her lower eyelids.

"Wanda... Kenny is... gone."

She backed away from the camera and grabbed the sides of her head. "What do you mean, *gone*?"

"He's dead. Something altered his mind. Perhaps the time changes affected him; I don't know..."

"I knew he was despondent, and I told you about his recent suicide attempt. How — how did it happen?"

Marshall looked away for a moment and wiped at his eyes. "He ran into a crowd of street people, the ones they call 'floaters'. He plunged into an angry, vicious mob, and they beat him to death and threw him in front of a semi-truck."

"Oh no, that's ghastly. I can't..." She moved off screen, and Marshall could hear her screaming at first, then sobbing, and finally whimpering. He envisioned Wanda ripping at her hair and raking her bare skin with her nails. Any words of comfort and support would ring hollow, so he simply sat and waited while she continued to grieve.

Several minutes later, she returned looking even more haggard, and her hand was tangled in a huge mass of hair.

"I can't believe it," she said while wiping her nose and dabbing at her eyes with a succession of tissues. "First Iglar, then Hayden and now Kenny. Are we all going to die? Marshall, I'm so scared."

"I really don't know, Wanda. We—I mean I—have a plan, but the probability of success is poor," he said. "Did you find out anything more about Munoz, Anston and Randall?"

"I was just getting ready to contact you. The one named Munoz met up with the other two at the house in Portland. They're all there together, and Wallace put alerts on their vehicles. Police cruisers only send GPS info when they transmit over the radio. We used that sporadic data to tie in with the cell phone transmission Munoz is using to stay covert, and now we're tracking that."

"You two have done an excellent job. I appreciate your thoroughness."

Her expression lightened ever so slightly. "Thank you, Marshall. That's very kind."

An urgent knock mercifully interrupted what might have been an uncomfortable moment. "Look, I have to go. If there's any movement at the safe house, please alert me."

"Of course. I'll talk to you tomorrow." She shook her head slowly before looking away from the computer's camera. "I still can't believe Kenny's gone. The whole Group is gone…"

"I know, Wanda. I'm grieving too."

She looked back at him and moved a bit closer to the camera. "Marshall?"

"Yes?"

"I love you."

"I, uh, I love you too, Wanda."

The screen went blank as the knocking outside grew more urgent. Marshall closed the computer, walked to the door and looked through the peephole. Sixtus stood outside shuffling his feet and looking around suspiciously. His jet-black hair, usually perfectly styled, looked ragged and unkempt. He sported several contusions and freshly scabbed over wounds. Marshall no sooner turned the knob when Sixtus pushed the door back brusquely and walked in with purpose.

Marshall stumbled backwards and tried to recover his composure. "Mr. Clayton, you look upset. Is something wrong? I thought you were tracking the detective?"

Sixtus dropped his bag and sat down on the bed. "I—I was, but then my wife called me."

"Based on what you've told me, I assume that is something you wanted."

Sixtus nodded in agreement. "It was. She talked me into letting her come out here. I knew it was wrong, but I agreed. But…"

"But?" repeated Marshall.

"She tried to kill me. Kara was the fourth Time Sculptor. She lived with me for five years, monitoring my actions and working to undo the damage to the time line. The Corporates must have known of the declension for decades, but they still kept sending us on missions to appease the elites."

"Where is your wife now?"

"In my room—dead. She stabbed me, Marshall. I was dying before time reset again, and I survived. These

329

episodes are happening more frequently, and it tells me we're in very deep trouble. One second the knife was buried between my shoulder blades, and the next second we were struggling again as though it never happened." He paused before continuing. "You said you experienced the reset too?"

Marshall nodded. "Yes, like I told you over the phone, it affected my best friend."

Sixtus sat at the table and brought his hands up to his eyes while shaking his head. "Kara's gone, and I killed her. I don't know if I can go on."

"Look, Mr. Clayton... Sixtus, I don't want to minimize your pain. But she attacked you. Why did she do that?"

"She may have been an agent of the Corporates, but she denied it. Daxtar Liss persuaded Kara and Glendar Raczor that diffusing the bomb was paramount. That only leaves the second Sculptor, and I don't know who he or she is."

Like a host who suddenly recognizes his rudeness, Sixtus turned and gestured toward his companion. "I'm rambling on. I'm sorry, Marshall. Tell me about your friend."

"Well, I guess Kenny was threatening to harm himself back in Phoenix unless my other friends told him where I was. Like I said before, he flew out here, and we went to a restaurant to talk. On the way back to the hotel time slid backwards, and after the reset, he ran into a pack of the vagrants who ripped him apart. He was screaming. It was awful..."

They sat in silence for some time; Sixtus weeping and wiping at his tears while Marshall stared blankly at the wall. Finally, Sixtus broke the silence.

"We've got to leave the hotel right now. We'll continue on with our original plan. Did you hear anything from your friends?

Marshall nodded. "I just talked with one of them before you knocked. Anston and Randall are still at the house in Portland, and the detective has also gone there."

Sixtus rose quickly from the chair. "All *three* are in the same location? Let's get on the road quickly. I assume you picked up a rental car because we'll both have to drive in case they split up."

"Yes, I got the car. It's parked on the third level." Marshall walked to the dresser and started to remove his clothes from the drawer and place them in his modest suitcase

"I'm going to get a beverage from the machine down the hall. I'll meet you in the parking garage." Sixtus left the room and made his way over to the vending machine. He put a dollar into the tray and received a soda, which he drank without pause. Even as he swallowed the sweet syrup, he couldn't shake the gruesome images of Kara from his mind. Once he reached the elevator, he heaved and expelled the soda and whatever else lingered in his stomach.

He managed to get into the cab and rode it down to the third level in the basement where he waited by the door until Marshall showed up, looking peaked and somewhat overwhelmed.

"Somebody vomited right outside the elevator door," Marshall said with a look of disgust. "The smell and content was utterly repugnant."

"Ah, yes, I saw it too. Probably some drunk conventioneer," replied Sixtus sheepishly. "But let's get moving, we have no time to waste."

Once his car was located, Marshall drove Sixtus back to the first level where the latter's car was parked. They sat inside the running vehicle as Sixtus entered the address Marshall had given him into the GPS.

"Look, Marshall, this is a simple drive, so we shouldn't get separated. I've entered a place in Centralia, it's about two hours away called *Joey's Once Upon a Time*. It's an all-night restaurant. We'll meet up there, grab a quick bite and then drive the rest of the way. The whole trip shouldn't take more than four hours. Are you up for this?"

Marshall nodded. "I think so."

"I need more than that from you. We have to get this done. There's probably going to be more floaters out there, and I can't guarantee the ride will be smooth. Are you going to be okay?"

"I hope so. I've lost three friends, and I'm terrified I may no longer exist at any moment. The fear paralyzes me. It's hard to even cope."

"You have to stay with this," said Sixtus. "We're committed here. Remember, I just killed my wife, and I'm suffering too."

"I understand, and I'll try."

Sixtus opened the door and stepped out of the car, bending over and leaning through the opening. "Okay, follow me to I-5, and then use the GPS. No matter how long it takes, I'll wait for you in Centralia at the restaurant. If you get there first, you wait for me. Don't let anything distract you, understand?"

"I do. I understand."

Sixtus smiled at him. "Good luck, and I'll see you there."

Once he was back in the car, Sixtus waved at Marshall, who looked like a deer in the headlights. As he rolled slowly toward the exit, he wondered how long he actually would wait at the restaurant if Marshall didn't show up.

The hour was late, which was both good and bad. Most of the floaters lay unconscious with anti-depressants and other mind deadening drugs coursing through their bodies. In the depths of the darkness between 1:00 a.m. and daybreak, the vicious crazies took over the streets. The chronically mentally ill, violent sadists and sexual predators looked for the innocent caught in the wrong place at the wrong time.

Sixtus took 26th street out to 200th, hoping to avoid as many of the floaters as possible. With Marshall following, he drove cautiously through the darkened streets looking to either side for signs of an imminent attack. Fortunately, he only saw a few men and a couple women lying alongside the curb. One couple was in the middle of a vicious fistfight while the others were too incapacitated to react.

The vagrants were more active on 200th, and Sixtus noticed several curious stares that morphed into looks of anger. He sped up, and Marshall followed, leaving the neighborhood and merging onto I-5 before anyone had an opportunity to act.

As they drove south on the freeway, Sixtus was unnerved by the lack of traffic even at this time of night. What had once been a bustling center of activity was virtually deserted, except for a couple semis that passed in the opposite direction over several mile intervals. Besides Marshall's headlights, Sixtus could see two other cars that seemed to have settled in with them, apparently looking for comfort in numbers.

To Sixtus, it almost felt like walking through an impending apocalypse. He could only wonder when the four-car caravan would draw enough interest to provoke an attack. The barrel fires were endless, and the underpasses had become their own cities. A kind of cast system seemed to have developed where social status determined if you slept under the bridge or outside of it.

The support pillars served as boundaries and a constant source of contentiousness between those under the bridge and those exposed to the elements. The crush of humanity pulsed at that point, and the pushing, shoving and verbal taunts were evident under every bridge. At various times, violence erupted on the fringes. Inevitably, a body, or sometimes several bodies, would emerge bloodied, beaten or dead.

With nerves on a raw edge, Sixtus drove carefully down the road, taking care to avoid the numerous potholes, abandoned vehicles, human waste, trash and other hazardous objects that littered the pavement. Uncertain of his companion's driving skills, he tried to cut a wide berth so Marshall wouldn't hit anything that might disable his car. Except for the occasional rock or bottle tossed from the side of the highway, the drive was uninteresting, at least until they reached the junction of the 705.

The extensive network of ramps provided an ideal place for the floaters to congregate in an area where they established a large tent city. The pungent smell of raw sewage mixed with body odor, decaying foodstuffs and rotting animal corpses blended together and wafted down the highway in all directions. The smell penetrated the cabin of his

334

car causing Sixtus to hit the button to roll down a window. Unfortunately, that only intensified the smell, so he closed it and tried to breathe through his mouth. He could only imagine what ultra-sanitary Marshall was going through.

As he approached the intersection of the two freeways, Sixtus sped up. While most of the camp occupants were sleeping or passed out, he noticed a dangerous group of young men who saw him at almost the same moment he saw them. He recognized the look of an "AntiPoss" group, which was short for "Anti-Possessions."

These anarchists evolved from several street gangs that worked hard to kill each other. However, as the state of society worsened, they eventually came together with a single purpose, which involved killing those with possessions beyond the basic necessities of food and a single suit of clothes. Members were identified by a long angry scar that ran from the top of their foreheads to the cleft of their chin. The deep, jagged lacerations came from wounds inflicted by the gang's leaders during initiation ceremonies.

Eyes smoldering with rage, the leader stared down Sixtus and then started running towards the freeway. Anticipating the danger, Sixtus hit the gas pedal, and the car lurched forward and pulled away. He looked in the rearview mirror for Marshall, who hadn't changed his speed at all. Sixtus honked and tapped his brake lights to get Marshall's attention but to no avail. His companion did not alter his speed as the two cars grew farther apart. He grabbed his cell and punched number one on the speed dial. After three rings, Marshall answered.

"Hello?"

"Damn it, Marshall! Look out your left window. Those guys are going to make you. Speed up!"

He looked back repeatedly as Marshall began to gradually accelerate. As Sixtus looked at the approaching AntiPoss gang members, he could see them waving their arms frantically, their faces contorted in a collective snarl of anger and ill intent. They carried clubs, bats and other weapons to slow or stop one or more of the vehicles about to pass by them. As he judged distance, Sixtus knew he would easily make it past the group, but looking in his rearview mirror, he realized Marshall might not.

Shaking his head and pursing his lips, Sixtus took his foot off the accelerator and allowed Marshall to catch up. When they were traveling at the same speed, Sixtus' speedometer read seventy-five, which was only five miles over the limit. He shook his head in frustration.

The first group reached the roadway while Sixtus and Marshall were still a good thirty yards away. They jumped onto the pavement, swinging their weapons and motioning for the vehicles to stop. Sixtus looked back and saw Marshall slowing down. This wouldn't end well without a severe change of strategy. Acting on instinct, Sixtus punched the gas and steered the car directly into the path of the one he identified as the leader.

Sensing it was a game of chicken, the head banger stood his ground and extended his middle finger in an act of defiance. While not as confident, his henchmen remained by his side, but their legs were bent and arches flexed, ready to run. Sixtus continued to accelerate as the car quickly closed the distance. About twenty feet before impact, the leader of the AntiPoss realized Sixtus was not bluffing. His cohorts arrived at the same conclusion moments before and peeled off in a mad scramble to the side of the road.

The leader made a desperate attempt to jump out of the way, but he was a moment too late, and his hip collided with the front driver's side of the vehicle. The point of impact was such that it sent him spinning in the air a few feet off the ground. Even with a shattered hip he might have survived, but when he stopped spinning and hit the pavement, he led with his head. His skull bounced along the roadway for several feet, leaving splatters of blood that looked like they belonged on an impressionist's canvas.

Sixtus cursed and continued to speed on ahead. He didn't want to draw attention to the car by damaging it. Fortunately, it seemed his left headlight survived the incident, although it looked slightly misaligned.

He glanced back and confirmed Marshall traveled straight through the carnage without incident — at exactly seventy-five miles per hour.

Chapter Twenty-Nine

Sixtus sipped the last of his coffee and stared at the half-eaten apple pie sitting on a chipped, oval plate. The neon sign flickered in the background, advertising *Joey's Once Upon a Time* 1950s-themed traveler's restaurant.

"So, as an apparition, Mr. Cox only seems to show up when someone is considering suicide?"

Marshall lifted his fork and sniffed at a small piece of peach cobbler before putting it in his mouth. He immediately grabbed his glass of milk and took a long swallow. "So far, that's the only time anyone has seen him," he said while still chewing. "My friends spoke about him right before they died."

"Indeed," said Sixtus as he handed the waitress the bill and a credit card. "As I told you earlier, I met him, but I wasn't trying to kill myself."

Marshall leaned forward. "Did he try to... Did he try and manipulate your mind?"

"Sort of. He did exhibit some telepathic ability, and it felt like he was trying to mentally probe me. I resisted, and that was the end of it."

"Why would he stalk my friends and me? You say he has psychic ability. Was he manipulating my friends to make them depressed? How can he travel to multiple places simultaneously?"

"I don't know much about him," said Sixtus. "He's very mysterious. Perhaps he believes you and your friends are a threat to his plans. Who knows, he might even think you're trying to persuade me to let the detective diffuse the Chicago bomb."

"Of all the things we've encountered, he frightens me the most. I sense a cruelty in him I can't explain. He has tempted me. I…" Marshall stopped talking and absently ran his fork through the cobbler.

"Tempted you with what?" The waitress returned with the bill before Marshall could answer. Sixtus grabbed the receipt, added a tip and signed his alias as his mind drifted elsewhere. "With all that's happened, I can believe almost anything," he said while placing the credit card back in his wallet.

As they walked through the restaurant's parking lot, Sixtus noticed how withdrawn Marshall appeared. He suspected if the young savant had it to do over again, he would never have pursued his alternative "memories" of the past.

"Punch in the second destination when you start your car. If by some chance you get there before me, park away from the house. Close enough to see if anyone arrives or leaves but far enough away to remain out of sight, okay?"

Marshall shook his head as he opened the door and got behind the wheel.

"And one other thing. I don't expect any more trouble because we're going to a residential area. But if you feel threatened, don't stop under any circumstances."

339

"Sure, I know. Just speed up and run them over."

"... Marshall, that's unfair. I had no choice."

"I know. It's just..." He didn't finish his sentence and closed the door.

Sixtus knocked on the window, but Marshall didn't lower it, so he rolled his eyes and pointed. "Pull over to the pumps. We're going to need to fuel up before we leave. I don't know if there's another station between here and Portland."

As Sixtus anticipated, the rest of the trip was uneventful. The long stretches of road between major cities were more deserted now than ever before. Most of the older gas stations were shut down, and the greasy spoons that dotted the road and provided emergency assistance were long gone.

The sky was dark, and there was an unusual chill in the air for July. Sixtus turned on the heater and adjusted the radio until he finally picked up a jazz station. He preferred classic rock, but most of the broadcast networks had permanently banned older songs with offensive lyrics. Every day that passed, the government became more oppressive in a desperate attempt to retain its authority.

***

The drive took only an hour and a half, but it seemed much longer since Marshall refused to exceed the speed limit. Nearly twenty miles outside of Portland, Sixtus turned off on I-84 and took the road to the town of Corbott, a small rural community near the Columbia River. The distance from the city helped them avoid the vagrant groups

340

that gathered in numbers throughout Portland proper.

He checked the mirror to confirm Marshall was still following before exiting onto Corbott Hill Drive. A couple of quick turns later and he was on Meyers Lane, moving slowly down the street until he found Munoz' brother's house. A floater wandered down the sidewalk while slowly pushing a grocery cart that held his meager possessions as he looked for an empty house to loot. Sixtus slowly drove down the street to ensure no one was watching and finally turned the car in the opposite direction before parking in the most inconspicuous place he could find.

Two vehicles sat in the driveway, and Sixtus assumed the large sedan was the detective's, and the smaller compact was the rental that belonged to Anston and Randall. Checking his watch, he wondered what was taking Marshall so long, but the Chevy Cruze turned the corner at that moment and quelled his impatience. Albeit clumsily, Marshall drove past, turned his car around, and parked directly behind Sixtus.

The moon was a small sliver in a cloudless sky, so the street was cast in complete darkness. Sixtus waited for several minutes, but Marshall didn't move from his car. Shaking his head slightly, he turned on the interior light and looked back while motioning for Marshall to join him.

In a scene plucked from a slapstick comedy, Marshall looked around as though he wondered if Sixtus was actually gesturing to him. He thrust a thumb in his own chest and mouthed, "me?" Sixtus nodded, and Marshall left the car, closing the door with a slam that should have woken the entire neighborhood. While the kid may have been a brilliant physicist, his stakeout skills left something to be desired.

Once he reached Sixtus' vehicle, Marshall grabbed the door handle but then ran back to his own car to retrieve something he apparently forgot. Another door slam, and this time he came back and actually got into Sixtus' car carrying his laptop.

"I'm going to hack one of the Wi-Fi networks in the neighborhood," he said. "Almost every house has one, and you'd be surprised at how many don't even bother with security."

"What are you looking for?"

"I'm going to hook up with Wanda so she can send me updates on the location of the vehicles in case we lose sight of them."

"Excellent. That sounds like a good idea."

Once he established a connection, Marshall conveyed his request through a series of text messages. Wanda responded within minutes.

Marshall, we've arranged to have the coordinates of the cars you're following sent to your cell phone. There's an app attached to an email I've just sent you.

That's great. Very helpful. Please also monitor the airports for activity if they try and book a flight.

I'll pass that on to Wallace. One more thing; remember, I'm leaving today on a trip.

Yes, I remember. Where are you going?

I'm leaving for Chicago. It's business, remember?

Marshall froze as he read her text. *Business in Chicago? I'm unaware of any conferences there this month.*

Yes, there is a conference on particle physics at the University of Chicago. Wallace is going with me.

Marshall felt a growing panic welling up within him. He knew Sixtus wouldn't approve of telling Wanda about the scheduled nuclear detonation, so he couldn't warn her not to go.

Let's discuss this later.

342

Why? We bought plane tickets. Scheduled to leave today at 1 p.m.

Ok.

After closing the lid on the laptop, Marshall sighed and looked out the window. He took another deep breath, interrupted by an audible sound of frustration that escaped from his lips. Sixtus sensed the distress in the utterance.

"Are you alright?

"Yes, I'm fine. My friends have figured out a way to track the vehicles we're going to be following. I'm sending you a link to an app. Just install it, and you'll see exactly where Randall's car and the detective's cruiser are heading."

"That's outstanding. Your friends are amazing, but you seem upset. Are you sure everything is alright?"

"No—actually, I'm not alright. I'm anything but alright."

"Did something happen to your friend?"

Marshall's head dipped, and he said softly, "She's more than a friend. And she's going to Chicago today, and I can't tell her not to."

Sixtus puffed out his cheeks and blew the air out slowly. "I see. And you care for this girl?"

Marshall nodded and turned away.

"Look, Marshall, I've lost my wife, and with that, I've lost any reason to live. I'm running on autopilot right now, and I haven't allowed the full depth of my despair to sink in. If you've found someone you care for, you should protect her."

"But the timeline…"

"Damn the timeline!" Sixtus snapped back. "What is the timeline, anyway? How do we know that every change we experience isn't supposed to happen? Look what all our meddling has done to the precious timeline.

Will a single change in travel plans affect anything? We have nuclear bombs detonating and distortions in space-time, so what's the difference if you talked your girlfriend out of going to Chicago?"

"I—I just don't want to see reality disturbed more than it is. I watched my friend get torn to pieces by a bloodthirsty mob. Where does this end?"

"It ends in Chicago. And hopefully your girlfriend isn't there."

"So, you've decided to try to detonate the bomb?"

Sixtus shook his head. "No, but I haven't decided not to either."

Marshall lifted the lid to his computer and sent out an alert to Wanda over Bleep, but she was no longer logged onto her computer. Instead, he opened an email message and began to type.

Wanda,

You can't go to Chicago. I won't go into detail, so don't ask me to. I know you're not going for business; you're going because Chicago was on Iglar's list. You must not upset the delicate balance that's holding everything together, and your presence in Chicago might do that. I'll try to contact you tomorrow if I can.

He hovered over the keyboard for some time before typing, *Love, Marshall.*

"Is this acceptable?" He pushed the laptop over to Sixtus without making eye contact.

After reading it, Sixtus smiled and gave the computer back. "Yes, Marshall, it's perfect."

As Portland emerged from the dead of night, the temperature dropped into the mid-fifties. Sixtus pulled a jacket from his bag and noticed Marshall already had one on. It was almost four a.m., and the eerie quiet of the residential neighborhood was somehow comforting. Marshall softly snored next to him, temporarily escaping the horror of this reality.

Weariness crept up on Sixtus as well, but he couldn't indulge in the luxury of sleep. He slid down in the seat and crossed his arms to fight the cold. His mind was nearly a blank, filled only with distorted images of Kara's anguished face when he plunged the knife into her chest and the feeling of dead, cold flesh when he wrapped her body in the shower curtain. There was no question he would eventually kill himself, for there was no recovering from the horror of killing Kara. For now, only finding the bomb in Chicago mattered.

Sixtus recounted a perfect day in November a few years back when he and Kara took a small paddleboat out on one of the private lakes inside McCormick Ranch. They planned a picnic, and the weather couldn't have been better. Bare feet touching, they sat together on lush grass on a little island in the middle of the lake. The sun was shining, and it warmed the air just enough that they didn't need a sweater.

Kara packed fried chicken and made one of those delicious cherry pies he loved so much. Her hair was radiant, and her complexion was so fair and clear he felt like he was looking into the face of perfection. He leaned up to touch her cheek, and she took hold of his hand.

This was reality. The other horror, whatever it was, never happened. This little island was where he wanted to stay forever. She smiled at him, but the loud sound of a car engine interrupted the moment. He looked around but couldn't find the vehicle, but the motor revved again from some hidden location.

Sixtus woke with a start, coughing and sputtering. He rubbed his eyes and looked around, trying to gain his bearings. The sun was just beginning to peek through the trees as daybreak approached. He looked across the street and saw the vapor of exhaust coming from the unmarked police cruiser in the driveway of the safe house. Sixtus elbowed Marshall and yelled, "Wake up!"

"Wha… What is it?" Marshall looked around as he emerged from a deep sleep.

"There's no time. Looks like Munoz is leaving. Get out right now. I've got to be ready to follow him."

"Okay, okay," said Marshall as he gathered up his computer and tried to gain his wits.

The cruiser began to back out of the driveway as Sixtus started the engine. "Marshall, get out — *now!*"

Marshall opened the door and set his foot on the curb, but Sixtus already started to pull away. The unexpected movement caused him to stumble, and he fell onto the sidewalk as the sedan drove off, trailing the cruiser at a safe distance to avoid detection. Fortunately, the fall only scuffed his computer, and Marshall got to his feet and stumbled back to his car just as Sixtus turned the corner and moved out of sight. In that fleeting moment, Marshall wondered if he would ever see Jeffery Clayton again.

Sixtus followed the unmarked cruiser as it made its way to I-5 and headed north. He unlocked his phone and touched the link to the tracking app Wallace and Wanda set up. The map took a second to load before coming up on the screen. A blue arrow moved slowly across the map, accurately tracking Munoz' vehicle. Sixtus nodded in acknowledgment to the brilliance of Marshall and his high-functioning autistic friends. Their capabilities were truly impressive.

Marshall sat in his rental car, shivering for most of the morning. Sixtus left a couple hours ago, and time crawled by ever since. Mercifully, the sun finally emerged around nine a.m., and the effect of the car windows magnified the radiant heat. He was rubbing his hands together when activity over at the safe house drew his attention. Anston and Randall were leaving and walking towards their car.

Nearly paralyzed by anxiety, Marshall sat motionless as Anston started the engine while Randell got in on the passenger's side. He tried to recall Sixtus' previous words of encouragement that helped him at the airport, but they weren't quite as motivational this time. Marshall felt like he was entering a full-fledged crisis. His hands were shaking as his finger missed the engine start button several times. As Anston backed out of the driveway, Marshall groped at the shifter before managing to put the transmission in gear, but his foot stomped hard on the accelerator, and the car lurched.

Focus on the moment, not the fear.

The small jolt to his psyche gave him a sense of perspective and rationality. Marshall was most successful when he worked through the anxiety by using logic.

He pulled out his phone and called up the GPS locator Wanda had set up for him. After confirming it was working, he followed their car out to I-90 as it made its way toward I-5. Soon, he was on the freeway traveling south, unsure of his destination and frightened to the point of debilitation. Moving cautiously down the highway, he periodically looked at the blue arrow as it moved along the colored map. Marshall didn't know if he would have another opportunity to talk to Wanda, so he placed his Bluetooth headset over his ear and punched the speed dial button.

"Marshall, are you alright?"

"I'm fine, but I need to tell you something. I can't answer any questions, so you'll just have to listen to me, and do as I say."

"What are you talking about? I don't understand."

"You can't go to Chicago. I sent you an email. Did you get it?"

"What? No, I haven't read my emails yet," she said.

"You're not going for a business meeting. You're going to try and find something in Chicago related to the time distortions, but you can't do it. Cancel your flight."

She waited for several moments before replying. "Why can't we help, Marshall? We think Chicago is a key to the mystery. Maybe we'll find something important."

"Chicago is a big city. The odds of stumbling on something useful are minimal.

"But *you* know something, don't you, Marshall?"

"It doesn't matter what I know. I just need you to promise me you won't travel to Chicago."

"Are you going there?"

He carefully measured his answer. "I'm sorry, but I can't tell you what I'm doing. But I need you to promise me you won't go."

There was hesitation in her voice. "I—I'm not sure I can do that."

"If you go, you'll die," he blurted out. "I need you to promise."

"How will I die, Marshall? What's going to happen in Chicago? You're scaring me."

"I won't say anymore. I need your promise," he said.

"Why is it so important to you?"

"Because I—care about you." Marshall's tone was low and desperate.

"Okay, you have my word," she said softly, "but only if you promise me you won't go there."

"No, I can't do that. I have no idea where I'm going and what I'll be getting into."

He heard her breathe softly and sigh. "Please, come home, Marshall."

"I have to go now. Let me know if you find out anything else on those people you investigated. And don't go to Chicago because… I love you."

He hung up before she could answer, and he resumed his pursuit of Anston and Randall.

Chapter Thirty

Munoz traveled north on I-5 for roughly three hours before reaching his destination in the upscale residential community of Edmonds, just north of Seattle. Sixtus had no idea why the man who was supposed to save the world would visit a residential neighborhood less than twenty-four hours before the Chicago bomb was set to explode, but he was there to observe, not judge.

After exiting his car, Munoz walked to the front porch of a magnificent mid-19th century Tudor home. He looked around but didn't ring the bell. Instead, he stood near the threshold and pushed on the oversized front door until it swung open slowly. The detective peered inside the house before entering and then disappeared from sight.

Sixtus kept his eyes on the door for several minutes, but if anything was happening, it was taking place inside the house. After several minutes of frustration, he tried to find a location where he could see through one of the windows. He got out of his car and checked the immediate area for signs of activity, but none of the neighbors were out yet.

Large yards separated houses in this area, so it wasn't hard to avoid detection. Still, he hurried towards the Tudor, fighting the urge to break into a run.

He came upon a dense row of hedges planted in front of a series of windows that spanned the length of the living room. Sixtus ducked behind the thicket, remaining motionless just long enough to confirm no one had become suspicious. He raised his head and shifted slightly to get a better look between the slats of the blinds.

The interior was relatively dark, so he could barely make out the people in the room. A man lay slumped over a desk, and another sat propped up against a wall with his hand covering his forehead. A third person stood away from the others, holding one side of his face and doubled over in obvious pain. On the opposite end of the room, Sixtus saw Munoz favoring one of his arms, and it appeared he was also bleeding from the forehead.

Should I intervene?

Sixtus knew Munoz was supposed to make it to Chicago, so the detective would likely survive this struggle. Still, with reality so corrupted, the outcome was far from certain.

Three explosive gunshots from inside the house caused Sixtus to jerk his neck awkwardly and duck. After the last echo faded away, he cautiously stood back up and looked through the window. One of the men was lying on the floor motionless, and Munoz was handcuffing the other to the banister.

The gunshots were loud enough that several dogs in the neighborhood were barking aggressively, and Sixtus imagined the neighbors were starting to take notice as natural curiosity overcame initial fear. Crashing through the hedges at a full sprint, he ran back to his vehicle and closed the door just before Munoz left the house. Someone must have called 9-1-1 because a police siren sounded in the distance. Waiting impatiently for Munoz to leave, Sixtus drummed his fingers on the steering wheel. After a seeming eternity, the cruiser finally pulled away from the crime scene. If the detective hadn't been focusing on his own escape, he might have realized how close he was being followed.

Munoz drove fast and reckless as he weaved through traffic, and Sixtus had trouble keeping up. Munoz wasn't heading away from Seattle; he was driving into the heart of the city. Eventually, the traffic became so thick the Time Sculptor had to give up the chase. He turned to the phone map Marshall sent him and followed the blue arrow moving north on 15th Avenue, ultimately arriving at the U.S. District Court building on Stewart Street.

Without warning, the arrow disappeared from the map. Panicking, Sixtus tapped the screen several times but couldn't reconnect. Either something interrupted the GPS feed, or Munoz parked some place where the signal was blocked. Sixtus chided himself for being too cautious and not following the other car more closely. Losing track of Munoz would eliminate any chance he had to affect the outcome of the Chicago detonation, assuming the detective was actually the one charged with deactivating the device.

He pulled up next to the court building and slowly drove around it, enduring the honks and profanity of motorists irritated by his slow pace. It was almost noon, and the floaters were starting to stir after having slept off the effects of the drugs and alcohol they consumed the night before. The police still patrolled the downtown streets of most major cities, so except for a challenging look or provocative gesture here and there, Sixtus drove through without incident.

When he saw the parking garage, he realized the thick concrete structure would probably block GPS signal transmissions if Munoz car was inside. He found the entrance on the west end of the building and entered. After taking a ticket from the dispenser, he started looking for Munoz' vehicle. The District Court building was bustling with activity, so the first two levels of the garage were full. By the time he reached the third level, he became anxious, wondering if Munoz was somewhere else. Just as he turned the corner and looked toward the exit, he saw the cruiser parked in the last space at the far end of the building.

The car faced forward, and the passenger's side was up against a cement exterior wall. As Sixtus drove past, he saw Munoz sitting in the front seat, and they briefly made eye contact. Not wanting to draw the detective's attention, he circled the perimeter until he was on the other side of the garage, where he found a parking spot between two large SUVs.

Sixtus crouched in the seat and looked out the window. A clear line of sight allowed him to monitor Munoz if he left the car, but his wait would be a very long one. He repeatedly looked over at his phone, but there was no signal. If the device had been working, he would have received a notification that Mr. Cox' first nuclear explosion detonated in Istanbul at precisely twelve p.m. Eastern Standard Time.

***

As Marshall continued down I-5, he became increasingly convinced that Randall and Anston were taking a long trip. They cruised through Oregon into Northern California, driving at a brisk pace. Marshall constantly increased his speed to keep up, and it made him uneasy. Fortunately, Wanda's GPS feed gave him the luxury of losing sight of the other car while still maintaining contact.

The road was almost free of floaters, since I-5 bypassed major cities. Marshall estimated he was about three minutes behind, and he began to feel a sense of urgency to relieve himself. When the blue dot on his phone stopped moving, he imagined Randall and Anston probably needed to use the facilities as well. This presented an excellent opportunity to reestablish visual contact.

Marshall alternated between looking at his phone and the traffic in front of him, eventually maneuvering off the freeway and pulling into a state-owned rest stop. Anston parked his car just ahead, so Marshall backed into a parking space three spots over from the other vehicle. The rest stop was about half full, and children played around a huge T-Rex replica as the adults bought refreshments and food from a snack bar.

Marshall scanned the area and noticed a small group of people were gathered near Anston's car. Arranged in a circle, they surrounded something or someone on the ground. More bystanders approached out of curiosity, so Marshall left his vehicle and walked tentatively toward the group via a circuitous route that drew the least attention.

He hated spaces packed tightly with people, but the revulsion didn't keep him from pushing past several bystanders. When he got to the front of the crowd, Marshall saw Anston leaning over the prone form of Randall, who appeared to be unconscious.

Mesmerized and confused, Marshall inched up even closer, drawn by an unidentifiable compulsion he could not rationally explain. He felt the power of an electrical charge pulsing out of Randall's body and coursing through his own muscles and tendons. The hair on the back of his neck rose and bent toward the prone man's still body.

For a moment, Marshall pondered the possibility he was experiencing a full-fledged nervous breakdown, but the thought evaporated as the vast dominion of his mind surrendered to a mysterious force of enormous potency. He found himself slipping into a kind of dreamlike state where he remained sentient, but powerful waves of energy permeated his brain and assumed control of his optical cortex. Without warning, he plunged into a surreal, murky kind of cerebral vision.

The substance and purpose of the image was difficult to understand. Somehow, he found himself inside a room where Randall was talking to a woman as she wept and moaned. She sat on the edge of the bed with an empty bottle in her hand. Some sort of apparition — the only accurate description — shimmered in the background. Marshall heard talking, but they spoke in a way he couldn't fully understand. He tried to interpret their expressions since he only heard their conversation sporadically.

Engrossed to the point of distraction, he was vaguely aware of Anston moving Randall off the pavement and into the car with the help of a few bystanders. Once his friend was inside, Anston sprinted to the driver's side, started the engine and backed out from the space.

Marshall remained immersed in the scene as his mind did its best to piece together the narrative. Based on their exchanges, he suspected Randall was trying to comfort the despondent woman. At times, he seemed to communicate with the shimmering apparition, but that transference was occurring on a level of thought Marshall couldn't comprehend. What he heard clearly in his mind was a repeated reference to *The Dark One*, and it chilled Marshall to the bone. How could Randall and this woman know about Mr. Cox?

The answer was right there in his brain, tantalizingly close, but despite enormous effort, the proper synaptic pathway wouldn't close, and the window of opportunity evaporated. As the car pulled farther away, the vision faded. The last image Marshall remembered was Randall unexpectedly turning and looking at him with a mixture of curiosity and suspicion.

Who are you? Randall didn't speak, but Marshall clearly heard the words. *You're not supposed to be here.* The last words tailed off as the vision faded to nothingness.

Dazed and disoriented, Marshall stumbled around, falling to the pavement on two occasions. Several of the rest stop visitors stared at him with a look that conveyed disgust as he appeared drunk or altered by drugs. He grabbed the arm of a metal bench and sat down, still reeling from the encounter. After some moments, he regained a sense of balance and stood up slowly before making his way back to the car.

By this time, Anston and Randall were long gone, and Marshall fumbled with his phone to find the tracking beacon. The blue arrow was again stationary and not that far away. He pinched the screen to expand it and realized they stopped only a couple miles ahead.

Slowly gathering himself, Marshall started his car and pulled out of the rest stop. A few people gave him passing side glances as he left the parking lot and accelerated back onto the freeway. As he tracked the arrow, he realized Anston and Randall unexpectedly exited two streets further ahead. Marshall followed and found several gas stations spread out over half a mile on the busy street. Fortunately, their car was not that difficult to find since they picked the largest station located right on the corner.

Marshall pulled up to one of the gas pumps while scanning the scene. He couldn't find Anston, who was either in the car or inside the convenience store. Looking past a couple rows of parked vehicles, he saw Randall leaning up against a decrepit pickup truck on the far end of the lot, engaged in an animated discussion with a young woman Marshall had never seen before. She paced back and forth while gesturing in a way that conveyed distress and obvious sadness.

Marshall went inside to use the facilities, avoiding the floaters who sat in front of the building and passed around cheap liquor and cheaper drugs. He waited until an aggressive floater cornered a woman, and he used the opportunity to slip inside the building to do his business.

When Marshall went back outside, Randall and the woman were still talking, but he seemed to have calmed her down. He put his arm around her shoulder, and they started to walk away, but another man approached from across the parking lot with an obvious sense of purpose. Well-dressed even in casual, his black slacks and black pullover polo shirt projected an air of casual professionalism.

He blocked the path of Randall and the woman, and they both stiffened. Based on their reaction, Marshall sensed this was an unwelcome surprise. The tall man stabbed a finger into Randall's chest, and judging from the change in body language, the conversation took on a decidedly more confrontational tone.

After a minute or so, they stopped talking, and the man in black grabbed the woman brusquely. She recoiled and tried to pull away, but he held her tight and leaned over and whispered something in her ear. Whatever he said had an immediate effect, and she backed up against the truck as her hands went up to cover her face. This only seemed to enrage the man, and he slapped her hard across the cheek. She fell to the pavement from the force of the blow, and he dragged her by the hair towards a dark sedan while muttering loud enough that Marshall could hear his hostile inflections.

The assailant turned back and motioned for Randall to follow, and he did so obediently. After pulling the woman up from the pavement, the tall man grabbed her hands and strapped them together behind her back. As he reached the car, he opened the rear passenger door and pushed her into the back seat by the back of the head.

Marshall couldn't make out exactly what was happening, but he watched the tall man turn to Randall and fasten his hands together in the same way. Once he finished, Randall started to get into the car, but the kidnapper used the occasion to push him into the seat with a foot to the back.

The assailant stood up and looked around for a moment, sending a challenging nonverbal message to anyone who might consider intervening. He placed his hands on his hips and thrust out his chest, scanning the area in every direction with squinted eyes and a clenched jaw. After straightening his shirt, he walked purposefully to his car and got in. Moments later, he pulled out of the station and onto the freeway.

Marshall sat motionless, wondering what he should do next. Out of the corner of his eye, he saw Anston driving away in apparent pursuit of the dark sedan, but the overweight accountant didn't look like the type of person capable of confronting a professional kidnapper. Marshall worried that the recent confrontation was an unanticipated deviation that could spoil Randall's plans. They were mixed up in something dangerous, and Marshall couldn't help but believe it related to the Chicago detonation.

He turned on his phone and located the blue arrow that tracked Anston's car. Marshall might not be able to keep up with the large sedan driven by the new character in the drama, but if Anston was chasing him, then Marshall must follow Anston.

The three cars continued to drive south for close to three hours, enduring their fair share of projectiles hurled from the bridges and the sides of the road. Just outside of Stockton, the blue arrow pulsated and remained motionless, which meant Anston's car was stopped and had exited the freeway yet again. Looking at his low fuel gauge, he assumed either the sedan or Anston's rental car needed to gas up. Marshall hoped it was the former because he was relying entirely on Anston to keep him in physical contact with the lead car. About a mile ahead, an exit ramp led directly to a complex that housed a gas station, convenience store and fast-food restaurant.

As he exited the freeway, Marshall moved past the store and spotted the sedan parked next to a fuel pump. Anston's car was on the other side of the building, and it looked like he was still in it. After pulling his own vehicle into the parking lot, Marshall stopped at a different set of pumps and walked outside to fuel up. Once he was in the open, he felt extraordinarily vulnerable. He fumbled with the credit card Sixtus had given him but finally got it into the slot.

After filling the tank, he got back in his car and drove to a corner of the parking lot that divided the distance between Anston and the assailant's sedan. He watched for activity, alternating between the two cars and the convenience store. Only a minute or two passed before the doors to the store opened, and Randall and the girl walked out and made their way back to the car with the mysterious man in the black polo following.

Marshall was so transfixed that he didn't see Anston approaching the kidnapper from behind until the last second. Randall's friend had what looked like a tire iron raised high over his head, and he struck the kidnapper somewhere between his neck and shoulder. The man recoiled and slumped, bringing his hand up to the affected area as he turned to face Anston. While the blow stunned him, it wasn't incapacitating.

The assailant rose to his feet, smoothed his hair and stalked Anston, who backed up and frantically swung the weapon. Without warning, the kidnapper rushed the small, hefty accountant, knocking him to the ground. He raised his fists and started pummeling Anston with blows to the face. Randall managed to get out of the car, and with his hands still bound, rushed the pair and plowed directly into the larger man, who toppled over and grunted in surprise. He got back up and glared at Randall, pulling him to his feet and punching him hard in the stomach.

Marshall felt helpless, but somehow, he found the mettle to make his way over to the altercation. A few people stared from a distance, but so far, no one moved from the landing. Randall and the kidnapper looked at each other for some moments without moving.

The stalemate ended when the large man started to scream, stumble and clutch the sides of his head. His eyes widened and mouth opened, and he let out a second terrified shriek that carried across the entire parking lot. Almost instantaneously, he fell to the ground and rolled around as the veins on his neck bulged, and his face morphed into a deep blue mask of pain.

As a wave of extreme heat washed over him, Marshall realized a concentrated portion of the directed energy burst was pointed right at the kidnapper. Drawn to the power like a moth to a flame, he robotically walked forward at the same time Randall was gathering Anston and moving away. A small crowd looked on with stunned curiosity at the thrashing of the tall man covered in blood that oozed generously from his ears, mouth and eyes. Meanwhile, Randall, Anston and the woman piled into their car and spit gravel as they drove out of the unpaved portion of the parking lot.

Marshall turned and sprinted to his vehicle just as the crowd began to turn their attention to Randall's retreating sedan. After starting the engine, he drove out to the service street and merged into traffic. Once clear of the scene, he breathed deeply to dampen his anxiety.

Hesitantly, Marshall switched on the radio, hoping to hear some calming music to smooth his frayed nerves. Instead, the somber tone of the announcer conveyed an immediate sense of concern. It took only a few sentences before Marshall realized the first nuclear bomb exploded in Istanbul, precisely as Sixtus predicted. The time on his digital clock read 9:16, which was 12:16 Eastern Standard Time.

So, it was all true. The sense of urgency was only surpassed by the sense of futility. And here he was, chasing a car whose occupants might have nothing to do with the entire affair. He gripped the wheel tighter and sped up.

Chapter Thirty-One

Sixtus woke up from a light sleep, startled by loud voices and the sounds of scuffling from across the parking garage. As he raised his head above the dashboard, he saw Munoz and another man in a heated discussion that bordered on conflict. With stooped shoulders, horned rimmed glasses and a briefcase, the man appeared scholarly. Obviously agitated, he gestured vigorously, but Munoz stood his ground with his arm extended and a palm thrust forward.

After some time, the scholar reached into his pocket and reluctantly handed over his car keys. They entered a large SUV, and Munoz took the wheel. After pulling out slowly, the vehicle ascended from below ground to street level. Sixtus waited a moment and followed, realizing he would no longer have the benefit of GPS to track their movement.

The two vehicles drove almost in tandem as the Navigator merged onto I-90 and traveled east for half an hour before exiting onto Garcia Road, well away from Seattle proper. Creeping slowly down the rural street, they pulled over to a remote area concealed by a thick grove of trees, and Sixtus wondered if he was about to witness a murder.

He hid his car in a vacant lot that bordered a tall fence less than 100 feet away from Munoz. The passenger's side of the Navigator was visible, but he was sure the occupants couldn't see him. Sixtus was parked for about ten minutes when the Navigator's door opened, and the captive got out and started walking away. Then he stopped and turned back as Munoz rolled down the window.

"That device will unlock everything," said the scholar. "You'll learn the entire command structure of the Network," Munoz replied, but Sixtus couldn't make out what he said.

The captive leaned in through the open window. "No, Moss reported to me. This is the real thing, but it won't help you. Mr. Cox will learn that I've been compromised, and I'll be dead within a day or so. Of course, so will you. I guess we both lose."

Again, Munoz said something inaudible in reply. The scholarly looking captive shrugged his shoulders. "You are law enforcement; I should have known. But it hardly matters. As I said, we're both dead men. I'm going to finish the job I started many years ago, but I want to say goodbye to my family first." He turned away and started walking down Garcia Road until eventually disappearing out of sight.

Sixtus leaned back in his seat and grabbed the wheel tightly. His heart raced and a cold sweat broke out over his entire body. The words were unmistakable; the scholar said *Mr. Cox* would know he was compromised. Finally, Sixtus had indisputable proof that Munoz was indeed the man who would disarm the bomb in Chicago.

Long after the scholar was gone, the Navigator remained motionless. Sixtus wondered what was going on inside the vehicle, and growing restless, he shifted uncomfortably in the seat. Dusk was just beginning to set in, and he nodded off several times but was woken by the periodic hooting of a barred owl and the grumbling of his own stomach.

After another long interlude, the sharp crack and muted sound of shattered glass startled him out of a shallow slumber. Munoz' SUV roared to life and swerved violently as it lurched back onto the road. Sixtus started his car and punched the accelerator, pulling out sharply from behind the fence. He knew he couldn't lose sight of the Navigator or risk being spotted in pursuit.

Once he turned onto I-90, Sixtus followed Munoz as he drove west back toward the city. Years of academy surveillance training alerted him to a trailing unmarked squad car some ten car lengths behind. As casually as possible, he slowed and let the vehicle pass. The last thing he needed was apprehension and interrogation by the police. If Kara's body was found, they'd be actively looking for Mark Simpson.

The three vehicles traveled in a silent convoy for several miles, staying equal distance apart without exceeding the speed limit. About a quarter mile later, the unmarked squad car swerved violently to the right and caught an exit ramp.

Two streets later, Munoz got off the freeway and pulled into the first service station he came to. Sixtus kept the SUV in sight, ultimately parking in an apartment complex across the street. After scanning his surroundings, he turned his attention back to Munoz in

365

time to see the detective holding out his badge in front of a frightened older man, who reluctantly walked to the passenger's side of his car and helped his wife get out.

Munoz said a few words and then sprinted to the driver's side, slammed the door and sped up onto the service road. Sixtus was close behind him, troubled by the fact he would have to follow yet another car. Still, he strongly suspected Munoz was running from law enforcement. Somehow, the detective persuaded his pursuers to discontinue the chase, but apparently, he believed they would be back. It appeared he was trying to thwart their efforts by frequently changing vehicles.

Once he reached the heart of Seattle, Munoz merged onto I-5 south in a last second maneuver. He pursued an odd asymmetrical course that ostensibly made no sense. He stayed on the freeway until he was well clear of the city, and slowly, Sixtus began to suspect the detective was heading back to Portland.

But why?

Using the cloak of darkness, Munoz commandeered two more vehicles from unsuspecting bystanders parked in obscure areas off the frontage road.

Only Sixtus' advanced skills kept him from losing sight of the cunning detective. Countless hours spent in a driving simulator preparing for every contingency in this barbaric past now paid dividends. Even so, he almost lost contact with Munoz twice. For many miles he wondered where they were heading, but Munoz' intentions became clear when a text unexpectedly popped up on his phone.

Per my instructions, Wanda and Wallace monitored flight reservations on the global distribution system. Detective Jose Munoz six-digit passenger name record showed up on Amadeus. Booked on DeliverMax cargo plane (D-146) leaving Portland International at 1:45 a.m. arriving at O'Hare at 7:45 a.m. Southwest cargo area.

Sixtus dropped the phone and sped up to keep Munoz in his line of sight. So, the detective was flying to Chicago after all. This served as the confirmation that Munoz was the one who would diffuse the bomb. He reached over and picked up the phone to dial Marshall.

***

Anston and Randall continued driving south through the vast expanse of California wasteland with Marshall following at a safe distance. Periodically, he sped up to gain a visual sighting but always dropped back. Every time he was in the car's line of sight, a strange sensation overpowered him. The feeling was difficult to describe, but he imagined he was momentarily transported inside the cabin of the car, which was physically impossible, of course. Still, the sensation was so unsettling he continued to fall back every time the hallucination started.

After traveling for several hours, his curiosity became overwhelming. The closer he moved toward Anston's car, the easier it was to see the woman, who was curled up in the corner of the back seat shaking uncontrollably. Anston continued to grip the wheel almost in a trance-like state, periodically looking over at Randall and occasionally peering at Sarah in the rearview mirror. That was her name: *Sarah*. Marshall didn't know how he knew, but he was certain of it.

Still, it was Randall's reaction that was the most disconcerting. Even while he spoke on a cell phone, he simultaneously looked around the cabin as though he felt the presence of someone else in the car. With rising anxiety, Marshall pushed the gas pedal and moved in even closer. His awareness intensified, and he looked around with a 360-degree panoramic view of the interior of the vehicle from the vantage point of the center console.

As he changed perspective, the piercing stare of Randall unnerved him. No matter which way Marshall looked, he couldn't escape Randall's steely gaze.

Who are you?

The words reverberated in Marshall's head with stunning clarity. He nearly lost control of the car, but the connection with Randall remained in place. Panicking to the point of hysteria, he pressed on the brake pedal, but he could not shake free of the other's presence.

Without warning, a loud *bang* erupted in his head, and Marshall was thrust firmly back in his own car. As he struggled to clear the confusion, he saw another vehicle aggressively closing in on Anston until it slammed into his back bumper, which sent both cars into a dangerous skid.

Anston fought to regain control while Marshall's car swerved in sympathy as the link to Randall shut down. The attacking vehicle moved into the adjacent lane and pulled up next to Anston. Marshall drove on in a state of abject horror, and he accelerated without realizing his foot had floored the gas pedal.

The next impact was even more violent as the left front fender of the larger car smashed into the right front fender of the small rental. The two cars drove in parallel as the gnashing and grinding of metal and rubber created an unnerving, piercing squeal. Marshall again drove parallel to Anston on the passenger's side, and he could see through their windows into the assailant's car. The man in the passenger's seat was the tall kidnapper from the convenience store, but he had a blank look on his face and stared ahead without blinking. The driver was fully animated, and his maniacal smile stretched from ear to ear. With eyes full of loathing, he glanced over at Anston and cackled insanely.

Marshall's mind was sharply drawn back inside Anston's car as he sensed a growing mass of telepathic energy pooling around Randall. Scorching heat emanated from his physical body and divided his consciousness. The skin on Randall's neck stretched tight, and his eyes narrowed as he looked directly at the snarling assailant.

Vibrant waves of hot energy pulsated, and Marshall could see it clearly as a dense cloud of glistening white smoke. He felt Randall's anger and raw unbridled rage, which triggered a sympathetic response he couldn't understand. Without reason, Marshall instinctively hated the driver of the other car. An odd stirring came from the depths of his own mind, and a thick quantity of thermal psychic energy ascended from his core and merged with Randall's.

The converged psychokinetic force leapt out in a reddish-orange jet that effortlessly passed through the physical barriers of metal and glass and struck the other driver directly. He immediately let go of the wheel and clutched the sides of his head as his car swerved. In that instant, the man looked over at Randall, and Marshall

369

witnessed a horror unlike anything he had ever seen before.

The driver's face was a hue of dark green, and ugly red patches grew and burned through the skin on his forehead and cheeks. His mouth opened, and he screamed as blood leaked from his nostrils and eye sockets. The agony continued for several seconds until he grabbed the wheel and veered radically to the left, purposely slamming the car into a concrete support pillar underneath a multi-lane bridge.

A horrible screech of tires, burning rubber and twisted metal started a chain reaction of dreadful accidents. Small flames licked the sides of the fenders before the vehicle exploded from the high rate of speed and unyielding nature of the massive support. Marshall, Anston and several other cars made it past the traffic catastrophe, and those who survived the wreck drove away in a collective state of shock.

Marshall continued onward even though part of his consciousness remained in the other vehicle. The intensity of residual energy leaking from Randall was immense, and Marshall was caught in the backwash of his extraordinary power. He tried to extricate himself from Randall's mind, but the sticky tendrils blanketed him and were slow to recede. In this state, he found himself drawn further into Randall's psyche to the point where he feared his entire existence might be appropriated.

The sensation was similar to suffocation, but just as he started to panic, the force pushed Marshall to the periphery of Randall's consciousness. The struggle to regain his composure ended when another presence of enormous influence drew his attention.

Are you a rogue? Marshall's skin crawled as the image of Mr. Cox emerged into the swirling mists of the surreal scene. The words weren't spoken, but they echoed in his mind with multiple reverberations.

(Cox) I – can you explain this? You are a rogue.

(Randall) What are you? What are you doing, and why are you here?

Marshall sensed that Mr. Cox pondered the question. *You have intruded into a place reserved only for me. From where do you come? How did you receive your gift?*

(Randall) I – I don't have answers. I search for them. And yet, you continue to try and kill the girl. Why?

(Cox) The girl belongs to me. You have intruded. You are a rogue. I have no comprehension of you. With whom do you stand?

(Randall) I am… alone. I only wish to learn why this has happened and what you are. Did you… There was an uncomfortable period where Marshall was blocked from receiving further communications, but he suspected they still were exchanging thoughts.

(Cox)… Purification, beautiful.

(Randall) Do you exist physically in Arizona?

(Cox) Yes, you shall come. I will wait for you there. I will allow your free passage to Desolation, but do not try my patience.

The vision snapped shut as Mr. Cox finished his final thought transfer. Marshall's mind reconnected with his body and the autonomic systems that controlled the vehicle during the encounter. He clutched the wheel tightly and burst into tears, trembling uncontrollably.

I'm losing my mind, there's no room for argument. I'm just like Iglar's friend, Jonathan, from the Lincoln House. The mental confusion that caused him to become catatonic is affecting me now.

He grabbed his cellphone and pulled up the map, typing *Desolation, Arizona* in the search box. It took only a couple seconds for the small flag to pop up. The town sat in the middle of the Arizona desert about halfway between Kingman and Phoenix, some distance off of Route-93.

Was the contact a hallucination, or did I experience an actual confrontation between Randall and Mr. Cox in the noosphere? The town is real, so maybe it wasn't a hallucination after all...

The unexpected ringing of the phone startled him from his anxiety-driven speculations.

"I am barely maintaining my sanity, Jeffery." said Marshall.

"I understand, and I can only imagine where your journey has taken you. I wish there was time to discuss all of it, but based on the text you sent me, I need to get to Chicago immediately."

"So, this is it then. You know where the bomb is."

"Not exactly, but Munoz booking a flight to Chicago makes it increasingly probable he's the one who will diffuse it. I need a flight out of Portland, and I need to get to Chicago before he does."

"Now that a bomb has detonated in Turkey, that's problematic," said Marshall.

"I know. But they can't close all the airports and cancel every flight. I have credentials with official clearance as a Special Counsel to the Arizona Secretary of State, which should help your friends get me through the FAA. I don't have the capacity to locate the departments or computers that I'd need to make it work, nor do I have the time."

"Okay. You'll have to either scan the documents or take pictures. I'll give you a secure address so you can forward them to Wanda and see what she and Wallace can do."

"Did you talk to Wanda about Chicago?"

"Yes, and I hope I persuaded her not to go."

"Good for you." There was a pause. "Marshall, I'm not sure if I'll be able to talk to you again. I wanted to thank you for your help."

"You're welcome. I—I'm not good with this sort of thing, but before you go, I'd like to know what you've decided to do about the bomb. Will you try to stop Munoz from diffusing it if you have the chance?"

"… I still don't know. I suppose I'm hoping for an epiphany of some sort. It hasn't happened yet."

"Well, you know how I feel. Please save us, Sixtus. The chaos and confusion in my brain is growing. I can hardly stand it anymore."

***

Sixtus disconnected the phone, reached into his shoulder bag and unfastened the zipper on one of the pockets. He dug around until he found the envelopes he took while changing cars in the warehouse back in Arizona. He rifled through them until he found the one labeled *Percy Campbell*.

The process used to secure authentic government credentials was relatively simple. History provided all the details required to identify those in high places who cooperated if the price was right. He opened the envelope with one hand and pulled out several official-looking documents, doing his best to smooth out the creases while simultaneously trying to keep the car in its lane.

Darkness enveloped the countryside some time ago, and finding the proper papers while keeping Munoz in sight was proving impossible. Mercifully, after another half hour of driving, the detective exited the freeway for gas, and Sixtus pulled up at a different station across the street. He used the occasion to arrange his certifications and government ID badge. After taking close-up pictures, he sent them to the email address Marshall provided.

Sixtus stepped out and hurriedly filled the gas tank. Several other people stood around the pumps talking in hushed tones under a single flood lamp while looking around suspiciously. As Sixtus approached, they collectively recoiled, and he forced a smile and waved.

"Hello. Anyone know if there's any trouble heading south?" he asked.

A man with a large pot belly and thick, black framed glasses shook his head as the others looked on. He apparently anointed himself the impromptu leader. "No, no more trouble than usual. But there's sure a lot of trouble going on in the world."

Sixtus shook his head. "Oh, you mean the nuke in Istanbul? Yeah, that's terrible."

The man shook his head again. "You haven't heard? Another one went off in India. The world's on the brink my friend. Be safe."

Sixtus stood silently for a moment and then checked his watch. It was half past ten. The second bomb exploded just over an hour and a half ago. "My God, it's really happening."

"What? What's happening?" said the de facto leader as the whole group turned toward Sixtus. Everyone thirsted for information.

"Ah, nothing specific. Just the whole world is going to shit, I guess."

The man nodded. "We're all scared to death."

After filling his tank, Sixtus waited until Munoz finished before driving back onto the freeway, trailing the detective at a distance. Keeping Munoz in visible sight was less critical now that he knew where he was heading. Sixtus caught up to the other car ten miles past the service station, and he remained just within visual contact.

The balance of the trip was eerily calm. Even the floaters appeared like they were affected by the two detonations. They huddled in large groups under the freeway overpasses, in the parks and around government buildings, swaying together in a kind of rhythmic trance as though they were all listening to the same drum beat. Their synchronized movements stopped whenever a vehicle passed, and they turned as one to stare at the motorists with malice. Sixtus found it particularly unnerving and kept his eyes focused on the road without turning his head. As expected, the groups grew larger and appeared more frequently as he approached the city.

Munoz exited on I-205, and the juncture at I-5 was packed with hundreds of floaters. Normally, they would be rioting by this time of night. Yet, they stood in tight groups, swaying to the same rhythm Sixtus witnessed for endless miles on the freeway. Though separated by great distance, they appeared to share a hidden frequency. The energy of the floater crowds was palpable, and at some point, he envisioned mobs across the world collectively exploding in uncontrolled fits of rage, prompted by the inaudible message they all seemed to be sharing.

As Munoz turned onto Airport Way, Sixtus breathed a sigh of relief. The detective found a parking spot near the cargo building, which was quite a distance from the passenger's terminal. Sixtus realized this was where he would have to break off contact and hope to arrive early enough in Chicago to locate Munoz before he left the airport. He nervously glanced at the phone several times, hoping from a confirmation from Wanda.

After parking in the passenger's garage, Sixtus took the elevator to the concourse level and walked over to the terminal. Upon entering, he looked for an arrival/departure board. Everything on it was blinking and displayed a red *delayed*, including Flight 745 to Chicago, originally scheduled to depart two hours ago.

He slumped down into one of the hardened plastic chairs that ran along the perimeter of the check-in area and sighed. No wonder Munoz was traveling on a cargo plane. The chaos from the nuclear detonations brought air traffic to a near standstill as the screeners checked and rechecked every passenger. Just as Sixtus wondered if the quest was hopeless, his cell phone buzzed with a new text message.

Hacked FAA domain controller in the Western Pacific Region at Marshall's request. You are on Flight 745 departing at gate C6 as Special Counsel to the Arizona Secretary of State, Percy Campbell. Doors close in 14 minutes.

Sixtus got up and alternated between a fast walk and a slow run as he moved towards the departing gates. Fortunately, C6 was adjacent to the TSA gate screener security checkpoint. He stopped in a restroom and pulled out the bi-fold ID and walked authoritatively toward the screener who looked the least confident. He moved to the front of the line and pulled her to the side. After he showed his badge, she nodded and directed him to the sterile area.

Sixtus arrived at the departure gate with eleven minutes to spare. His flight left almost forty-five minutes before Munoz.

Chapter Thirty-Two

When Randall's car turned off Route-97 onto Route-96, Marshall knew there was no way to continue following it visually. The single lane road was dark and deserted, and his headlights were a dead giveaway. As he sat on the shoulder of Route-97, the GPS beacon pivoted onto a side street called Lindal Road.

Randall, Anston and the woman entered Desolation, and Marshall retraced their path as he contemplated what to do next. Perhaps they led him to a dead end, but in his hallucination, Mr. Cox invited Randall to Desolation, and he had come. That reality gave Marshall hope he wasn't losing his mind after all.

The landscape was barren and dreary, but he couldn't help feel as though he'd been in this place before. The howl of a lone coyote added to the sense of isolation. A dull throbbing in his temples camouflaged a low-level probe that crawled slowly through his mind. Without being fully aware of it, Marshall tried to block the incursion, although the residual effect only raised his level of anxiety and gave him a headache.

Back inside his car, the arrow on the GPS map was now stationary. Marshall drove cautiously until he reached the intersection with Lindal Road. He turned off the headlights and crept forward with only the parking lights to guide him. Fortunately, the moon was relatively bright, and it illuminated the pavement for a few yards ahead. The brush here was thick, and something scorched the land until it became inhospitable. The shadows cast by the moon were ominous and foreboding. As he reached the Burro Creek Bridge, his anxiety escalated into a sudden swelling of irrational fear.

The old bridge was wooden, and Marshall doubted it could hold the weight of a man, let alone a car, so he parked in a small cove that provided cover from a massively overgrown mesquite tree. Once the car was secure, he approached the bridge and took a few tentative steps across the expanse. Every squeak and groan caused his anxiety to spike and served to convince him that at any second the bridge would collapse. After a seeming eternity, he reached the other side and calmed a bit.

The fine dust on the dirt road silenced his footsteps as he approached the crumbling town. Desolation was dimly lit with a few low-powered street lamps that flickered intermittently and lit up the old buildings in a dull glow that cast exaggerated shadows. Faded gray paint and rotted wood peeled away from compromised framing. Broken glass littered the ground, and the windows, while still intact, were covered with so much grime they were opaque.

The town square was deserted except for a couple stray curs that slunk along the dusty streets in the moonlight, their coats matted and ribs showing. Inside, a few of the buildings had single bulbs that shone a muted light through dirty glass, but most of them were dark. Marshall had an ominous feeling as he walked past an old gas station toward a building with a faded sign that advertised the *General Store*. He sensed multiple sets of eyes following him as he moved down the road. The entire town comprised four streets, so he covered the area quickly, looking for signs of Randall and Anston.

As he turned a corner at the farthest street from the town center, he saw two shadows walk past a lit window inside the second story of a nondescript run-down building. Near the doorway, muffled voices could be heard from the entryway. The conversation cut through the thin night air and reached Marshall's ears with surprising clarity as he stooped behind a tree.

"Keep 'em locked in all night; make sure they don't get out. The door is flimsy. A woman could break it down."

"And what am I supposed to do if they *do* break the door down?"

"Jugo is just outside their door, right?

"Yes."

"Tell him to say he'll shoot them, but not really do it. The Benefactor wants to see them in the morning. Hefe knows one of them is a big shot."

"Ok, Hefe. I'll be here all night, and it's the only way they can get out. I'll make sure they stay inside."

"Call the radio if there's a problem, but Hefe hopes there won't be one. Right?

"Yes, Hefe, I understand."

A small man opened the door, allowing light to escape and illuminate a larger man with a lit cigarette hanging from his mouth. The smaller one looked around for a moment, waved, and then walked toward the center of town before entering a different windowless building. Marshall moved out from behind the tree and crept away from the room that apparently housed Anston, Randall and the one named Sarah.

With guards covering the entrance, the captives were inaccessible. However, when the small man entered the other building, Marshall didn't see anyone else around, so he followed and crept up to the door. The rusted hinges squeaked as it opened, and he held his breath before going inside a large circular room, which looked like a 1970s relic. The furnishings were scant and old, and it appeared rats were the primary occupant since they had pulled stuffing out of the chairs and couches and used it for nesting material.

Doors to several other rooms lined the perimeter, and most looked like they hadn't been opened for years. Oddly, a lit lamp sat on a modern desktop along with an active computer whose monitor gave off an otherworldly green light. The room wasn't occupied, but Marshall wondered if he was under surveillance.

With slow, tentative steps, he stayed close to the walls to avoid detection. Across the other end of the room, a small glowing orange ring stood out in contrast to the dirty gray walls. Marshall walked over to it and recognized the lit ring as a pressure-sensitive call button. Against his better judgment, he pressed it.

Despite its conventional appearance, the door slid open to reveal a modern elevator. The interior was lit with LEDs, and the walls were upholstered in fresh fabric and plush cushioning. Two buttons populated an otherwise blank brushed aluminum panel. Since the

381

building was a single story, Marshall pressed the down button. The doors closed quickly, and he immediately felt the sensation of falling.

After an unsettlingly long ride, the elevator slowed and then stopped. The doors opened, and he stepped into a lavish room of unimaginable opulence. As a pseudo expert in the field of art authentication, Marshall recognized disturbing, but genuine, Medieval Gothic paintings by Bonaventura Berlinghieri, Duccio di Buoninsegna and Jacopo del Casentino. Drawn to the gruesome wood carvings of gargoyles, demons and other wicked underworld creatures, he tried to look away but couldn't fight the compulsion.

On the far side of the room, huge curtains shrouded a second chamber. Above it, a camera was attached to the ceiling and pointed toward the doors. Until now, Marshall hadn't seen any security equipment in the building, but if he wanted to remain undetected, he couldn't take a chance on a guard watching him on a monitor.

The lack of surveillance was a sign that the authorized list to this facility was limited, and they fully trusted those people. He turned back toward the elevator just as the doors opened again. Two men stepped out and walked toward the curtains concealing the second chamber. He couldn't hear everything they said, but one man was called *Delgado*.

Marshall's eyes darted around the perimeter until he found a single exit off the main room that didn't appear to have a lock. He moved quickly in that direction, and the door silently closed behind him just as the two men walked past.

Did their footsteps slow as they walked by? He struggled to breathe, but after several minutes, his vitals finally returned to normal.

Tentatively, Marshall looked around the room, allowing his eyes to adjust to the darkness. Numerous rows of very old books sat on shelves that lined the long walls, illuminated by a soft security light. The etymological origin of the writing seemed to be primarily in Latin or ancient Hebrew dialects, and the majority of the books were in remarkably good condition. This was a library of some sort, and it housed priceless editions of lost masterpieces.

In other circumstances, Marshall might have spent weeks in the room studying these precious ancient manuscripts. Some titles from authors like Miles Cloverdale, Geoffrey, Chaucer and Dante were unfamiliar.

Could these be undiscovered originals? Who assembled such a collection in an isolated underground bunker? … Mr. Cox. The name burned even when he thought of it.

Once the profound intellectual euphoria of the discovery faded, Marshall realized there was nothing he could do except find the most inconspicuous place in the room and try to remain undetected. The night would pass slowly...

***

When he arrived at O'Hare, Sixtus exchanged pleasantries with the flight crew before disembarking and making his way over to the rental car stand. He encountered little resistance as he paid for a vehicle as Percy Caldwell. The short shuttle ride dropped him off at the rental lot where he tipped the driver, found his car and sat inside while typing the address of the freight terminal into the GPS on his phone. The drive down Snowtunnel Road from Terminal 2 was swift, since airport traffic had thinned considerably after the first blast in Istanbul. By the second detonation in Mumbai, it disappeared almost entirely. The thorough implementation of screening procedures had kept some planes flying, but they sent most of the ground crews home while security people were at full strength and pulling double shifts.

Twice during the brief trip from the passenger terminal to the cargo area, security personnel stopped Sixtus. Each time, he only had to show his ID as an Arizona government official before being waved on. He pulled into the parking lot and found a spot in the front row, which was close to the terminal. There couldn't have been more than two dozen cars in the expansive lot. His watch read, 7:35. Even if Munoz' plane arrived on time, he should have almost ten minutes to spare.

Once inside the terminal that housed DeliverMax, Sixtus walked over to the freight counter on the far west end. A burly clerk typed furiously into a computer, trying his best to act busy. Through experience, he apparently acquired the talent to ignore a customer even when the patron looked directly at him. Finally, after a period that was just long enough to ensure irritation, the man looked up.

"Can you tell me when Flight D-146 is scheduled to arrive?" said Sixtus.

Visibly annoyed, the clerk looked at his computer and made a few keystrokes. "It's arriving in five minutes at the gate right behind me. If you're receiving freight, you're in the wrong place."

Sixtus shook his head. "No, I'm meeting someone."

The clerk looked over his glasses and shrugged. "Okay, you can wait over there. We have more passengers on the flight than usual. Times are, uh, strange."

Sixtus nodded and moved away from the counter into a hastily constructed temporary waiting area, joining three other people. Two women traveling together spoke in low tones. A man dressed in business attire scrolled through his phone. They went to great lengths to remain anonymous, but there was suspicion in their eyes. As the clerk said, these were strange times indeed.

The roar of the jet pulling up to the cargo terminal made an uncomfortable situation more palatable as it drew everyone's attention. Sixtus watched as the plane taxied to a halt, and the mobile stairwell moved into position. About a dozen people exited the aircraft and started towards an entrance into the freight terminal.

Once the plane disembarked, Munoz was the second one through. He kept his eyes straight ahead and walked with purpose before turning a corner and moving out of sight. Sixtus took a step forward but noticed a man in a business suit looking around suspiciously. He followed Munoz with his eyes firmly fixed on the detective. Sixtus waited until they were far enough ahead and then shadowed them.

As he turned the corner, he almost ran into Munoz standing near a bank of courtesy phones. The business suit had caught up with him, and they were talking in low tones. Recognizing it would look suspicious if he stopped, Sixtus walked by them without breaking stride, allowing only a quick side glance. The suit was gesturing, and deep frown lines creased his forehead.

Munoz' eyebrows arched, and he stroked his chin as the other man spoke.

However Munoz was going to diffuse the bomb, it appeared this other person was part of it. Sixtus reached a restroom with a recessed area in front of the entry. This allowed him to peer out at them without being discovered. About a minute later, they started walking toward the exit out to their car. Sixtus waited a few seconds and then followed.

The sun was just peeking out from the horizon, so it was easier to see Munoz and his companion as they got into a nondescript dark-green Ford sedan. It looked plain, but the engine had a deep growl, and Sixtus suspected it was an unmarked police vehicle. He walked casually over to his car and waited for them to leave.

They pulled out of the parking lot and maneuvered through O'Hare's security checkpoints until reaching the entrance of the Eisenhower expressway, which eventually merged into I-90. Trailing them was challenging as Sixtus constantly monitored his distance and speed.

The freeway was relatively clear, but the crowds of floaters, vagrants and psychotics were unnerving. They now gathered in concentric circles and swayed together in the exact same rhythm as their brethren in Portland. The early morning Chicago air was damp as a brisk wind blew, but the crowds seemed unaware. They collectively chanted something unintelligible, and although Sixtus couldn't make it out, he sensed the angry and desperate tone that permeated their inflections. As the green sedan drove by, Sixtus watched the mob turn as one and stare until it passed.

After a short ride, the car exited the freeway, and after a few turns through the narrow streets of Chicago, it pulled into the unpaved lot of an old church in what seemed to be a poor neighborhood. They parked close to the building, and Munoz and the other man got out and walked around to the back entrance.

Sixtus parked across the street in a liquor store lot, and after several minutes passed, he crossed at the stoplight and went to the west end of the church farthest from the street. He moved quietly to the back of the building, which bordered an alley, and pressed his face up against an old, single-pane window that was slightly ajar. Listening intently, he could make out most of the conversation from inside.

"Well, what about this Cardinal, his name is Riggs? It looks like he's a ranking member of both the church and a lieutenant in the stealth organization. If the bomb *is* in a church, wouldn't he know about it?" Based on the tonal qualities he remembered from Curtis Roberts' trailer, Sixtus suspected Munoz was talking.

"Risky at best." This was a different voice that sounded older and bone-weary tired. "Cardinal Riggs will be surrounded by an army of bishops and priests. He lives in a compound, which is called the Holy Church of the Flame on State Street. It's like a fortress, almost impenetrable."

"Could the bomb actually be in Riggs' church?"

"No, we've already swept the area. No sign of radiation there." A third person spoke. His voice sounded younger and slightly agitated.

There was a pause and some shuffling. Muffled conversation about coffee or something, but Sixtus couldn't quite make it out.

"Father?" Munoz spoke again. "Father, we may need your help. Do you have enough standing to get us an audience with Cardinal Riggs?"

"I suppose I could if that's what Chad wants. But what on earth do you need to see the Cardinal for?"

"I wish I could say for certain. Maybe it's nothing, but we have to talk to him," said Munoz.

"I'll phone them and ask the Cardinal for a meeting. I believe I have the standing. What should I give as a reason for the audience?"

Sixtus heard footsteps approaching and ducked down below the windowsill. The room must have become uncomfortable as the outdoor temperature was cold for July. Someone closed the window, and the voices inside became inaudible.

Sixtus crouched for a moment and then hurried back across the street to his car. He went inside the liquor store and bought two doughnuts and a small carton of milk. As he sat inside the vehicle eating the food, he wondered what led Munoz and the other men to conclude someone planted the bomb in a Catholic church.

Of course. Why didn't I think of it sooner? The first bomb detonated in a Muslim country, and the second was in a Hindu country. Were the bombs planted in a Mosque and Pagoda? If so, attacking a Christian church would be a logical next step.

How did Munoz stumble on the plot to begin with? A pedestrian detective from Seattle was at the epicenter of an event so significant the future hinged on the outcome. And how were Randall and Anston involved in the grand scheme? These were answers Sixtus would probably never completely understand.

He was tired and reclined in the seat as his mind drifted to Kara. So many vivid memories of her etched deep in his memory, but the earliest times were the ones he remembered most fondly. He closed his eyes and pictured her in a simple print dress, her hair perfectly framing her face and shining in the midday sun. They were walking through an open market in Portugal. The street vendors were friendly, and luscious fruits, vegetables and sweets were in abundance. Kara purchased handmade jewelry, soaps, ceramics and colorful clothing that reflected the spirit of the culturally rich European country.

He watched her from behind as her hips swayed in the gentle breeze, and Sixtus felt at peace.

Chapter Thirty-Three

Sixtus saw Kara up ahead in the Portuguese market, and he tried to catch up, but somehow, she kept increasing the distance between them. He called out, but she must not have heard him because she never turned around.

Dark clouds closed quickly and began to roll in from the south, obscuring the sun and sending the vendors scrambling to cover their goods. A pouring rain started to fall, but no matter how fast he walked, Kara kept moving farther away. Sixtus broke into a run, but his legs felt heavy and sluggish. From the shadows, someone reached out and jerked his arm, which almost caused him to trip. He stopped and turned around to face Daxtar Liss, who looked at him with a mixture of pity and contempt.

"You killed her, Maras. You know that. In fact, you killed us all."

Sixtus felt a different touch on his other arm, and he turned around to see Kara standing within inches, only this time her face had a horrible blueish tint, and foam spittle pustules caked the sides of her mouth. A large wound in her abdomen bled freely.

"Yes, Jeffery, you have killed us all." Her breath stank of rotted flesh and sulfur. "Why would you want to do that?"

Jerking forward with a start, Sixtus realized he'd dozed off, but the unsettling images stayed fresh in his mind. He tried to focus and purge the dream by looking over to the church parking lot. Fortunately, the Ford sedan was still there. The need to shake the lingering cobwebs sent him into the liquor store for a cup of coffee. He sipped the hot liquid and felt the first caffeine surge just as Munoz and two other men walked outside and got into their car.

Sixtus started his vehicle and called up the GPS on his phone. He already entered the Church of the Holy Flame into the address box, so he didn't need to follow Munoz closely. Watching as they pulled out onto the street, he started his pursuit only after they were safely out of sight. A summer rain started to fall, and the intensity increased as he weaved through the early morning traffic that was already backing up because of the weather.

In terms of miles, the drive was quite short, and only the heavy traffic made the twelve blocks seem like ten miles. The church was right off State Street, accessible by a private driveway hidden by tall walls and dense vegetation. Sixtus drove past the exquisitely manicured bushes and a garden filled with the fragrant smell of orchids. After passing the rectory, he found a spot in front of the building and parked as far away from the police sedan as possible to avoid detection.

After waiting outside for several minutes, he still wasn't sure what he should do next. The church bells chimed ten times, which signaled there was less than an hour before the next bomb was set to detonate.

How can I confront Munoz when he has two people with him who are probably fellow cops?

Sixtus couldn't overpower them without a weapon, but even with the obvious obstacles, he knew he must act. The element of surprise was an ally, so a stealthy approach was paramount. He stepped out of the car without much of a plan, but the unmistakable sound of gunshots coming from inside the church made planning irrelevant.

***

Marshall remained hidden in the strange library overnight, dozing occasionally despite his best efforts to stay awake. The hunger and thirst were oppressive, and his body odor was nauseating. For hours he debated whether to try and free Randall and Anston, but there was no way of knowing if that was the right thing to do. From a practical standpoint, he couldn't overpower the guards, anyway.

Throughout the night, the building buzzed with preparations and activity. Periodically, Marshall opened the door and peered out into the main banquet hall. The attendants pulled a large conference table out of a side storage room and surrounded it with about a dozen chairs. A lectern sat on top of a high pedestal in anticipation of a presentation of some sort. The freshly scrubbed tile floors gleamed, and all the lights in the room were replaced. The nervous commotion foretold of something important coming soon.

Perhaps the strangest item brought into the room was a large metal cage set on a hoist and placed slightly to the right of the conference table. The enclosure was large enough to accommodate several medium sized primates. Once the maintenance worker positioned it properly, he checked the latch and hung a chain with a thick iron bracelet on one of the bars. The workers tidied up and dimmed the lights before leaving.

Marshall sat quietly on the floor for some time until he was certain he was alone. Mustering his waning courage, he crept out from behind a stack of books and walked over to the cage. He felt something threatening and dark lurking inside and was drawn to the chain with the open lock on the bracelet. He reached inside his pocket and pulled out scraps of paper and receipts, ripping them into smaller pieces and rolling them up into little balls he stuffed into the hole that housed the locking mechanism. Hopefully, if someone tried to close the lock, the paper would prevent the shackle from engaging. The cage could only be there for the captives, and Marshall wanted the option of helping Anston and Randall escape if the situation presented itself.

The sound of the main door opening sent him scurrying back to the library. He crouched down and peaked out as a number of people walked slowly to the conference table where they took the seat directly behind their name placard. These people might not have been instantly recognizable, but their dress and mannerisms hinted of great wealth and power. Traditional business suits, religious attire, thobes, capes, tunics and colorful headdress gave the gathering a distinct international flavor. Whatever this meeting was about, Marshall sensed the participants were very important global figures.

As the procession ended, Marshall watched a guard roughly shove Jarad Anston inside the room followed by Sarah. Two burly men dragged Randall in, each having draped one of his arms over their shoulders. His head drooped and legs slid lifelessly across the floor. They brought him over to a hard wooden chair and pushed him into it gruffly. Anston tried to break free to help his friend, but his restraints held him firmly in place.

One of the security men grabbed a chain and led Sarah to the cage. She showed only minimal resistance as they instructed her to get inside. One of the captors picked up the chain and wrapped the bracelet around her wrist as she shook her head vigorously in protest. As he pushed on the u-shaped bar to shut the lock, Marshall wondered if jamming the paper in the mechanism had worked. He imagined they set the cage up for something nefarious, and they proved him right.

After the guests were seated, the lights came up, and the long curtains covering the second chamber slowly parted. Everyone at the conference table stood up while the attendants stiffened. A security staffer grabbed Anston and forced him to his feet, but Randall remained slumped over in the chair. After a dramatic pause, the shadow of a short, slender man grew in size as he approached. His face was shrouded in a wide hood attached to a dark robe that covered his body.

Upon reaching the lectern, he lifted the hood and revealed his sickly pale face, blood-red lips and unnaturally white teeth. Marshall cringed and drew back into the deeper recesses of the library. His breathing intensified, and he pinched himself hard to bring his exploding heartbeat under control. Fear-sweat formed on his brow, and he cowered behind a stack of books. There was no mistaking who walked out from the shadows…

Mr. Cox.

Marshall breathed deeply and slowly until he was able to recover a small measure of control and discipline. The terror ran roughshod through his mind, and it took all the fortitude he could muster to crawl back to his viewing spot.

A thick layer of kinetic energy now permeated the room, probing, learning and acquiring. Marshall fought off the urge to capitulate and open his mind to the deep intrusion. Instead, he tried to project a sense of invisibility, and the energy flow changed course and moved around him like fog hugs a solid object.

With some hesitancy, Marshall leaned over and peered through the crack in the door. Mr. Cox walked over to Randall, who seemed to have regained some semblance of consciousness. The room was so quiet it almost existed in a vacuum. When Mr. Cox spoke, his voice radiated with such intensity Marshall had to cover his ears.

"Welcome back, Mr. Randall. We all were worried that you might not, uh, have your wits about you, so to speak."

Anston reached out and touched Randall's shoulder. "Zach, are you alright? Do you know where you are?"

"I..." Zach stumbled for words. "What... happened?"

"I will tell you what happened. You attempted to resist me," said the Benefactor. "You have unusual abilities, my friend. Similar to my own, but somehow different. Still, you are weaker and no match for me. In fact, you are no threat whatsoever."

Randall looked around the room as he appeared increasingly cognizant. Marshall imagined the Dark One had physically beaten or mentally ravaged him. Whatever happened, he looked disheveled and disoriented.

"Ah, how impolite of me," said Mr. Cox. "We have assembled a team of the most distinguished leaders in politics, religion and business from around the world. Seated to my right is our Director of Security, Mr. Delgado. To my left is our Director of Field Operations, Mr. Watts. Next to him is the Emir of Bukara. Then we have the President of the Global World Bank; the Chairman of the Federal Reserve; the Archbishop of the Greek Orthodox Church; the President of the People's Bank of China, then... I could continue, but I think you get the idea. These are the most influential people on the planet, and they have pledged their loyalty to me."

"I still don't understand. What is it that you want?" said Randall.

"What is it that I want? What is it that *I want?* I *want* — everything. I want the world to suffer as I did. I want to see humanity drop its pretentious conceit and sickening facade of compassion and concern for the plight of the disadvantaged. I want to see an end to the hypocritical words of empathy that hide the hope that some horror will plague one's neighbor.

"You are all so disgusting with your false mask of kindness while you secretly revel in the misery of others. It's time your actions find harmony with your thoughts."

"How have you accomplished this anarchy?"

"Our success was a result of my genius. I provided the ideas, and my associates carried out the plan. It has been magnificent."

"How large is this organization?" asked Randall.

"We are everywhere. In every country, government and religion. Our ranks grow each year by at least a million. In fact, you were invited to join us, Mr. Randall. Do you remember?"

"What do you mean? I would never join you."

"Ahhh, but you almost did. I sensed a certain familiarity with you from the first time we encountered one another. I couldn't quite place you, and it bothered me because I never forget a face. Yet, you were different in many ways. I needed to search through your mind for something that would remind me of who you are. And I did find it. You tried to commit suicide, did you not?"

"Yes… I did. How would you know that?"

"I remember because I was there. I am always there when they are ready to take their own lives. If they are of use to me, I provide an alternative, a chance for salvation. You were offered that chance, Mr. Randall. You were offered salvation, and you declined.

"I couldn't place you, and that bothered me immensely," said the Benefactor. "It was irritating to me. But you — you are different. I made you an offer, do you remember?"

Randall shifted uncomfortably in his seat. "Yes… I do remember now. You were going to give me wealth and return my wife to me."

"That's right. I would have given you those things and much more for your loyalty. But you declined my offer." Marshall watched Randall nod slowly.

"And that meant you had chosen to die. If they turn away from me, they must finish the act. I watched you take the pills and the alcohol; it was enough to kill three people." Marshall recoiled as Mr. Cox grabbed Zach by the shoulders and shook him. "You were supposed to die. Why are you still alive, Mr. Randall, and how did you acquire such capabilities?"

Randall shook his head and refused to answer until Mr. Cox released him. "I'm not sure what's happened to me, and I don't know why I survived since I was clinically dead. They told me at the hospital that for some unexplained reason, my heart started to beat again even with the poison coursing through my system. When I regained consciousness, I realized I was different somehow. Sometime later the visions started. I was delirious and supposedly brain dead. It's no wonder I forgot about you."

Cox paced the floor. "Why are you able to see certain suicides? Since you see some, why can't you see them all? This cannot stand. You are a rogue that threatens everything we have worked for."

He turned to the people sitting around the conference table and his voice grew louder. "Ladies and gentlemen, I'm open to suggestions. What should we do with them?"

"Kill the other two and dissect this one's brain!" shouted someone with red hair and a bad case of acne. "I have probes that can be inserted into his skull that will record his encephalographic activity while he's still conscious. We'll learn a lot about him and inflict tremendous pain at the same time."

Delgado folded his hands and tapped his forefingers together. "That is just violence for the sake of it, Alan. We must first extract the information we need from them. How did they find us, and who else knows of our existence?"

"I agree," said Xavier Watts. "We have a lower-level breach we are following up on in Seattle. I suspect these three may have been involved.

The Benefactor's lip curled into a snarl. "Have you successfully apprehended the miscreant lawman?

"No. The Seattle police detective has, uh, evaded capture so far. I believe this one," said Watts while pointing at Zach, "is responsible for our recent failures. We tracked these three from Washington through California. I put Thomas Abernathy, the

Director of the Western region, in charge of apprehending them. And according to Alan, he fried Abernathy's brain."

Mr. Cox stroked his chin thoughtfully as his eyes blazed. "I will deal with this later, but such a breakdown in security is unforgivable. Turning back to Zach he continued. "Still, I must admit your presence was impossible to prepare for, Mr. Randall. While your capabilities are different and less impressive than my own, your ability to manipulate behavior threatens the success of my plans."

Mr. Cox stood up and began to pace. "So, I offer you a second chance to join with me. Our combined power would be formidable. I will even spare the life of your friend and the whore." The Benefactor gestured at Sarah. "You would experience wealth, prestige and power beyond your imagination. In fact, you could assume Mr. Watts' position as my second in command."

Watts' back stiffened, and his eyes widened. Delgado could barely contain his glee.

"Well, Mr. Randall, it is time to make a decision. Will you join us in ruling the world, or do you choose to die? I promise you that if you choose death this time, I will make certain you succeed."

Marshall froze just inside the door. Unbridled power and an incomprehensible mental capacity to manipulate others had magnified and accelerated the effects of the time changes. This man, or entity, had capitalized on the impact of those events to further his ambitions and power by adding the elements of hopelessness, violence and despair into the mix. The coordinated effort couldn't be random.

Chapter Thirty-Four

Sixtus climbed a flight of cement stairs until he reached a landing that led to the inner sanctum of the massive church. Apparently triggered by sensors, forged bronze doors swung open slowly revealing the interior of the immense cathedral. He stepped inside cautiously and strode down an aisle with a polished travertine floor. His footsteps echoed off the building's high walls and extraordinarily detailed 19th century architectural features.

As he continued forward, Sixtus glanced at a vestibule surrounded by either thick plate glass or protective hard sheet plastic. A small stream of blood ran across the side of the main aisle, emanating from the front of the vestibule. As he followed the trail, something drew his attention to the prone body of a priest in full religious attire. Another dead body dressed similarly lay nearby, and as Sixtus came closer to the space between the seats and the pulpit, he discovered several other dead clergymen. Crude weapons littered the area, including razor sharp crucifixes, swords, spears and lances.

Sixtus shuddered as he saw the two men who accompanied Munoz. Viciously mutilated, each suffered multiple fatal puncture wounds delivered from the medieval armaments. One man was almost totally disemboweled, his intestines splayed all over the floor in a bloody pile of pungent gore. The other suffered complete decapitation and dismemberment; his head and limbs spread haphazardly around a small area near his still twitching torso.

There were several people within the expanse of the nave who were clinging to life, moaning and chortling through bloody spittle in the throes of agonizing death. Sixtus examined several of them closely, their expressions of anger and pain imprinted on his mind forever. One man reached up and grabbed his shirt at the midsection, leaving a red smear on the garment, which gave the impression Sixtus himself was wounded.

Wobbling slightly from shock, he surveyed the slaughter while nervously running his hands through his hair and trying to comprehend the inconceivable. At that moment, the doors from an adjacent hallway burst open, and Munoz ran through the archway with a look of abject terror on his face. Eyes wide and mouth curled back in a primitive scowl of survival aggression, the detective ran toward the main entryway at the front of the cathedral, encountering a surprised Sixtus who stood in his path while holding his hand against his bloody shirt. Munoz must have assumed Sixtus was part of the clergy assault mob, and he shoved him aside roughly before continuing toward the exit.

As he stumbled and fell to the floor, Sixtus watched as Munoz tried futilely to open the huge bronze doors, but they wouldn't budge. Rising to his feet, the Time Sculptor's attention was drawn back to the hallway that connected the cathedral to the rectory. A large group of angry clergymen desperately chased Munoz, and their frothing profane-laden rants signaled their ill intent. Sixtus turned and ran toward Munoz, who dove through a stained-glass window just as a frocked priest swung a sharpened crucifix that missed the detective by mere inches.

The glass shattered, and the priest's momentum pulled him past the window while Munoz tumbled to the ground outside. Momentarily stunned, Sixtus turned in time to see a priest running straight at him with a spear extended in a threatening position. The mob was only twenty feet behind him, so there was no room for error.

Nimbly dodging the thrust of the weapon, Sixtus used an open hand to chop down hard on the man's neck, which sent him sprawling to the ground as the spear clattered along the slick tile floor. Turning and sprinting as fast as he could, Sixtus leapt through the hole in the glass and followed the detective's path out to the parking lot. His own car was several spaces down from Munoz, who was busy dealing with the rabid clergy mob in hot pursuit.

While they pounded on Munoz' roof and smashed the windshield with their weapons, Sixtus started his car and pulled away almost unnoticed. A few of the fervent ecclesiastics looked in his direction with a puzzled expression, but they quickly focused back on Munoz as he floored his vehicle and created a deadly pathway by plowing through the clergymen that stood in his way. The bodies fell to either side as they impacted the car with sounds of cracking bones and tearing flesh.

Now that Munoz left the grounds, Sixtus drew their attention, so his foot pushed deep on the gas pedal. The tires squealed, and the car swerved from side to side as he tried to avoid hitting anyone. While traversing Munoz' path of destruction, Sixtus blocked out the echoes of human bodies crushed and snapped like dry kindling as he ran them over a second time.

With the wheel clutched tightly, he cringed when another near-dead casualty shrieked in agony. The front driver's side tire ran directly over the deacon's head and crushed it as the pressure sent brains, blood and cranial fluid splashing across his windshield.

Munoz made a hard turn on State Street, and Sixtus followed, barely avoiding a collision with a cab as he veered left and accelerated. If time permitted, Marshall's friends might have zeroed in on the unmarked squad car's GPS, but at this rate of speed, contacting anyone was out of the question. Munoz made another radical turn on Pierson Street and drove a couple blocks further before pulling up inside a "no parking" zone. He exited the car without closing the door and ran up a flight of steps toward a neighboring building.

Sixtus pulled up behind him and sprinted after the detective. He glanced up at the large brass sign fastened to the structural metal that read, *Wulfric University, John Howard Student Center and Holy Trinity Chapel*. He entered the building just in time as Munoz moved away from the stalled elevator towards the emergency stairwell. Sixtus immediately followed, slowing down for only a second until the entry door clicked shut. He looked at his watch as he climbed the stairs. The time was 9:41, which meant Munoz had nineteen minutes before the bomb was set to detonate.

He heard Munoz' footfalls on the steel grating echo through the isolated cement stairwell. Just past the second floor, a door opened above him. Munoz exited on the third level, and Sixtus knew he could no longer afford to maintain a safe distance to avoid detection. The enormity of the decision he faced descended like a dark cloud of noxious gas, sucking the air from his lungs and causing him to gasp.

Liss or Zir. Which one told the truth?

As he entered the third floor, there was no sign of Munoz, so Sixtus ambled down the hallway looking through the small rectangular glass portals set inside each door. He quickly realized these were classrooms of various disciplines, but they were mostly empty because school was out of session. Occasionally, a student or teacher eyed him suspiciously as he looked around. The sheer number of classrooms was daunting, and it was entirely possible Munoz would deactivate the bomb before he even got there.

Rounding a corner, Sixtus peered down another hallway that looked identical to the others. After quickly surveying the empty passage, he took a step forward before stopping short. A frocked priest appeared out of the shadows from the opposite end of the hall and walked swiftly toward one of the rooms. In one hand he held a heavy golden scepter, and he pulled open an arched set of double doors with a silver cross and the words, *Holy Trinity Chapel* imprinted above them. Sixtus saw the same look of hatred and anger he witnessed on the faces of the clergymen who attacked Munoz back at the Church of the Holy Flame.

The situation took on a sense of urgency, and he stepped out into the hallway, but the distinctive echo of high heels on the tile floor stopped him in his tracks. Even at a distance, Sixtus could see the outline of an attractive woman. She moved cautiously forward, emerging from the shadows, looking distraught and slightly unkempt. Sixtus could hear her talking to herself in hushed tones. At first glance, he wondered if she was suffering from some kind of mental impairment.

What is she doing here at this place and time?

Who knew what role she played in the grand scheme of deception that would lead to the destruction of Chicago when the bomb detonated? She stopped, straightened her clothing, and with a sense of purpose, walked into the same room the priest had just entered.

***

From behind the door to the reference library, Marshall continued to watch the scene unfold before him as the Benefactor stood over Zach Randall. All conversation ceased, but their changing facial expressions made it appear as though they still communicated. Random words and thoughts bubbled up in Marshall's mind as though they traveled through deep water before reaching the surface. Focusing tightly, he tried to find their frequency, almost as though he was tuning an old analog radio.

After shifting back and forth, he located the wavelength that carried their conversation, although the sound was small and tinny. Whether it was real or imagined, he couldn't be sure, but the words were clear and unmistakable.

So, Mr. Randall, you decline my offer? A pity, a pity indeed.

I could never join you, Cox. For whatever reason I was chosen, this gift is meant to be used for good. You're an abomination. You have abused the gift, and you disgust me. Tell me where you came from.

A sudden explosion of blackness brought temporary blindness, and Marshall's hair stood on end. His skin tingled as though he absorbed a massive jolt of electricity.

You dare call me an abomination? You know nothing. You know nothing of what I endured. You want to know where I came from? The bowels of hell, Mr. Randall. The bowels of hell itself.

"It is time," said the Benefactor out loud. "Time to finish what you started. If you will not join me, then you must die. You are the rogue, and you must be neutralized." After a momentary pause, Marshall peeked through the doorway and saw Randall start to shake as his face grew scarlet. Soon thereafter, his limbs flopped around, and it appeared he was having a grand mal seizure.

Just as it seemed Zach might experience an aortic rupture or massive aneurysm, Marshall heard the girl in the cage whisper, "So, it was you after all. I would have never guessed." A slow smile spread across her lips.

Almost instantaneously, Marshall experienced a blinding explosion of white light that caused him to grab reflexively at his eyes. The power of the energy was so pure and pristine that it completely enveloped the dark aura surrounding Mr. Cox. A momentary pause ensued as Randall seemed to free himself from Cox' mental grip. As the white light faded, Marshall saw the image of Jarad Anston shimmering through the parting mists. Once again, he understood the communication that crossed into his mind without the exchange of actual words.

You, Cox sputtered, *how?*

We have been aware of you for some time. This new thought stream originated from Anston. *We needed to understand the depth and breadth of your power. It would take someone with the gift who was unaware of our presence. Someone who could draw you out and expose your considerable capabilities so we might find you. Individually, you are far too powerful for us. But collectively, with the element of surprise, we felt we might be able to channel and focus our own power to defeat you.*

Who – who are you?

We are the Suicide Society – a small group of survivors. Like many who serve you, we all have tried to take our own lives. Yet, within the depths of that despair, we were given an extraordinary gift.

But… but I know of everyone who commits suicide. I know them all.

You assumed you knew them all. Anston's mental projections were calm and confident. *But your arrogance has proven to be a fatal error. You never became aware of those few who actually died but came back from the dead. After we received the gift, we remained hidden from you.*

Anston turned back to Randall. *Zach, I am so sorry. If there was another way, we would have taken it. Your ignorance of our existence persuaded the Dark One that you were acting alone. It pains us terribly that your own free will was sacrificed this way.*

My God, Randall and Anston executed a perfect Trojan horse, and they snared Mr. Cox in it, Marshall thought to himself. *While the Benefactor focused his attacks on Randall, Anston waited patiently to spring his trap.*

At that moment, Cox howled in anger, followed by a subsequent explosion of colliding waves of telepathic energy that nearly knocked Marshall from his feet. He recovered momentarily, and as he focused once again on the confrontation, he could sense the force and volume of Anston's pure energy had overwhelmed Mr. Cox before he could even respond.

Anston turned his attention to Randall, and Marshall could again hear the transfer of thought communication in his mind. *Zach, I have the location of the bomb, but there is only six minutes left until it detonates. There is one more task we must ask of you. One of Cox' thought tendrils is still in place. You must use it to locate a person who has influence. We pray that there is someone in the vicinity of the bomb who has attempted suicide and failed. The tendril is attached to a person under his control, someone who is closest to the bomb. You must summon the strength to travel through the portal and into that person's mind, and you must disarm the bomb with the code I will give you.*

Yes, conveyed Randall weakly.

Zach, you must understand the tendril will dissipate when I finish with the Benefactor. You may not return from this.

Marshall sensed intense sadness, but there was no further communication. Instead, Anston swathed Mr. Cox in an enormous shroud of intense mental energy. Thick threads of the kinetic-laden mass darted through his brain, reshaping neurons and reforming synaptic pathways. He finished the entire process in less than a second, and when it was over, Mr. Cox sat with an idiot's smile on his face and a blank look in his eyes, babbling like a moron.

Chapter Thirty-Five

When Sixtus entered, it took a few seconds to process the scene unfolding before him. Munoz was on the ground gasping and wheezing as the priest who followed him into the room choked him violently.

The woman with the high heels leaned against a wall in a corner. She stared at her shaking hands and repeatedly turned them over as though they weren't her own. "Whaa—What? My God, someone is in my head. I'm going insane."

She looked up and examined the room, looking confused and bewildered. For a moment, she watched the two men locked in a life or death struggle but then suddenly ran towards them and lunged at the priest. Startled, he turned around in time to catch a punch full force in the face. The impact stunned the combatant, and he loosened his grip on the detective so he could backhand the woman, which sent her sprawling in the opposite direction.

Munoz used the opportunity to launch his own punch to the priest's Adams apple, causing immediate and substantial distress. The clergyman clutched his throat and struggled for breath as he made choking and gagging sounds. Munoz pushed him away and grabbed the shaft of a sharp golden cross embedded in his chest just below the shoulder. The weapon apparently pierced the detective's lung because he labored with every phlegm-ridden breath.

The woman sat up and looked around. Her movements were jerky and robotic like an animatronic character from a theme park. She reached out and tried to talk, but only a squeaking croak came out. Finally, she gained enough control of her voice to speak in a tone that sounded artificial and mechanized. "Jo-se... Jo-se... it's me, Zach Randall."

Sixtus took a step backward, which drew the attention of both Munoz and the woman. They looked at him dismissively, recognizing they didn't have time to deal with another threat, no matter what his intentions were.

"How—could this be?" said Munoz in almost a whisper.

Yes, how can it be? How can Zach Randall be controlling this woman's body? Sixtus looked at her with a mixture of puzzlement and fear. If Randall was here, where was Marshall?

She shifted her gaze between the two men. "Please. I can't remain in her body without killing her. I am Zach, I swear. My—my mind is fading. Bomb—you must—disarm the bomb."

"I can't," said Munoz. "I don't have the code. It would explode immediately if I tried."

"The—code—is 8778-5584. That's 8878-55..." The woman collapsed to the floor without finishing the recitation, either passed out or dead.

Munoz immediately shifted his gaze to Sixtus. "It doesn't feel like you should be here. Please don't try to stop me from disarming the bomb."

"Was that really Zach Randall, and who is the woman?"

Munoz shrugged. "I hope it was Zach. I've witnessed him do things with his mind I couldn't begin to explain. No idea who the woman is, but I imagine she's connected to whoever planted this bomb." He glanced over at the timer and swallowed hard. "There's no time left. I have to do it now."

Sixtus nodded slowly and watched Munoz punch numbers into a small keyboard. A long moment passed before the detective leaned back and exhaled. "It's over," he said. "Chicago is saved."

Sixtus remained standing in the same spot he occupied since entering the room. His heart was beating so fast he was certain it would fail. Had he made the right decision? In a moment of naked honesty, this wasn't how he envisioned it playing out, and a strange feeling of depression descended on him. When given the chance to change the course of history, he passed. Somewhere in the future, he prayed the Corporates were no longer in charge.

***

Marshall watched as Anston reached out telepathically to each of the men and women seated around the conference table. Throughout the ordeal, and especially after Anston had modified Mr. Cox, the conference participants appeared dazed and disconcerted since they were no longer connected to their leader. As Anston soothed those fears, Marshall left the safety of the library and started cautiously making his way out to the main hall. He would need to reveal his presence and introduce himself to Anston anyway, and this was as good a time as any.

The girl was free of the cage and tending to Randall as Marshall started walking out into the main room, but he only took a few steps before stooping over as a familiar cold chill ran through his body. The augury grew in intensity, and he knew what followed. With clammy skin, he stumbled as a fetid blackness closed in.

No, not now!

Marshall grabbed the door frame to steady himself as he fought against a slight disorientation that felt similar to vertigo. After the sensation passed, he opened his eyes and blinked rapidly as his vision came back into focus. He looked out to see Randall and Anston seated while Mr. Cox stood over them, his face thrust within inches of Zach's.

"It is time, Mr. Randall. Time to finish what you started. If you will not join me, then you must die. You are the rogue, and you must be neutralized…" Mr. Cox abruptly stopped talking, stood up, and jerked his head toward Anston.

Instantaneously, Marshall realized time had rebooted yet again. The glitch left them at the moment just prior to Anston unleashing his Trojan horse surprise. Everyone in the room, including the captives, seemed oblivious, but Mr. Cox glanced around to see if anyone else was aware of the reset.

Cox stared at Anston; a wide smile parted his glowing red lips. "So, all along you were the one with the real power, Mr. Anston. Your scheme has failed, but you don't know why, do you? Neither of you know what just happened." He laughed and without waiting for a reply unleashed a virtual explosion of squalid black energy focused directly at Anston.

The stunned telepath appeared bewildered but tried to fend off the potent attack. The tendrils of the competing psychokinetic projections danced and crackled through the room, powering the lights to an unimaginable brightness for a moment before circuits blew and fused, plunging the room into blackness before the emergency system engaged.

Bathed in a dim light, Marshall looked at Randall, who appeared to be trying to help Anston, but his aura was weak and ineffectual, and he looked panicked and befuddled. Judging by the size and depth of the competing energy masses, Anston was quickly losing ground against Mr. Cox.

You cannot defeat me, nor can your silly Suicide Society. The Benefactor's cerebral communications were curt and forceful. *Yes, I know all about it. I will destroy them after I destroy you.*

Marshall cowered against the back wall of the library. *Randall and Anston were oblivious, but Mr. Cox experienced the time reboot just like I did. How could that be? He certainly isn't autistic, which means he must be....* Marshall curled into the fetal position and shivered.

***

Sixtus wobbled a moment and adjusted his eyesight. He once again stood at the end of the hallway on the third floor of the John Howard Center in Wulfric University, listening to the high-heels of the woman clicking across the tiled floor as she approached the chapel. As his brain unscrambled, he realized that time had once again skipped backwards. The time resets were happening with increasing frequency, and at some

413

point, it would deteriorate into an endless feedback loop.

In that moment, the unexpected glitch served as a catalyst, and in its aftermath, he knew exactly what he must do. Unlike the first reality when he felt confused and hesitant, a certainty of purpose and righteousness coursed through his body.

Time reset back to this moment so I might have another chance to do the right thing, and I will not squander it.

His facial expression hardened, and his hands wrapped tightly into fists. The answers to troubling questions converged with stunning clarity. The Corporates used Kara to spy on him to ensure reality conformed to their specifications. Protecting this reality meant they would remain in power.

The timeline itself was crumbling, that much was a certainty. Sixtus was not an expert in physics, so he didn't know what the consequences would be if time collapsed upon itself. Yet, even a layman understood such an event had the potential to become the final, ultimate catastrophe.

The woman appeared out of the shadows and smoothed her rumpled business attire as she prepared to enter the chapel. She didn't see Sixtus running at full speed until it was too late to react. He plowed into her with such force they both went toppling to the floor. Her head hit the hard tile with a dull cracking sound. He cocked his arm back as his hand balled into a fist, but when he looked down, he saw her eyes rolling into the back of her head. She was either knocked unconscious or dying. Either way, she wouldn't interfere.

He burst through the chapel doors with single-minded purpose. The priest was sitting on top of

Munoz, and he relaxed his grip on the detective's neck for a moment as he looked over at Sixtus. As expected, Munoz used the opportunity to punch the priest in the throat, just as he had in the previous reality. On cue, the ecclesiastic gasped and grabbed his neck as the airway constricted, and Munoz pushed him off, briefly looking over at Sixtus. He started crawling toward the bomb, a task made infinitely more difficult because of the golden shaft that protruded from his chest.

As he reached the device, Munoz let out a small gasp and furrowed his brow when he looked at the digital counter. Turning to Sixtus, Munoz' eyes conveyed utter desperation. "There's less than a minute before this thing explodes. I don't have the code. Tell me you have it."

Sixtus shook his head and smiled. "No, no I don't have the code." He flicked a thumb over his shoulder toward the door. "The woman lying outside had the code, but I killed her."

Munoz cocked his head sideways. "Why? Why did you do that?"

"Why? Because this reality is too painful."

"Too *painful?* You're willing to let millions of people die because you think life's too painful? You selfish bastard."

Sixtus opened his mouth to reply, but an unimaginably bright flash burned out his corneas just before the fireball that emerged from the exploding nuclear device incinerated him. Twenty-six thousand people in the immediate vicinity died instantly, and another 100,000 were given a death sentence from the fallout or other serious injuries. As chaos gripped the city and infrastructure and law enforcement capabilities broke down, the death toll would ultimately exceed half a million. The final body count might be slightly less than the larger explosions in Istanbul and Mumbai, but the carnage would prove to be more than enough to plunge the entire world into utter chaos.

***

Marshall's level of angst and panic was unimaginable, and yet, a certain calm grew from his core and radiated waves of warm confidence. He knew he couldn't shrink from the occasion and live with himself. Flushed with a sense of poise he didn't fully understand, he hesitantly stood up and walked out of the library. The clashing telepathic masters were so deeply engrossed in conflict they didn't see him approaching. Unaware of the depth of his power, or if he really had any for that matter, Marshall summoned all the strength and focus he had in his mind and projected those thoughts at Mr. Cox with ill intent.

His effort was clumsy and undisciplined, but the eruption of a third stream of youth-infused psychokinetic energy startled the Benefactor. The battle waged on with relentless force and fury, but within seconds it became apparent they had reached a protracted stalemate. With no chance of a triumphant outcome, the standoff ended as the two main participants nearly collapsed from exhaustion, and the theater of subliminal thought evaporated. Anston slid off the chair to the ground as Mr. Cox fell to his knees. They both looked over to Marshall, who staggered forward while trying to regain his balance.

"Mr. Anston, take Mr. Randall and get to the elevator," he said. Anston paused and looked up at Marshall curiously.

"Who are you?"

"No time for that. Please, we have to get away from here *now*." Marshall emphasized the last word in a surprising voice of authority.

Mr. Cox was breathing heavily and desperately trying to recover his strength and composure. He was panting to the point of hyperventilation, and his normally pasty white complexion had morphed into a morbid shade of gray.

"You!" he said as he pointed at Marshall. "How — how did you get in here without detection? I offered you what you wanted, and this is my repayment?"

"You offered me a life of servitude to you, which is no life at all." Marshall talked as he sprinted over to the cage and pulled the lock off, grateful his primitive jamming method had worked. He reached inside and grabbed the frightened woman by the arm and pulled her out. She appeared somewhat reluctant but offered little resistance.

As he moved toward the entryway with Sarah in tow, Marshall looked back at the Benefactor and the stupefied men and women seated around the conference table. While Cox was still recuperating, several of them began to stir, slowly recovering from the deep shock of untethering from their leader.

"Hey, don't let them escape. We need to stop them," mumbled the younger man with the flaming red hair and bad acne as he rubbed his temples. "Man, I have a mega headache. I feel like I just woke up after drinking a quart of cheap tequila."

Marshall looked over and squinted at them. "Anyone who tries to stop me will have their brains

417

turned into mush. If you doubt me, just try it." The threat was sufficient enough to cause them to pause, and he watched as a man in a crisp blue suit put his hand on the arm of the red head and pulled him back into his seat.

Marshall caught up to Randall and Anston as they reached the doorway, and he ushered them out into the main foyer. Just before the doors swung shut, he heard Mr. Cox cackle in the distance. The unnerving sound echoed off the walls of the entire building and somehow seemed to amplify with each reverberation.

"You're too late!" The Benefactor shouted between gasps for breath. "The bomb in Chicago has exploded, and the beautiful anarchy has begun. You may escape this day, but I will be ready for you in our next encounter." He laughed with such gusto that Marshall could still hear the sound as the elevator opened, and the four of them left the subterranean bunker.

They exchanged no words while riding up to ground level. Moving into the street, a few scattered townspeople stopped and stared at them in an unnerving uniformity. While Marshall scanned the surroundings for any evidence of aggression, none of the malnourished, indigent inhabitants made any attempt to stop them. He let go of Sarah and broke into a sprint while she struggled to keep up with the slow pace of Anston and Randall.

Marshall reached his car outside the town's main square, and without angst, he drove back over the old bridge to pick up his companions. Just beyond Randall, a group of men from the bunker had recovered enough to start pursuing them on foot. He jumped out of the car and almost shoved

Randall and Anston into the rear seat before getting back in and flooring the gas pedal. A fist impacted the trunk with a loud *bang* before the thrust of the engine put them out of reach of the Benefactor's security team.

He checked several times in the rearview mirror as they drove down Lindal Road, but no other car was in sight. After turning onto Route-96, Marshall leaned back and let out a long, deep breath. Everything seemed relatively calm until they reached Route-93 and made the turn toward Phoenix. That's when the shock set in.

The only sound inside the cabin was the steady hum of tires on pavement as they continued east toward Phoenix. Route-93 wasn't an interstate, but oddly, there wasn't a single floater alongside the roadway. Marshall didn't know what else to do, so he instinctively followed a route that took them to his house in Glendale. Throughout the trip, there couldn't have been more than a handful of cars out on the road, but the complete absence of floaters was most unnerving.

At some point, they awkwardly exchanged pleasantries but said very little. More importantly, no one tried to probe for information telepathically. Marshall did his best to erect a defensive barrier around his thoughts, but he suspected either Randall or Anston could easily crawl inside his mind if they were so inclined.

They pulled up to Marshall's house, and after going inside, he tried to make them as comfortable as possible. Sarah lay on the couch with her legs pulled up to her chest and quietly wept. Randall was well enough to talk in full sentences, at least to Anston.

Once he offered them the obligatory beverages and use of the bathroom facilities, they sat down in Marshall's living room. After an uncomfortable silence, Anston was the first to speak.

419

"Marshall, there's so much we need to learn from you. How did you come to know about us? How did you end up in Mr. Cox' lair?

Marshall closed his eyes and massaged his temples. "It's hard to know where to begin. I — my friends and I remembered certain things differently than everyone else. You see, we have what's known as high-functioning autism, and it made us more sensitive to changes in space time. We documented some of these changes, and it just became bigger and more complex..."

When Marshall finished explaining the strange path that led him to Desolation, Jarad looked over at Zach, raised his eyebrows, and shook his head. "I'm stunned that we approached this entire affair with such naiveté. Time changes? Curtis Roberts was a Time Sculptor? If what you say is true, Marshall, we have utterly failed. We were unaware and could not have known about disruptions in the timeline."

"I would still like to have your story corroborated," said Zach. Slowly, his synaptic pathways seemed to have reconnected, and the scrambled signals largely sorted themselves out.

"That's fine," said Marshall while crossing his arms. "Check on the name Jeffery Clayton from Scottsdale. Also check the police blotter for a Mark Simpson. He killed his wife in self-defense in a hotel near the Seattle airport. You can also talk to my girlfriend; she'll tell you everything."

Anston tapped the side of his head with his forefinger. "There's an easier way, and one that will provide us with details you may have inadvertently omitted or forgotten... Let us probe your thoughts and memories."

420

Marshall recoiled. He hardly knew these two strangers, but he certainly was aware of their enormous telepathic power. Individually, he was no match for either of them. Collectively, they could obliterate his brain in almost an instant. There was no point in resisting them, so he nodded and allowed them to enter the deepest recesses of his conscious and subconscious mind.

Chapter Thirty-Six

"Don't worry, Marshall, these are good people. They won't hurt you; I promise." Sarah reached over and took Marshall's hand in hers. He waited for the usual sense of anguish and dread that usually accompanied human contact. Yet, this time, his body didn't flinch, stiffen or recoil. In fact, he welcomed the touch of this stranger. Her hand felt warm and gentle, and she radiated kindness and compassion.

"Okay, if you say it's safe, I'll let them do it."

Anston looked over at Randall, and they both closed their eyes simultaneously. Marshall suspected he should do the same, so he shut his eyes as well. Thin wisps of energy approached from opposite sides and converged into a single stream of flawless white light. The energy coalesced and hovered in front of his eyes for a moment before plunging into the four lobes that held the history of Marshall's distant and recent experiences.

The sensation was not unpleasant and actually had somewhat of a calming effect. Before they accessed any word, image, encounter or thought, Anston asked for and received Marshall's permission. He allowed them to relive his experience with the Group as they worked through the process of discovering the time changes. They watched Iglar's horrific suicide followed by Hayden's and Kenny's. Marshall revealed every encounter with Sixtus from the death of the man he pushed into traffic until they parted for the last time in Portland. The only memories that were off limits were his intimate experiences with Wanda.

In fractions of a second, the probe was over, and they withdrew from his mind gently and with great care.

Anston and Randall communicated telepathically, shielding their thoughts from both Marshall and Sarah. Anston eventually turned back to him and spoke in a hushed tone. "We're sorry we doubted your story, Marshall. Your memory confirmed the details exactly as you recounted them. Your insight is astounding and changes everything for us. We even wonder if diffusing the bomb was the right thing to do. While it may benefit those in our time, perhaps letting the bomb detonate might actually be better for those in the future."

Marshall nodded. "It's the dilemma Sixtus struggled with throughout the entire affair. Ultimately, he made a decision…"

"But only after time slipped," said Randall. "In the original reality, he must have helped disarm it."

"The timeline was falling apart," said Marshall. "After the slip, he clearly changed his mind. Perhaps he took it as a sign."

Randall turned to Anston. "The bigger question is what do we do now? Chicago is decimated and there will be chaos."

Jarad stared far off for a moment before answering. "We need to consult with the entire society. Perhaps we

423

do nothing. It will take a collective effort to figure this out."

"And what about Marshall?" asked Randall.

"Wait a minute," said Marshall while crossing his arms. "From now on, only I decide what's best for me. I've told you everything about myself, but you haven't told me anything. What is the source of your power, and what were you hoping to accomplish?"

Anston smiled. "You have every right to expect answers. We will give them to you at the appropriate time. Right now, we must prepare to leave for New Mexico first thing in the morning. The global energy feels—corrupted. We need the sanctity of the others."

Turning to Randall, he continued, "Marshall is now one of us." Randall started to speak, but Anston waved him off. "I know. We don't understand the source of his abilities. Still, he has the gift, and we need him." Randall thought for a moment and then shook his head in agreement.

Marshall looked at his three companions with a mixture of apprehension and reverence. He was utterly confused and knew he needed their guidance. Still, there was one more piece of unfinished business he had to address.

"Please, make yourselves at home, but I have to leave for a while. I'll be back before dawn, and I'll go wherever you want after that. I have nothing here, and honestly, I don't even feel like I belong in this reality." Marshall got up from a chair at the breakfast bar and pulled the car keys out of his pocket.

"Please be careful. It's dangerous out there, Marshall," said Sarah.

Marshall smiled reflexively as he walked out the door.

The drive to Wanda's apartment was nerve wracking and horrific. Fortunately, she lived at 51st Avenue and Bethany Home, so the trip was just under twenty minutes. He avoided the freeway and took 43rd all the way. Even this alternate route was like a terrifying adventure in a dystopian horror film. He saw a man and woman stark naked, chewing chunks of flesh off each other while fornicating in the street as cars passed by at high speeds. Marshall watched a man disemboweling himself and cackling insanely at the corner of 43rd and Orangewood, a pleasant neighborhood in times past.

He tried to block out the two stabbings and a gang rape he witnessed as he drove on with a single-minded purpose. Finally, turning on Bethany Home, he arrived at Wanda's apartment complex. After pulling in, he parked the car and sprinted up the steps of her building. When he reached the second-floor landing, he could see hundreds of fires burning throughout the Phoenix metropolitan area. He pounded on her door, hoping there was no one looking for blood sport in the immediate vicinity.

"Wanda, it's me, Marshall. Let me in." Turning back to the street, he saw several floaters staring at him. Apparently, the noise and activity had drawn their attention. They snarled and swore, and two of them began moving slowly toward the stairs near the side of the building.

Marshall looked down and scratched his head, and that's when he noticed the corner of a white envelope poking out from under the door jamb. He reached down and freed it, hastily tearing at the sealed flap. A single folded piece of paper was inside. His hands shook as he opened it.

Marshall,

I went with Wallace to Chicago after all. He's convinced he knows where the bomb is planted. We came up with a formula based on the time change events that corresponded with the explosions in Istanbul and Mumbai. Wallace believes it's hidden in an area near downtown. You know how he is; I couldn't let him go by himself. He's never even flown on an airplane because of his fear.

Marshall, I hope we both survive. I love you, and I can say it without reservation. Maybe you feel the same way. I'll send you a text and email when we're safe, but the systems are so unreliable, I wonder if they'll get through. If you are reading this, I guess we didn't succeed.

Please be careful. I love you,

Wanda

Marshall slid down against the wall of the building until his backside pressed against the wooden floor. He brought a hand up to his eyes and pressed inward, but it wouldn't stop the free flow of tears. His other hand held the letter, which he crumpled into a tight ball. Pent up raw emotions rose to the surface, and desperate wails soon replaced the tears. He sat there for some time before exhausting the emotions. Emptiness filled his heart and left him tired and numb. Wanda was lost forever, and he wondered how he could survive such an intense feeling of pain and despair.

Walking slowly down the stairs, Marshall dodged a rock and pushed away a floater as a gang prowled the street and eyed him suspiciously. By the time they were within striking distance, he was already inside the car, and they knew they couldn't

426

get close enough to stop him. The drive back to his house seemed surreal as the shock and grief forced his mind into automatic pilot. The crazies were out in full force, but he couldn't deal with it right now, so he took several detours while retracing the route back up 43rd Avenue.

Marshall reentered the house and found Randall asleep on the couch. Sarah was dozing but woke when she heard the door opening. Anston sat straight up in a different chair, his hands folded, eyes closed and fingers pressed against each other in a scholarly manner.

"You look terrible, Marshall. Is it—Wanda?"

Marshall nodded, and the tears started falling once again.

"I'm sorry," said Jarad. "I have a wife who I love and miss very much. The feeling of loss is universal."

"What now, Mr. Anston?" Marshall sat down. His shoulders slumped and head dropped to his chest.

"Please, call me, Jarad. Tomorrow, a jet will take us to a place where we'll be safe and can plan our next course of action with the other members of our organization."

"Jarad, who are you, and what is the organization you speak of? I heard you and Mr. Cox call it 'The Suicide Society'."

"All in good time, Marshall, all in good time."

***

The Hawker 900XP took off from the executive runway at Phoenix Sky Harbor early the next morning. They left Marshall's house at daybreak, just as the floaters were crashing and before the intense heat woke them up. Even so, the drive as treacherous as Marshall could recall. The vagrants routinely stopped

427

cars on the frontage roads, pulling the drivers out and beating them senseless. They drove the commandeered vehicles back onto the freeway and parked in the middle of the road. A massive collision occurred near Camelback, and a flaming semi-truck was on its side. Several crushed vehicles were underneath the trailer, and the bodies of the passengers lay on the pavement looking like bloody rag dolls.

Fortunately, at least from the traveler's perspective, many of the floaters dispersed through the city, looting indiscriminately as an overwhelmed police force consolidated to protect the upper-income neighborhoods. That made the drive a little easier, and they arrived at Sky Harbor intact.

The actual flight was almost as difficult. The airport was nearly shut down on the commercial side, and thousands of irate passengers stranded in Phoenix soon reached their breaking point as the bottleneck worsened. Fortunately, money was still persuasive, and Anston transferred gold bullion certificates into the personal account of a nervous booking agent who arranged the chartered transportation. The plane was waiting when they arrived with an FSS approved flight plan.

Once on board, Marshall noticed the pilot fidgeting constantly and checking for rogue aircraft. The flight control network was losing its authority, and small craft pilots who wanted to escape big cities grew frustrated with the delays. Many of them took off without a flight plan or working instruments. Already, nine planes collided in midair. One involved a major commercial jet carrying 212 passengers, none of whom survived.

About an hour and a half after takeoff, the Hawker 900XP began its descent, landing on a short runway in a remote area. Marshall looked over at a metal sign attached to a small brick building. The Portales Municipal Airport looked vintage 1950s. Two large metal sheds served as hangers, obviously the most recent additions.

The plane taxied up to the buildings, and the airstairs unfolded. The group descended quickly, and Marshall saw a large late-model electric Lincoln Navigator waiting for them. Randall, who now seemed to be alert and fully recovered, ushered them into the vehicle. He held Sarah's hand, and she pushed up against him in the car, her head in the space between his neck and shoulder. It appeared they were definitely a couple.

The Navigator left the airport, traveling about ten minutes before reaching the town of Portales, a small, isolated area in Eastern New Mexico about three and a half hours away from Albuquerque. They drove slowly down the nondescript main street until the vehicle turned a corner and pulled up to an old factory that appeared shuttered and run down.

Anston motioned for everyone to exit, and he led them up to a large electronic keypad that seemed out of place against the rotted wood and brick building. A faded signed painted on the exterior identified a previous tenant. If Marshall was reading it right, it said, "Yang Textiles."

The keypad sounded a single chirp and turned green while emitting a whooshing sound reminiscent of a sealed airlock. The faded door opened, and he realized the wood was a façade. In fact, the assembly behind the wood was about six inches thick and made of solid metal.

The interior of the room resembled an abandoned factory. Old sewing machines cluttered the floor along with rusted carding and spinning equipment. The dust was decades, if not centuries, thick, and Marshall strained to see through the clouded windows that rimmed the upper edge of the ceiling. Anston pulled out his phone and accessed an app, and with a push of a button, the interior lit up. He motioned Marshall and the others over to an elevator near the center of the building.

The doors slid open effortlessly, and inside of the car was clean and modern. They rode the elevator down for about 30 seconds until it reached its destination, which was a small room with a single conference table in the center. It could accommodate twenty-five people, but only a few surrounded it. Marshall felt uneasy as the eyes of these strangers focused on him as they approached.

"Speaker Anston, we welcome you." said a petite woman with a classically beautiful face who looked to be in her mid-thirties.

"Thank you, Sasha. I wish we greeted you under better circumstances. We have failed in our mission and the consequences are dire. We'll need every resource at our disposal to work through this threat. I hope you are all prepared to leave this place. We have an aircraft waiting for us as soon as we finish our business here."

"What is the threat, Speaker? Is it related to the one called, 'Mr. Cox'? Are we in danger here?"

"The threat is extraordinarily serious. I believe we are in imminent peril although I can't precisely say why at this point. We should be hidden, but the kinetic energy suggests we are exposed."

Turning to Marshall, he continued, "I have brought a friend with us. You know of Zach Randall even though you haven't met him. We also brought someone else who can help. His name is Marshall Beiner. He's an overseer and has a fantastic story that explains why our efforts were so lacking."

Hello, Zach, hello, Marshall.

They spoke in perfect synchronization, except they didn't use words. It took a second for Marshall to realize they transferred their thoughts collectively.

Anston held up his hand. "Marshall, let me introduce you to the Suicide Society. Seated around the table from left to right are Sasha, Rogelio, Jacques, Liu Wei, Aminah and Yasin." Not knowing quite what to do, Marshall avoided eye contact and waved.

"Before we continue," said Anston, "it's important that we share the essence of our purpose with Marshall and how we came to be in this place. Please, everyone clasp hands, and Zach and I will each take one of Marshall's hands." The group followed instructions, which created a closed circle of collective consciousness.

As Anston and Randall slipped their hands into his, Marshall felt a familiar revulsion, but it was only momentary and much less intense than he imagined it would be. Perhaps his contact with Wanda... The thought of his companion, no lover, made him tear up yet again.

"Open your mind to us, Marshall," said Anston quietly.

Marshall did what they asked of him. He opened the gates to his mind and relaxed. A flood of mental energy rolled carefully through his thoughts and memories, releasing warm, soothing endorphins that calmed him. The effect seemed cumulative but also singular, and he felt oddly familiar with these people on a deeply

431

personal level. They shared their histories, emotions and unique experiences that helped Marshall understand the content of their souls.

The temporal lobes in his brain filled with memories he actually never experienced, including the origin and centuries-old history of the Suicide Society. Their missions, successes, persecutions and tribulations transferred to Marshall in their entirety, and he marveled at the extraordinary impact the Society had in affecting the outcome of so many crisis events through multiple centuries.

Implanting the entire history of the group in Marshall's brain only took several seconds and included the present and most recent events. They revealed Mr. Cox' foul plan for world conquest and its spectacular evil and cunning. Residual traces of his rancid black energy filled Marshall's nostrils, although there was nothing real to smell. He saw Zach and Jarad as they progressed through the various levels of the plot, and he understood the mass deception the Society used to try to defeat the Benefactor.

The comforting energy withdrew like evaporating fog cover, and Marshall blinked as he reemerged into reality. He looked at each member of the group, and they smiled back at him. In that instant, he knew he belonged here.

"So, you understand that we had half of the mystery solved, but without the other half, we couldn't succeed," said Anston. "And the world is disintegrating because of our ignorance."

"I have no doubt it was Sixtus who stopped Munoz from disarming the bomb," said Marshall. "The detective must have succeeded the first time, so we're in a new reality."

"Certainly, our society in this new reality is degraded and collapsing. Should we have sacrificed our time for a better future?" asked the one named Aminah sitting a few seats away from Marshall.

"I don't have the answer," said Anston, "I don't know…." He stopped mid-sentence as the elevator door chimed and started to open, drawing the attention of the entire group.

"Who found us?" asked Randall. He looked over at Anston who was wide eyed and clearly unnerved. Several of the members rose to their feet and moved toward the subdomains as they sensed a threat.

The doors opened, and a man stumbled out, looking disheveled and agitated. His eyes were wide in panic and abject fear. He clutched his throat and fell to his knees, extending his arm and reaching up in a vain quest for help.

"The future—there is no future. Horrible—not worth living," he stammered.

Zach rose from the table and took several steps backward. The man on his knees was thin, old and smelled like death.

"My God, man," said Randall while moving towards him. "Who are you? Where have you come from?"

"Get this man some water," said Anston.

The stranger continued to grab his throat and coughed in deep, phlegm-ridden spasms. "There's no time to explain," he rasped. "You must leave here before it's too late. They know where you are. You're trapped, and there is no time." His face contorted, and thin black lines began to snake through his countenance, which distorted his features and clearly caused him great pain.

"Who knows we're here? How did you find us?" asked Anston.

"There is a traitor in your midst... Marshall... It's 2132364..." He slumped over, and several seconds later his body went limp as he hit the floor face first.

Randall bent down to check for a pulse and then shook his head slowly. "He—he's dead."

Marshall stepped from the shadows and approached slowly. "He died from the Epstein-Rosen transfer. Too much radiation," he said tentatively. "Turn him over. I need to see his face."

Zach reached down and grabbed the man by the shoulders and rolled him on his back.

Once he saw the man's countenance, Marshall stumbled backwards while bringing his hand up to his mouth as though he might be sick.

"What is it?" said Zach. "Marshall, he said your name. Do you know who this is?"

"This—this is too much for me to process," said Marshall. "They must have an entirely new historical record in the future. Those in positions of authority know who you are now, and of course, where to find you. How could he have...?"

Anston turned to the group. "We must quickly scatter to the winds to survive, my friends. Make haste, for we are leaving immediately. I'm implementing the epsilon protocol."

A collective gasp broke the silence.

"Speaker Anston," said Liu Wei, "Will we survive this thing, this madman?"

Anston shook his head. "I don't know my friend. I simply don't know."

The End

Sign up to my email list:
https://authorwbk.com/contact/

Visit my website: www.authorwbk.com

Facebook:
https://www.facebook.com/WilliamBrennanKnight

Twitter: https://twitter.com/Williambrennank

Instagram:
https://www.instagram.com/wbkauthor/

Books in the Suicide Society Series:

Prequel: Desolation (novella)
Book One: The Suicide Society
Book Two: Rational Insanity
Book Three: Kill it to Death
Book Four: Resurrection of Death

If You Liked the Book, Please Leave a Review

If you enjoyed this book, would you mind taking a few minutes to leave a review on Amazon? The process is very easy. Scroll down on the book page until you see the reviews section. On the left side, underneath the ratings, you'll see a button that says, "Write a Review." Simply click the button and a box will pop up where you can leave your review. If you're uncomfortable with writing, not to worry. Most review readers are just looking for your general impressions and how much you liked the book.

About the Author

William Brennan Knight is originally from Chicago and settled in Arizona in the 1980s. In his life, he has been a father, musician, salesman and business owner. His passion for writing began early in his childhood and flourished as he grew older. He enjoys reading horror, thriller and science fiction as well as memoirs and biographies.

Knight currently lives in Southern Arizona and spends most of the summer in Ruidoso, New Mexico.